BETHANY
COLLEGE
LIBRARY

THE SPY NEXT DOOR

A NOVEL BY
LAWRENCE KESSNER

Arlington House Publishers
Westport, Connecticut

Copyright © 1981 Lawrence Kessner
All rights reserved. No portion of this book may be reproduced without
written permission from the publisher except by a reviewer who may
quote brief passages in connection with a review.

Kessner, Lawrence.
    The spy next door.
    I. Title.
PS3561.E717S6   813'.54   81-12871
ISBN 0-87000-521-9   AACR2

Manufactured in the United States of America
Production services by Cobb/Dunlop, Inc.

To Audrey;
to my parents, Paul and Miriam;
to my brother, Ricky, and sister, Ellen,
and to my grandmother, Tessie.

· · · ● · · ·

813.54
K486s

Acknowledgments

This book was inspired by, and to a great extent is based on, the true story of the family of KGB Col. Rudolph Albert Herrmann, who lived in Hartsdale, New York from 1968 to 1979.

My efforts to contact and interview the Herrmanns, and to gain access to U.S. intelligence files on the family, were thwarted by the FBI when I began to research the book in the spring of 1980. I was, however, able to interview neighbors and friends of the family, those who knew Peter Herrmann during and after his college years, and U.S. intelligence officials, both active and retired.

Much of this book is true, but much is fictional, and for that reason, the names of the family members and other names have been changed, and the book should be considered a work of fiction. Some of the characters are composites, and some are entirely my own creations.

I would like to express my appreciation to Richard J. Bishirjian, former Senior Editor at Arlington House, who read a newspaper story and saw a great story in it, and who helped make it possible for this book to be written; to Tom Bell, who devoted the month of June 1981 to helping me reorganize and refine the manuscript; and to my future wife, Audrey Bernstein, whose intelligence, unerring good taste, honest criticism, and loving encouragement have been invaluable.

Thanks must also go to Ernest Imhoff, whose fine editorial insights helped me through the difficult early stages of the book; to the neighbors in Hartsdale and others, whose lives met with those of an unusual family; and to certain members of the intelligence community who helped me better understand, I hope, some of the material touched on in this book.

Contents

The soul unto itself
Is an imperial friend—
Or the most agonizing Spy—
An Enemy—could send—

—EMILY DICKINSON

1
...

Obligations

.... ❡ ....

Mark traced his right index finger along the trap's jagged steel teeth, trying to imagine what it would feel like if he were running through the woods and suddenly a steel jaw clamped down on his ankle and dug into his flesh.

But, the ten-year-old boy reassured himself, these traps were only for small animals.

In the woods, a hundred yards beyond the last split-level house on Sycamore Road, he set the trap, which he had bought through an ad in *Boy's Life*. He placed it on the cool ground behind a rotten log and then sat on a rock twenty yards away, watching the trap and trying to keep as still as he could. When an hour had passed and no animal had come near the trap, he went home for dinner.

At eight o'clock, he returned to the woods, his lank blond hair plastered to his head, damp from the heat of the early September evening and the excitement of what might be waiting for him behind the log. With a flashlight from his father's workbench, he threaded his way through the trees to the clearing. He could hear the rustling before he reached the trap. The sounds made him clench and unclench his empty hand, pressing his fingernails into the flesh of his palm.

He took a quick breath, and trained the beam of his flashlight on the trap. What he saw made him stare in silent fascination, repulsed yet unable to avert his eyes.

A rabbit the color of Nestle's Quik was caught by its right hind leg. The creature's eyes were wide with fear as its front legs beat against the earth in a steady but futile march.

Mark stepped toward the struggling animal, but caught the tip of his sneaker on a root and stumbled. As the flashlight fell from his hand its yellow beam traced an arc across a distant tree's branches. Groping in the darkness around his feet, he found the light, and again trained it on the trap. The animal seemed to freeze for a moment, then began to gnaw furiously at its own trapped leg.

Mark turned away to vomit, and when he turned back to look at the trap after he had finished, all that remained in its jaws was the stub of the rabbit's lower leg.

· · · ● · · ·

At first Mark thought it was part of the dream he was having and then, as he turned over in his bed, he realized that loud voices were coming from the kitchen. One voice was his father's. He did not recognize the other one, which was harsh and insistent. His father, Walter, was speaking partly in English and partly in another language that the other man spoke better than he did.

"It is a stupid thing for me to do," said Walter. "They will trace the letter to me somehow, and everything will be ruined. We are not even settled into Woodvale yet."

"You must," the other man said. "There is no one else to do it. And the task is simple. The message will be complete, and all you need to do is type it and send it to the name of the NASA official we provide you with. We have enough information on the program so that the space shot will surely be delayed until they investigate the letter. It will be a supreme embarrassment to the Americans."

Why, Mark wondered, would Dad want to embarrass the Americans? Before they moved to Woodvale, Walter had come into his room one night and explained to him why they were moving to America. Not because they believed that America was the land of the free or the road to riches. There were many people still in a kind of slavery in America, Walter told him. There were many things wrong with the American system. But, he said, there were also some good things about America, and if you were of a certain class of people, if you had certain skills, as he did, and could afford to live a certain way, then America could be a pleasant place for a young boy to grow up. He could receive a good education, but should not believe all they tell him in such subjects as history and civics.

But the main reason they were moving, Walter said, was so that he could do very important work that could be accomplished only in that country. Mark guessed that Walter meant work with his camera. Mark was proud when he told his friends in school that his father was "an independent film producer" who owned a company called Documentaries, Inc.

Mark left his bed and stood in the darkened doorway, rubbing the sleep out of his eyes, and wondering why his father would be talking to a gruff sounding man who was telling him he had to do something to embarrass America.

The strange man kept pounding his fist on the top of a kitchen countertop and saying "Nyet, nyet." Mark remembered the words from a television cartoon called "Rocky and Bullwinkle," in which a squirrel and a moose were always being plotted against by a couple named Boris and Natasha, who spoke with funny accents. Boris sometimes said "nyet."

Walter raised his voice more as he said, "there is nothing more to talk about. You can just tell them I don't think it is a wise suggestion."

There was silence for a long time, and then Mark heard the man call his father "David."

"As long as you are David," the man said, "it is not your decision whether or not something is wise. And I hope, for your health, and your family's, that you will be David for a long time to come."

"Goddamnit, you bastard, you can't threaten me like that. Don't think that I can't cause trouble for you also."

The man's voice became soothing, and so soft that Mark had to strain to hear it. "Why, my good comrade David," he said, "I wouldn't even dream of threatening a man so fine and valuable as you. After all, there is no need to threaten you. For aren't our goals the same as the goals of the great Communist party, and of the struggle against capitalist nations. Aren't we all fighting for the same thing, comrade?"

"What is your point?" Walter asked.

"Do you concede that our goals are the same?" the man asked.

"They certainly should be," Walter said.

"Then don't we agree that it is necessary to sabotage the rocket launching in the manner prescribed by the Center?"

"We do not agree on that point, comrade," Walter said. "We agree on the goals, I'm sure, but not on the methods with which to reach the goals. Now, if you'll please leave, I'm quite tired and would like to join my wife in bed. We can resolve this problem at a later date, I'm sure."

The two men stepped from the kitchen into the hallway in front on the stairs. Mark could only see the man's wide back and shiny black hair.

"It must be resolved now," the man said. "Yasikov insisted that all arrangements be made tonight so that the Center can be alerted in time if there are to be any problems. I assured Yasikov that there would be no problems, and I'm sure you can understand the position I'm in. I'm sure of that."

Mark was not sure what was happening, but he knew that it was something he probably was not supposed to know about. Was "Comrade David" a name his father used in business? And what did he have to do with the Communist party, Mark wondered. Mark had a sick feeling in his stomach.

The man placed his arm around Walter's shoulder, and began to lead him down the stairs to the entrance landing. "We will have to go see Yasikov tonight. This must be resolved immediately."

Mark could not see them without risking discovery, but he had to know what was happening. So he crept quietly down the hall, and flattened himself against a wall to peer around the edge.

He saw Walter push the man's hand from his shoulder and open the front door. "You'll have to leave without me, comrade," Walter said. "I'm sorry, but I just can't go now."

"It would really be in your best interest to go with me to see Yasikov."

"You'll have to prove it to me, I'm afraid," his father said.

The man placed his right hand on the doorknob and leaned forward so his face was inches from Walter's. "Very well," he said, and began to speak in near-whisper. Mark could not hear the words, but he saw them make Walter look frightened in a way Mark had never seen before in anyone.

After the man finished, he opened the door and Walter followed silently behind him. Mark waited a moment, then ran down the stairs to the landing and opened the front door to see head-lights shining on the house across the street as a car pulled away. He threw the door open wide and heard it bang against the side of the house as he ran down the flagstone steps, through the hedge and down the driveway. But it was too late. The car was gone.

He sat on the curb, his chest heaving, and began to shiver in his light pajamas. A thousand things came into his head, all of them horrible. Then he sensed something moving behind him and turned to hear his mother shout his name as she ran down the driveway, her nightgown flapping behind her. He ran to her, and hugged her around the waist, and his deep breaths soon turned into dry sobs. Else asked why he had run out of the house like a crazy boy, and why he was crying. When he told her what he had heard and seen, he felt her stiffen, but all she said was "Oh."

She led the frightened boy back into the house, tucked him into bed, and, laying across the foot of his bed, waited for the sound of his steady breathing. But Mark was unable to fall asleep. Though he knew that there were certain things he was not sup-posed to ask about, and that what he had just witnessed was one of those things, he could not keep himself from asking.

"Where did the man take Daddy?" He whispered the words, startling Else out of her near-sleep.

She sat up, began to rub his back, and told him to try to fall asleep, but he repeated the question louder.

"Where did Daddy go? I want to know."

"He must have had to leave on business. I don't know. He didn't tell me."

"Who was the man?" Mark asked.

Else sat up, resting her forearms on her knees as she thought of what to say. She felt intense anger welling up inside her, the same anger she felt before when she finally realized who her husband really was. She had told him then that his business was his own, but under no circumstances was it to involve the family. She had said she would leave him and take the children with her, and that he could play all the spy games he wanted once that happened. But Walter had explained that such a thing could never happen, and that his superiors would take great efforts to see that it didn't, and they both knew that Else was just venting her rage in a bluff and would never leave him.

Else knew Walter would disapprove if he found out what she was telling Mark that night, because he had arbitrarily decided that it ought to wait until Mark's thirteenth birthday: "if his Jewish friends can become men then, so can he." But Else decided that it would be easier later if he learned now that there were certain things that just couldn't be fully explained, at least not right now.

"The man shouldn't have come here," Else began. "It was part of the agreement your father had with him. They do business together . . ."

"What kind of business?" Mark interrupted.

"Just business."

"Making films? His new business?"

"Your father is involved in more than just one business, Mark. He is a very busy man, and he will have to tell you all about it someday soon because you're too smart to hide things from for too long. But you must promise me one thing right now. You must promise."

"What?"

"Never, ever, under any condition, to tell your brother about anything you have seen tonight or about anything we may ever talk about that has to do with these things. Stephen isn't the same as you. He can't know."

"I promise. I swear."

"You must understand that there are certain things I can't tell you, and it's not because I don't trust you or don't love you. But I will tell you this. The man that came to the house tonight is a business partner of your father's. I do not particularly care for him or his type."

"What language was he speaking?" Mark asked. "Was it Russian? It sounded like Russian to me."

"It was," Else responded. "And he is an impulsive fool. Sometimes your father and he don't agree on certain business decisions. But he should have known better than to come here and expose us like that. What he did was very foolish, because he could have been seen. And if anyone should know that, he should, with all his training. But I suppose impatience got the best of him, and he could not help himself. It worries me."

"I don't understand what you're talking about, Mom."

"Just keep in mind what I'm saying," Else said, "and don't ask any more questions about it until we decide the time is right.

This is family business, and it stays right here. Now go to sleep, my love, and rest peacefully." she stood up, then leaned over and patted Mark on the head before she left the room to return to her bed.

· · · • · · ·

Mark felt wet drops of sweat on the back of his neck as he turned in his bed. He tried to go to sleep as his mother had told him to, but the picture of his father's face as the man whispered to him kept returning. His eyes reminded Mark of the rabbit he had seen in the trap. They seemed so large they were almost bulging from their sockets, and the pupils had seemed to grow in size.

How could it be that this man had such power over his father, Mark wondered. If the man was in business with his father it must have to do with making films, but what could it be? Besides, the man had talked about the Communist party, had called his father "comrade," and had asked, "Aren't we all fighting for the same thing?" It had to be more than just something to do with a film. What could make his father so fearful? The only time Mark could remember that his father had seemed to show fear was when Mark had been in a bicycle accident. It happened right in front of his house when he carelessly went wobbling out into the street on the new bicycle his parents had bought him. He didn't look both ways, as Walter had taught him, and didn't see the oncoming car until it was too late to pedal out of the way. The car's brakes seemed to shriek as it slid to a halt, bumping him just enough to throw him headlong onto the street and leave him scraped and bruised.

His father had been making one of his rare efforts to subdue the hedges with electric shears, and later told Mark he looked up just in time to see the accident, but too late to call out. Mark remembered being on his back with his father leaning over him, his father's hands moving rapidly over his body to see how badly he was hurt. The expression on his father's face had been almost the same then as it was tonight when the man whispered to him. It has to do with me in some way, Mark thought. He has loved me and been good to me. He is a good person. I must help him now. Whatever he needs that I can do, I will do.

· · · ● · · ·

"This is not merely your first assignment. It could also be your last." Yuri Iosifovich Kanayev looked evenly across his desk, as he directed the words toward the blond young man seated in front of him. The director of the Illegals Department of the KGB paused to let his words sink in thoroughly. Only silence and the light filtering from the afternoon sun over Moscow through the curtains in the office of the Soviet political police building filled the room.

"You were a brilliant student at the Institute of International Relations," Kanayev continued, "even if you did gain admission because of your father's influence. And your personal background contributed magnificently to your potential for intelligence work. Because of your father's travels for the Education Ministry, you were able to do naturally what we have to work very hard to do here: to become so familiar with languages and cultures that you can move invisibly within a foreign nation."

The blond man sat without replying, relaxed but alert.

"But there are drawbacks," the KGB officer added. "You have certain qualities which raise questions about your value in our endeavor. In your dossier, it says that as a student in India, when your father was stationed there, you were superb in individual track and field events, particularly the high jump and the javelin throw. But it also notes the disruption you caused at the rugby and soccer matches because of your difficulty in functioning on a team. And in the capitalist countries you developed a taste for luxury which you seem unwilling or unable to discard."

The man continued to sit without responding, though his eyes displayed complete concentration on Kanayev's words.

"We have considered your case," said Kanayev, "and have decided upon a course of action. Would you like to know what it is?"

The man leaned back slightly, head cocked to one side, and surveyed Kanayev's expression. Slowly and evenly the man nodded.

"It is obvious that despite your superior intellect and education, you cannot work in the central office," Kanayev said. "And because of the unfortunate incident in which you were involved last week, it has been suggested that you be tried on a criminal charge." Kanayev paused again. Still no response. "We are aware that the man made certain inflammatory remarks about your work, but we do not consider yours a measured response. And because you failed to maintain control, one of our number died.

"However, witnesses noted that you were amazingly patient during his insults until he slapped your face. Perhaps your chief difficulty is that you lack a certain sense of proportion in physical matters. But I have reviewed the matter and believe I have reached a satisfactory solution. We shall turn your limitations into assets. There is a place within our organization for someone who enjoys travel, physical activity, solitary assignments, and yes, even luxury.

"Here is how you shall redeem yourself. You will take on today the first in a series of assignments which require that you travel widely and that you operate generally according to your own devices, and which will give you an opportunity to enjoy life well. You will answer only to me, and you will answer with immediate and absolute obedience. Otherwise discipline will be immediate and of a maximum nature. Do you understand?"

The blond sat up slowly until his back was absolutely straight. "I understand exactly," he said, and smiled.

"We will give you the code name 'S'," Kanayev said, "for the winding way the letter curves as it pursues its alphabetical mission. That will be needed often in your new work, though sometimes you may operate in a more direct line. Your mission will be to trace and eliminate those individuals whose activities are counter to our own, particularly those who once were aligned with us and turned."

"Exactly," said the blond man.

· · · ● · · ·

Maria Halvorsen was so excited she couldn't keep from jumping up and down in her bed. She ran to the window of her sunny bedroom and looked down Tordenskiolds Street to the wharves which jutted out like square fingers over the shimmering waters of the great Oslo Fjord. A few shrimp boats were already tied up at the wharves in front of City Hall, and she knew that passersby would soon be stopping to buy fresh boiled shrimp, just as they had been doing each morning since her family had moved to Oslo four years before.

She ran back to her bed and grabbed up the large stuffed Bengal tiger which Grandmother Halvorsen had sent last week from St. Paul for her eleventh birthday. When it arrived, she had complained mildly that grandmother could have sent something more grown-up, but she really loved the tiger, especially its big, mysterious green eyes. When she was alone in her bedroom, though only then, she would hug it close and think of nice things.

Lots of them would happen today, she thought, as she dressed and brushed her long ash-blond hair. Astrid was coming, Astrid Halversen, the girl she had met four years ago in Möslund, the small fishing village on the south coast of Norway, where Grandfather Halvorsen had taken her during his visit the summer before he died at his home in Minnesota. Even though they spelled their last names differently, Maria was convinced they were related.

Astrid was one of the reasons Maria was glad her father, a career foreign service officer for the American government, was transferred from his post in Jakarta to the more prestigious one in Oslo. The promotion particularly pleased his aging parents, Harold and Sonia Halvorsen, who lived in a large white Victorian house in an older section of St. Paul, where Maria had spent several happy summers. Grandfather Halvorsen had just retired from his medical practice when he learned of the transfer. The eighty-year-old patriarch had made plans immediately to visit his son in the land of the family's ancestors.

"It's almost like home," the old man had said to his slender granddaughter as they strolled along the Oslo waterfront. "Why, it's just like some Scandahoofian burg in the middle of Minnesota, except they have more people and water. I guess that's why all of us back a hundred years ago became farmers instead of fishermen."

"It's tough to fish in the middle of all those fields," said Maria.

"It's the Land of 10,000 Lakes, my dear," replied her grandfather. "At least, that's what they advertise on the license plates. But you need a big sea like this to do it properly, the way my great-grandfather Olaf used to talk about."

"Tell me about great-grandfather. That means he was my great-great-great-grandfather?"

Harold Halvorsen had laughed warmly and squeezed his granddaughter's hand, then stopped in front a wharf where people were buying boiled shrimp at a small stand in front of a boat moored there. "First of all, he was about 93 years old when I was a kid," said Grandfather Halvorsen, "and to me he looked like a little white prune. Second, you have that Latin blood in you, so you don't really look quite like the rest of us Halvorsens, though you're the most beautiful girl I know."

Maria had felt a twinge of sadness when her grandfather said she didn't look quite like a Halvorsen. She had always felt closer to her father's family than to her mother's family, who were Portuguese immigrants living near New Bedford, Massachusetts where they fished commercially. She had had little contact with them.

"I want to know more about the Halvorsens," the girl said, tugging at her Grandfather's strong forearm. "You promised you would take me to that town someday."

"Möslund," the man said. "We'll go next Sunday." And they had.

She remembered Möslund now as she looked out through the window of her home, watching boats move like toys across the fjord. The weather had been the same that crisp, bright day four summers ago when Grandfather Halvorsen took her on the ferry boat across the fjord and down the coast until it docked at Skien. From there a taxi had taken them the ten miles to Möslund.

When they had arrived at the small fishing village, the Lutheran church had just finished Sunday services, and people were milling about in front of the stark white structure. Harold Halverson had dusted off the Norwegian he learned as a child in Minnesota, located the church's pastor, and introduced himself. The clergyman had smiled at the old American and his olive-skinned, but otherwise Scandinavian-looking, granddaughter.

"I have seen the name of your ancestors in our church's records," he said. "One always wonders what happens to the descendants of our townspeople after they leave for America. All we receive are occasional letters from your Minnesota and sometimes from North Dakota and a place called Sheepshead Bay in New York. We're glad to see you."

"Thank you," said Grandfather Halvorsen. "Are there any Halvorsens still living in Möslund?"

"Yes," said the pastor, "though they spell the name differently. I will take you." Bidding the members of his congregation goodbye, he had escorted Maria and her grandfather to a house next to the village post office and knocked on the door.

Karl Halversen, the postmaster, had opened the door and welcomed them inside where they met his daughter Astrid. "Perhaps this is your long lost cousin," the pastor had said as he made the introduction to Maria.

Except for the difference in skin tones, the pair might have been mistaken for sisters. Astrid had the same regular facial features that Maria did, and the same graceful neck. Though her bone structure was not delicate, there was about her developing body—the same balanced combination of bone and flesh—that could simultaneously evoke the image of both an athlete and a fashion model.

Astrid and her father had taken Maria and her grandfather on a tour of the village, stopping at an ancient cemetery, where headstones which bore the name HALVERSEN rested in the ground, with dates on them spanning more than four centuries. "We are the only Halversens now," said the postmaster as he gazed down at the grave of an ancestor. I am widowed, so soon there will be no more here. Astrid is my only child." When the group left the cemetery, they had returned to the postmaster's home to eat and visit, and by the time Maria and her grandfather had left to board the ferry back to Oslo, the two men had determined that they were related through Olaf, the old emigrant.

Maria and Astrid had decided to call each other cousins, and vowed to write each other and visit whenever they could.

The friendship had deepened over the last four years, and Maria hoped that her father would never have to be transferred to another diplomatic post. But the day before her eleventh birthday her parents told her they would be moving soon to Copenhagen, reassuring her that they would visit Norway and Astrid often.

When Astrid arrived late in the morning, Maria met her at the pier and told her the bad news. The girls cried, embraced each other, and promised always to be best friends, cousins, and even more.

"It's almost like we're twins," Astrid said.

"Yes," echoed Maria, "twins."

· · · ● · · ·

They took the Holmenkollen train to the stop at Voksenkollen, and hiked up a hill to the Tryvanns Tower, the highest point in Oslo. It was their favorite spot in the whole city, because from the top of the tower, they could see down the length of the sixty-mile-long fjord on one side, and across the forests and lakes into Sweden on the other.

They rode the elevator to the observation deck on top, and as the doors opened, Maria noticed a man who seemed to be walking directly at her, from the deck into the elevator. Perhaps he didn't see her because his right hand was partially raised to his face and blocked his view. Maria couldn't see his face because of that but something she did see riveted her attention. Others might not have noticed, but she did because it made her think immediately of her new birthday present, the stuffed tiger she had named Lief.

On the little finger of his right hand, the man wore a ring of heavy gold with a raised signet in the shape of a tiger's head. A pair of tiny emeralds sparkled from beneath its ferocious brow. In the second the ring flashed past her, it made her shudder because the tiger seemed cold and hard instead of soft and cuddly like Lief.

The fleeting moment unnerved her, but not nearly so much as what she and Astrid encountered when they stepped out on the observation deck. A crowd was gathered around the railing, staring down at the ground hundreds of feet below, and speaking excitedly among themselves. Astrid approached a man and asked what they were looking at.

"A man just went over the side," he said. "Some say they heard a shout. I didn't hear anything."

Astrid rushed to the railing where the crowd was staring down, but the man grabbed her arm gently and said, "Please, young lady, it's not a pretty sight. It will ruin this lovely day for you."

Maria agreed. "Let's leave, Astrid," she said. "I don't want to look over the side with those other vultures."

The next day there was a brief mention in the newspaper that an unidentified man "apparently fell to his death from the observation platform of the Tryvanns Tower yesterday afternoon at two-thirty."

Later that night, however, when Maria was in her bed trying to fall asleep, she heard her father tell her mother what he had heard at his office. "They said he was a recent KGB defector, and they don't think it was an accident."

Maria hugged her tiger to her, trying to push the unpleasant thoughts out of her mind, and wondered what the KGB was.

13

2
Golden Legends

At the age of twenty-four, the man who would become Walter Gottfried Scholz was a lieutenant in the State Secret Security of East Germany, stationed in the Soviet sector of Berlin. The year was 1952, and the young man, Tomas Most, still bore vivid memories of World War II. He came, by way of the German army, from the small village of Decin in the Sudeten mountain chain, where for centuries its peaks had been pushed like stacks of game chips back and forth across the table of international politics. The village was under Czech rule at Tomas' birth in 1928, though the Most family was of German origin, as were the bulk of the families in the Sudetenland. Tomas had the air of an unaffected country boy, though he was determined to move ahead, to live a different life than he had known in Decin. Even amid the rubble of war, he found city life attractive.

And besides, there was nothing to return to in Decin since Dieter Most was dead. He had been Tomas' father, and served as a German infantry officer in World War I, returning to Decin with the Iron Cross pinned to his breast and his left tunic cuff pinned to his shoulder. Both decorations he won in the Second Battle of Marne, on a rainy July day in 1918 when he had led his unit in an assault on a French tank. He had slipped in the mud as he reached the clanking contraption, caught his sleeve in its wide steel treat and felt his mind go black as his arm was stripped from his shoulder like a twig from a branch.

He regained consciousness in a field hospital where the first face he saw was that of an American doctor. Until that day Dieter Most had been a warm and expansive person with a lively interest in literature and the arts. He returned to Decin with eyes set in a perpetual squint, with a mouth that seldom opened except to expel bitter venom against the nearest target, which was often Tomas. He ran the only inn in Decin, which had come under Czech rule with the signing of the Treaty of Versailles.

He commonly spent his evenings in the inn's small bar, where the more he drank the more he cursed. The Czechs were regular targets, but late at night, as his words began to slur into a muddy facsimile of speech, he would curse the Americans. "What business was it of theirs?" he would ask as he leaned on the bar with his one arm. "They fought to shake free of the British 200 years ago. Then they helped tear my arm from my shoulder."

Dieter Most both cheered and wept on January 30, 1933. That day he learned that Hitler had been appointed chancellor of Germany, and that his wife had died of diptheria contracted while nursing a neighbor's child. Though he had treated her more like a servant than a spouse, Sigrid Most cared for Dieter, and he for her. The day after he buried her in a mountain meadow, cursing himself while Tomas dug the grave with the shovel Dieter was unable to wield, he sat down and wrote the first of a series of long epistles to Hitler. In them he chronicled the ills of the modern world for pages, always ending with a diatribe against, "the Yankees who stole my arm." Sometimes he posted the letters and sometimes not. But he continued to write them even after he began organizing a cell of the Sudetenland Separatist party, which because of his drinking soon slipped from his control. Hitler never answered his letters personally, but Dieter Most found the Führer answering his prayers in the Munich Agreement of 1938 as Hitler took back the Sudetenland as part of the price for peace in Neville Chamberlain's time.

After the smouldering embers of international resentment broke into the flames of war, Tomas Most left his father to wear a German soldier's uniform. The father died in his bar, bleeding from shots fired by a Russian soldier. Tomas Most survived the same situation near Dresden where he also weathered the rain of fire from American bombs.

At the end of the war, Tomas Most—having learned of his father's death—settled near Berlin, where he joined the security police. There were many qualities he possessed that suited him for intelligence work. During the war his superiors in the German army had noticed and cultivated them. He had the uncanny ability to recall the slightest detail, he was disciplined in his actions, and he was amazingly strong for his medium height. Therefore it was natural that he would be asked by a former comanding officer to join the State Secret Security, better known as the MfS by East Germans, when it was formed after the war, and just as natural that the Soviet secret service, the KGB, should later call for his services as its members began—not so subtly—to exert influence on the agencies of their satellite states in the first chilling days of what would be remembered as the cold war.

Unlike many intelligence officers, Most found it easy to laugh and to draw others into his confidence, frequently throwing his arm around a person's shoulder as he talked expansively. An innocent might have thought him naive. He was not. He had explained himself but once in his life, and that time to a drunk passed out on a park bench the night after he learned of his father's death: "I have no mother. I have no father. I have no home. I have no land. I have no God. The strong rule because they are the strong. The weak do what they must." Then he vomited on the grass.

· · · ● · · ·

In April 1952 Lieutenant Most met a dour middle-aged Russian named Ivan Filikov. The introduction was performed in Filikov's Berlin office by Most's immediate superior, who knew that Filikov was one of several KGB "advisors" to the MfS. Despite the official denials, it was Filikov and his Soviet comrades who set MfS policy.

One of Filikov's duties was to recruit officers from the MfS to work directly for the KGB, and although the East German police resented the skimming of their best intelligence talent, they cooperated without spoken complaint in the KGB's talent search. The Soviet satellite nations were learning, often in blunt terms, that they were pawns of the Politburo in Moscow. Enlisting persons such as Tomas Most helped drive that point home.

Filikov was impressed even more by Lieutenant Most's personal interview than by the young man's file. The interview lasted seven hours, spread over two days, and at the end of it Filikov—who prided himself on his ability to determine the true nature of a person—concluded that Most was ideologically sound. To Filikov, there were different levels of Communist belief, and Most's, Filikov had no doubt, was among the highest.

This was crucial. Regardless of a recruit's skills, if his political reliability was remotely suspect, he was rejected. There could be no chance that on some distant day doubts might lead to defection, and defection to disclosure of KGB procedures and practices to a foreign power.

Filikov nodded slowly as he looked across his desk at Most at the end of the second day. He will do well, Filikov said to himself. Again I have made a good catch.

· · · ● · · ·

"Sit."

The word was spoken softly, almost inaudibly by the uniformed, graying Russian officer. Tomas Most sat down in the chair directly in front of the desk of the tall lantern-jawed man in his early sixties. Leaning back in his leather chair, the KGB officer studied Most's countenance for perhaps two minutes before he glanced down and picked up the manila folder which contained Most's file. He studied it silently, with several minutes more passing before he spoke.

"I am General Petrov," he said at last, again in a whisper. The senior KGB officer in East Germany took pleasure in intimidating subordinates by periods of uncomfortable—for them—silence. He found the technique useful in evaluating a man's worth. Most, he noticed, did not display any nervous mannerisms. He sat with his hands folded calmly. Petrov liked that.

"You are not a Soviet citizen?" the general asked quietly.

Most examined the question before he responded. "No, Comrad General, you are entirely correct," he said, "I am not a Soviet citizen. But I am a Communist, and the citizenship of a Communist knows no national boundaries."

The older man's lips turned up at the corners slightly, and he continued to leaf through Most's file.

He looked up again. "You are not a particularly well-educated man, Lieutenant Most?"

"I do not have the benefit of a university education, Comrade General, that is true. But my home was a cultured one, and I am familiar with music, art, and good literature. I speak several

17

languages and I would have liked very much to attend a university. Unfortunately, the war prevented me from doing so."

General Petrov already knew what Most was saying. There was little he had not known about Most before the Lieutenant stepped into his office. It was not the content of the responses that interested General Petrov. It was the nature of the responses.

"Lieutenant Most," he said, pointing to the large window which overlooked the street, "would you be so kind as to open that window. It is stuffy in here."

Most walked to the window, and pushed on its heavy wooden frame. It did not budge. He tried three more times, with General Petrov quietly watching. No luck. Slowly Most turned to face the general.

"I believe there is a problem with the window," Most said. General Petrov displayed no sign of hearing the statement and stared at Most for a full minute. "It is stuffy in here," he repeated evenly. Most realized he was being tested. Without hurrying, he turned back to the window and ran his fingers around the frame until he felt the smooth head of a nail. Inwardly he smiled.

"I wonder, Comrad General," he said without turning to face General Petrov, "if you would have in your possession a pliers or other such instrument for removing a nail that seems to have become embedded in your window frame?"

"Never mind, Lieutenant Most," General Petrov said sharply. "Just have a seat. There are matters to attend to."

· · · ● · · ·

Ten days after the interview with General Petrov, Tomas Most received his orders to begin his KGB training. One set of papers informed him of his honorable discharge from the East German state security police; the other directed him to report to KGB School 65. The latter set was personally signed by Semen Denisovich Ignatiev, director of the KGB. The next day Most departed for Kiev, where School 65 was located in the largest city of the Ukraine.

The training took one year, and Most was the only non-Soviet in his class of thirty-two students. The school, he learned, was under the First Chief Directorate of the KGB, which was responsible for all clandestine operations abroad. The school's major task was the training of agents for the Illegals Department, known as Directorate S, which directed the activities of KGB agents who lived illegally in foreign countries under false identities. Most himself thought it strange that he should be surrounded by men who had been his enemies only a few years before, and that he felt no animosity toward them. They had won the war, and Most believed they would soon overpower the United States. Most wanted to be on the side of the winner.

His training concentrated on preparation for the Illegals Department. As a member of the East German security police, he had developed the mind of an investigator. Now he learned the skills of a spy. The schedule was demanding. Inside a fortress-like stone building in a residential section of Kiev, Most and his classmates studied "special disciplines." They ate in the building and slept there, three men to a room. Most had anticipated an atmosphere of easy comraderie, much as he expected a university to have. That did not develop at School 65.

Close friendships were not encouraged. Each man learned to think of himself first, and each was advised by his instructors that he should monitor the behavior of his classmates carefully. Some were voluntary informers. Such a position carried no onus. It was part of the training.

The special disciplines which occupied the first few months of training were varied and thorough. They included classes on the operational activities of the KGB; the intelligence and counterintelligence departments of the KGB's primary enemies, the United States, West Germany, Great Britain, France, and Israel; intelligence activities of the KGB; and activities of the KGB during war (the last was the area that especially interested Most and the project paper he researched was enthusiastically forwarded by his instructor to headquarters in Moscow).

Other subjects, taught in the manner of university survey courses, included misinformation, anti-Jewish work, counterintelligence techniques, and strategies to discredit anti-Soviet spokesmen. Seminars covered the creation of false identities, cover stories and occupations, methods for integrating oneself into a new community, and—most important—communications.

"Never forget," the communications instructor said as he tapped a piece of chalk against his blackboard, "if you cannot communicate with your superiors, you are of no use to us."

The intriguing part of the training to Most was devoted to learning how to establish a false identity or, as it was called in cryptic terminology, "a legend." A student would be given an identity to assume, perhaps that of a Finnish freelance journalist residing in West Germany. Working from a brief biography committed to memory, the student would be interrogated by a succession of instructors. The interrogations sometimes lasted nine hours at a stretch. Sometimes three instructors would ask questions at the same time: "Where was your mother born? . . . Her maiden name sounds Jewish. What was it, Kornblatt or Kornblum? . . . A dairy farmer? I thought you said your father raised chickens?"

Only three students never failed in the sessions. One was Tomas Most. His legends, remarked another student, were golden.

· · · ● · · ·

The heading on the file Filikov handed to Most read: WALTER GOTTFRIED SCHOLZ. Seated at the table in the conference room of School 65, Most opened the file and scanned the biography it contained as Filikov continued his explanation of Most's new assignment. Outside, Kiev traffic honked in the late fall afternoon.

"Forget that you were ever Tomas Most," Filikov said as he paced slowly around the table. "From this day on, you are Walter Gottfried Scholz." He stopped and leaned across the table, placing his hands on its surface as he stared full-face into Most's eyes. There was a trace of a smile on his lips as he said, "To the KGB, Tomas Most is dead."

The man across from him returned Filikov's gaze, and recalled a scene from years ago: a young boy was digging a grave while his one-armed father stood at the edge of the hole, cursing the world and himself.

So be it, he thought. From now on, I am Walter Gottfried Scholz.

· · · ● · · ·

"He's a charming gentleman with a sharp mind and a keen wit," said Frau Hertz to Else Liselotte Stroesser in the parlor of the boardinghouse where both lived in East Berlin. "You really should give him a chance."

"Frau Hertz, you will be a matchmaker till you die," replied the slender girl with the flaxen hair as she arranged flowers in a green glass vase on the end table by her chair. "What is he this time? A bottlemaker?"

"No, no, no," said Frau Hertz. "He is a soundman with the radio station where we work. His office is just a few doors from yours. I was talking to him the other day and he commented that he found the women of Berlin mostly dull, and I said to myself, he would never say that about Else."

"You flatter me," Else laughed. "Where is he from?"

"I'm not sure. Perhaps if you go out with him you can find out and tell me. He's quite handsome, you know."

"All right," said Else, and she finished arranging the flowers. "I will see him if he wishes. You win again; you always do."

"Very good," said Frau Hertz, brushing a wisp of gray hair back from her forehead. "You will like him, I'm sure. His name is Scholz—Walter Gottfried Scholz."

· · · ● · · ·

Else Liselotte Stroesser was born near Dresden, the daughter of a municipal land records clerk. From him she learned the gift of laughter and the value of discipline. From her mother she learned domestic skills, patience, and survival.

Else's father had been a confirmed bachelor who married late in life, after he encountered a petite, quiet woman in a floral shop. She was seventeen years his junior, but Greta Frölich caught his eye because of her gentle manner, and the fact that she always wore a flower—either in her dark hair, or on her dress. Else grew up in a small house in a village near Dresden where her parents seldom spoke and never fought. Her mother had fragile health, and frequently took to her bed, though she never complained about her ailments. As a child, Else's favorite part of the day was when her father first came through the door from work.

"Where is my Else?" he would shout and she would run and throw herself into his arms, and the pair would play animatedly until dinner. After they ate, the household became solemn, and Else soon learned that each thing in life had its place. If she tried to coax her father into play after dinner he would frown and say, "Not now. I will play with you tomorrow."

He died during the Allied bombing which destroyed Dresden, and Else's mother took her to Berlin. Shortly after Germany surrendered, the mother's health failed for the last time. Else donned a black armband for the second time in two years, taking it off only when she found a clerical job with the state radio station in Berlin nine months later.

. . . ● . . .

Walter and Else fell in love almost at once. She was entranced by the friendly, smooth talking man who had certain of her father's mannerisms, and who always seemed to have plenty of money to lavish on her. When they went out, which was almost every night after the first two weeks, Walter did most of the talking. He was a masterful storyteller, and would spend hours recounting details about events he covered for his radio job. Else sometimes thought he mixed equal parts of fact and fiction, but she never questioned his stories.

Walter displayed a lively interest in politics, and he often tried to draw out Else's opinions on political issues. But Else displayed no interest in such topics.

"What do you think of the protests against the Soviet moves in East Germany?" Walter asked one night at dinner in a small restaurant.

"I have no control over these things," Else said, with a trace of petulance in her usually sweet voice. "They are events and circumstances much larger and more powerful than I am, and I don't see what good it would do me to become involved. I know many would disagree, but I can't help it. That's just how I am."

"But certainly Hitler proved what influence one person could have," said Walter. "And now the Communist Russians control our lives."

Else put her fork down by the wienerschnitzel on her plate. She looked at Walter and sighed. "I have no strong feelings one way or another about our communist state, or about the Russians," she said. "If they let me live my life peacefully, I support them, and God knows our lives have not been peaceful. Maybe things will be better, maybe not. If not, I suppose I will want a change for the better." She picked up her fork and resumed eating. Walter did not comment on her words, and two weeks later he asked for her hand in marriage.

"You must understand," he said as he proposed, "I have the type of job which might cause me to be stationed elsewhere."

"I will go anywhere with you, my love," said Else. "I would like to see a little bit of the world."

$\cdots \bullet \cdots$

"You can't change my mind," Walter said to Galetkin. "She'll make a fine wife. And there is certainly no cause to worry about her politics. She has none. She loves me and will learn to hold the opinions I have."

"Which we know are correct ones," joked Walter's KGB superior as the pair debated Walter's future in Galetkin's tiny Berlin office.

"Of course," said Walter, "so you shouldn't worry about a thing. I am not such a fool that I can't be trusted to select my own wife. And you needn't ask. I understand perfectly well the importance of a reliable mate in my situation."

"You know what you are being groomed for," said Walter's handler. He reached down on his desk and picked up a heavy paperweight and began examining it as he talked.

"Yes," said Walter.

"And you know," Galetkin continued as he turned over the paperweight to study its base, "that your wife must not only be reliable, but must—eventually—become acquiescent."

"Of course."

"We would prefer that you not be so hasty."

"I do not regard my actions as hasty, and I find the women you have suggested in the past of no interest to me."

Galetkin returned the paperweight to its former place on his desk. "I suppose there are some decisions a man must make for himself," he said. "But at the proper time you shall have a child. Only after its birth can this woman become aware of the full extent of your situation. There are reasons for that, reasons which I am sure you understand."

Walter stood up to leave. "It has to do with the nature of women," he said.

"Exactly," responded Galetkin.

$\cdots \bullet \cdots$

Else Liselotte Stroesser became Frau Walter Gottfried Scholz in a civil ceremony in January 1955, and settled in a large, comfortable apartment not far from the radio station. In the winter of 1956, Else quit her job, and began learning to knit so that she could make warm mittens for the child she would soon bear.

The boy was born on October 10, 1957, and was named Mark Conrad Gottfried. Walter chose the English spelling for the middle name, explaining to Else. "It might be more convenient for him in later years."

Four months after Mark's birth Walter told Else, over dinner, "There have been some changes in my work, and we may be moving soon."

"Where?"

"To Munich. To the Federal Republic."

Else rubbed her hands on her apron and Walter reached across the table, taking her hands in his. "My love," he said, "things have changed a bit at work, and I think you should know about them."

Else heard Mark cry out in his bedroom and pulled away from Walter. She walked to the door of Mark's bedroom, peered into the darkened room for a moment, and then returned to the dinner table.

"When I was in the military," Walter explained as she sat down again, "I was assigned for a while to the intelligence units. I acquired some expertise in photography and electronics which helped me to get the network job."

"What are you telling me?" Else asked, cocking her head at a slight angle and frowning.

Walter looked intently into her eyes and continued. "They have asked that I put my skills to use for the state intelligence services again, and it would require that we live in the West for some time."

Else laughed uneasily. "You mean that you would be a spy," she said.

"No," he said, shaking his head for emphasis, "not exactly a spy. We will be working and living and raising a family like anyone else. There will be no funny business, I promise you. But the only way we can do this is to go to the West as ordinary refugees, emigrants. And I should be able to secure the same type of job in radio, or perhaps television."

"Have you thought about this carefully?"

"It is what I have to do," said Walter. "You will understand better in the future. Trust me to do the right thing."

"I always have," said Else, "and I always will." She stood up and walked back to Mark's bedroom door, then turned back toward Walter. "He's sleeping nicely," she said. "Whatever was bothering him, it's gone now."

· · · ● · · ·

There was no doubt the boy was precocious. His eyes began following Else whenever she entered his room almost as soon as she returned with him from the hospital. He was crawling within a few weeks. And after Walter, Else, and Mark settled in Munich as refugees in early summer, he was trying to walk during outings in the neighborhood park when other infants his age were still crawling. He learned to say "Father" and "Mother" just past the age of one—in both German and English.

Else too was learning English, at Walter's urging, "to broaden your horizons." Occasionally he hinted that she might have need for it in the future.

By the age of four, as Walter had predicted, Mark was equally at ease in German and English. That made it easy for him when Walter moved the family to Canada, settling in Toronto. Mark was quite at home in the nursery school, where his teacher found his progress in developing fluency in English "quite remarkable."

Toronto was pleasant enough to Else, though she was homesick from time to time. Even so, it was a part of the world that bore no scars of war. Perhaps, she thought, it is better for the children to live in a less troubled country. Else did not, however, like the decline in the family's standard of living. She didn't like living in a small apartment in an immigrant neighborhood, but Walter was careful to explain that he had taken a job as a meat cutter in a delicatessen to appear to be a normal immigrant. They had money to live better, he told her, but it would be unwise for a delicatessen clerk to live in a grander fashion than people expected.

Such subterfuge disturbed Else. During the past several years, she had learned more about Walter's background, though she still did not fully understand his connection with the KGB. Besides, she felt there was little she could do about it. Divorce was not an alternative, partially because she truly loved the man who had systematically deceived her since they had met eight

25

years before. So she really had no choice but to follow the advice Ann Landers gave to a woman ("Distraught in Denver") who complained that her husband was occasionally unfaithful.

"Dear Distraught," advised Ann, "Sorry, honey, but there's no easy way out of this one. Lover boy has just told you point-blank that he's going to keep on romancing. Either give him up or stop your bellyaching and get used to it."

· · · ● · · ·

Two years later, in the winter of 1964, a second son was born to Walter and Else. They named him Stephen Thomas, a name Mark selected from a list given him by his parents. Else had been reading a rash of child care books, which all suggested that children should play an important role "in welcoming the new arrival into the family." She was becoming increasingly concerned about seven-year-old Mark's development. One night after dinner, while Walter was reading the newspaper in the living room, she came in and asked if he thought the boy was growing normally.

"But of course he is," Walter said. "He's the brightest child in his class. He's healthy, and he appears to be quite happy. I don't see why you worry so much."

"You don't see him like a mother does. He has these long, strange periods of silence, as if he's thinking of something so important that the fate of the world hinges on it. And another thing . . ." She paused in mid-sentence.

Walter looked up from his newspaper. "What is it?" he asked. "It seems he has taken to examining your equipment when he thinks I'm not looking. I saw him the other day, but he didn't see me. He was fascinated by it. I could tell that he thought it was all rather secret."

"I have tried never to give him that impression," said Walter, laying the newspaper down on the sofa beside him.

"He understands more than you think he does," Else said. "He is a very intelligent boy."

"I know that," said Walter. "My superiors know that too. What was he looking at?"

"Your Minox camera, and the microfilm containers. And the transmitter. He was utterly fascinated by the transmitter."

"I'll talk to him," said Walter. "He's old enough to know a few things."

· · · ● · · ·

Just after Stephen was born, Walter was hired by the Canadian Broadcasting Company as a television soundman. The timing was just right, his new handler in Ottawa, an aide name Barinov, told him during a rendevous soon after he landed the job.

With the higher salary that the job brought, the family bought a house in a middle-class neighborhood of neat homes called Leaside. In a pattern that he was to follow until his discovery more than a decade later, Walter quickly became friendly with his neighbors, entertaining them with stories about his job, such as the time when he was following the Canadian prime minister on a trip through the Western provinces and had to carry his drunken wife up to her room from a hotel lounge. Walter was a fine fellow, the neighbors often said, and weren't the Scholzes a lovely family? It was with a touch of sadness that their friends on quiet Sutherland Drive bid them farewell when Walter announced four years later that they were moving to the States. Walter left Toronto in his new Ford station wagon, loaded to the top with household possessions, at midnight on August 10, 1968.

At the Niagara Falls customs station, Walter presented his Canadian passport and his immigrant visa. The immigration officer, noticing toys in the car, asked Walter if his wife and children would be following soon after him.

"They should pass through at mid-morning," said Walter. "The children have difficulty sleeping in the car, so we thought it was best if they traveled during the day. Anyway, I'd like to supervise the movers and get things a bit organized before they arrive. Ah, what a pain in the ass the whole thing is."

"Sir?" asked the immigration officer.

"Moving," said Walter, with a disarming grin. "You sell your house, it's a pain in the ass. You buy a new one, it's a bigger pain. Higher mortgage payments, higher taxes, higher everything. It's always higher, higher, up, up."

"Welcome to the United States," said the officer, stamping Walter's papers. "I'll leave a note for the next shift about your family. Maybe we can speed up their entry a bit."

The officer leaned closer and said, in a confidential tone, "You know, we see all types on this job. We see the dregs, the scum, people who don't know a word of English. They can't make it in Canada, so they come here. Then we see good hardworking people, they've learned how to get along, if you know what I mean. "We're glad to welcome people like that into America, Mr. . . ."

His soliloquy tapered off as he checked the papers again for Walter's names.

"Mr. Scholz, it's people like you we welcome."

. . . ● . . .

When Walter arrived at his new house in Woodvale at nine-thirty that morning, the movers were already there, unloading furniture on the blacktop driveway. Like a field marshal, Walter directed the three moving men: "Couch in this corner, table in the center, a little to the right—you got it pal—no, a little to the left . . ." If Walter had not gone and bought two six-packs of beer the men might have mutinied. But Walter Scholz had a fine sense for knowing just how far he could push.

A combination of lack of sleep, the long drive, the heat, and four bottles of beer had Walter feeling a bit lightheaded when Else and the children drove up the long driveway in the late afternoon. The old Checker cab was not air-conditioned, and a day of driving in the summer heat had left Else looking worn and tired. Strands of light brown, fine-textured hair were plastered to her forehead with sweat, and her clothes, normally fresh looking, were limp and wrinked.

In the roomy back seat, four-year-old Stephen slept soundly. Mark was out of the car almost before it stopped.

Walter helped his wife from the car, kissed her briefly and remarked, with a smile, "You look like you just took a tour of Calcutta during monsoon season." Else smiled wanly.

"Please, I'm not in the mood for your joking."

"What you need is a good cold beer, Else Liselotte Scholz," Walter said in a tone of admonishment. He sometimes liked to address her by her full name, because unlike many other important things in his life, his wife's name had not changed. It was Else Liselotte before his "involvement," as he liked to think of his lifetime commitment to the KGB, and it was Else Liselotte after it. She had taken the name Scholz not knowing it to be an integral part of Walter's carefully constructed "legend." That would come later; there would always be time for her to learn the truth, and at a time when it would be nearly impossible for her to do anything but accept that truth as her own, and learn to live with it.

These thoughts played fleetingly on Walter Scholz's mind as he drove down the hill to buy beer for himself and his wife, and soft drinks for his sons. When he returned, the family sat underneath a tree in the backyard of their new home, and, like any hopeful family of immigrants, they talked about their first day in America, and of days to come.

· · · ● · · ·

While the other kids his age were trying to ignore the troubled summer of 1968, Darrell Ventura spent hours in the family room of his home in Des Plaines, Illinois reading newspaper accounts of Robert F. Kennedy's assassination in June and watching, in bloody living color on TV, the riots during the Democratic convention. It was a lot for a thirteen-year-old to take in.

As the Chicago cops battled more than 10,000 anti-war demonstrators in the streets just fourteen miles away from Darrell's house, the boy remained in his cozy room. He was fascinated by the way the television and newspaper reporters could make the violence even more livid than it already was, and fantasized that he was not skinny little Darrell Ventura sitting alone in his house reading and watching television, but instead, a fearless journalist out there in the hot, bloody streets and parks of Chicago, recording events with a quick pen and even quicker mind.

That fall he joined the staff of the student newspaper, and told everyone that he was going to be a journalist when he graduated from college. But he realized that it was in the nature of his character to dream about great things more than to accomplish them. He took pleasure in imagining all sorts of great acts, but when he had to venture away from the fertile field of his imagination, it was not nearly so much fun. Why bother with all the effort, he sometimes thought, when you can just sit back and think whatever you want.

But he was no loner. He was, in fact, quite the opposite. People enjoyed having him around because he managed to make them feel better about themselves. Mostly it was because of his way of slighting his own accomplishments. He sometimes seemed like a soap opera character. He made people feel better about their own lives after they watched him for awhile.

"Poor guy," some would say. "He means so well."

And he did mean to be a journalist. That was one dream, he said to himself, that he would make into a reality.

3
Family Business

It was a sticky hot day in early September, a week after school had opened, and the twenty-six students in Martin Caglieri's tenth grade biology class at Woodvale High School were not ready to start working yet.

The teacher, however, was not about to allow apathy to interfere with his carefully planned schedule, which that day called for a lecture on how planaria reproduced.

Mr. Caglieri outlined the lesson on the blackboard, including in it several minutes at the end of class in which he would contrast the reproduction methods of the tiny flatworm planaria with those of his prized fantail guppies, which lived in three tanks in the back of his classroom.

"Planaria," began Mr. Caglieri, "are flatworms. Who can tell me their genus and species?"

"I must assume," the teacher continued, "that all of you bright young people are familiar with the terms genus and species."

"Well?" He paced silently behind his desk.

"Can anyone tell me what genus and species are?"

At a desk in the back of the room, near the guppy tanks, Mark Scholz pretended to pay attention to the teacher as he sketched geometric forms in his notebook. He looked up as Mr. Caglieri repeated his question.

"What are genus and species? Does anyone know?" he asked impatiently.

Mark smiled, and said under his breath, "Yeah, I'm a genus." The only one who heard him was Doug Engel, who usually sat next to Mark in the classes they shared.

The two boys spent much time together, often discussing their academic interests as well as taking weekend bicycle trips and going cross-country skiing.

They saw humor in the same things. With their small group of friends, they would attend a Friday afternoon pep rally for the football team only to snicker at the loud revelry.

To them, a clever prank was nothing so ordinary as throwing a water balloon at an unsuspecting teacher, or pulling down someone's gym shorts as he ran laps around the football field. Rather, it would be in passing the humorless principal, Mr. Cochran, in the hall and asking him in rapid French, "Is it true that you molest young boys in your office?"

Twenty minutes into the planaria lecture, with another twenty to go, Mr. Caglieri asked if anyone would like to diagram and label the flatworm on the blackboard. No response. And, as was usual after getting silence as the response, the teacher asked if "perhaps Mr. Scholz or Mr. Engel could help us out a bit."

The pair, although they spent most of the time paying no attention to what was going on in the front of the room, were frequently called on to provide answers that the other students could not. This amused Doug, but Mark did not like having to put his knowledge on display for those who did not appreciate it.

He disliked making a public spectacle of his displeasure, however, so when Mr. Caglieri said "Mark, why don't you give it a shot," he walked to the front of the room and began to draw on the blackboard. It was all going just as he had planned.

A minute later, the silence of the classroom was broken by a series of popping noises at the back of the room.

A fat girl named Sheila Berman, who was sitting in the back row, suddenly shrieked, "Icch, someone spit on me!" as she brought a hand to her face to wipe away the offending substance.

It was a delicate, inch-long guppy, plastered to her cheek like a wet leaf on the pavement. By the time she had discovered this, the rest of the class had turned around in their seats to see what the commotion was about.

"What is going on here?" the teacher demanded. "Who is shouting?"

As he strode to the back of the room, a plume of green-tinted water shot up from the center of the fish tank arrangement. It sprayed several feet into the air, ejecting half a dozen guppies in the process.

At the front of the room, standing quietly with a piece of chalk in his hand, a smile played across Mark's mind.

The teacher watched in frantic amazement while his fish tanks, as if in choreographed sequence, bubbled and boiled as they spewed his beloved guppies into the air.

The bizarre display lasted only a minute or two, before subsiding as abruptly as it began. In its aftermath, guppies flopped helplessly on the floor, several boys were bent over in convulsive laughter, Sheila Berman had thrown up in a corner, and Mr. Caglieri, scooping up the dazed fish with a small net, repeated the words, "Sombody's gonna fry. Umhmm! You can rest assured, young people. Somebody for *sure* is gonna fry."

But no one ever did.

· · · ● · · ·

Later, eating lunch with his friends in the student cafeteria, the talk was of nothing but the fish tank incident. Mark was not unusually quiet, but neither did he express much interest in the affair. While the boys proposed one theory after another as to whom or what might have been responsible, Mark chewed on a sandwich of German salami on pumpernickel bread. He drank dark beer from his thermos, which amused his friends. He was always quiet and well mannered, so they left him alone.

"Who do you think did it, Mark?" Doug Engel asked. "We were sitting back there the whole time; it must have been set up before class."

"I guess so," Mark replied. "Some jerk, some greaser must have gotten waterproof cherry bombs or something. Who would do a thing like that, anyway?"

"Somebody pretty smart," Doug said, "because it was pulled off beautifully. I don't know how Caglieri could ever catch the guy."

"What guy?" asked Mark, distractedly.

"The guy who blew up tanks. What's the matter with you? Did you do it or something?"

"Yeah, sure," Mark grinned. "I've got nothing better to do than blow up some poor little guppies. Give me a break, will you?"

"The whole thing sounds really weird," said David Gordon, an editor for the school newspaper. "I wish I could've been there to see it—it would make a great story. How'd you like to write it up, Mark? We could use it on the front page: 'Anonymous Psycho Bombs Fish Tanks—see inside for exclusive photos.' How about it?"

"No, thanks," Mark said. "I don't see what the big deal's about anyway. There are so many important things going on, and you guys are worrying about some foolish prank. I've got better things to do."

"One thing, though," he added, pausing to swallow a bite of his sandwich, "I can honestly say that I got a laugh out of it. But enough is enough."

"You didn't get a laugh out of it, Mark," Doug Engel said. "A smile, maybe, but certainly not a laugh. Didn't you once tell me that laughing takes up too much energy?"

"Yeah," Mark replied. He smiled broadly. "Yeah, you're right. I did say that, didn't I?"

Mark excused himself from the table before the lunch period was over, and went to one of the boy's bathrooms. He was alone there, and lit up a thin, brown Player's cigarette. Leaning against the wall he slowly puffed on the cigarette, and was halfway through it when he felt it coming. He could have controlled it had he wanted to, but he didn't. He thought he deserved it, so he laughed and laughed, and bent over double until the tears started to roll down his cheeks. When he had laughed enough he splashed cold water on his face, combed his hair, and hurried to be on time for his next class.

"They'll never know," he thought to himself as he threaded his way through the crowded halls, "and that's the way it should be."

· · · ● · · ·

Walking home from school that day, Mark thought about Doug Engel's offer to spend a weekend with him and his brother in the mountains. Mark wanted to go, but things were never simple. There were always the unexpected trips with his father on "family business." Before Mark had left for school that day, his father told him a message would be arriving at noon to tell them if a weekend trip was necessary. It was not that Mark minded the trips. They were often pleasurable, more so than his tenth grade classes. What he disliked was the uncertainty involved, the fact that he couldn't make summer or weekend plans. Sometimes he felt so old, so responsible.

But what bothered him most about "family business" was a feeling he could explain to no one, except perhaps his mother. That was because, he was beginning to realize, she often felt much the same way. The feeling had to do with control, with having it and losing it, and not knowing whether or not one had the opportunities to make choices. "Take charge of the situation," Mark's father always told him. "You be the man in charge. You control what happens."

And, Mark thought, maybe his father really did believe that was how it worked, that his father was in control of the situation, which for his father was "family business." Mark wasn't sure he saw things the way his father did; there seemed to be so few choices. Just as in many cultures a farmer's son becomes a farmer, and a baker's son a baker, in the world that Mark was born into, it was expected that if he exhibited a certain amount of native ability and was properly nurtured, he would take up his father's occupation. These were not things that were said in words. They were transmitted by what Mark saw and learned to understand in his family's comfortable home at 16 Sycamore Road.

Mark walked up the long driveway to his house, past the row of overgrown shrubs which his father never trimmed. As he unlocked the door he could hear his parents arguing in German. "It's not necessary," he heard his mother say. "At this age, he should be doing other things. He can wait, Walter. What is the hurry?"

"Else, dear heart," his father said, "sometimes I don't know why I bother to explain these things to you. You're always protecting him, and there's no need to. This is not his first trip, and it will not be his last. He enjoys traveling with me. It's good for a son to learn his father's business."

His mother laughed derisively. Still standing at the front door, Mark reflexively put his hands to his ears. That tone in his mother's voice made him wince. He knew what it did to his father. "His father's business," she said loudly. "Do you think all the other fifteen-year-old boys in town go traveling around the world with their fathers on such 'business trips'?"

Mark rattled the front door knob and opened the door to slam it noisily. His parents fell silent.

"I'm home," he called out, and immediately felt embarrassed. He seldom yelled, and never about such an obvious thing as his arrival. I'm home, he thought for a moment, was the sort of thing happy children on television comedies said. "I'm home," Beaver Cleaver would yell, and Mrs. Cleaver would bustle in from the kitchen with a tray of cookies and a glass of cold milk while Mr. Cleaver patted him on the back and asked him about school.

No, Mark thought, the Scholzes are certainly not the Cleavers.

Walter walked out of the kitchen and into the living room. He nodded to his son and asked, "Do you know the sour beef song?"

"What?" asked Mark.

"An old country favorite," said Walter. "You sing it just before eating any meal containing sour beef."

"Is this a Walter Scholz do-it-yourself instant song?" asked Mark.

"Just listen, you little wiseass and show some respect," Walter said, and smiled. He began to sing with an oompah rhythm: "Sour beef with red cabbage, dumplings, and beer. Have you tried it? Did you like it? Was it tasty? Was it pasty? Was it . . ."

"Stop! Enough." Mark commanded, cutting into the singing. "I get it, Dad. You don't have to sing anymore."

"Well, then go wash up for dinner, ingrate. Imagine, my own son doesn't appreciate my musical talent. Maybe I'll send for a new one."

"I'm sure they'll oblige you," said Mark.

"What are you talking about?"

"You know," said Mark. "Just send a message back to the Center: 'I am not pleased with present eldest son, Mark, known to you as Hoffnung. He gives us nothing but trouble and has capitalist tendencies. Send replacement as soon as possible. Yours truly. David.'"

Walter Scholz frowned, making deep furrows in his forehead. He studied his son, then placed his hands gently on the boy's narrow shoulders. "Try to be careful with your humor, Mark," he said. "You may think these things are funny, and on occasion, so may I, but I doubt many other people would." He paused. "Okay?" he asked.

"Okay," said Mark. Else brought in a casserole dish of red cabbage. "Stephen will not be here for dinner," she said flatly as she placed the dish on the dining room table. "He is having dinner with the Franklin boy."

The three sat down and began eating, with Walter taking a large serving of red cabbage. As he wiped a spot of cabbage juice from the corner of his mouth he pointed at the bread plate in front of Else at the other end of the table.

"The bread?" he asked.

Else looked up from her plate.

"I would like the bread," Walter said.

"Then why don't you ask for it properly," said Else, holding her fork stiffly above her plate.

Walter's jaw clenched, and Mark noticed the muscles under his ears tighten. Laying aside his napkin, Walter stood up, walked around the table to where Else sat, removed the unsliced loaf of rye bread from its plate and returned with it to his chair.

"Would you please pass the bread, Else dear," he said.

"You infant," she replied. "You spoiled little baby."

Mark wanted to say something, but he continued eating in silence. He was grateful that Stephen was eating elsewhere since his brother had a talent for turning a scene such as this into a monumental blowup.

Walter turned to Mark and said sharply, "While your mother is attacking my character—in silence, I hope—I will tell you about our weekend."

"The message came?" asked Mark.

"It came."

"And?"

"And you must arrange to be absent from school on Friday. We will take one of those early flights to California. I'm getting a special rate for you because we're buying Disneyland tickets as part of the package. If a businessman brings family members along and takes them to Disneyland, the kids get a special rate."

"I'm not putting on any mouse ears," Mark said.

"What family?" Else interrupted. "The family isn't going, not even to Disneyland. I will not subject Stephen to this."

Walter shook his head slowly from side to side. "These moods, Else," he said. "These moods. Sometimes I think another person has taken control of your voice box. Why can't you just relax? It's not as if you've never heard of these things before. Don't play such the innocent."

"We'll be careful, Mom," said Mark. "You know we will. Dad and I are always careful."

Else brought her napkin to her eyes, which were beginning to well with tears. "Mouse ears," she said softly. "Mouse ears, and he says he'll be careful."

Walter returned to his meal. Else held the napkin to her face for a moment, then sat upright, turned to Mark, and said, "What do you think about on these adventures?"

The question startled Mark. Sometimes, he thought, she asked questions which had no appropriate answer.

"I think about the same things I think about any other time," he said.

"Which is what?"

Walter answered for Mark, with annoyance in his voice. "He thinks about what any other boy his age thinks about, except in a smarter way," he said.

"I asked Mark," Else said.

"He thinks about sex," said Walter. "Okay? Isn't that what he should be thinking about at his age? Right, Mark? Don't you think about sex?"

"I . . ." Mark began.

"I asked Mark," Else shouted, almost shrieking. "Why don't we let Mark say what he thinks? What do you think?"

Mark stood up from the table. "I think that I'm not hungry anymore," he said flatly. "That's what I think." Then he turned and left the room.

· · · ● · · ·

The smog, usually bad in September, was lighter than normal as the airliner carrying Mark and Walter began its descent near Los Angeles International Airport. Sitting at the window Mark could see around a dozen surfers riding the waves off Venice Beach as the craft glided in for the landing. As the pilot reversed the engines to bring the plane to a shuddering stop, Mark recalled reading about Los Angeles ("El-Lay," as a friend whose father was a film studio executive always called it) and deciding the city was too new to be really interesting.

Disembarking with their baggage in hand, they went straight to the car rental counters. Walter glanced at the signs stating the various rates and went to the counter where a young blond with dark eyebrows wore a green suit with the company's name stitched over her left breast. He liked the way she looked; besides, she seemed to flirt back. Walter signed for a small sedan, and took the packet and keys the girl handed him.

When they reached the car, Walter opened the trunk and Mark put the bags inside. Then they got into the car and Walter withdrew a map of Los Angeles. Seated behind the wheel he unfolded the map on the seat between him and Mark to plan the route.

Maps were among Walter's favorite objects. He could spend hours pouring over maps of any type—world maps, nautical charts, road maps, geological surveys. The map's subject was of no consequence. Its lines, numbers, names, and symbols fascinated him.

He recalled, as he traced his finger along the path he and Mark would take, a soldier—a German corporal pointing to a map pinned to a bulletin board in a gray, wooden barracks. Then he remembered who the soldier was. He had given Walter instructions in map reading and orienteering during the abbreviated training he received after being drafted into the German army. That had happened in 1943 when he was fifteen, in the wake of the disastrous Nazi losses at Stalingrad and the surrender of Italy. The image of Mussolini hanging like a side of beef after the war flashed through his mind. He had seen the photograph of Mussolini's execution long after the war had ended, in a bound copy of *Life* magazine which he was leafing through in the New York City Library while he waited to make a contact. He remembered thinking then that no matter how high one rises in life it is all the same in the end.

Mark shared his father's fascination with maps. He liked the sense of order he felt when he looked at one, the feeling that he could eliminate the unexpected. In his room at home, he had a bound thirty-two page road map of Westchester County. With it he had no need to depend on anyone else for directions. He couldn't get lost that way.

As he listened to his father explain directions, he felt the same fascination again, and realized that he wasn't really paying attention to the instructions. He reached into his father's brief-case and fished out a marking pen.

"What are you doing?" Walter asked.

"I was going to trace the route," he said.

"You're not thinking, Mark," said his father. "Why trace the route? What if we get stopped by a policeman, or we're in an accident and they see a big red circle around Silverado Canyon? Think, Mark. Think."

"I should have known better," said Mark, as he returned the pen to the briefcase. "I'm sorry."

· · · ● · · ·

Walter drove south on the San Diego Freeway, with Mark following their progress. At each interchange, he checked to see if the exit signs read the same as the road map.

"Segundo Boulevard," he said, looking at the map and then at the sign. "Rosecrans Avenue," a mile later. Redondo Beach Boulevard. Long Beach Freeway. Lakewood Boulevard.

They turned off at Rossmoor, drove seven miles east on Garden Grove Boulevard, and then three miles north on Harbor Boulevard through Anaheim until they reached Disneyland.

At the huge amusement park, Walter seemed to enjoy himself more than his son. Narrating from a guidebook he bought at a shop near the entrance, he touted the wonders of New Orleans Square, Frontierland, and Adventureland.

They rode the Matterhorn roller coaster, Walter yelling in mock terror, and Mark feeling nauseous and saying nothing. In the haunted mansion, Walter accompanied the background music by making scary noises, until Mark turned to him and said, deadpan, "I'm scared Dad. I'm real scared, okay?"

After lunch, they went to a souvenir shop.

"Now you get to buy your mouse ears," said Walter to Mark, as he watched people load their arms with cheap mementos of their visit to southern California.

"Are you serious?" asked Mark. "You really want to get this crap?"

"When in Rome," said Walter, smiling.

Mark laughed. "Okay," he said. "But how about just a T-shirt for me? You can get the ears for Stephen. I think he'll appreciate them a bit more."

"Dopey kid," said Walter. "He'll love 'em."

· · · ● · · ·

In the Disneyland parking lot, Mark, under protest, changed into his souvenir T-shirt.

"Do I really need it, Dad?" he asked. "What's the difference?"

"Look," Walter said. "Don't give me a hard time. I've got enough on my mind. Just put on the shirt. I told you already, there's nothing more perfect than a kid in a Mickey Mouse T-shirt. So we got a little lost, who's going to say anything to a tourist loaded down with cameras and a skinny kid who just came from Disneyland? Now tuck that shirt in, so you don't look like a slob."

They got into the car, and Walter started the engine and turned on the air conditioner. As the engine warmed up, Walter reviewed the plan with Mark, who listened attentively.

"Boris Alexevitch Deev," said Walter, "forty-two years old, a bachelor. They should have known better. Bachelors are bad risks. He impressed the Center with his devotion to party ideals. In his youth, he was known as a ruthless informer. He had his uncle sent to Lubyanka Prison for meeting with westerners without authorization. His first assignment was with the mission in Tunis. By the age of twenty-six, he had advanced to second secretary in Rome. He was sent to New York in 1967, and was given the title of chief information officer with the U.N. Mission. In 1969, as far as we can tell, he was recruited after being caught in a compromising position, shall we say. It seems that Mr. Deev has a penchant for little boys. He did severe damage; it is believed that he is responsible for the arrests of two of our agents who had attained sensitive positions in the National Security Agency; "Formulator" and "Ellipsis," they were called. The Center became aware of his defection about two years ago, but watched him for a while instead of arranging for his elimination. It was a mistake. The CIA apparently had good information, and soon the FBI had him placed in hiding. However, it has been almost unmistakenly determined that our friend is living the hermit's life, with protection from the U.S. Justice Department in a small cabin on a dirt road near this place called Silverado Canyon."

Walter removed a U.S. Geological Survey map of the northern section of Cleveland National Forest, in which Silverado Canyon was located. The map showed a town of Silverado, population 900. Silverado Canyon Road, a narrow blacktop road, according to the map, stretched four miles east of the town before ending. Exactly three-eighths of a mile before the road ended, the map showed, a dirt road turned off to the south. It crossed the creek and kept running for miles into the forest. Just after it crossed the creek, about a quarter-mile, another dirt road ran east. Two miles down this road, if the information Walter received from Moscow on the receiver in his basement was correct, Mr. Boris Alexevitch Deev hid in fear.

"Memorize it," said Walter. "Then close your eyes and describe the route to me."

Mark studied the map for several minutes, concentrating at the important turn-off junctures. He noted the altitude rings on the map, and imagined the slope of the terrain. Finally, he encoded the route into a line of numbers and letters that he was able to memorize in less than a minute. It was simply "R18S4neg38s15e2." Route 18 to Silverado, four miles, and then back three-eighths, one-quarter south, two east.

He folded the map and tore it into four pieces. Then he got out of the car and walked around the parking lot, leaving shreds of the map in different garbage cans.

Following the road map, Walter drove east through Orange and Villa Park until he found Santiago Boulevard. In a few miles, it turned into Santiago Canyon Road, and the dry suburban landscape turned into barren brown hills that stretched fifteen miles east to the peaks of the Santa Ana Mountains.

The road curved gently through the hills for ten miles before turning south just before the town of Silverado.

After passing through the town, which was little more than a few stores and an old gas station, Walter pulled the car over to the side of the empty road.

"I forgot," he said, "to show you this."

He took from his wallet a small, faded photograph, on which the name "B. A. Deev" was printed. It showed a grim looking blond, blue-eyed man whose high cheekbones and narrow eyes gave his face a somewhat Oriental cast. He had a small mole on the left side of his chin.

"That's probably gone by now," said Walter, "and you can bet his hair is black as the ace of spades."

Mark nodded. Walter got out of the car and walked around to the passenger side, away from the highway. He crouched next to the door as Mark watched for cars on the road, then burned the photograph with his cigarette lighter.

"Is there anything we forgot to do?" he asked Mark, getting back into the car. "Anything we should get rid of?"

Is there anything on film?" Mark asked.

"Just Mickey and Goofy and the gang," replied Walter. "I think we're okay. Let's go."

In a matter of minutes they were on the second dirt road, driving toward the cabin. Mark was the first to see it. It had been painted red many years before, but the color had since faded to a murky brown. It sat behind a stand of pine trees, 100 yards back from the road. A worn footpath led to it, and a new pickup truck was parked next to it.

Walter stopped the car. "We got lost on our way to San Diego," he said to Mark. "We wanted to get off Interstate 5 for a while to see the canyon country, and now have no idea where we are. By the way, could you give us a jug of water or something? It's hot as hell out there."

"Take it easy," said Mark. I don't need a goddamn script. I can handle it. Don't worry."

As he walked down the path to the cabin, a man opened the front door and started towards him. Mark felt his throat tighten for a moment, and then took a deep breath. From fifty yards, away, the man shouted "What do you want? Stop right there."

Mark stopped, and waited for the man to come to him. He was about six feet tall, maybe thirty-five years old, and solid looking. There was a bulge at his right hip. A gun. He looked all-American, Mark thought. Not Deev, no matter what they did to his face.

"What do you want?" The man stood at arm's length from Mark, and spoke with a flat midwestern accent, eyeing Mark suspiciously.

"We must have gotten lost," began Mark.

"Who's we?" the man asked.

"My father and me. See." He pointed to the blue car parked on the road. "We just came from Disneyland and wanted to see some of the countryside instead of just taking the highway down to San Diego. We're going to the zoo," he said, smiling. "I heard it's great."

The man looked at Mark's T-shirt, at his narrow frame and smooth face, then at the car, with its middle-aged driver.

"You live out here by yourself?" asked Mark.

The man ignored the question. "Do you want directions back to the highway?" he asked. "Go back over the creek, left on the hardtop road, about six miles past town, left on Peters Canyon Road for five miles until you hit the freeway. It'll take you to San Diego."

"Thanks," said Mark. The man turned and walked back to the cabin.

Mark walked to the side of the car. Walter looked through the window at him angrily. "Why didn't you go in?" he asked. "Why didn't you try to go in?"

"Dad?" asked Mark. "Does Deev know of your existence? He wasn't a contact, was he? I got worried. I thought maybe he had access to our files and knew what we looked like."

"Deev doesn't know me," said Walter. "I made sure of that. Do you think I am a fool?"

Mark didn't answer.

"But smart thinking anyway," continued Walter pretending not to notice the glaring silence. "I'm glad you're careful, but you should trust me. Only me." He reached through the window and patted his son's arm.

Mark ran back to the cabin, reaching the door before the man could stop him. When he realized Mark was back, he came out and grabbed the boy firmly above the elbow.

"What do you want now?" he asked, raising his voice.

"I forgot," Mark said, his eyes wide, "to ask if you could give us a jug of water. Dad's really hot and he has high blood pressure, and we just don't want to take any chances."

The man, annoyed but no longer suspicious, opened the cabin door and told Mark to sit down at the kitchen table. Mark saw a powerful two-way radio on a table in the living room.

"Are you a ham?" he asked, using the slang for a ham radio operator.

"Yeah," the man said. "You want a half gallon? That enough?"

Mark heard a door at the back of the living room open. The all-American walked quickly out of the kitchen, toward the source of the noise. "That you, Bill?" he asked, raising his voice slightly. "We have a visitor. Maybe . . ."

It was too late. Before he finished his sentence, the man had entered the living room. He looked at Mark.

The man's hair was dark, but his blue, Oriental-like eyes had not been altered. "Who's this" he began to ask the all-American, with a distinct Russian accent.

"The kid and his father got lost coming from Disneyland," all-American said. "But they're leaving now to go to the zoo in San Diego."

He handed Mark a plastic milk jug filled with water. "Sorry I'm so edgy, young fellow, but Bill and me like to come here to get away from our wives and the hustle-bustle. We kind of like our privacy."

"Sure," said Mark. "Sorry to bother you. Thanks for your help."

· · · ● · · ·

Driving back to Los Angeles, Walter Scholz was a happy man. Everything had gone according to plan. No problems. He would report back to the Center at the scheduled time on Sunday. In a while, maybe weeks, maybe months, or maybe longer, Mr. Boris Alexevitch Deev would have a most unfortunate accident.

"You did well," he told Mark, who sat silently beside him.

"What will happen to Deev?" Mark asked.

"Don't worry about it," Walter said sternly. "It's not our concern."

· · · ● · · ·

Mark made several more trips with his father during the fall of 1972, and gained considerable skill in the art of making quick and neat "dead drops."

It was quite simple, he thought, to walk to a statue in Washington or Nashville, casually check your compass bearing as you began to walk away, and then, after you paced off the correct distance, to bend over as if to tie your shoe and slip the container of money or film or microdot instructions under a rock or tree branch.

In December, during the semester break, Mark traveled with his father on a "real" business trip to Indianapolis to shoot footage for a sales film an insurance company had commissioned, using the Indianapolis 500 as a motivator for salesmen. Mark found the sleek race cars exciting, and hoped they would return for the race later in the spring. They arrived home to find Else in tears.

"The police were here yesterday," she said.

"What?" asked Walter. He tried to seem alarmed.

"Yes," she said. "They caught Stephen near the Peterson's house. He and his friend Jimmy had broken out almost all the windowpanes in their den windows. Walter, you have to do something about that boy."

"What did the police say?"

"Only that they want us to come in with Stephen and talk to some people at the police station. I'm so upset."

"I will deal with him," said Walter.

Walter made Stephen help him replace the windowpanes the next Sunday afternoon, and confined him to his room for a week.

"Why did you do it?" he asked Stephen, as the boy sat on the side of his bed.

"I don't know," said Stephen. "I just felt like it."

"You must learn to control yourself," said Walter. "In life you cannot do only what you feel."

Stephen turned his back to his father. "It doesn't matter," he said. "No one cares, anyhow."

"Your mother and I both care. But you must live by the rules. Wherever you go there will always be rules."

"I don't care about rules."

"You have to care about rules," said Walter. "You cannot live without rules." He stood up and left the room.

4
Pretending

In late February, during the week Mark and his brother had their mid-winter school vacation, Walter was called to Ottawa on business. The instructions said that he should come alone. Mark told his father that he was very disappointed, that he thought he was to be included in everything.

What he told his mother, however, was different.

"Let him go," Mark told Else while they were shopping for new ski boots on a snowy afternoon. "I can use the rest."

Else took a pair of reflector ski goggles from a display rack, and pantomimed a skier *schussing* down the slopes.

" 'What say we hit the slopes?' Isn't that what they say, Mark?" she said.

"Yeah," he said. "You want to?"

"Just me and you, kiddo," he added.

"What about Stephen?" Else asked.

"I guess we can't just leave him in his room for a week, can we?" Mark replied.

"No," said Else, laughing. "The little meatball would eat the house. We better take him."

Mark and Else loaded the old Rambler (which Walter bought because, as he liked to tell his neighbors, he made "an unbelievable deal" on it) early Friday afternoon when Mark got home from school.

Both had expensive, European-made skis and accessories. Stephen, however, didn't have his own equipment.

"Can I buy skis yet?" he asked Else. "Please."

"Please, please, please, please," he added for good measure.

"No," Else replied firmly. "You're still growing too fast, and in the wrong direction, if I must say so. And you're not a good enough skier yet. You never pay attention to the instructors. You're always thinking about getting back to the lodge for a cup of hot chocolate; isn't that it?"

"My feet get cold," the boy whined, "because I have to wear those crummy boots they give you at the rental shop. They're tie-up boots, they're too cheap even to give you buckles. How do you expect me to ski with those?"

"We'll see how you do this week," Else told Stephen. "I'll sign you up for the five-day course at the ski school. If you pay attention and I get a good report from your instructor, we will think about buying you your own equipment. But only then. You have to earn things, Stephen. They don't come to you for doing nothing. You'll have to learn that."

"Don't yell at me," Stephen whined.

"I am not yelling," said Else. "Did I raise my voice? No. I am simply telling you some things for your own good."

"You're always yelling at me," said Stephen.

By the time the three were ready to leave, it was nearly 4 P.M. With a light snow already falling, and a forecast of heavier snow in the mountains, Else was anxious to get started on the five-hour trip to the Stratton ski area, in southern Vermont.

Stephen sat in the front seat with his mother, and Mark stretched out on the roomy back seat and watched the bare tree branches, lightly dusted by snow, whiz by as they drove north on the winding Taconic Parkway, through the Hudson Valley.

Watching the exit signs, Mark began to play a favorite mental game. It consisted of imagining what a certain town was like, who lived there, and what they did. By the time he was finished he would know every last detail about the subject of his imagination.

The sign on the highway said "Poughkeepsie-Amenia." Poughkeepsie seemed too big, so he chose Amenia, a small town, the map showed, near the Connecticut border.

Amenia, he thought. Must be named after a family of Swiss-German Lutherans named Amen who came over in the early 1800s. Deeply religious people, they walked around saying "A-men" all the time, so they called them Amen. Bill Amen is the sixth generation of Amens in the town. A dairy farmer, thirty-three years old, he has a dumpy wife who smiles a lot and teaches Sunday school and bakes sugary fruit pies. They make it together every Friday night, but that's it. No monkey business during the week, and not on Saturday night either, because it's too close to Sunday, and you can't do it on Sunday. Three kids: Bill Junior, whom they call Junior, and Bob, whom they call Buck—the kid's got tremendous hands and feet for his age and plays good basketball. Then there's little Mary, whom they call Mary because she's too plain and simple-minded for a nickname.

"Mark!" Stephen screamed into his older brother's ear, startling him out of his silent world.

Mark jolted inwardly, but didn't flinch as far as his brother could tell. That was Stephen's favorite game; to sneak up on Mark when he was deep in thought, and to scream in his ear to make him jump. But it never worked, much to the frustration of the younger boy.

"Won't you ever stop that nonsense?" Else asked Stephen. "One day Mark's going to belt you in the face, and I won't blame him."

Stephen ignored his mother and continued to lean over the seat, hanging above Mark. "What are you doing?" he asked Mark.

"Don't bother me," said Mark. "Sit down."

"What are you doing?" the little boy asked again.

Stephen was short for his age, and overweight. "Fatball," his classmates called him, or "Potatohead." His fine blond hair, cut in the "Dutch boy" style, framed his round face, with its small straight nose and light blue eyes. His pink complexion and sensitive mouth, the lips usually parted, gave him the look of an innocent.

"ANSWER ME!" he demanded of Mark.

"I'm thinking," Mark said quietly.

"What?" asked Stephen.

"I said you sometimes don't think very much."

"Shut up!" Stephen spat the words out.

"Let's have a peaceful ride, boys," said Else threateningly. "Please. Don't make me stop the car."

"I didn't start it up," said Mark, still lying on his back with his head on an armrest.

"Did too," taunted Stephen.

"Stephen, I have a few questions for you," said Mark cheerfully. "I'm not kidding. Let's play a game together. You answer these questions."

"Here they are," Mark said. "One, why are you so stupid that you can't even do the idiot work they give you in school and Mom has to go in and see your teacher?"

Tears started to well in Stephen's eyes. "Shut up," he said softly.

"Stop it, Mark," Else said sharply. "I'm warning you, stop it."

"Two," he continued calmly, "Why are you so fat and spastic that you're the only kid I know who can strike out in softball, and you can't even stand up on a pair of skis?"

"SHUT UP SHUT UP SHUT UP," Stephen screamed, as he climbed over the seat and began to flail his fists at Mark.

· · · ● · · ·

The southern Vermont skies were cold but clear and blue during the days, and several inches of dry snow fell almost every night, creating ideal skiing conditions.

Stephen complained relatively little about the ski school instruction, and seemed happy enough if Else and Mark accompanied him down the gentle "bunny slope" a few times in the morning before he had to report to his Austrian instructor, Josef.

Else Scholz had learned to ski as a child, before the war made travel from her family's home near Dresden to the Austrian Alps impossible. At the age of forty, she still radiated vibrant health, and was an excellent skier. Walter didn't ski, and was uninterested in learning, but Else had made sure that both children learned at an early age.

Mark had taken to the sport naturally, and could handle almost any slope by the age of twelve. Stephen, however, was still not advanced beyond the safe "snowplow" stage.

On the last day of their vacation, Mark and his mother tackled some of the most difficult slopes on the mountain. By midday both were tired, and Mark would have been content to have a good lunch and go back to the motel to pack for the trip home. Else, however, had earlier proclaimed that she wanted to ski until "I drop dead or it gets dark, whichever comes first," so Mark said nothing.

They ate together in the crowded base lodge, which smelled of wet wool and smoke. Instead of buying the bland cafeteria food, Else had prepared a meal of imported cheeses, pears, apples, and dark bread. They shared part of a thermos full of wine, "but not too much," Else warned, "or you'll ski into a tree."

Sitting opposite each other at one of the picnic-style tables, they leaned toward each other to talk, every now and then touching hands, or laughing at the same moment as they recalled the events of the morning. An observer could sense that there was a special bond between the mother and son, and if that same observer were to view the pair from behind Else, without being able to see her face, but still able to view her athletic body and loose, windblown hair, he could easily have thought that the teenage boy was on a date. Sometimes, alone together and away from the tensions of the family, they would forget to play the mother-son role, and would talk to each other almost as contemporaries. Else saw a lot of herself in her elder son, much of the same reserve and stoicism, but she also saw a much keener intellect and a sometimes cruelly cynical and sarcastic wit. Those traits, she thought, the boy must have gotten from his father.

The thing that she sensed most deeply now was a certain ambivalence toward his new situation. It was something that she believed her husband was unaware of, and that Mark intended for him to be unaware of. To Walter, the boy was a "trooper," as he liked to say. But to his mother, he was just a teenager who wanted to please his father. Or was he? Sometimes she wasn't sure.

They spent more than an hour over lunch, and then checked on Stephen, whose instruction group was on a small hill near the lodge practicing parallel skiing. The chubby blond boy, his ski poles pressed tightly to his sides and his mouth set in grim determination, moved slowly down the hill with his skis almost parallel.

Upon seeing his mother and brother, Stephen waved a pole at them, shouted "Look," and skied slowly but steadily to where they stood.

Mark laughed. "Not bad, little brother," he said. "We'll have you on the slalom course yet."

They skied several times down a challenging, two mile long wooded trail before the sky started to darken.

"One more run," Mark said to his mother at the bottom of the mountain, "before the lifts close for the day."

"Okay," she replied. "We might as well take it all the way to the top."

Halfway up, at a point where Mark and Else were dangling about forty feet in the air, the lift stopped with a jolt. It could mean a cold wait of anywhere from a minute to an hour, Mark worried.

From their perch, the white countryside unfolded in peaks and hills westward toward the border with New York State. The sun had already dipped behind a distant mountain, and the sky was beginning to turn purple.

They remained silent for several moments, until Mark's feet began to get numb and cold. He stamped his skis, resting on a bar outside of the enclosed bubble, up and down until the tingling subsided.

"Are you okay?" Else asked him.

Mark didn't answer; he was looking down the mountain, past the town, at the endless white, broken here and there only by evergreen trees. Maybe this is what it's like, he thought. No, it would be flatter, at least in the part east of the Urals, where the camps were. It would probably be colder, too, and they wouldn't be allowed to wear warm ski clothing. Would they keep the whole family together, or would Mom have to stay at a camp for women? Or is there really no such thing as the Gulag system? Was it manufactured by the warmongering western press?

"Mark?"

He wondered to himself why he was thinking such things, anyway. Wasn't the family loyal? Hadn't they served well so far? Wasn't Hoffnung eventually going to become the most damaging mole the KGB ever had? They would never have any reason to punish us, would they?

"Mark, I'm talking to you!" said Else, grabbing his arm and shaking it.

"Oh," he said. He pushed the thoughts away. "Oh, I'm sorry. I guess my mind was wandering."

"Isn't it always?" she asked. "I think you spend too much time alone with your mind and your father and not enough with people your own age."

"I have friends. I do things with people."

"I worry sometimes, Mark," said Else. "I know you bring some of your classmates to the house every now and then, and you play sports, and take pictures for the newspaper, but I think maybe you do those things just to please your father. Do you do them because you really enjoy these things? A boy your age should be having a good time, meeting girls. You should make an effort to develop friendships, Mark, and that doesn't mean just people who you discuss school things with."

"I have friends," said Mark, hunching his shoulders in response to the icy air blowing through the stalled lift; "just like everybody else. It's just we're not the rah-rah types you probably think all American kids are like. I have friends, and they invite me to do things with them, and everything's perfectly normal, Mom, so don't worry about anything. I don't know since when you've become so concerned about being normal, anyway. What's the big deal about normal?"

"You're a fifteen-year-old boy no matter what, Mark, and I'm very worried that your normal development isn't hurt by . . ."

"By our obligations, is that what you wanted to say?" Mark interrupted.

Shivering, Else rubbed her gloved hands together. The lift jolted forward for a second, and then stopped again.

"What the hell's wrong with this thing?" Mark asked.

"Have you ever kissed a girl, Mark?" Else looked straight ahead at the long line of empty lift cars, rocking from side to side in the cold air.

"That's a strange question," said Mark, calmly. "And I don't think that it's any of your business to know."

"I just want to know that you are doing the normal things for your age."

"You want me to be normal." Mark said this as a declaration rather than as a question.

"Yes. Is there anything wrong with wanting my son to be normal?"

Mark leaned forward, resting his elbows on his legs and his chin in his hands. "In computers, Mom," he began to speak softly, "I know you don't know much about computers, but let me try to explain it in simple terms . . . You can program a computer to perform certain functions, like addition, or multiplication, and it can only perform those functions on what you feed into it, the data. It can come up with answers that are the result of a certain function, or series of functions, being performed on the data it has, but it can't do anything with what it doesn't have . . . In the same way, the computer can have been fed all the data you have, all the information, but if it isn't programmed to perform a certain function on that data, it won't. It really doesn't work all by itself."

"So," Else said sharply. "you're a computer, and you haven't been programmed correctly or you are missing some data or something like that. Is that what you're telling me?"

"Not exactly," said Mark, in the detached manner of a professor explaining his subject, "but there are parallels."

"Will you stop talking to me like that," Else demanded.

"Like what?"

"LIKE A COMPUTER," she screamed. "I ask you a simple question, which is, do you associate with boys and girls your own age in the way you should, and you answer me with nonsense about computers. I don't want to know about computers. I want to know about Mark."

"About who?"

"Will you stop that!"

"How do you know my name is Mark?"

"Stop being ridiculous," said Else. "Of course your name is Mark."

"How do you know?" he asked. "How do I know? How do I know they didn't tell you. Mark sounds like a good name, so why don't you change it to that from Alexei, or whatever it was. You know Mark sort of sounds like it'll fit in more where you're going, Walter. See, Dad named me Alexei to get in good with the guys at the Center, but it was all for naught, wasn't it?" Mark laughed.

"You're acting like a crazy man, Mark. Stop it right now!"

The lift lurched again, and this time continued to move. Mark, however, responded to his mother's demand without hesitation. "Don't worry about me Mom," he said, in softer tones.

"I'm all right. I'm really okay. I'm not going to jump off a bridge or anything like that, if that's what you're worried about."

"That's not what I'm worried about, Mark. You would never do anything like that. It would be out of character. You would never admit that you were unable to handle your problems."

"I don't have problems," Mark said, "I have certain pressures, perhaps, but I wouldn't call them problems."

"I think you would feel better about these pressures, Mark, if you began to develop some real friendships with your classmates, if you began to feel like you belonged, instead of just watching them and saying, 'Oh, it's so interesting to see how these odd Americans behave.' You must stop being an observer, Mark. You have to participate."

"But I do," protested Mark.

"You pretend to," said Else. "You join in name maybe, but not in spirit. People can tell when you do that. You can fool people about some things, but not about matters of the heart. Attitudes are often easy to detect, Mark. People can sense it when you're not one of them."

"Well, we do a pretty good job of it, don't we?"

"It's not the same thing," Else said. "We are what we appear to be, and more."

"You want me to have friends, to belong," said Mark, almost wistfully, "but don't you realize that if I do that, if I really forget about what I really am, and pretend that I belong . . ."

Else sat quietly as her son's voice grew louder in the cold, airborne bubble. She kneaded her strong hands, and listened.

". . . all I can do is pretend," he continued. "Because I can't be real, because if I was . . ." He paused a minute.

"How can you even say such a thing?" he asked. "How can I be real, How can I belong? You have to keep your distance, don't you. When it gets below the surface, you have to keep your distance."

"In the end, you do," Else said, after a moment of silence. "You are right."

It was dark when they got to the mountaintop. They skied down the empty slope by the light of the reflected snow, Mark following closely behind his mother.

· · · ● · · ·

For the next several weeks, Mark thought about the conversation on the ski lift. He knew his mother's pleas for him to be "normal" could not be satisfied, and he knew that what mother, who was often freer with her words than he thought she ought to be, had talked about were things that he had been thinking for a while.

So maybe it would be good to try, he thought, to do some of the things that the other kids at school did, even if they didn't appeal to him. He could try, and if he didn't like it, it could be counted as just another academic experience.

Lisa Keller, a girl in his neighborhood, was a year ahead of him in school but often sat next to him on the school bus. They would exchange sarcastic comments about school, or make fun of people in the neighborhood, but never discussed anything of real importance. Lately, however, Lisa had been quieter, and seemingly more contemplative than usual.

On the bus to school one morning, she asked if he had ever been to "Encounter Experience," or "N-X," which she said she had been going to for several weeks and "getting my head together."

"Yeah, I know about N-X," said Mark. "Isn't that where all the drug addicts go to spill their guts about how messed up they are, and then that shrink with the frizzy hair—what's her name?—Dr. Winston—then she tells you it's because your mother didn't let you play with your shit when you were three years old."

"Hey, like take it easy, you know" said Lisa, who had taken to wearing long, shapeless cotton dresses with fringe on the bottom that was always dirty from scraping the ground when she walked. "Like maybe you should stop being so critical of things you're not into, okay?"

"You're one to talk," said Mark. "Since when are you so peaceful?"

"At N-X, you realize that you just put things down because you're insecure, and like that's something you have to work out with yourself."

"Like mellow, mellow," said Mark, affecting what he supposed was a "druggie" voice.

"Like maybe you could get something out of N-X, have you ever thought about it?" the girl asked.

"I don't think so," said Mark. "I don't really see what the point of it is, except to get out of going to class a few times a week. I have other things to do with my time."

"It's always worth the time to find out who you really are, what makes you tick, and like, people are really supportive to you. Like everybody really wants to help you, it's sort of like having another family," said Lisa, breathlessly.

Just what I need, Mark thought, but said, "The people who go to that aren't really my type, for the most part."

"Don't be such a snob," she said. "You really should try it. It's not like going to a shrink or anything, it's just that you get to hear other people talk about what they're going through, and it's sort of nice to know that you're not the only one who feels bad sometimes, and that other people are going through the same thing you are, you know?"

"I don't think so."

"Why, you think you're so much different from everybody else just because your parents are foreign or something?" Lisa asked.

"That's not what I meant," said Mark, surprised that the girl understood his response, almost the meaning he intended her not to pick up. "I meant I don't think I'm too interested in the whole thing."

"Try it just once," said Lisa. "Try it, you'll like it," she said, unwittingly repeating the punch line of an Alka Seltzer commercial.

"Are you a missionary, or what? Why do you care so much if I go?" Mark asked.

"Just come once," the girl said, with a beatific smile. "I'm going this afternoon, seventh period. Meet you at the water fountain outside the room. You don't even have to say anything. Just listen. It's really no big deal. You don't have to make like any big confessions or anything. You'll see."

The cardboard sign on the door read, in carefully lettered India ink script, "Welcome to Encounter Experience. Leave your image at the door, enter and find the real you."

Mark thought to himself as he walked into the dimly lit, smoke-filled room behind Lisa. They sat down on a huge, over-stuffed pillow on the floor, and listened as Frankie (no last names were used in N-X) talked in angry tones about his father.

"It's not like I don't try or nothing, you know, like I try to make the guy happy, but all he fuckin' does is bust my chops. Fuckin' is always on my case, no matter what. My older brother Jimmy, he can't do no wrong in the old man's book, it's like Jimmy's King Shit or something."

"You must resent that," said the leader of the group, a graying, angry looking psychologist named Sara Winston ("Just call me Sara"), whose job was constantly being threatened by a combination of disgruntled parents and budget cuts.

"I could kill the guy sometimes," said Frankie.

"We all have aggressive feelings," said a red-haired girl wearing a T-shirt with the name of the rock group Crosby, Stills,

Nash and Young emblazoned on it. Sounds like a Wall Street law firm, Mark thought.

"So I come home after some partying Friday night, and the motherfucker grabs me by my neck and says I smell like dope, what did he raise me to be, a fuckin' dope addict. So I was a little high, right, so I says get your fuckin' hands off my neck before I spit in your eye, and anyway, you don't get addicted to dope, you stupid fuck."

"Maybe your father would like you to speak to him more respectfully," said Sara. "Did you ever think of that"?

Mark smothered a laugh. The kid talks like he was raised in a sewer, he thought.

"Fuck respect," said Frankie. "Motherfucker never gives me any respect, treats me like a piece of fuckin' shit, then he wants respect."

"Have you shared your feelings with him?" asked the red-haired girl.

"Lay it on the line with the old man?" asked a tall, thin black boy named Curtis.

"Think about it, Frankie," said Sara. "Think about why you come home after smoking pot when you know your father will smell it. Think about why you smoke it in the first place, why you need it. Maybe you're really hoping for your father to react like that."

"Fuck that," Frankie said.

"Get angry," implored Sara. "Tell us what you really think, but not now. Think on it for a while. We'll always be here for you."

"You know, I really appreciate that," Frankie said.

"We're your friends," said the red-haired girl. "We really care for you."

"That's what Encounter Experience is about, people," said Sara, looking directly at Mark. "We're about helping, and caring, and sharing our feelings. We're about growing as people." She paused a moment. "Lisa, why don't you introduce your friend? We're always glad to welcome someone new."

"This is Mark," said Lisa. "He's in tenth grade. He's from my neighborhood."

The fifteen people in the room turned toward Mark, and nodded at him. He nodded back. He recognized most of them, and knew a few of their names, but did not know anyone well.

"What's on your mind, Mark?" asked a girl wearing round wire-rimmed glasses.

"Nothing," he said. "Lisa said I could just watch."

"No problem," said Sara. "We won't put any pressure on you. But remember, whatever you hear in this room stays in this room. That's the golden rule. We have to trust each other."

"Dig it!"

"Trust is the name of the game, Jack," said Curtis.

For the next hour, Mark listened as his schoolmates confided in each other, often startling him with their sometimes brazen confessions and professed feelings. He could not understand how they could sit there, calmly puffing on cigarettes, as they revealed the most intimate details of their lives to each other. There was the girl with the bad acne who told how her father would come into her room at night when she was a little girl and touch her under her nightgown until her mother found out and threatened to kill him, and that now she can't stand the thought of even kissing a boy because she can't get out of her mind the "creepy" look on her father's face when he would "do those things" to her.

Then another girl remarked, laughing, how she wished her father could do something like that, because at least it would be better than passing out drunk on the dinner table and throwing up all over himself and making her mother call up his boss in the morning to say he's sick and can't come to work.

What, Mark thought to himself, would he say about his family? That his father was a Commie spy and they were in the process of making him one, too, and that he spent his summer vacations learning how to subvert the U.S. government someday? Why not? He imagined what would happen. An earnest looking girl would say "Thank you for sharing that with us, Mark, like we know what you're going through, you know?" And another one would chime in with something like "Yeah, like that must be a really heavy head trip, like being a spy and everything. I can really relate to it." Oh, can you? Mark thought, laughing to himself at the absurdity of such a question.

Though the idea of Encounter Experience held little appeal for Mark, the things that he heard in its smoky confines fascinated him. He was by nature a voyeur, an observer and listener, eager to learn secrets but loathe to betray them. He enjoyed sitting back quietly on a floor cushion, listening to the recountings of sometimes bizarre, sometimes ludicrous incidents, experiments with drugs and sex, and of the family secrets that were intended never to leave the house.

Two days after his first N-X session, Mark returned. The next week he returned again, this time without his sponsor, Lisa. He lit one of his Player's cigarettes, and blew smoke out between a small space in his front teeth, waiting for Sara to start the conversation.

"I want to start off today," the psychologist said, looking in Mark's direction, "by emphasizing how important it is that Encounter Experience not be a one-way street for some people. The experience can only be truly appreciated by those who are willing to give as well as take; by people who will not only listen, but who will also share with us their thoughts and feelings. Imagine what would happen if everybody listened and nobody talked; there would be nothing to listen to."

Gems of wisdom, Mark thought, that broad must have taken basic logic.

"Understand, people," continued Sara, "that I'm not pointing fingers at anybody. I can't force anybody to do anything that he . . ." she paused a moment, then continued, "or she doesn't feel comfortable doing. But it seems to me that if we can trust each other, we can talk to each other, and to everybody's benefit. That's all I have to say."

"Tell it like it is, Sara," said one boy.

"Lay it on the line, sister," said Curtis, who seemed to spend most of his time at N-X.

"I've been thinking the same thing as Bill," said the red-haired girl, whose name, Mark had learned, was Carolyn.

"Like, for example, and this isn't to put you down," she said, talking at Mark, who sat across the room from her, "but, like, I'm just being honest with my feelings, and it sort of seems to me that you . . ."

"Who?" asked a girl who had been looking at the floor as Carolyn spoke.

"Mark." replied Carolyn. "It just seems to me that you'd get a lot more out of N-X if you would share yourself with us."

As the girl spoke, Mark felt his throat turn dry, and his mind raced as he began to think of a response.

"Could you tell us how you feel about what I've just said, Mark?" asked Carolyn.

He looked down at his hands, which were playing with the extinguished remains of his half-smoked cigarette. He briefly chewed on his lower lip.

"Take your time," Carolyn said, as the others in the room directed their attention at Mark.

He lit another cigarette, and dragged on it. "I guess it just takes me a while to get used to things like this," he said. "I'm not used to talking to people like this."

"Why don't you start by describing your family to us, if you'd like to, Mark," said Sara, who sat in a corner of the room on a tattered green vinyl armchair.

"What kind of description would you like?" Mark asked.

"That's entirely up to you," said the psychologist, twisting a strand of her hair around a finger. "Whatever you feel comfortable with."

I shouldn't be doing this, Mark thought. It's not right. It's none of their business, even the things I can talk about. He had been told countless times by his father and by his handlers at the Center to avoid at all costs getting into a situation where he might be tempted into saying the "wrong" things. Not necessarily anything that would have drastic consequences, but just enough to get people thinking about you more than they should. Also, it was simply bad form. There was no practical reason for it. If you want to talk about personal matters, his father had told him, talk to your mother and father. There is no one else who needs to know.

"Cat got your tongue, man?" asked Frankie.

"Easy, Frankie, take it easy," said Carolyn.

"The man can't sit there like a fuckin' mummy, wrapped up in himself all the time," Frankie said, laughing at his own retort.

"You ought to write for Carson, Frankie," said Sara. "You have a real subtle wit."

Mark leaned forward on his pillow. "All right, take it easy, everybody," he said, startling his schoolmates with the commanding tone of his voice.

"There's really not much to say, but I'll try," he added.

"There's always something to say," Frankie said.

"Let him talk," said Sara.

"I guess one thing that sort of bothers me is that I come from a pretty high-achieving family, and they expect a lot from me. They want me to do well in school, and sometimes it sort of bothers me."

"Is that all that bothers you?" asked Sara.

"Mostly," said Mark. "I suppose it's because they're foreign-born; you know, America, the land of opportunity and everything. I guess immigrants are always like that, they want the best for their kids."

"It's not me so much, I guess, but it'll probably be harder on my little brother, the older he gets. My father, he's a freelance filmmaker and photographer, and I do a lot of work with him, and I think my little brother, he's nine, I think he feels left out sometimes, especially because he has problems in school and isn't all that brilliant when it comes to his schoolwork. Sometimes my father lets him know that he's disappointed in him, and I'm always the star of the family, and I think he resents me for it and feels like he could never compete with me."

As he spoke, a wave of nausea swept through Mark. Why, he thought, am I doing this? Why am I suddenly such a weak person that I have to say these things to people I hardly know to say hello to in the halls? What's the point? So they'll like me? Does it really matter if they like me or not?

"That's really all there is to say," Mark said.

"It is?" Sara asked.

"Yes," said Mark. "And anyway," he added, glancing nervously at his watch, "I'm supposed to meet someone in a few minutes, so I should get going."

"Not so fast," said Sara. "Don't you think it would only be fair to flush out what took you all of a minute to say? Tell us how you feel about this, and not just the bare facts?"

"I really have to go," said Mark. "I'm sorry."

"COP OUT," shouted Frankie.

"Why don't you shut up," Mark responded in a steely voice.

"Hey, like no need to get hostile," Carolyn said to Mark.

"Maybe Frankie has a point," said Sara. "Maybe you are copping out. Maybe you would feel better if you tried to deal with your feelings."

Suddenly, the room became a surrealistic blur to Mark; the faces of his interrogators—Carolyn, Frankie, Sara, and the rest of them—seemed to hang suspended from the air in front of him, thick streams of blue cigarette smoke swirling around them as they chided him.

He sprang up from the floor, sweeping his books under his arms in a fluid motion, and said, "I have nothing more to say."

Frankie, sitting on a chair near the door, stood as if to block Mark's exit. "Cop out," he said.

Mark brushed past him, and stumbled over pillows, books, and empty soft drink cans toward the door.

"It's okay," said Carolyn, as Mark reached the door and began to turn the knob. "He'll be back. I can tell; he needs us. Just give him time."

Mark's face flushed, and he turned to confront them. His fists were clenched, and he struggled to control the emotion in his voice. He took a deep breath, and then said, "I won't be back. I don't need you, and I won't be back."

"COP OUT," Frankie shouted after him, as he left the room.

· · · ● · · ·

Just before dinner that night, as Mark was watching an old Bogart movie on television downstairs, the telephone rang, and he answered it. Walter, upstairs in the kitchen, had picked up the receiver at the same time, but Mark said "hello" first, and Walter remained silent.

"Hello," the female caller said. "May I please speak with Mark?"

"Speaking."

"Hello, Mark, this is Sara Winston."

Mark's hand tensed on the telephone receiver. "Yes?" he said.

"I'd like to apologize for what happened in Encounter Experience today," said the woman. "Perhaps I shouldn't have let the kids get on you like they did. It's difficult to talk about your family."

"Yes?" asked Mark again.

"I hope you'll come back soon. We're happy to have you with us."

Mark remained silent.

"Mark?"

"Yes?"

"I hope you'll come back. Will you?"

"I don't know," he answered. "But I don't think so. I just don't think it's for me."

"Well, why don't you think about it for awhile," said Dr. Winston. "Please give it some thought."

"Okay," said Mark, hoping she would end the conversation. "I will. Okay?"

"Okay, please do. Goodbye, Mark."

"Bye."

Walter was unusually quiet during dinner. Instead of his normal banter and storytelling, he looked down at his plate, ate slowly, and occasionally glanced across the table at Mark.

The ground floor of the Scholz's typically suburban split-level house never failed to fascinate the classmates Mark sometimes brought home. Each of the four little rooms downstairs, he would explain, has something to do with his father's job. One room was for taking pictures of small things like insects or even microscopic objects, and was full of miniature cameras. Some would even fit in the palm of your hand. Another room was the developing room, and it had shelves full of chemicals and papers, and an aluminum tub about four feet long.

The largest room was the projection room, which was really like a small movie theater. Standing against one wall was a gray metal floor-to-ceiling shelf that contained four large metal boxes with knobs and dials on them. Walter would often show the apparatus to neighbors and explain that he was a radio buff and that is was just "some old equipment I've been playing around with."

The fourth room was the one that Mark told his friends was called the exposure room. This room was always kept locked and airtight, he said, because his father had film in there that was under a special kind of treatment. Once he showed them a movie his father had made; it was one that had gone through the special process in the exposure room. It was called "Birth of a Child," and featured amazing scenes of a fetus in the mother's womb. The film used in the movie was so sensitive, he said, that it had gone through a dozen different processes and had to dry for nearly a week.

The exposure room, Mark would tell them, was strictly off limits.

· · · ● · · ·

After dinner, Walter and Mark went downstairs "to develop some film," they told Stephen when he asked. Walter told the little boy that he wished he could come and help them, but that there was really not enough space in there for all three of them. He promised Stephen to teach him how to develop film soon.

Inside the little room, the "exposure room," Walter flicked on a bank of fluorescent lights recessed in the wall. Mark, in three quick motions, opened the door of a safe hidden beneath a floor panel, and extracted a metal box the size of an attaché case. Inside it was a radio transmitter strong enough to reach Moscow from anywhere in the world.

Employing a complicated number-base code, Mark used a dial like that on a telephone to record eight digits at a time. When each message segment was complete, he pressed a button that systematically scrambled the numbers and then sent them through the atmosphere so rapidly that radio detectors would not be able to determine where they were sent from, even if they were intercepted.

After each segment was sent, it had to be repeated backwards. A tiny green light flashed each time the transmission was received in Moscow. The process was repeated for nearly two hours, Mark performing the task as his father, Walter to some, Colonel Walter Gottfried Scholz or "David" to others, watched and nodded his approval.

"You did a good job," said Walter when the transmission was completed. "It's obvious that you learned a lot last summer."

"Thank you," Mark said.

"However," said Walter, scratching his cheek with his left forefinger, "it seems that one of the things you have still not learned is how to keep your mouth shut about certain things."

"What?" Mark felt panicky. Could he know? he wondered. Does he know what I said? How could he have found out?

"I overheard your conversation with that woman who called before dinner."

"You overheard?" Mark began to ask.

"I picked up the phone at the same time . . ." Walter began to apologize, but stopped himself. "That's not the point," he shouted at Mark. "The point is that someone will always be trying to listen. You never know when someone is listening. You have to be careful."

Walter slammed his open palm on the formica counter. "What the hell is this 'Encounter Experience' business?" he demanded. "Who was that lady? What did you say about your family?" Walter's eyes were wide and his lips pursed as he waited for Mark's answer.

Shame. It swept through Mark like a searing red heat, dimming his eyes for a moment, making him wish he was anywhere else than where he was. He could think of no proper response, no answer that could explain what he did.

"Answer me?" Walter demanded. "What is this business? What did you say?"

"Please," Mark said softly, tears beginning to well in the corners of his eyes. "I didn't mean that."

"What did you do?" shouted Walter. "Tell me this instant!"

Mark felt his voice cracking. "It's just a place—Encounter Experience—where kids at school go to talk about things that bother them, you know, problems at home and school and things like that."

"You don't have any problems," Walter said brusquely. "You have no reason to go to a place like that."

"I just went to see what it was like," said Mark, poking at his wet eyes with his knuckles. "I was just going to watch. It was interesting, to see what kinds of problems most kids have. I didn't mean to say anything. I was just going to watch."

"WHAT DID YOU SAY?" Walter barked the question directly into Mark's face.

"I said I was just going to watch," said Mark.

"I meant, what did you say in front of all those people at this Encounter Experience place, you fool. What did you tell them?" Walter yelled.

"Oh," said Mark. "Nothing. I didn't really say anything important," he said quietly.

Walter grabbed Mark by the shoulders, and tightened his grip until Mark began to wince. "Did you say anything about family matters? Did you open your mouth in the middle of all this crap, all this free love business, isn't that what the kids are doing these days?" Walter talked rapidly, as if he was about to lose control.

"It's not what you think . . ." Mark began.

"Shut up," Walter snapped. "You don't know what I think. I think you're starting to lose sight of some very important facts, young man, and I think you better get on the right track before you do some real harm, if you haven't already. I think you better stop trying to follow the ways of your American counterparts to such a point that you begin to think it's fine to go around talking about anything you want to. They are morally corrupt, don't you understand? Their system is ready to collapse, and there is no purpose to their lives, so they must resort to this search for meaning in these encounter groups and drugs and wild behavior. Look at what they are doing at the universities! Destroying them, spitting in the eyes of their educators, burning buildings. The youth are seed, Mark, and when the seed is damaged, so is the fruit. Look at the craziness of the young people in this country, Mark; watch, listen, and understand them, but do not allow yourself to become one of them. That must not happen. Do you understand?"

"Yes," Mark said softly. "I understand. But I don't know if it is all as bad as you say."

"It's worse," said Walter. "Believe me, Mark, I am a student of this country, and I can see what is happening to it. And it's all beginning with the young people. But enough with that." He paused a moment.

"Now tell me, Mark," Walter implored, "what exactly did you say in that group today?"

"I just said," Mark declared, "I swear, I just talked for a few minutes about how sometimes I feel pressure to do well in school, and how Stephen and I are so different."

"And that's all you said?" asked Walter.

"I told them you were a freelance film-maker," Mark said. "I swear. That's all I said—you know I'm not foolish. I wouldn't say anything wrong to anybody. I thought you could trust me."

"I thought I could," said Walter. "Until I found out you are involved in these groups where people sit around and talk, talk, talk, just to make themselves feel better. It's such a weakness. I never imagined that you would have any desire to become involved in such a thing. And I trust that this is the end of it, and that you will make sure never again to place yourself in a situation that could lead to trouble."

"Yes," Mark said. "I'm sorry. I knew I was doing the wrong thing the moment I opened my mouth. It's better just to listen."

"It's always better to listen," said Walter, "but I'm not saying you can't talk to people, that you can't be a normal person. What you want to do is create the appearance of being what they used to call 'hearty fellow-well hailed.' "

"Something like that," said Mark, unwilling to correct his father's error of idiom.

"Like Lyndon Johnson, L. B. J.," said Walter. "A backslapper, a handshaker, a real wheeler-dealer. Boy, did that guy know how to operate. He would make you think that he was as wide open as the Texas skies, but he never really showed his hand. You could never figure out what he was thinking. Why, the guy would smile at a fellow and ruin him the next day. A very private person, but not by any means shy or quiet. That's how you want to be."

"Okay," said Mark, "but do you still trust me?"

"I trust you," said Walter. "You're my son. I know you would never do anything to hurt us. But when you're young, you are more prone to errors of judgment, and I just want you to learn how to avoid them. Because, Mark . . ." his sentence trailed off.

"Yes?" Mark asked.

"Because," Walter continued, "we cannot afford to make any errors."

· · · ● · · ·

Exactly forty minutes after the final message segment was sent, Mark removed another receiver from a wall safe and activated it. The instructions took only seven minutes to arrive, but the deciphering process was a tedious one. It was not until midnight, almost five hours after they had entered the little room, that Walter was confident that they had received a correct message.

It read:

Arrive with Hoffnung in Dallas, Texas airport, April 27, before noon. Travel to Grapevine Reservoir northwest of city, proceed to boathouse where you will find a park bench. Microdot following message, place in magnetic container, and attach to underside of bench. Message to say: Abandon plan to recruit "Horace" at NASA. "Horace" has been planted by FBI. Watch him, but do not establish contact with him. End message. Rent rowboat with Hoffnung and stay 100 yards offshore until man wearing yellow shirt and red hat removes container from bench. End

"You will microdot the message," Walter told Mark. "Make sure you are careful about it, but it's not necessary that you show it to me. I trust you to do it correctly. After all, to the Center you are Hoffnung, the Hope. Just as I am David, who slew Goliath."

5
...
Twenty-five Year Plan

On July 4, 1973, Walter Scholz and his family boarded a Lufthansa flight for Frankfurt, Germany, landing early the next morning.

"Riding on airplanes is no fun," said ten-year-old Stephen, as he stood in line to be checked through customs. "I couldn't sleep, and the trip was too long."

Else Scholz reached over and patted her irritated son on the head. "But you said you wanted to see Germany," she said.

"Yes, but I didn't want to miss the Fourth of July. The Scanlons, down the block, said they were going to shoot off a lot of fireworks."

"You can do that next year," she said. "Right now you get to take a train ride."

Else explained that the two of them were not staying in Frankfurt, but would be taking a two-hour train ride to Coburg, where they would stay with relatives whom the boy had never met before. Stephen's father and Mark, Else said, would be traveling throughout Germany for the next three weeks, making a film about rural mountain life. They would meet in Munich at the end of the month.

Stephen was unhappy about the plans. He wanted to stay with his father and brother, and maybe help them with the movie. But he decided it would do him no good to complain and anyway, the boy enjoyed being alone with his mother. She let him do pretty much as he wanted.

The family separated after a breakfast in the airport restaurant. Else embraced her husband quickly, and then turned to her blond, handsome son who was looking more and more like a man every day.

"You are still too young," she said to him. "I hope you are ready. Please be careful, Mark. Your mother loves you."

The father and son registered at a small hotel in Frankfurt under the names listed on their passports: Walter Gottfried Scholz, age forty-four, and Mark Conrad Scholz, age sixteen. They spent the night there, and the next morning tore up their passports and flushed them down a toilet. They then registered at another hotel using names appearing on a second set of passports. This way, if any suspicions were ever raised, the authorities would be unable to determine where they had been for the ensuing three weeks.

Early the next morning, July 6, the pair took an express train to Munich, 200 miles to the south. They arrived in the Bavarian city at 1 P.M., and enjoyed a lunch of bratwurst and beer at an outdoor beer garden. After a leisurely walking tour of the city, they took Munich's modern underground train system, the U-Bahn, to the residential southwest section, and quickly found the Hotel Holzkirchen, a deteriorating four-story structure.

At precisely 4 P.M., a short, middle-aged man dressed in an ill-fitting dark suit slowly walked around a corner and approached the hotel. Walter Scholz immediately recognized him as Ivan Filikov, the man who had recruited him into KGB service. Filikov was now a highly placed officer in the Illegals Department, the section of the KGB responsible for training and monitoring agents who live in foreign countries under false identities.

Without a flicker of recognition, the older man walked within several feet of Scholz and began to light a cigarette. He tossed the wrapper from the cigarette package to the sidewalk, then turned to Mark and said, "The city is so full of tourists this time of year."

Hesitating only a moment, the boy responded. "Yes," he said, "that is why we are leaving for the mountains Thursday."

· · · ● · · ·

The three Soviet agents, if Mark could be counted as one, arrived late that evening at the Czechoslovakian border, near the village of Lenora. They presented their credentials and passed quickly through customs.

Walter was afflicted with a certain sadness on the few brief occasions he had to return to the land of his birth. He could not understand it. The sadness always took the form of a vision in his mind; a vision of a high-spirited young man named Tomas. The scene was always the same. There would be the young Tomas, his arm linked with that of a smartly dressed girl, and they would be strolling on a leafy boulevard in Prague, watching the river Vlatava flow by.

It would take some effort to get these thoughts out of his mind, but he knew they were silly ones. Still, they persisted. Walter decided that maybe he was just mourning his fading youth.

The next afternoon, July 7, Walter, Mark, and Filikov flew from Prague to Moscow's Vnukovo Airport on an Aeroflot jetliner. They dined that evening in a dark wood-paneled, high-ceilinged room in the director's wing of the KGB Center, enjoying the freshest caviar, cold sweetmeats, and vodka served in heavy crystal goblets. After the meal, as they sat in comfortable leather chairs smoking cigars (Mark declined), they were visited by Yuri Iosifovich Kanayev, deputy director of the KGB Illegals Department.

A tall, courtly man with polished manners, Kanayev was the highest ranking member of the KGB hierarchy who dealt directly with illegal foreign agents. He had been looking forward to meeting the Scholz father and son, especially the son.

Kanayev had spent the previous week reviewing the files of Major Scholz and his son Mark. It especially pleased him that young Mark maintained the highest academic standards. Also, it was good that the young man had become involved in athletics, and was a member of several after school clubs. He understood the importance of cultivating friendships, and of having diverse interests. He would be quite useful someday soon, Kanayev believed.

The three men rose as Kanayev entered the dining room. After formal introductions, they engaged in small talk for several minutes, and then the deputy director removed from his carrying case a detailed schedule that Walter and Mark would be following for the next three weeks. The first week would consist mostly of debriefing sessions. Mark and his father were to be interviewed separately. The information each furnished would be compared to determine whether the father and son exhibited similar patterns of observation.

Later, there would be training on newly developed communications equipment, and Mark would be instructed in the use of microphotography, a process by which a normal-sized page of writing is reduced to the size of a period at the end of a sentence.

There would be much to learn, Kanayev said while looking directly at Mark, and much to think about during the forthcoming days.

The Scholzes were furnished with an elegant apartment on Kutozovsky Prospect. Leonid Brezhnev and other members of the Politburo, including Yuri Andropov, the KBG director, lived on the same shaded street only two blocks from the Kremlin.

Much of their work would take place in the apartment. They could come and go as they pleased, as long as they were in the apartment at designated hours. They were to be cordial to the neighbors, but were not to engage in any long conversations. The neighbors would know not to ask questions.

During the long debriefing sessions of the first week, Mark sometimes became bored by the questions of his interrogator, who was usually Filikov. At such times his mind would wander, and he would be reprimanded by the senior officer. A long lecture would often follow.

"I quite understand, Mark, that these questions may not seem terribly interesting or important to you," Filikov would begin.

"One's daily life, especially to a boy like you who has known no other kind of life, does not always appear eventful to he who is living it. But, Mark, you must at all times remember that everything you do, no matter how trivial you may think it, will one day enable you to serve in a capacity that will make you one of our most highly valued men."

Mark's comprehension of the Russian language was perfect, but he often had difficulty understanding the meaning of Filikov's discourses. The man spoke in vague terms, and had a habit of smiling conspiratorially at Mark when he said such things, almost as if he expected him to read his mind.

On the final day of debriefings, Filikov handed Mark a typed sheet that read across the top "Hoffnung—Twenty-five Year Plan." Mark at first thought it was a joke, but quickly remembered that Filikov was not given to humor.

"I always thought that a five-year plan was considered suffi-cient," Mark quipped.

"Well, then we will start with the next five years," Filikov replied grimly. "The first order of business is to gain admittance to Georgetown University, which has the finest foreign service studies in the United States. You will accomplish this goal through conventional means, which you are certainly capable of doing. You will remain there five years, and earn both the bache-lor's and master's degrees. During that time, you will become active in an organization called the U.S.-China Friendship Soci-ety, and you will befriend visiting students from the People's Republic of China. You will learn what they think of their Soviet neighbors, and what they think of their country's recently devel-oped warm relations with the United States. When your studies are complete, you will seek employment with a security-related agency of the United States government, preferably with the Central Intelligence Agency or the National Security Agency. You will become a hard working, responsible employee, and you will steadily gain promotions. By the time you are forty years old, you will hold a top-level position."

Filikov looked up from the folder he had been reading from. This time he had spoken plainly. He addressed Mark severely:

"You are a very talented young man, Mark. You should have little difficulty in accomplishing these goals. We are counting on you."

Mark suddenly felt dizzy. Never before had he thought in detail about the course his life would take. He had just assumed, as most teenagers do, that it would go along pleasantly enough by itself. His father had hinted at such things as Filikov had just read from the folder, but it had always been in generalities. Now he knew exactly what he had to do. There were few choices. In one way it was a relief, though a rather overwhelming one.

· · · ● · · ·

At breakfast the next day, Filikov entered the apartment and announced that for the remainder of their sessions Mark and Walter would be separated so each could receive different types of instruction. Walter would stay at the Center, he said, and Mark would go with Filikov after breakfast to a secret location some-where outside Moscow. Walter did not appear to be particularly pleased by the arrangement, and did not hesitate to make his feelings known to the elder spy.

Filikov, however, reassured the father that his son would be in good hands, and that there was really no way in which he could receive this special kind of instruction in close proximity to Walter. "But if you're so concerned," he told Walter, "we will make arrangements for you to talk to each other on the telephone every night." The special training for Mark would last approximately a week, Filikov said.

Mark was excited though apprehensive about leaving his father for training outside Moscow. Filikov declined to be specific about the training during the automobile trip out of the city, except to say that the boy would "experience certain things." This he said with a slightly leering grin, adding, "you will experience things that will come in very useful as you go on in life—things perhaps you have not yet experienced."

Mark closed his eyes, let some wild thoughts run through his mind, smiled to himself, and then looked at the scenery outside the window of the small Volga sedan.

Filikov drove fast and not too steadily on the Skolkovskoje Highway, one of the radial roads that extends out of the capital city. It would only take them about an hour, the spy trainer said, to get to "the very comfortable little cottage where you will stay."

"Will you stay with me?" Mark asked.

"No, that won't be necessary," said Filikov. "You'll be in quite capable hands, believe me."

Driving northeast from the city, they passed through the small town of Osajevskaja, driving parallel to the sloping green fields bordering the Kl'az'mu River. Several miles outside of the town, the open fields merged into thick forest, the road veered away from the river, and Filikov turned off into the narrow road that seemed to lead in the direction of the rapidly flowing stream.

At the end of it sat a small, red and white gingerbread-style cottage which looked like it had been around since the Czar's rule or had been lifted from the illustrations in a book of nineteenth century fables.

Filikov drew the vehicle up to the cottage door, got out of it, and stretched his arms wide.

"Ah, the wonderful, beautiful country," he said. "What a lucky young man you are to be able to spend your holidays here in such a tranquil setting. I wish I had been able to enjoy such things when I was your age."

"What wonderful, beautiful things will I be doing out here in the tranquil country?" Mark asked, using a Russian idiom that Filikov was surprised the boy had command of.

The man grinned, put his arm around Mark's shoulder, and said "My boy, sometimes it is better not to know exactly what awaits you. It is much more interesting that way."

"You have a way of frightening me when you talk like that," Mark said. "I wish you would be more explicit."

Filikov picked a blade of long grass from the ground, and began to play it through his teeth, which had small spaces between them. He wove the thin green blade in front of one tooth, behind the next, and continued until it was woven into his upper teeth, with the ends protruding from each corner of his mouth. Then slowly, with the precision of a technician who performed the procedure regularly, he removed it.

Mark watched, but said nothing.

"You think I'm a little strange?" Filikov asked him.

"What were you doing?" Mark responded.

"Just flossing," the man said. "Removing the plaque. Very important for dental hygiene." He paused, then said "Now!"

"Yes?" Mark asked.

"About me being frightening. Funny, but I never thought of myself in that way. It distresses me," he said, drawing his eyebrows down in a gesture of consternation, "that a fine young man such as you would be frightened by me. Maybe it is a family trait, who knows? I remember back twenty years or so when your father was under my care, and he often expressed similar feelings. He always would want to know exactly what he was doing, where he was going, who was what and what was where. But you will learn that sometimes it is just better to trust those who have responsibility for you. We wouldn't let any harm come to you. We have a lot invested in you, young man, and we intend to see that our investment pays off."

Mark frowned, but remained silent.

"Excuse me for putting it in those terms," Filikov said. "I just meant to say that we are all comrades and we all look out for each other's well-being. Okay?" The man smiled broadly, but without conviction.

"Now," Filikov exclaimed again. "I really should get on my

way." He took a key from his pocket, walked to the door of the small house, and opened it.

"Come in, Mark, let's get you settled in here," he said.

Mark removed his bags from the back seat of the car, and followed Filikov into the house. The interior was decorated with modern furniture which looked Scandinavian in design; it was remarkably fashionable and un-drab, Mark thought, by Soviet standards.

On the walls were mounted photographs of street scenes from various Soviet cities, and several framed museum posters. Thick, white area rugs added an aura of luxury to the large living room, and a refrigerator hummed in the background.

"I trust you will be comfortable here, Mark," said Filikov. "It is really a very nice place. Your bedroom is in the rear, and I'm sure your trainer will get you settled later."

"When is my trainer coming?" Mark asked.

"Soon," said Filikov. "Just relax on the sofa and wait a few minutes, and you will be introduced. Filikov turned and left. He started the Volga and rumbled down the narrow road, and Mark was alone.

Obediently, he set about relaxing. From his overnight case, he drew a paperback copy of a book that had recently become popular among his friends, *Mother Night,* by Kurt Vonnegut, Jr. He flipped to the middle of the book, and continued reading the story of the American Nazi, Howard Campbell, Jr., the son of a General Electric engineer who became a broadcaster of Nazi propaganda during World War II.

Mark read the book, in part, so that he could nod his head in agreement when his friends would say "Isn't Vonnegut unreal? The guy must be out of his mind!"

As he began the first page of a chapter entitled "The Polygamous Casanova," he heard a rustling in a back room. He put the book down, and stood up, his heart beating rapidly. A moment later, he heard a door open, and then light footsteps coming down the hall.

"Hello, Mark, I am your trainer," she said. "I am Natanya. It's good to meet you."

She stood across the room from Mark, smiling kindly, her hands on her shapely hips. She was perhaps 25, and beautiful in the way that few American men appreciate. Almost six feet tall, she was wearing fashionable leather boots with heels that made her tower over Mark. Her long, thin legs were sheathed in tight, high-quality denim jeans, which were available in the Soviet Union only on the black market. Her lips were narrow, her stomach flat, and her small breasts high on her lithe frame.

It was her face, however, that riveted Mark's attention; the cheekbones high and Oriental, of the type particular to Siberians and Finn Laplanders. Her wideset eyes were pale gray, the distance between them in perfect proportion to her broad face. Her nose, small and finely sculpted, was lightly freckled, and her mouth was gentle and inviting. Her jet-black hair hung loosely to her shoulders, and she brushed a strand of it out of her eyes as she laughed easily and said, "Surely you've seen a woman before, Mark. It's not polite to stare so."

"Sorry . . . I'm . . . It's just that . . ." the words stumbled out of his mouth.

"No need to apologize," Natanya said briskly. "I know you must not have expected me to barge in on you like this."

"I expected some crusty old man, really. I thought maybe they would send me Colonel Abel," he said, referring to the famous Soviet agent who had spied in the United States for many years before being captured by the FBI in 1957, convicted on espionage charges, but then returned to the Soviet Union in 1962 in exchange for Gary Powers, the U-2 pilot. Abel had returned to Russia as a hero, and became a master spy trainer at the KGB Center. He was especially known for having trained agents who worked in the United States.

"Colonel Abel is busy with other matters," she said. "I'm afraid I will have to do."

"You're really a trainer?" Mark asked, knowing as soon as the words were out they were ill-chosen.

Natanya walked over to where Mark stood, and peered down at him. Her expression became severe. "No," she said. "I'm a housemaid. I was sent to cater to your every whim. What do you think? This isn't America, you know. We have had your 'women's lib' for a long time."

"I didn't mean . . ." Mark began.

"It happens that I am a graduate of the Institute of U.S. and Canada Studies, and of KGB specialty schools too numerous to mention. I look younger than I am, though I shan't bother to tell you my age. Soviet women have their vanities too, you know."

"Anyway, these matters are not important. The important

thing is that you take full advantage of your time with me and learn all you possibly can. I will be carefully monitoring your progress. The work will be demanding. Understood?"

"Yes," Mark said.

"There is an American phrase for it," the woman said. "I'm going to bust your balls," she said in perfect English, laughing.

Mark laughed also. He wondered if she was serious.

· · · ● · · ·

That night, as they ate a dinner of salmon and boiled potatoes, she outlined the work that would occupy them for the next several days.

Walter called at about 9 P.M., asked Mark how he was, and said he had heard that Natanya was a well-respected trainer. "I wouldn't mind trading places with you, you punk kid," he told Mark laughing. "Work hard and behave yourself. And don't tell your mother about it." He laughed again.

Natanya showed Mark to his room, told him she would wake him at seven, and said goodnight.

The next morning, after breakfast, they began to review cryptic terminology, some of which he already knew and considered rather silly. He learned that a "legend" was a cover story, a "music box" was a radio transmitter, a "shoe" a forged passport, and that "illness" meant arrest.

"I think we can skip this stuff," he told Natanya. "It's so cloak-and-daggerish," he said in English, which the woman spoke fluently.

"Listen here," Natanya said sharply. "There are certain ways we do things, and there are reasons for everything we do, even if they are not clear to you."

"Think carefully about that," she added. "Because it pertains to everything that we will do here until you leave. There will be a reason for everything. Remember that."

"Okay," said Mark. "It's just that . . ."

"Don't argue," Natanya commanded. "Just listen."

· · · ● · · ·

During the next several days he learned to master the fine points of invisible writing, and received advanced training on how to encipher and decipher messages reduced to tiny dots through microphotography.

The technical instruction, however, was not as interesting to Mark as such topics as disinformation and the recruitment of Americans and other Westerners into Soviet service. *Dezinformatsiya,* or disinformation, Natanya explained, by which the KGB could surreptitiously foment disorder and strife in and between capitalist nations, was one of the most effective espionage tools. It could also be used to discredit a government or an individual who threatened to harm the Soviet system, such as an outspoken dissident living in a western nation.

Recruitment, she said, was an important duty of every KGB agent, and the utmost attention should be given to understanding the theory and practice of it. Those in the best position to recruit westerners with access to important information, she said, were Soviet agents attached to trade delegations or agents with diplomatic cover. The most successful recruitments, Natanya told him, are often carried out not in the native country of the person being recruited, but a third country where the chances of detection and apprehension are not as great.

"Many of your father's trips to Canada are for recruitment purposes, although he does not do any direct recruiting, for obvious reasons. There is a certain professor friendly to our cause who David has used to considerable advantage."

"Who?" Mark asked.

"David, your father."

"Oh, yes. I forgot. That's his code name, isn't it?"

"Surely you haven't forgotten yours, also?"

"No," he said.

"You are the hope. That's why we're here this week. Now pay attention," she said, placing her hands gently on his shoulders, her long fingers reaching toward the back of his neck.

Mark stiffened, then relaxed.

"If you learn your lessons well, you may learn more than you bargained for." She smiled winsomely for a fleeting moment, and then clapped her hands together like a drill sergeant.

"Tell me," she commanded, "who are we looking for when recruitment is our goal in the United States."

Rapidly, with obvious command of the subject, Mark began to answer: "Employees of government agencies who have clearance for secret political, military, technical, and intelligence information. Also, employees of private firms who perform work on contract to the government, especially the large defense-oriented companies, which operate practically as government agencies.

Also, students and others who are preparing for service in the intelligence agencies . . ."

After nearly thirty minutes of these recitations, Natanya told Mark that he had done very well, and that he could be excused from his lessons for a little while.

"It's a beautiful day outside," she said. "Why don't you go and enjoy it."

Relieved, he left the cottage and walked down a trail through the woods to the riverbank. He sat on a grassy knoll, then leaned back and stretched out and watched the thin wisps of clouds float through the sky, changing shape or disappearing.

He could not rid his mind of the thoughts that had been creeping into it since he arrived at the cottage five days before. They were natural, he supposed, but he dared not mention them to Natanya. She was beautiful and brilliant, everything that he had never seen before in a woman, and he desired her. He wanted to understand her, to become friends with her, to love her, but he knew that he was just a little boy to her. A clever one, perhaps, but a boy all the same. At least, he thought to himself, he was practical about it. There's no use in pursuing her like a fool, he thought. Why waste time? On the other hand . . . He closed his eyes and smiled, and breathed deeply of the heavy summer air.

"Mark." Natanya whispered the name into his ear. Startled, he opened his eyes and flinched at the sight of his trainer, who had crept up silently behind him, and watched him for a moment before she spoke.

Not knowing how to react, Mark simply said "Hi."

"You look so peaceful lying there," she said, sitting down on the soft grass and leaning over him.

"I was just thinking," Mark said.

"So was I." She lowered her head, placed her hands behind his ears, and kissed him gently on the mouth. His eyes remained open, and he looked into her eyes, but did not respond to her kiss.

She smiled, and ran her fingers through Mark's fine hair. "Have you ever kissed a woman before? You look surprised."

"I didn't expect it," Mark said softly. "I was hoping, but I . . ."

"Hoping for what?" Natanya interrupted.

"That you would kiss me."

"A silly little kiss," she said, "like I was your older sister, is not something to get excited about."

He groaned in exasperation, and said to her, as matter-of-factly as he could, "That, my dear, was no sisterly kiss."

"And that," she retorted, looking down the length of Mark's reclining body, "is no brotherly lump in your pants."

"Mark turned over onto his belly immediately, blushing. "You have a way with words," he said.

Natanya stretched out next to Mark, moving close to him and running her hands over his back. "You should learn not to fluster so easily," she said. "You have to react with a level head at the hands of a seductress. Because a man's penis is the way to his secrets, you know."

"And I think it's time that you learn how to maintain a level head in even the most delicate situations," she continued.

Mark's heart began to race and his breath came in rapid, shallow intervals as he began to realize what was about to happen. He turned his head toward Natanya, and asked: "You are the seductress?"

She smiled, her cat-gray eyes shining with excitement. She embraced him, drew his lips to hers, and flung a jeans-clad leg over his hips.

Soon they were naked, and the brilliant sunlight played on their bodies. Mark was transfixed by the fluid motions of Natanya as she made love to him, and nodded silently in response when she made the statement: "This is your first time."

It was over rather quickly, as Natanya had expected it to be; Mark, however, didn't know what to expect, and asked his mentor sheepishly, "Did I do all right?"

"You were just fine," she said, amused at his concern. "Now I think you should get back to studying your work."

Her abrupt, taskmaster's tone shocked him. He had expected the time afterwards to be different. "Shouldn't we just lie here awhile and talk about what just happened?" he asked, suddenly embarrassed at his nakedness and reaching for his clothes.

Natanya laughed derisively.

"How sentimental!" she pronounced. "The young lover wants to talk about his first . . . let's call it his first experience. That's delicate enough, I think."

"Why are you behaving like this?" Mark asked, his face showing clear hurt. "Why are you taunting me?"

"But I'm not. I just want you to take certain things for what they're worth, and not to make too much of them."

"But," Mark began to stammer, unsure of his words, "I love you, we love each other, in a way. Isn't that why we did it?"

She moved close to him again, and took his face in her hands. "Don't delude yourself," she said. "I told you before, there is a purpose for everything we do together. The purpose was not for you to fall in love with me, and I seriously doubt that if you had had more experience with this sort of thing you would not have become so overwrought. Don't act so silly. Believe me, by tomorrow you will have forgotten all above love."

"I want to stay here with you," Mark said, gently tracing her lips with a finger.

"No," she said. "There will be more young Marks for me to train. Some of them will react like you. Some will have already learned not to let lust weaken them. You too will learn, and I hope this will have served as a valuable lesson. You don't love me, Mark, and I don't love you. But we can be very good friends. I'm fond of you; you're really a very sweet person. It's rather touching to see some qualities in you that I'm sure won't be there next time we meet, if ever. Once your service begins in earnest, once you stop looking at it as a big adventure that other boys don't get to have . . ." Her voice trailed off.

"Once you realize with certainty what your role is, then you will understand what I am telling you."

"That I can never love anyone?" Mark asked.

"You can, but it will be a love tempered by a thing more important than merely the love between two people. There are greater things to love. There is love of the system, of the party, of the cause.

"It sounds phony," Mark snapped. "Don't tell me you've never loved anyone."

"Okay. I won't tell you anything, except for this: Never be compromised. If you can love without compromise, then you are an unusual person. But I need not say anything; you'll find out for yourself. Just make sure that your first mistake is one that can be easily mended. In this business, there are all too often no second chances."

"I've heard that before," Mark said.

"Remember it."

Suddenly, they embraced again.

6

American Friends

"I trust that your training with the young lady went without adverse incident." Ivan Filikov spoke the words quickly, his bland face revealing no expectation of the response he anticipated. As the pair sat in Filikov's office, Mark suppressed a smile, and in a fleeting moment decided it would be unwise even to hint at certain aspects of the instruction he received at the hands of his trainer. It was very likely that Filikov already knew all the details of Mark's stay at the cabin, and that he was just testing Mark to see what he would reveal. Regardless of what Filikov already knew, Mark thought he would only hurt himself by saying more than he had to.

"None that I can think of," said Mark. "Everything went according to plan, I am sure."

"I'm sure," Filikov responded, in the same flat tones. "Would you care to tell me about some of the more interesting things you learned?"

"There was quite a bit of discussion about ideological matters," Mark said, maintaining a serious air. "The subject of who makes the best candidate for successful recruitment is really fascinating. We spent much time on that. It appears that those who will come to our side for the promise of money only are not the ones we are looking for, even though in capitalistic nations one would assume that money is the best motivator. But we have learned through trial and error, regrettably. . . ."

"Fine, Mark," Filikov interjected. "There is no need to recite the vast amount of knowledge that I'm sure your young mind has absorbed in recent days."

"But I thought you wanted me to tell you about my training," Mark said, trying to look disappointed.

"Yes, yes, yes. Some other time, perhaps." Filikov began to shift uncomfortably in his chair. "Are you okay?" Mark asked. "What's wrong?"

"Nothing really," said Filikov. "Just this," he added, as he waved his hand around his cluttered office. The table against the wall to Mark's left was stacked with file folders. Two wastebaskets were filled to overflowing; in the adjacent file cabinets, two drawers were open with folders stacked on them so they could not be closed.

"The directorate has decided in its infinite wisdom," Filikov explained, "to computerize the files. There is no time to do all which needs to be done when you have to spend half of each day going through files to decide what to save and what to destroy."

He winced. "Especially," he added, "when you have gas pains."

"I'm sorry to hear that you have such problems," Mark said politely.

"It's all right. It's just that sometimes it gives me problems in the bathroom. Either it's the job or my wife's cooking. I've had them both for so long I can't tell which it is."

Mark allowed the remark to pass without comment.

Filikov stood up. "I guess I better go down the hall before things get out of hand," he cackled.

"Just stay where you are. If you weren't Walter's son I'd make you leave while I go to the toilet. But you're all right. You're the Hope."

The old man trotted out of his musty office, dragging his slightly crippled left leg behind him with an obvious swishing noise as he made his way to the bathroom.

Crazy, Mark thought to himself as he rose from the chair, already ignoring Filikov's instructions. The old bastard is absolutely out of his head, carrying on with his ridiculous bathroom jokes. What do I care about his diarrhea?

Mark was surprised at his own boldness as he walked around the perimeter of the room, observing it with detached curiosity. Listening carefully for the sound of Filikov's feet dragging down the hallway, Mark walked to an open file drawer and pulled it out another six inches. Perhaps he would chance upon his file, he thought or the one marked "David." It would make for a few minutes of interesting reading and he could return the files to their original state and be seated quietly, as Filikov had told him to do, by the time the aging spymaster returned.

His Russian had improved remarkably during the last year, and he read the faded markings on the envelopes with little difficulty. Some simply read "SECRET," others "TOP SE-CRET," and one bulky envelope stuck in the back of the drawer was unmarked.

Mark opened it, and almost laughed out loud when he discovered an issue of *Playboy* magazine, dated March 1968. "How un-Soviet," he said quietly, smiling at the thought of poor old Filikov being sent to Siberia to have his mind purified of the thinking that led him to buy such a sick manifestation of the capitalist way of life. Mark opened the magazine to the center-fold, and laughed again when he thought of Filikov drooling at the sight of the busty Miss March. He considered for a moment hinting to Filikov humorously that he knew of the Russian's penchant for American decadence, but decided that Filikov really didn't have a very good sense of humor.

He returned the drawer to its original position, and then tried the handles on the other three drawers in the cabinet. All appeared to be locked. Mark balled his right hand into a fist, and pounded firmly on an area near the handle where he thought the locking mechanism was. He heard something spring open behind the handle, and pulled once again on it. It opened.

Like the other one, this drawer was stuffed with closed brown envelopes, except that these envelopes seemed to be grouped under the heading scrawled on a tab pasted to a cardboard divider at the front of the drawer.

It said *Amerikanski Droogi*, "American Friends."

Mark quickly flipped the divider back, and began to examine the fronts of the other envelopes. Again, there was writing in smeared pencil, but instead of the Cyrillic alphabet, the words were written in English. The words were names of the American states, and the one closest to the front of the drawer read "Arizona." Mark counted sixteen envelopes.

Mark opened it, a light sweat starting to form on his upper lip and forehead.

Approximately fifty yellowing pages were bound together.

On the first page was the date, "April 18, 1972." The text was in Russian, and Mark began to read it laboriously, but sure of what he read.

"This family," began what appeared to be the introduction to the report,

> is led by MORGAN, who was recruited into our service while an officer in the American OSS, stationed in France, during the Great War. Morgan had been tested and proves to be reliable. Immediately after the war, when MORGAN returned home to the United States, he established residency in the city of Tucson. Although the city was not important to our purposes then, we had good reason to believe it would experience a substantial growth, and we thought it best that our man establish himself in and grow with such a city. Our expectations have been met, if not exceeded.
>
> Let us just say that MORGAN's occupation is involved with the silver trade, and that his business often causes him to travel to Mexico. Of course, thousands of Arizona businessmen have valid occasion to travel to Mexico, so it is not surprising to us that MORGAN's actions have aroused no interest in him by the authorities.

Still listening nervously for Filikov, Mark continued reading.

> MORGAN has established important links with embassy personnel in Mexico City, and has, more importantly, facilitated the illegal immigration of numerous native-born Mexicans who are in our employ. MORGAN has also helped us pass several important KGB agents into the United States.
>
> MORGAN has functioned very effectively as the control for the families of PICKERAL in California, TORRENT and PASSAGE, both in Texas, and JOSEPH SMITH, In Utah.

Turning several pages at a time, Mark stopped when he came to the heading SPRINTER.

"This boy," it read,

> promises to do great things for us in the future. He is fifteen years old now, and seems to suffer none of the rebellious outbursts that all too often appear in middle-class American

youths. SPRINTER became fully aware of all his father's involvements on his thirteenth birthday, though he claimed at the time that he had known for several years that MORGAN had some secret connection to our agency.

SPRINTER's loyalty to his father and family is, at this time, stronger than his loyalty to international socialism, but that is to be expected. He has been placed on a stringent reading program that should do much to shape his still impressionable mind.

While training in Moscow last summer, SPRINTER impressed us as having a keen intelligence and a high sense of adventure, which he apparently acquired from his father. He expressed a desire to accompany MORGAN on more missions, and was particularly quick to master several types of highly sophisticated equipment.

SPRINTER is now in the second year of high school. He is an accomplished athlete, and one of the more popular young men in his school. Academically, he is just above average, which is something of a disappointment to us. However, SPRINTER has many other qualities that lead us to believe he will, at his full maturity, be one of our more valuable and trusted agents in the United States.

The telephone on Filikov's cluttered desk rang, and Mark was suddenly jolted out of his almost total absorption in the "American Friends" file. It rang again, and he walked over to answer it.

"Filikov's office," he said.

"Filikov?" a voice asked. "Who is speaking?"

"This is a visitor," Mark cautiously replied. "Filikov has left his office for a moment."

The voice crackled with laughter. "For a moment, eh? That's the fourth time today he hasn't been in his office when I've called. I'll bet old Filikov is having a bout with his bowels again. He'll be gone an hour, if I know him. Just tell him that Mikhail Telenko, from the technical directorate, called. Goodbye."

His heart pounding, Mark walked across the room to the thick wooden office door and locked it by pushing down on the button near the doorknob. He would tell Filikov that he received an odd phone call, and that for his own protection he thought it best to lock the door until Filikov returned. It was a strange excuse, he thought, but Filikov was a strange man and might not think anything of it, he hoped.

He returned to the MORGAN file, and continued to turn the pages past the entry on SPRINTER. There were several pages about MORGAN's wife, whose code name was MAYBELLE. She was born in London in 1926, and met MORGAN during the war. She was responsible, to a great extent, for MORGAN's recruitment into the KGB, but the report furnished no details on that.

TURQUOISE was the name assigned to the seventeen-year-old daughter. "Forget TURQUOISE," Mark muttered to himself, anxious to move on to some of the other folders. Before replacing the MORGAN report in its envelope, he made a mental note to remember all he could about SPRINTER. Someday, he thought, they might be able to get together and compare notes. It would be like meeting a long-lost brother. Maybe even a twin.

He skipped over the envelope marked California, and opened the one marked Connecticut. Closer to home. Maybe someone he had heard his father discuss.

ELITE was the first word on the paper, also dated from the previous year.

"His background cannot be described as other than perfect," it began,

because it is so typically American upper class. His type is often referred to as 'eastern establishment' in the United States, and what that term means is that he is from a long-established New England family, and he attended a prestigious boarding school as a youth and a university of the type called Ivy League.*

Mark followed the asterisk to the bottom of the page. "*Of course, it is inadvisable to be more specific about the schools ELITE attended, or to be specific about many details in this report. The companion report contains such information."

Continuing to read the report, Mark found ELITE was of such value to the KGB

because of his extensive and well-rooted contacts among the class of people who run the vital government organs. It is well known that this type is over-represented in the CIA and other intelligence-related agencies in the United States.

ELITE has close friends in these agencies from his school days and from family connections; in fact, in his social circles the two are almost inseperably intertwined.

One of ELITE's cousins is a deputy director of the CIA. His college roommate is a congressional representative, and has a seat on the intelligence subcommittee. Both men have invaluable access to intelligence secrets. ELITE has access to both men, as well as others.

Our man is the superintendent, or what is called 'headmaster' of a boarding school in this state. He was formerly an executive with a large multinational corporation, but his vast family wealth allowed him to take the position he presently holds, which pays very little compared to his former position, but is a much more leisurely one.

We are quite pleased with it, as it offers ELITE much more time to satisfy his obligations with us.

ELITE is most valuable to us in that he apparently has done an excellent job of transmitting socialist values to his twenty-year-old son, HOMER. This young man has already served as a summer worker in the National Security Agency, and has virtual assurance of permanent employment with an intelligence-gathering unit of that agency upon his graduation from a prestigious university next year. His major field of study is eastern European affairs, and he has impressed his professors and superiors during his summer job with his command of the field.

Mark jammed the report back into its envelope. His pulse was racing, and he felt himself hyperventilating. He sat on a chair next to the filing cabinet and took deep breaths. He slowly rose from the chair, unlocked and opened the office door, and peered down the long, dark, barren hall in both directions. Filikov was not there. Checking his watch, he found that the old man had been gone ten minutes.

Mark closed the door, and again locked it. He returned to the forbidden cabinet, and once again began turning the folders.

Nothing for Delaware. Two for Florida. Nothing for Georgia or Illinois; one in Chicago. He turned, and turned again. New Jersey. New Mexico. New York.

His hands were trembling slightly as he opened the folder. The front page had printed on it, in thick, black letters, DAVID FAMILY.

He turned the page, and began to read:

Certainly our most valuable asset in all of North America, if not at the moment, then certainly in the potential they hold. DAVID was recruited from the intelligence services of the German Democratic Republic military in 1952. In the more than twenty years he has been in our service, he has operated strictly according to the plan set for him and his family almost from the beginning, after his marriage to MARY.

DAVID has blended in very nicely with the typical American suburb in which he lives, a town where many of the residents work in nearby New York City. His legitimate business interests have fared well, and, like those established by some of our other American friends, provide an excellent base of operation for his more important work.

The KGB has invested more in DAVID and his family than it has in any other family in this category. In our opinion, DAVID and his family members have perhaps not as great an opportunity to penetrate the highest levels of U.S. government as do one or two other families, in particular ELITE and SUSAN.

However, the very circumstances that allow ELITE and SUSAN the greatest chances to perform the ultimate also make them a greater security risk to us than the DAVID family. As native-born Americans, they are more inclined to suffer a change of purpose.

"Conversely, it would be more difficult for DAVID or his immediate family members to cause problems of this type. There are presently family members in socialist nations of sufficient closeness who could be adversely affected by unwise decisions on the part of their American relations. More importantly, there is HOFFNUNG.

Mark's eyes remained focused on the last word for several seconds. HOFFNUNG. The hope, the boy who could do everything. The boy who would do everything, whether he wanted to or not. The boy for whom there were great possibilities, and even greater plans. He read on:

HOFFNUNG was born on October 10, 1957. His development was rapid. He showed signs of extreme precociousness by his first birthday. At age seven, his intelligence quotient was tested at 165. Later tests confirmed this figure.

The boy in many senses is a typical American teenager, but this is manifested only in his day-to-day behavior with his counterparts. He has a keen awareness of his true function, and understands that appearing as he does to his American neighbors, schoolmates, and others, is a very important part of his job.

HOFFNUNG has mastered just about all the technical points that he will ever need to, and shows great ability in the use of photographic equipment. DAVID reports that the boy has been fascinated with photographic gear since he was very young.

HOFFNUNG is at once both the pawn and the king: he can be used as a device to keep tight control on DAVID. In the next several years, as his training intensifies, he will be called upon with increasing frequency to visit the Center, on occasion for extended periods of time. His visits will of course be necessary to ensure his progress, but they will also serve to send the message to DAVID and MARY, especially the woman, that HOFFNUNG is in fact a subject of the Soviet state.

Eventually it is expected that HOFFNUNG will attain a position in the U.S. government which would make it inadvisable for him to travel to the Center. By that time, we will have determined exactly what his value is.

In a flash of anger, Mark stuffed the report back into the envelope, and then back into the file cabinet, unaware of the fact that he had placed it between the two envelopes marked Texas instead of between New Mexico and Texas, where its proper alphabetical place was.

He was suddenly angrier than he had been in as long as he could remember: angry that it was all so perfectly planned, angry that the forces that controlled his life hesitated not at all to use the term "pawn" when referring to him. Mark slammed the file drawer shut, and sat down again to think for a minute, to decide whether or not to go on reading his destiny in cold, detailed print. But there was no time to think and no time to get angry, he suddenly realized as he quickly sprang to his feet, opened the office door, and scanned the corridor for his aging mentor. It was clear.

Mark, his palms sweating, opened the file cabinet again. He took deep breaths to fight off a choking sensation. He could feel the heat from a large, bare, globe-shaped lightbulb against the back of his neck.

But something inside him halfway between a gnawing curiosity and an uncontrollable compulsion made it impossible for Mark to stay away from the thirteen reports on the "American Friends." He decided to go through the folders rapidly, just long enough to remember some vital strands of information that would be enough for him to start from, when the time came.

Skipping MORGAN, from Arizona, he opened the PICKERAL folder just long enough to see that the family lived in San Diego, where PICKERAL was employed at the Navy base in an unspecified job. He had two young sons.

ELITE, from Connecticut. Mark flipped past the folder. SUSAN, of Washington, D.C. SUSAN was thirty-three years old, divorced, and had a daughter. The report did not say what she did for a living, but alluded to the fact that she was very close companion to a ranking member of the Senate Subcommittee on Intelligence.

PARABUS, who lived in the Florida Keys, had "close ties to the Cubans. Married, three sons, a commercial fisherman, and a pillar of his community."

REFUGE, also from Florida. MIKE, a minor politically appointed civil servant in Chicago. Two daughters, one son, not involved, wife had been successfully co-opted into service.

FORTUNE, a New Jersey man who imported marble from Italy.

LUKE, a ski school owner who lived near Taos, New Mexico. Church member, family man.

PASSAGE, from Brownsville, Texas. DAVID, from New York. He looked at it again. DAVID.

As he held the folder, he became aware of a faint dragging sound in the hallway. It was, he estimated, perhaps sixty or seventy feet away, and he was sure it was Filikov.

There were, at most, thirty seconds remaining before he would reach the door. Mark rapidly looked at the two remaining folders, TORRENT, from Texas, and JOSEPH SMITH, from Utah.

Quickly he replaced the folder, unlocked the door and sat down. He tried to breathe normally as Filikov entered the office.

"Ah," the man signed. "It was necessary to be away longer than I thought. I hope you kept your mind active but your hands folded."

"Of course," Mark replied softly. Ever the obedient child, he thought. Play along and everything will work out. But when Filikov did not speak, Mark said, "I was reviewing in my mind the excellent instruction that I have received here during the last two weeks, and how much I've enjoyed myself. Boy, will I have something to tell the guys back home!"

Mark braced himself for Filikov's reaction, barely concealing his glee as the KGB officer began to redden at the cheeks and exclaimed "Have you lost your mind?"

"Only kidding," Mark said. "Can't you take a joke?"

"Yes, a joke indeed," Filikov spat back. "Some joke." But then, in an apparent change of mood triggered by nothing Mark could discern, Filikov began to laugh heartily and pound his desk with his meaty fist.

"Yes, indeed," he wheezed, between sputters of laughter. "He'll tell all the boys back home in the USA. Wouldn't that be something! Wouldn't that just be grand! Oh, what a sense of humor you have, my fine young man."

7

The College Kid

The years Maria Halvorsen spent at the Lycée Internationale in Lausanne, Switzerland, were more fun for her than for the administrators of the venerable and somewhat stuffy boarding school. "This place needs a sense of humor," she said shortly after her arrival, and proceeded to supply it with one.

She had the reputation of being a bit wild. One night, a housemother walked into Maria's room while she was entertaining a boy. The woman was not amused, and reported Maria's offense to the headmaster. The next day, Robert Halvorsen was on a plane from Copenhagen to Geneva, and had to muster up all his diplomatic skills to prevent his bright, lovely, but sometimes unmanageable daughter from getting expelled by the imperious headmaster, Monsieur Henri Malveaux.

Later, Maria was seen by a teacher at a local cafe, and the teacher had reported back that the girl had been "raucous and drunken, and in the company of older boys."

Again threatened with expulsion, Maria wrote a contrite letter to the headmaster and promised never, ever, ever again to do anything that would reflect poorly upon the good name of the esteemed Lycée. But Maria and her father managed to save her place in the class of 1975 because she was a diligent and brilliant student, and because her peccadilloes did not affect the quality of her academic work.

At the beginning of her senior year, she was ranked third in her class of fifty-seven. Her classmates, many of them the children of American businessmen and diplomats, spent the fall of their final year reading catalogs from American colleges and universities and deciding where to apply. For Maria, there were only a few places she would even consider: Carleton College in Northfield, Minnesota; Harvard, and Georgetown.

Carleton was her emotional favorite because of the romantic notion she had of returning to Minnesota and rediscovering her Norwegian-American roots, but her parents wanted her to go to Harvard, "to follow in the Halvorsen tradition."

Robert Halvorsen, though not a domineering tyrant, encouraged his only child to attend Harvard not only because he and his father had, but because he believed it to be the finest institution of higher learning in the world.

"Too stuffy," Maria told him in a letter. "Not my style. I appreciate your idea of the Halvorsen tradition, but mine is to go back to Minnesota. Also, Carleton is a first-rate college."

"My dear daughter," Robert Halvorsen replied,

I can understand your not wanting to attend Harvard, even though I think it is a mistake not to consider it more seriously. I can assure you admission; as you know, the dean is an old friend. Carleton, in my opinion, is a fine school, but somewhat removed from the mainstream of things. I don't think you could stand the homogeneity of the student body, or the lack of cultural stimulation, relative to what you are accustomed. You have mentioned Georgetown, which I propose as a good compromise; it is not Ivy, of course, but we can overlook that shortcoming (only kidding). Many colleagues in the diplomatic corps have been through Georgetown and recommended it highly. Also, Washington is a lively and stimulating town, and is infinitely more international in flavor than Northfield, Minnesota, though Northfield has its own fine qualities. I will be in Geneva in a few weeks, this time not, thankfully, to bail you out of a mess with that imperious prick who runs your school. Until then, love, your dad.

Maria applied to, and was accepted by, all three schools, as well as by two lesser universities. In May she decided to attend Georgetown with a few misgivings, but also with much anticipation.

· · · ● · · ·

His KGB superiors had directed Mark to get his college education underway as soon as possible, so he doubled up on his academic courses during the next year in order to graduate after the eleventh grade. His guidance counselor, a short, thin, man named Julius Perratta, suggested that he wait and graduate "with the other boys and girls in your class."

"Whattaya wanna rush for, Mark?" he asked, leaning back in his cheap swivel chair. "Why hurry? You'll only be sixteen if you graduate this year, and ya know what?"

"What?" Mark asked.

"I'll tell you what. You'll be sittin' in your dorm room, twiddlin' your thumbs on Saturday night while the older guys have all the girlie action. You know why?"

"Why?"

"I'll tell ya why." Perratta leaned closer to Mark, and in a hushed tone of man-to-man confidence, said: "Because girls like older guys, that's why. These big college men, Mark, they swoop down like a buncha chicken hawks and steal all the action from right under your nose. You need another year to fill out a little, put on a couple pounds, a couple inches. When you're sixteen years old, you're still a kid, no offense intended. Now if you were a girl, that'd be a different story, it'd be all right for you to go to college at this age. You know why?"

"Because guys like younger girls," Mark deadpanned.

"That's right," Perratta bellowed.

"I appreciate your concern, Mr. Perratta," Mark said, "and you're right, I'm sure. My social life won't be the greatest for a while, although you never know. I'm pretty adaptable. But I'm really eager to challenge myself, and I don't think there are any more challenges for me here at Woodvale. So if you could just write those recommendations for me, I'd really appreciate it."

"You're the boss," Perratta said, with an air of resignation. "The kid wants to go away to college so young, I guess all I can do is offer some friendly advice."

· · · ● · · ·

Mark was accepted by Harvard, Yale, M.I.T., Cornell, and Georgetown. When he selected Georgetown, his teachers and friends were mildly shocked.

"You just do not turn down Harvard," commented Mrs. Nadelson, a history teacher who was particularly impressed with Mark.

"I want to be in an international city," explained Mark, "and besides, there are a lot of courses in international studies and foreign languages which I can take. Georgetown seems like the best place for me to study international relations, even if it doesn't have the Ivy League seal of approval."

"I suppose so," said Mrs. Nadelson.

· · · ● · · ·

"Play it straight for awhile," Walter advised Mark while the family spent a relaxing week at a lakeside cabin in the Adirondacks before Mark left for Georgetown.

They were fishing for largemouth bass in a small aluminum rowboat, as they had been for three days, with little luck.

As he sat in the bow of the boat Mark nodded at his father, sitting in the stern. Over his father's shoulder he could see Else on the sandy beach, reading in a chaise longue. Stephen, who usually went fishing with them, had become bored with fishing and was ashore with a friend. Leaning back, dangling his arms in the water as Mark fished, Walter began to talk about "the vital importance" of Mark's upcoming years at Georgetown.

"There will be your studies, and your work for the Center, and your socializing. You can't underestimate the importance of socializing, Mark, of making friends and becoming popular. Because at this university, the people you make friends with will be very useful to you in later years. They will be ambassadors, and cabinet officers, and subcabinet officers, and people who have access to a lot of classified information. It's the old-boy network, Mark, and becoming part of it is probably as important as anything else you will do at college."

Mark nodded his head in agreement, then leaned forward to pull back on his fishing rod, which had begun to jerk convulsively. As he reeled in, the small bass at the end of the line flopped across the surface of the water, making ripples that broke into concentric circles ten and even twenty yards away. Walter grabbed for a mesh net as Mark drew the fish closer to the boat. When the creature was just a few feet away, it broke free of the hook and swam away.

"I was sure I had him," said Walter. Mark said nothing.

· · · ● · · ·

The expensive foreign cars that line the streets of George-town section of Washington don't necessarily belong to the people who live in the $300,000 row houses the cars are parked in front of. Many of the cars, BMWs, Audis, and Volvos, have Connecticut and New Jersey license plates with personalized messages such as "MARCI-1" or "TIPPY." Their faded bumper stickers proclaim "Sailing is a Way of Life" and "I'd Rather Be Sailing."

Many students at Georgetown University are conspicuously affluent, and, if they are from such places as Darien, Connecticut, or Potomac, Maryland, they wear the right uniform: Sperry top-sider loafers, khaki pants, and cotton polo shirts with little alligators above the left breast. When the weather turns cold, a long sleeve, all cotton, button-down collar shirt is added, and maybe a Norwegian ski sweater and a brightly colored down vest. The outfit is worn by both sexes.

The equally, if not more, affluent foreign students, many from Latin America, some from the Middle East, dress with more flair and at greater expense.

For the first few months, Mark quietly observed the way things worked at the university, the patterns along which friendships were formed and the way that certain types of people seemed to attract friends because they exuded power. The latter were not necessarily wealthy, or overly bright, or gregarious. Rather, they were those who at a very early age had managed somehow to develop a solid self-assuredness, a sense of well-being independent of the fads and fancies that left most of their peers grasping for something to hold on to.

Mark had always sought to develop these character traits, and on one level he had. He seemed a mature young man destined for more than the ordinary. But he was never sure that others didn't know his secret. He often wondered if others sensed him to be a fraud, a person whose friendship might be genuine or might be carefully planned, a person about whom you really never knew.

He didn't want to be like that. He didn't want to be two

people at the same time, one the college kid and the other the spy, all neatly rolled into one person so that either one could be called into action, depending on the circumstances. He wanted to work it out so that he could leave the secret part somewhere when it wasn't needed, but hold onto the college kid part even when the spy was working. He liked the college kid part better, because it didn't leave him with the terrible feeling of uncertainty that the other part did. It was simple: You do your work, you make your friends, and things are pretty much set for you. For the part that worked for the Center, things were never set: "There is nothing," Walter often told him, "that we can depend on. There are no assurances. Whatever peace of mind you have must come from yourself."

Mark adjusted well and rapidly to college life. There were few of the usual traumas suffered by many freshmen—no home-town honey syndrome, no problems with the workload, no inability to function without mother to cater to him. He even managed to get along reasonably well with his dorm roomate, a tall, blond tennis player from Summit, New Jersey named Brian Flanagan.

The son of a Wall Street financial executive, Brian was undecided between a major in economics or history; he would choose the one, he said, that would assure him the best chance of landing a job with the State Department after graduation, or perhaps after taking a master's degree at the School of Foreign Service.

On an evening in the beginning of May, Mark and Brian were having a late night snack of pizza and beer at a place called Nicky's, two miles up Wisconsin Avenue from Georgetown. During the second pitcher of beer, Brian became more talkative than Mark had ever seen him.

"I'm the kind of guy, Mark, I'm the kind of guy who you would never guess what I'm really like."

"Oh?" Mark asked.

"Yeah. I have all these plans that I never talk about with anybody. You'd never guess what I'm talking about."

Mark smiled, and poured down the remaining half of a glass of beer. "I probably never would," he said. "I can't bend spoons and I can't read minds."

"You know when I talk about working for the State Department?"

"Yeah?"

"Well, that's what you're supposed to say if you work for the Company, that's what they call the CIA. Nobody ever admits to working for the CIA, unless they're a secretary or something."

"You're learning quick, Brian," Mark said. "Washington has gotten to you already. But you know, half the people around here want to work for the CIA."

"I know," said Brian. "But you can't talk about it too much, because they give you all sorts of mind tests when you apply and if they find out that you've been telling everybody you want to work for the CIA, they won't hire you."

"Is that how it works?"

"Yeah. So don't spread it around."

"Okay," said Mark. "But when I'm skiing in Germany in six or seven years, and I see this blond guy with a Jersey accent skiing with a two-way radio, a trench coat, and dark glasses, I'll know who it is."

Brian, in the middle of a swig of beer, began to laugh at the image Mark conjured up. He managed to swallow the liquid before spitting it out.

"It's not like that any more, Mark. You shouldn't get the wrong image of modern espionage. I've been talking to this spook. That's a spy."

"Who's the guy?" Mark asked.

"This professor in foreign service."

Mark decided not to press for the professor's identity. There would be plenty of time to find out who he was.

"Spies these days," Brian continued, "are just ordinary people, like bankers or lawyers. You know, just regular guys in boring business suits, like my Dad or yours."

"My father doesn't wear business suits," Mark said.

"Whatever. They're just people doing a job. They don't all resemble macho men like James Bond or anything. As a matter of fact, a wimp would probably make the best spy. Just a meek little guy running around collecting the dirt on Russia—nobody would ever suspect him."

"Well," Mark said. "I never thought spies were such a big deal anyway. But if your thing . . ."

"Beats going to law school," Brian said.

Mark laughed, refilled his beer glass, and thought to himself that he had chosen the right place to go to college. Or was it part of the plan? The answer escaped him for the moment.

· · · ● · · ·

At the end of his freshman year at Georgetown, Mark returned to Woodvale. There, he spent the end of May and most of June doing nothing except visiting local roadhouses with his friends, most of whom were finishing up their last year at Woodvale High School. He spent most mornings at the town pool, reading, playing chess, and swimming only when he got bored. In the afternoon he worked in the basement with Walter, developing new codes and devising plans for what he would be doing during his second year at college.

The first year, Walter said, was just for him to get to know his way around; to become an accepted and well-known member of the campus community. Once everyone knows who you are, he said, you will never again be suspected of doing anything mysterious. Keep a fairly high profile, and you can steal state secrets from right under their noses.

"And by now," Walter added, "you have laid the groundwork to do just that."

· · · ● · · ·

In the beginning of August, a message came from the Center ordering Mark to report to Moscow immediately, and by himself. "Hoffnung shall be unaccompanied," it said. He was there in three days, having passed through the Iron Curtain at a predetermined border checkpoint between West and East Germany, using a forged passport.

His usual host, Filikov, was not there to greet him. Filikov, they told him, was on extended vacation but sent his warmest regards to Mark and his family.

Upon his arrival, Mark was ushered into Kanayev's large, formal office. The deputy director greeted him cordially, then said, "I'm sure you are wondering why we called you here in such great hurry."

"I'm sure you have a good reason," Mark said.

"We do."

Mark remained silent, unsure of what to say. He didn't want to venture a guess and perhaps sound presumptuous.

"Aren't you curious?" Kanayev asked.

"I am." Mark softly answered.

"We just wanted to see if you would show up," said Kanayev. "We were sure you would, of course, but we can never be too careful. It is important to issue these kinds of tests to our most valuable operatives every now and then, just to be certain of their reliability."

"Do you have any doubts about mine, or my family's?" Mark asked, struggling to control his voice and his emotions.

Kanayev lowered his eyes, and jutted out his lower lip a bit. His right index finger tapped slowly on the smooth, bare surface of his desk. He looked up again after several seconds and said, in a tone that sounded to Mark like one of fatherly concern, "That is a good question, Mark," he said. "You're no longer a child. It is important that you understand that you will be responsible for your actions."

Mark's mind raced. Could they know? It had been two years since the day in Filikov's office, and there had been no indication that they knew about it. Could they possibly?

"Pay attention to what I am saying, Mark," snapped Kanayev. "You have performed well for us, and I'm sure you are as proud of your service as we are. You have done a great deal to further the cause of world peace, and we expect even greater things of you. You should know, however, that your actions are closely monitored, for our mutual protection. We must be very careful that western counterintelligence stays a very safe distance from certain information, and through it, certain operatives. We just want you to feel safe in the knowledge that we are never too far away."

"Yes, sir," Mark said. "I'm very thankful for that." Maybe they didn't know. Maybe it was just a bluff to scare him, or to keep Walter in line; they were counting on him to tell Walter of the odd meeting. He wasn't sure of anything, except that the less he said, the less he reacted visibly to the blunt message Kanayev was sending, the better off he would be.

"Very well," said Kanayev. "Enjoy the rest of your visit, and keep up the good work."

"Yes, sir. Thank you, sir."

"Dismissed."

TO: Y. I. Kanayev
DATE: September 15, 1975
AGENT: Hoffnung, Washington, D.C.
IN REFERENCE: Academic Endeavors.

Hoffnung has enrolled in the following courses of study for the first half of his second year at the University:
Islamic History
Introduction to Literary Arabic
Emerging Modern America
Symbolic Logic
German History
Hoffnung has been thoroughly briefed as to his responsibilities during the next year. We have had opportunity to become well acquainted. Our meetings have been conducted under secure conditions. There has been no indication of surveillance. The signal system has proven reliable. Hoffnung is scheduled to begin the military operation soon. Further details will be furnished when available. Hoffnung has done nothing to merit suspicion concerning Friends.

V. A. Romankin
WASHINGTON, D.C.

"I'm sick of meeting at these overpriced Georgetown bistros. I'm sick of hanging around my dorm room with my pig of a roommate there hovering over us. Isn't there any better place for us to go, Mark?"

"I suppose we could think of something."

Maria Halvorsen winked suggestively, her sky blue eyes narrowing and her wide mouth forming the suggestion of a smile. She had met Mark only three weeks before, but was sure that she was on the verge of falling in love. She and Mark were the same age, even though she was a freshman and he a sophomore. She called him "the boy genius." He called her "the Portuwegian," and would joke that she looked like a product of miscegenation, with her olive-beige skin and otherwise Nordic features, including the ash-blond hair that hung halfway down her back.

They had discovered each other the first week of classes at a meeting for students interested in working for the *Voice,* one of

Georgetown's two campus newspapers. He looked slightly different to her from the apple pie, good Catholic schoolboy type that
seemed to predominate. He looked—she knew it was a cliché—
interesting.

Although she was born in Minneapolis and had been made,
at times, painfully aware of the fact that she was an American in
some of the less pro-western countries she had lived in, Maria
had always felt that she was more of an international citizen than
a citizen of the United States. Her college friends found it hard
to believe, and thought her something of a put-on, when she said
that she really felt more at home in Paris or Oslo than she did in
Washington or New York.

She spoke with the accentless voice of a television newscaster
when she spoke in English, which she had listed as her native
language on the college application forms. But she was equally
fluent in four other languages, and could read an additional two
or three with relative ease.

Mark, she realized soon after meeting him, was more like the
people she had known at the American schools she attended. The
students at these schools were sons and daughters of international businessmen, diplomats, and occasional movie stars. She
found them much more stimulating and not nearly as provincial
as the real Americans she knew, like her Halvorsen cousins in
Minneapolis. Americans bored her. Mark didn't.

They sat across from each other at a small table in the rear
of an M Street café, sipping cappucino and staring at each other
intently. Mark felt slightly foolish, like he was a character in a
daytime soap opera, but he knew it was all part of the game. So
he played.

"You don't take hints very well, do you?" Maria asked.

"If they are given with the proper degree of subtlety and
allure, I do."

"Maybe I'm not alluring enough for you," she said.

"I didn't say that."

She took his hand in hers, and squeezed it until he grimaced
in mock pain, "Let's stop playing games," she said. "You have
your own apartment, no roommate, and great view of the city.
And you haven't even invited me over yet."

"It's a mess," Mark said. "It would make you sick the way it
is."

"You can clean it up for me. That's no excuse. And what makes you think I don't enjoy a little creative slobbery, anyway?"

Mark smiled. "Okay," he said. "Dinner Friday night at my place."

"And?" asked Maria, raising her left eyebrow.

"And what?"

"Only dinner?"

"Didn't daddy teach you any diplomacy?" Mark asked.

· · · ● · · ·

It was a nondescript efficiency apartment in a nondescript apartment building in Rosslyn, Virginia, just across the Key Bridge from Georgetown. Mark and Brian Flanagan had moved in together at the beginning of their sophomore year, but then Brian joined the tennis team. Much to Mark's relief, Brian soon moved into a large house with other members of the tennis team, apologizing to Mark that they couldn't room together any more.

"But you know how it is," he said. "We're all on the same weird schedule, with out-of-town matches and everything, so it's really more convenient."

"That's okay," Mark told him. "I'm going to be keeping such strange hours myself that it would probably be better if I lived alone."

As soon as Brian moved out, Mark installed a heavy deadbolt lock on the door, and built a reinforced shelf into the main closet that would be able to support a small safe full of miniature espionage equipment, microfilm, and documents. The bathroom was modified so that it could be converted into a darkroom within minutes.

At seven on a Saturday morning in mid-October, Mark rose from his bed and looked at the still-sleeping figure of Maria beneath the blanket. He leaned over her, and was about to kiss her gently on the cheek when he stopped himself. It was too soon to show such obvious affection, especially in the morning. The morning was when you were supposed to wake up, see who was sharing your bed, and feel regret, nausea, or both.

He smiled as he remembered what a young gym teacher at Woodvale had once told him: "I've never gone to bed with an ugly girl. I've awakened with a few, though." But Maria was by no stretch of the imagination ugly, and he had felt no regret on any of the half-dozen occasions they had slept together in the last month. Still, he was not yet ready to kiss her at seven in the morning.

He washed up in the bathroom, and then converted it into the darkroom. There were pictures of the Chinese-American Friendship Society to develop, for delivery to Romankin the next day. The people at the Center were anxious to learn more about the influx of students from the People's Republic of China, and were pleased at Mark's success in becoming friendly with them. The day before, he had taken individual and group photos for publication in the yearbook. Romankin was to get the first set of prints.

· · · ● · · ·

They sat on a fallen tree in the northern section of Rock Creek Park, a mile east of Chevy Chase Circle. Romankin seemed anxious.

"They are putting pressure on me," he said. "They want more use out of you. More results. They want more than pictures of Chinese students. Kanayev himself has been quite insistent."

Romankin, in his mid-thirties, was short and powerfully built. He wore specially altered suits from Brooks Brothers with cuffed trouser legs, and wing-tip shoes from Church's of England. He wanted to look like a young American lawyer or banking executive, but his chronic five o'clock stubble and thick, dark features gave him the appearance of a stevedore who had been forced into a suit. However, his rough looks belied a sophistication and grace that allowed him to function effectively as an information officer at the Soviet embassy on the few occasions he had to. Like many others officially listed as Soviet diplomats in Washington, he was a KGB officer, and it was clearly understood that his KGB duties came before any diplomatic functions that he might be called on to perform.

"I think they have been following me," Romankin said nervously. "There is no solid evidence of it, and if they are doing it only sporadically, it's just to make me nervous."

He pulled an ulfiltered Camel cigarette from a box in the inside breast pocket of his suit, and jammed it in his mouth. He did not light it.

"But don't worry," Romankin said. "They didn't follow me today. I'm sure of it. I was staying at a safe house we have in northern Maryland, north of Baltimore. Perhaps you'll go there one day.

"What it comes down to is this, Mark. You are safer than we are. You'll have to do some of our work on this one. We've made all the arrangements with our man, but you'll have to be the intermediary. If it works properly, he won't have to even see you. If he does see you, he won't be difficult to silence."

"How long will it take?" Mark asked. "I don't want to be too conspicuous in my absences from school. My girlfriend will start to ask questions."

"Fool," Romankin spat out. "You have a girlfriend already? Some silly girl to watch over you and ask questions all the time? I should report this."

"Screw you." Mark said. He no longer cared if he didn't do every little thing they wanted him to. "Would you rather I be a homosexual?"

"I'm sorry," Romankin said. "In our business, it would be best if we were eunuchs, I suppose. We need as few complications as possible."

"This is one complication that you'll just have to tolerate. Don't worry, I'm not love-struck or anything. I won't start telling all in moments of passion."

Romankin extracted a business-size envelope from the same pocket that held the Camels. He opened it, and spread out in front of them a U.S. Geographic Survey map of King George County, Virginia.

"This is the Naval Service Weapons Center," he said, pointing to an area along the Potomac River near the small town of Dahlgren, about sixty miles south of Washington.

"We have a man there, a boy really, who has access to information we want desperately to have. He has been effectively convinced, shall we say, that it is to his benefit to provide us with the material. He has much to lose if certain authorities find out about some illegal activities he engages in. Also, we pay him. That always helps. Bucky is what we call him. Has a ring to it. A stupid ring, if you ask me."

Mark kneeled in front of the map, and looked at it carefully. The Dahlgren Center was near the U.S. Route 301 bridge that crosses the Potomac between southern Maryland and Virginia.

They had driven through the area several years ago during an end-of-August family trip to Williamsburg. Walter had wanted to avoid the interstate and "see what America is really about."

"We will procure a rented car for you, and you will drive Wednesday morning down to Dahlgren. You won't go near the weapons center, of course. On Route 301, just before you cross the bridge over the Potomac, there is a public picnic area, an overlook, they call it. Park the car there, and walk down to the river."

Romankin reached into his pockets again, and came up with a small, round object with a clip on the back and a gauge on the front. "Take this pedometer with you, and attach it to your belt. Walk .43 miles north along the river, and then turn into the woods. Bring an accurate compass with you, and walk .21 miles west. There will be a fallen oak tree, much like this one, and it will be covered with leaves. Walk along the tree and push against it as you walk. You will find a section that will move when you push it. Bucky was supposed to take care of this. Push it forward, and remove about a foot-deep pile of leaves. You will find a zippered plastic folder there. Leave two pennies in its place, so Bucky will know you've been there."

"What's in the folder?" Mark asked.

"Dahlgren is a naval weapons center, Mark. Use your imagination. They work on developing submarine-based nuclear weapons, things like that. Things that we need to know about."

"Did you develop Bucky?"

"I did." Romankin beamed proudly. "And I consider it one of my greatest achievements. If it comes to bear fruit, that is."

"Bucky has access to these documents on Tuesdays only, and he must photocopy them and return them to their files Tuesday night. He will have them buried under the tree by sunrise Wednesday morning."

"You mean this isn't a one-shot deal," Mark said.

"It will occupy your every Wednesday for as long as our man can provide the documents. Perhaps you'd better arrange your schedule to accommodate the trips."

"It's not so easy."

"You'll find a way," Romankin said. "You're a bright young man."

. . . .

TO: Y. I. Kanayev
DATE: November 3, 1975
AGENT: Hoffnung, Washington, D.C.
IN REFERENCE: Bucky

Hoffnung has made all the proper connections and is to be commended for his performance.

V. A. Romankin
Washington, D.C.

. . . .

8

A Spy Unveiled

"Watching these two guys is about as exciting as watching caterpillars on rose bushes," said Ed Cohn to his partner.

Jack Waters scratched his red hair as he sat on the sofa in the small apartment they had rented to monitor the activities of persons at the Soviet Embassy.

"At least with caterpillars you could be outdoors in the fresh air," he said.

Both men worked out of the FBI's field office at Buzzard's Point in the southwest section of Washington. During the spring of 1976 Jack and Ed were assigned the task of watching the comings and goings at the Soviet Embassy, an imposing edifice four blocks directly north of the White House on sixteenth Street.

They were both tall, athletically built, and in their late thirties. Both had degrees from second-rank law schools, and had always wanted to be FBI agents.

Ed grew up in northeast Philadelphia, the son of a wholesale kosher butcher. Whenever he told his parents that his burning desire was to be a "G-man" like the smooth, confident men in the gangster movies, his father would say "Sure, Eddie." His mother only said "You'll be a lawyer, Eddie." So he became both, to the specifications of J. Edgar Hoover and the displeasure of his mother, who would say at the end of phone conversations, "You can still go into practice with your cousin, Alan, you know. It's never too late."

The oldest of five boys in a family headed by an Irish cop, Jack lived in a noisy triple-decker house in south Boston until he left at seventeen via a football scholarship to Notre Dame. Three of his brothers had become cops, and the youngest, Bobby, was in his last year of seminary.

They often drove into Washington together from their homes in suburban Virginia, trading ethnic jokes or talking shop.

The apartment was only a half block from the embassy, and from it most entrances to the building were visible. The shades were drawn, and the small camera that poked through could not be seen from the outside. The movement around the embassy was transmitted onto a screen in the apartment, so that the agents wouldn't have to sit with their eyes glued to a telescope all day.

Watching the screen, Ed and Jack studied the file containing pictures and brief biographies of Soviet embassy personnel. At first they saw nothing unusual about the persons coming and going, but after a week of boredom the behavior of one man captured their interest.

"Have you noticed the constant little sideward glances?" Ed asked. "It's as if he always thinks he's being followed."

"They all do," Jack replied. "They're trained that way . . ."

"I know, I know. But this guy is really hyper. Check the file and see who he is."

Ed sorted through the file and pulled out a photograph. "This must be the man," he said. "He's the embassy information officer, Vasili Alexevitch Romankin."

Romankin's FBI file said he was a "possible" intelligence operative. But so were two dozen other embassy staff members. So were all of them, depending on how broad the definition of intelligence was made.

"Should we trail him?" Jack asked.

"Not yet. Let's watch him a while longer. See if there are any patterns in his movements. Start keeping a log on him."

"Where does he live?" Ed asked.

Jack looked at Romankin's bio sheet. "A high-rise on upper Connecticut Avenue. Near the National Zoo."

"My favorite place," said Ed.

"Yeah, it's a great place to take the kids."

"Not the zoo," Ed said. "This restaurant, it's called Arbaugh's. Best ribs and barbequed chicken I've ever had. They have these real old timey waitresses who call you 'Hon.'"

"Sounds good. Let's have a watch put on this guy's apartment building."

"Okay, but we should lay low for a while. We don't need any complaints of harassment from the ambassador. No car chases, no show biz."

Jack laughed. "We could use a little excitement, Ed," he said. "Life hasn't been a bunch of thrills lately."

"Why not shake him down right on Sixteenth Street?" asked Ed, with more than just a trace of sarcasm in his voice.

"Not a bad idea."

"You and your Irish cop mentality. I have a friend over at the Company, an Ivy League type, he and all his pals over there think we're just a bunch of cops with a few initials after our names. Maybe he's right."

Jack smiled, and slapped Ed playfully on the shoulder. "Maybe what we need around here is more Irish cops and fewer Jewish lawyers. Okay, we'll just watch him for a while."

"And where he leads, nobody knows," said Ed. "Yet."

· · · ● · · ·

Mark and Maria played a little game that kept them amused when they were tired of studying, eating, or making love. The game was best played in the spring, when throngs of tourists invaded Washington with their cameras and doubleknits and flocked to Capitol Hill and the monuments like so many pilgrims to Mecca.

A tour bus would pull up to the Lincoln Memorial or the Washington Monument. People from all sorts of places like Peoria, Illinois, or Stillwater, Oklahoma would pour out—people to whom Washington was more than just a city with an abundance of single women and trendy bars, to whom it was still a symbol of freedom and might.

Mark thought it a bit silly, but Maria seemed to get such a kick out of the game they dubbed "yokeling." They would drape cheap Instamatics around their necks, and blend into the crowd as they walked toward the monument.

"I'm Marge Hardin," Maria would say. The name evoked in her images of women who worried themselves sick over ring around the collar. "And this is my husband Bob. We're on our honeymoon. Isn't Washington just wonderful!"

Mark smiled broadly, and affected a midwestern accent. "Bob Hardin," he would say, thrusting out his right hand and pronouncing the name like "Bahb Haredin."

After determining where the couple was from, they would invent a home town—French Lick, Indiana was one of their favorites—and spend the next twenty minutes pretending to be naive young newlyweds from the hinterlands. Thus, "yokeling."

The game may have been silly, and certainly condescending, but it provided Mark with much-needed comic relief from a demanding schedule. In addition to the six rigorous courses he was taking, there were the regular Wednesday excursions to Dahlgren, and the occasional and often hastily called meetings in various parks around Washington with the increasingly demanding Romankin.

· · · ● · · ·

On the first day in May, a warm, cloudy afternoon, Romankin and Mark walked along the jogging path on the Arlington side of the Potomac, on Columbia Island.

Romankin walked slowly, looking at the river, and at the college crew teams practicing in their long, graceful shells. "I would like to do that," he said. "They move so well together, as if they were a single being. It is fine teamwork, just like our teamwork."

"I don't quite see the parallel."

"To be colloquial," said Romankin, "they're all pulling for each other." He laughed, and slapped Mark on the back. "Little humor?" he asked, clearly disappointed at Mark's lack of response.

"Very little," Mark said, somewhat brusquely. "I don't mean to be rude, but I really have a lot of studying to do. My finals start in a few days, and I'm not well prepared. And I have several papers to write. I'm under some pressure, so I'd like to get back to my studying soon."

"We won't be long, but something special has come up," Romankin said. "There will be some very important information available to Bucky on May 6, and as usual, he will have to deliver it to one of our drop sites that evening. It must be recovered the following day, and I trust that you will be able to handle the assignment."

"But I hadn't planned on it," Mark said. "I have final exams scheduled for that day."

"It's highly sensitive microfilm of plans for a nuclear weapon that is very far advanced over present technology. It's not just to keep you in practice, Mark."

Mark was annoyed, and unafraid to show it. Why must he be made to bear the burden of things as important as nuclear secrets? Wasn't there anyone else who could pick up the damn microfilm? Why not just hire the Speed-O-Messenger service?

"Can't it wait?" Mark asked. "My German history final is very important to me."

The normally reserved Romankin nearly exploded as he clasped Mark's wrist tightly and jerked him to within inches of his face. "Your German history final is a piece of shit," Romankin said. "You're giving me heartburn. It is not a question of whether your schedule permits you to make this pickup; you will make it if you have to pay someone to take the examination for you or if you have to pay a doctor to sign a note saying you are sick. I don't really give a damn how you do it, but that pickup will be made. Have I made myself clear?"

"Maybe if you shout it a little louder I'll understand better," Mark said.

Romankin lowered his voice to a growl, and asked again: "Have I made myself clear?"

"The pickup will be made," Mark said. "You'll have your secrets on the seventh."

· · · ● · · ·

"Dad?"

"Is that you, Mark?"

"Yes, Dad, I need your help. I'm in a little bit of a bind."

Walter's throat tightened for a moment. He didn't like the sound of that phrase, "a little bit of a bind," especially coming from Mark. He rarely asked for help. He was not one to cry wolf.

"What kind of bind, Mark? Please be direct."

"It's not really a big deal, but I thought you might be able to help out if you can get away from home for a day or two."

"What is it?" Walter's voice was tense.

"I'm supposed to make a pickup in Virginia and deliver it to a drop site in Washington on the seventh. I have a German history final that day, and would really hate to miss it. I hope you understand."

"Of course," Walter said. "Sometimes our friends are too anxious about the game of the day rather than thinking about the future."

"Yes," Mark said. "But they think plenty about the future, believe me."

"You would like me to take care of the job for you? Is that it?"

"If you could," Mark said. "Sometimes I just need the time to take care of the other part of my life."

"We'll have a great time," said Walter, his voice picking up. He sounded almost cheerful. "We'll go out on the town, you can show me all the hot spots, hey? We can be a couple of swingers! And maybe I can finally meet Miss What's-her-name, your girl-friend."

"Maria. I don't think so, Dad. She'll probably be very busy studying. So will I, as a matter of fact, so maybe we'll have to limit our swinging time. I'm sorry, but I'd really like to do well on my exams."

"Sure," said Walter. "Whatever. I'll enjoy myself just being with you. Wait a second. Hold on, your mother wants to talk to you."

Mark heard the sound of the second extension being picked up. "I've got it," he heard his mother shout through the house. "You can hang up now, Walter." Click.

"Mark? How are you, darling?"

"Fine, Mom. Everything's just fine."

"Are you sure? I can hear something funny in your voice. What were you talking about with your father?"

"Nothing. Just the weather, the Yankees, nothing important. How have you been?"

"Mark, you worry me. You have too much in your head, too much to worry about."

"I don't worry, Mom. Please."

"I know. That's what worries me. Mark?"

"Please, Mom. Everything is just fine. Can't we talk about something else?"

· · · ● · · ·

Walter arrived on the Metroliner too late for them to have a full evening together, so instead of rushing things they stopped at a liquor store and bought a fifth of good vodka.

"It's good for a son to get drunk with his father once in a while," Walter said. "It's a good old tradition."

"I have to study," Mark protested. "You go ahead and drink."

"What time is your exam?"

"One in the afternoon."

"You can study all morning. I'll show you my special trick for not getting a hangover."

So they drank the potent, clear liquid, and before thirty minutes had passed, Walter's cheeks were glowing, and he had to brace his arms against the arms of the chair when he stood up from it to avoid falling back. Mark, who had judiciously drank about one-fourth as much as his father, began to ask about how things were going at home. He soon regretted it.

Stephen, Walter said, was nothing but trouble. He was twelve now, and not a baby anymore.

"Since you've been away, he's gotten very difficult to control."

"He always was," Mark said. "He was blowing up frogs with firecrackers when he was six years old. He's just a little J.D."

"What?"

"A juvenile delinquent."

"I'm not worried about that," Walter said, as he poured another three fingers of vodka into his glass. "I don't care if he's an active boy, if he gets into mischief every now and then. That's normal; it's even a sign of some character. The problem is, I think he knows about everything. The entire situation. I had been planning for quite some time to explain things to him in a way he would understand . . ."

Mark interrupted Walter, who was sipping from his glass between every sentence. "Of course he knows," Mark said. "What did you expect? There are certain things you can't hide from the family."

Walter's eyes widened, and he began to clench and unclench his fists. His emotions seemed to be swinging erratically, from melancholy to anger to worry.

"You told him?" Walter's tone was accusing.

"No, Dad. I didn't tell him," Mark replied in an even but obviously annoyed voice. "I didn't have to tell him. If you had understood him, or even watched him, as Mom and I have over the years, you would have realized a long time ago that he was well aware we weren't just like all the other families in the neighborhood. And don't you think that his personality is some indication of how he grew up? Just because people don't say things, or don't understand why they act the way they do, doesn't mean that there aren't very good reasons for the way they behave."

"What nonsense are you talking? I don't want to hear it. Have you taken a beginning psychology course and now you think you understand the way everybody behaves?"

Walter's voice was getting louder, and his train of thought less cohesive, but Mark had seen him act like that before. He had never known his father to drink like that regularly; only when something was troubling him and he wanted an excuse to talk more than his normal reserve would permit.

"Dad," Mark began gently. "What you're worried about is that Stephen understands the situation and will tell someone about it; that he doesn't really understand how serious it is. Is that it?"

"Yes," Walter answered, after a brief silence. "He is an ass, a moron, and he thinks it's some big fun game, and for some reason, he seems to be very angry at me. Maybe he'll decide to get back at me, and say or do something that everyone of us will regret for the rest of our lives. Our very short lives, I should add."

"Don't get carried away," Mark said. "He would never betray us. But don't you understand why he's angry? Think of what you just said: 'He thinks it's some big, fun game.' Well, do you remember when you were a child and your older brothers wouldn't let you play with them? Or when you were too young to go out somewhere with your parents, but your big brother could go?"

"But this is different. This is not a game."

"To him it is," Mark said. "And it's a game none of us lets him play. He's angry about it. He was always the big, dumb baby, and now maybe he wants to get even for it. So he gets in trouble, he hangs out with the hoods, he's doing everything he can to get our attention."

Tears began to well at the corner of Walter's eyes. Embarrassed, Mark lowered his head to avoid looking at his father.

"Maybe," Walter said drunkenly, "someday he will understand and forgive us. Hopefully, before he causes our ruin."

· · · ● · · ·

Romankin made sure to do his own "dry cleaning" every day.

In Romankin's profession, "dry cleaning" is the process by which one makes absolutely sure that there is nobody watching or following his movements. It can mean careening through a red light at a busy intersection, or driving the wrong way down a one-way street, or doing what Romankin did one morning in April 1976.

The Soviet intelligence agent did not know that Ed and Jack were very interested in where he was going that day, nor was he aware that for the past several weeks his activities had been monitored much more carefully than usual. He did not even know who Ed and Jack were, and he would never know.

The change of seasons, the dramatic blossoming of the Washington cherry trees, and the fuzzy, pale green halo of new growth that hung over the city's parks and boulevards triggered memories of springtime in Moscow, when the bleakness of winter retreated before the advancing greenery in the poplar trees that lined its streets and filled its parks. The sight put Romankin in a buoyant mood as he walked out of his apartment building in the morning, and though his first inclination was to look around and expect that he was being watched, he was not as careful as usual.

First there was the taxi ride around the neighborhood, just to see if there was anything suspicious. He hailed the cab in the 4300 block of Connecticut Avenue, and instructed the driver to take him to Thirty-fourth Place and Observatory Circle, where the Norwegian Embassy was.

"Take Woodley Road," he told the driver. "And go down Thirty-fourth Street to the Circle, then make a right and go one block." He admired the large, handsome brick homes lining the street on the short ride, and remarked to the cab driver, a middle-aged black man, that there must be many wealthy people in Washington, because so many of the areas in northwest Washington had such beautiful homes and fancy cars.

"You must be from outta town," the driver said, "because if you had been here awhile, you would've seen the other parts.

Ain't no rich folks or limosines in Anacostia, or up New York Avenue. But yeah, I guess you right. They is a lot of rich people. But mister, they is lots more poor people."

Romankin told the cabbie to stop at Thirty-fourth Street and Observatory Circle, a block east of the Norwegian Embassy. He didn't really want to go to the embassy, but planned to make one of his switches in a quiet neighborhood surrounding it. It would be much easier to spot a trail. He walked east on the circle, constantly checking around him. There were many places to hide, but few cars once he walked a few blocks. His steps were brisk as he reflected on Bucky's latest success. It was a fine day, he thought.

At the corner of Davis Street, a red Fiat sports car made a right turn onto the circle and drove past Romankin. He looked quickly at the driver, a woman in her thirties wearing a tennis dress and a scarf. He was unconcerned; there were hundreds of such women in neighborhoods like this, he was sure.

Romankin was wrong. He had also been wrong when he walked out of his apartment onto Connecticut Avenue and assumed that the helicopter hovering above with the call letters of a local radio station was what it seemed to be.

He walked a block past Davis Street, and then west on Calvert Street two blocks. At Wisconsin Avenue he boarded a southbound bus, and rode it for ten minutes to Q Street in Georgetown. Ed and Jack, who had been informed of his movements, watched the intersection from the top floor of a nearby building, and took down the number of the bus that Romankin boarded. Jack quickly checked its route, and within three minutes the two FBI agents were in the old blue Ford Galaxy, following two blocks behind the bus. Ed drove while Jack lay prone in the back seat. It always looked better if there appeared to be just one man in the car.

The bus moved slowly westward on MacArthur Boulevard, past Georgetown Reservoir, and then past the intersection of Arizona Avenue. Romankin had still not gotten off, but the last stop was at Sibley Memorial Hospital, at the very edge of the District, next to Dalcarlia Reservoir.

He stepped off the bus and looked carefully around him before walking briskly down a dead-end street, toward the Potomac. At the Chesapeake and Ohio Canal, he turned back toward the District line, and walked for several minutes with the B & O railroad tracks on his right and the narrow canal on his left. When he reached the drop site, which nearly straddled the border between Washington and Montgomery County, Maryland, he spend a few minutes searching the area, just to make sure. He could always walk away, and they would still have a hard time finding the exact spot.

Satisfied that he was alone, he located the rusty muffler buried under a layer of dirt and leaves, and lifted it up. Underneath were the documents that Mark had carefully placed the day before in a plastic envelope. He slipped them in his coat pocket, still darting his eyes around nervously.

The following Thursday morning, Romankin again took the same route to the drop site. Ed and Jack were surprised that he did not alter it at all, except for taking the cab all the way to Wisconsin Avenue instead of stopping at Observatory Circle. He was getting less cautious. He did it again the following Thursday, and this time the two agents were puzzled by Romankin's carelessness. Could it be that he was sure in his mind that he couldn't possibly have been followed? Or that he was safe because he would have been asked to leave the country already if they had known what he was doing? With each successive pickup, Romankin grew bolder. Ed and Jack finally concluded that he was just stupid.

The day that Walter was to relieve Mark in his duties and make the trip to Dahlgren and back to the drop site in Washington was the first day that the FBI instituted a full-force stakeout of the area Romankin had been frequenting for the last several weeks.

Walter made the pickup in Virginia without difficulty, and was reviewing Mark's directions for the drop-off as he drove through southern Maryland in the early afternoon. As long as the maps were accurate, he thought, there would be no problems.

As thoroughly as he dry-cleaned, Walter was not clean enough when he kneeled to place the plastic-encased documents under the rusty muffler. Cameras silently recorded his movements and a small legion of FBI agents quickly moved into action to determine who the short, middle-aged man was.

On the way back to Mark's apartment, Walter performed a few perfunctory checks to make sure he wasn't being followed, but his caution did not go as far as checking the envelope he recovered from under the muffler. He hadn't expected to find anything there, but at the last minute Romankin apparently decided to leave instructions for Mark concerning a task he wanted him to do that week. So Walter placed it in his coat pocket, unable to notice the transparent strip of metallic tape that would send a signal to a tracking device from anywhere within a fifty-mile radius. Of course, the telltale tape was affixed to the envelope by an FBI agent, not by Romankin.

Within less than an hour after Walter arrived at Mark's apartment, Ed and Jack knew that it was rented to one Walter Gottfried Scholz, a freelance photographer and filmmaker who lived in Woodvale, New York. They also learned, soon thereafter, that the apartment's main inhabitant was Mark.

A rather youngish looking FBI agent, a recent academy graduate named Natalie, spent the next day doing many of the same things that Mark did. Carrying textbooks, she walked across the Key Bridge from Rosslyn to Washington, and even smiled at Mark when he noticed that she was walking the same way he was. There was nothing unusual about it. Hundreds of Georgetown students who lived across the bridge in Virginia walk to school on warm spring mornings, and Mark had often traded smiles with attractive young women.

Studying in the library that morning, Mark noticed her by the soft drink machines, but that was the last time he saw her. It was unnecessary to follow him all day; by the time he reached the library, Natalie knew enough so that Ed and Jack could complete the rest of their investigation of Mark without her assistance.

A certain high-ranking Georgetown administrator was not shocked when he was asked to release Mark's records to the FBI; he had cooperated with the Bureau on other matters before, though not on any precisely like this one. Ed and Jack were pleased at the thoroughness of the file, which included complete records on the family's birthdates and birthplaces, and chronicled where they had lived.

The file included letters of recommendation and one, by Mrs. Ruth M. Nadelson, was of particular interest to them. She called Mark "one of the brightest young men" she had taught in her eleven years at Woodvale High School, and added:

> He shows a perception and understanding of historical affairs far beyond that to be expected even from a good student. I understand he has traveled a great deal and it

shows in his work. It is almost as if he were a participant, rather than a passive observer, in the events and trends we have studied.

One particular incident in class stands out clearly in my mind, and you may make it what you will, but in my opinion it indicates that Mark is intellectually curious and adventurous. One day in class, I was showing newsreels of the Nazi atrocities. These films are quite graphic, I hasten to add. Let me also tell you that I'm Jewish. By the time the film was over, several students had become so upset that they left the classroom in tears. The others just sat there in stony silence when the lights came on. I asked if anyone had any comments on what they had just seen. A girl raised her hand and said she could not believe that people actually did these horrible things to other human beings, and said that the Germans must be some sort of monsters, subhuman. Mark politely raised his hand, and I called on him. He said very calmly something like "I don't think it's fair to classify any one group of people as subhuman because of what happened in Germany." It is well known that Mark is from a German family, and it must have taken a great deal of courage for him to speak that day. Many of the students at our school are Jewish, and Mark has many Jewish friends.

When Mark began to speak, a boy in the back of the class, a troublemaker, muttered something about Mark being a Nazi. I'm sure Mark heard him, but pretended not to notice. He continued to speak, saying something like, "What happened under Hitler was disgusting, a complete human tragedy. But I think we all would understand it better if we didn't just label the Germans a bunch of barbaric lunatics." I remember what he said because it impressed me so much coming from such a young person that I wrote it down after class. He said, "There are lessons to be learned from history, and particularly from the holocaust. But we have to understand the social and economic conditions that preceded it, and how Germany got in that position, and what role scapegoats like the Jews in Nazi Germany have played all throughout history. The Romans slaughtered Christians, Americans the Indians, and Turks the Armenians. There has been slaughter of one people by another since the beginning of recorded history. Any group could be murderers, and any group the victims, if the conditions are right. That's why we have to learn more about how it happened, instead of just making emotional statements."

Mark sat down, and for the rest of the class period we discussed some of the things he said. After class, the boy who called Mark a Nazi apologized to him.

I thought this example might illustrate that Mark Conrad is unusual, but in a positive way. I predict a great future for him. Incidentally, Mark consistently received the highest grades in the class on both tests and papers.

· · · ● · · ·

Ed and Jack continued to leaf through the file, making note of the courses Mark was enrolled in, and his professors. He graduated ahead of his high school class, third in a class of 198. His scores on the SATs, the scholastic aptitude exams relied heavily upon in college admissions, were 690 in the verbal section and 782 in the mathematical section, both scores placing him in the upper one or two percent of all college-bound high school seniors.

· · · ● · · ·

All mail addressed to 16 Sycamore Road, Woodvale, New York was steamed open and examined. The telephone lines were not immediately tapped, but any radio communications between the Scholz house and the rest of the world were carefully monitored. The messages were intercepted, but it took several months for decoding experts to make sense of them. However, they were able immediately to determine the destination of the messages: Moscow.

Three dozen agents were assigned to gathering information about the Scholzes, and it was reluctantly decided at the very highest levels of the Bureau to ask for the assistance of the Central Intelligence Agency.

There is more than a friendly rivalry between the two security agencies; it is more like a class war, with the often blue-blooded, pin-striped Company prototype pitted against the image of the straight talking, middle American, landgrant college graduate FBI agent. They don't like to ask each other for help, but in the case of the Scholzes, which involved investigation both in the United States and abroad, it became urgently necessary.

By June, when Mark returned to Woodvale from his sophomore year at Georgetown, the Scholz dossier was hundreds of pages thick. There were stacks of photographs of drop sites in

Washington, Virginia, and New York, photos of Mark with Romankin, and gaping holes in vacation itineraries, as documented by travel expense records.

Ed and Jack hoped that their work on the Scholz case would vault them from the Washington field office, itself a good assignment, to any one of a number of prestigious positions at headquarters. Their involvement in the case the last several months had given them the opportunity to have extensive contact with the Soviet desk, and they had become intrigued with the business of spy catching. It was one of the more glamorous jobs in the Bureau, with a high probability of attracting the attention of the higher-ups. Catching a spy, especially one without diplomatic immunity, could mean a lot to a career. Catching two generations of them could mean even more.

The New York and Westchester County field offices kept close watch on the movements of Walter, Else, and even young Stephen. Although Ed and Jack were getting anxious to make the arrest before the family became aware of their interest and attempted to leave the country, and had convinced their superiors of the same, the pressure from the CIA was to wait and to watch some more.

So they waited, and watched, and watched some more, with increasing nervousness, until their patience was rewarded the last Wednesday in June, when Else was seen entering a travel agency on Mammaroneck Avenue in White Plains.

She booked four seats on a Lufthansa flight to Frankfurt for July 16, all of them first class because the tourist season was in full swing and the other classes of plane seats had already been sold.

A pair of CIA agents silently and secretly escorted the Scholz family through Germany, until, as was the usual pattern, Walter and Mark left Else and Stephen with "relatives" and continued on their journey through the Iron Curtain.

When they arrived at the Center, a military attaché from the American Embassy was near the entrance on Dzerzhinsky Square to watch them, and even managed to take several blurry photos with a Minox secreted in a pants pocket without being noticed in that activity by a KGB agent, who had been obviously following the American for months. The Soviet, however, had no indication that the attaché was watching for Mark and Walter, and in fact did not even know of their existence.

Their movements were recorded for every one of the sixteen days they stayed in the Soviet Union, and CIA agents were able to ascertain exactly what route and methods they used to make their way back to West Germany and meet up with Else and Stephen.

When the family returned to Woodvale on August 8, Ed and Jack were certain that it was time to make arrest. Their superiors agreed, but the CIA did not. The Company wanted to wait some more, to watch some more.

But Ed and Jack and the people who decide things in the inner sanctum of the new FBI building at Tenth and Pennsylvania won the tug-of-war after the director reviewed the Scholz dossier, smiled, and said:

"The bastard will have to talk. He'll have to cooperate. Why, once we tell him how many times he took a piss on the ninth of July, he's ours. And the boy will follow. Good work."

9
A Knock at Noon

The line of sweat started at his solar plexus and ran in fat little beads, almost like dewdrops, down to where the round well of his navel hung over his blue jeans. His fine hair, the color of Kellogg's corn flakes, lay in wet strands over his reddened forehead.

It was hot, maybe eighty-five degrees, and the heavy air tasted like the wet towels they give you at a Chinese restaurant after you finish the spareribs.

But Stephen Scholz was glad that at least he was hot outside with his shirt off instead of hot inside a math class at school where he wouldn't understand what was going on too well, and the teacher would ask him wasn't he Mark Scholz's younger brother, and hadn't Mark done brilliantly in math? And wasn't Mark doing so well at college?

The school year was only two days old, but at least it had started on a Thursday, and at least he was only in seventh grade and did not yet have to face the high school, where the older boys would want to tease him and throw him in the filthy pond behind the cafeteria.

It was a Saturday, and Stephen was usually happiest on Saturdays, when his father would tell him to get out of the house and get some fresh air. Saturday would be even better now that he had what he had been begging and whining for since he was nine —a minibike.

The machine was yellow and shiny, from Sears Roebuck in

White Plains, with little knobby wheels and an engine that looked like it would go better on a lawnmower.

"But if you ever get caught riding that goddamn thing on a public road, so help me, I'll break your neck," his father told him when he bought him the bike for his birthday. "Walk it to wherever you're going to ride, and for chrissake don't ride over people's lawns so I get a bill for a couple hundred bucks."

"Sure," he said happily.

Donald Whitman lived near a large plot of cleared but unused land on the other side of town, and had fashioned out of it a crude racetrack, an eighth of a mile around. He had started the "Saturday Derby" last spring, and about a dozen kids usually showed up to start racing at about ten or eleven in the morning.

This was Stephen's first day and he didn't want to be late. He wanted to show them what he could do with his "Mean Machine." But Donald's house was two miles away, across Commerce Avenue, and it would take him forty minutes to walk the bike over. If any of the guys saw him walking it, they'd call him a punk and say he was scared of the cops, so he rode through the neighborhood and cut across Commerce Avenue when nobody was looking, and rode through the winding paths of the canine cemetery to Jefferson Avenue, where there was little traffic.

It was hot, but a lot of his sweat came from being scared about being caught by the cops and having the shiny new bike confiscated until his father went to the police station and promised Stephen would never ride it again on the streets.

Eight of the guys were already at Donald's house when Stephen got there, watching a new kid from Georgia named Jimmy Switt race around the track on a bike almost large enough to be a motorcycle.

Jimmy liked to play the good old boy, and claimed he had been riding dirt bikes since he was old enough to walk. When Stephen drove his small machine up to the track, he attracted only sidelong glances from the others. Jimmy, however, took one more lap and then roared to a halt a few feet away.

"Well, look what the cat dragged in," he said, smiling at Stephen.

Stephen smiled back, not understanding his expression.

Donald Whitman walked over from his expensive bike, and put an arm around Stephen's shoulders. "I invited him over," he said. "He's been bragging about it all week, so I thought we should see what it can do."

"Y'all better be careful," Jimmy drawled. "Mike here's gonna bring down property values in the neighborhood if folks catch sight of that thing here."

The other boys laughed raucously, partly because they laughed at anything Jimmy said, and partly because it was always okay to laugh at Stephen Scholz.

"I'll take you on," Stephen said loudly to Jimmy. "You and your hick machine aren't worth shit." Stephen's boldness had a hollow ring to it. He knew his small bike was no challenge to Jimmy's more powerful one, or to the boy's more formidable skills.

Jimmy sat on his haunches in the grass by the side of the track, picked a dry blade, and worked it between his teeth. "Tell you what, Steve," he said. "I'm sort of tired, been taking her around the track all morning. I don't know that I want to get all geared up for your mighty challenge just right now. Why don't you take it around yourself a few times so I can see what you can do?"

This was his chance, even though he wouldn't be going up against anyone else. They would all be watching him.

"Okay," said Stephen. "Fair enough."

He positioned himself on the sweaty vinyl seat, pull-started it, and turned the throttle hard so that the bike jerked forward.

"Go on Scholz," one of the boys shouted. "No bullshit, just get the thing moving."

Stephen eased on the throttle again, and increased his speed until the small machine would move no faster.

"What a hog!" "What a slow turkey!" He could hear the derisive shouts, but he told himself that they didn't matter. He rode around and around the bumpy track, the wind cooling his round face, and he showed them what he could do.

As he slowed to a stop in front of the gang, Jimmy applauded. "That was great," he said, and winked to his friends. Stephen felt great.

"But if you really want to prove what you can do, show us what you can do on the street. I'll bet you can't get to Peterson's Drug Store and back in five minutes."

"It's a bet," said Stephen and roared off.

· · · ● · · ·

Walter was in his workroom when he heard the doorbell. He quickly put the miniature camera he had been unloading into its hiding place, locked the room, and answered the door.

As he saw the two policemen in front of him, his heart jumped.

"Are you Walter Gottfried Scholz?" asked the tall one.

Walter resisted the urge to slam the door and run. "Yes," he said evenly. "What can I do for you?"

"Have you lived here long?" Walter wondered why they were asking. Surely they didn't suspect anything.

"Around eight years, yes," he said, his mind raced through the possible reasons for their call.

"Well, you better come with us," said the tall policeman. "We have your son down at the station. If you've lived here that long he should know not to ride a minibike on a public street."

"I'll get my coat," said Walter, barely able to conceal his relief.

· · · ● · · ·

"I'll be gone most of the day, Walter," Else told her husband as she reached for the keys to the car, that sweltering Saturday morning.

"Stephen asked me to get him some school supplies, and I have to do some shopping. Is there anything you want?"

"What did you say?" Walter asked from behind a face lathered with shaving cream. "The water was running."

"Do you want anything from Klaus Hohner? I'm going there."

"Tell the old Kraut to give me two pounds of his freshest bratwurst," Walter said. "And send my best."

Else drove three blocks to an old stone-and-shingle house set far back on a heavily wooded lot. She often took Beverly Rosenfeld, a friendly, talkative woman who had never learned to drive, to White Plains for shopping on Saturdays. The two women would go to their favorite stores alone but meet for lunch at the Showcase Delicatessen where old men with Yiddish accents sliced corned beef and pastrami from behind display counters full of New York-Jewish delicacies.

The lunchtime conversations inevitably turned to their children, one of Beverly's favorite topics. Sometimes she thought that getting Else to talk about her children was like pulling teeth. Not that she wanted to pry, of course; she was used to the fact that Else was not likely to start a conversation of much substance, but, as Beverly said to a friend, "She always says what's on her mind, in a quiet way."

Beverly took a bite of her dripping Reuben sandwich, wiped her mouth, and said. "So, I hear Mark is doing very well in college."

Else smiled faintly and replied, "Yes, quite well. But you know how Mark is with his school work. It was never any trouble for him."

"Everybody has their own talents. Thank God we aren't all gifted in the same things. Take my two boys, for example. Jeffrey will probably be the most brilliant law student in his class . . ."

If you don't say so yourself, Else thought.

"But he has no common sense, he'll do some of the dumbest things you can imagine. On the other hand, Jonathan was never too interested in the academic part. So I worried for years, I thought it would be nice if both my boys were professionals, but Sherm always said don't worry, he has a good business head and you don't need a wall full of diplomas to be a success in life. I guess he's right."

"Of course he is," Else said. "Book smarts aren't everything."

Beverly brought her right index finger to the corner of her mouth to wipe away a spot of Russian dressing. "Walter," she began, "Walter didn't go to college in Germany, did he?"

"No," said Else, softly. "Not during the war. Not many young men went during the war."

"And Walter's done quite well for himself, hasn't he?"

Not waiting for Else to respond, Beverly continued, "And you know why he did so well? Because he has a talent, a knack for photography. His films are just marvelous. And you know the other reason he is so successful?"

Else was amused. "Please tell me," she said.

"Because he has such a way with people, he's such a charmer, and people like him. That's the key to success in life, Sherm always says. You have to get people to like you."

"Yes, that's what Walter always says, too," Else said. "You

have to get people to like you. But sometimes I wonder if there aren't more important things in life."

As Else fell silent, Beverly thought back to a weekday afternoon three or four years before; she couldn't remember exactly when. It was at the elegant Scarsdale home of a member of the Synagogue Sisterhood, and Walter had spoken so charmingly and wittily. It was unusual, she thought; a German who had fought under Hitler in the war speaking to a group of Jewish women in Scarsdale, but she hadn't thought much about that. It just seemed that he would be an interesting person to have at the monthly gathering, so she invited him and he accepted, refusing to accept a fee. She still remembered the invitation she had worked on so long, to make sure it was just right.

"Our guest speaker, Mr. Walter Scholz," she recalled writing, "freelance producer of filmed documentaries, has worked for various scientific and technological companies. His camera has focused on Yehudi Menuhin and presently is filming the artist, Alexander Rutsch, who painted portraits of Dali and Picasso. The topic will be 'Personal Relfections on Personalities.'" The program drew considerable praise.

"Does Walter still give lectures?" she asked Else.

"I don't know," said Else. "I guess so."

· · · ● · · ·

Walter finished his work downstairs a few minutes before noon, and went to the kitchen to make himself a combination of breakfast and lunch, since he had not yet eaten. Else had often told him that it was uncouth to mix two meals the way he did; a large bowl of seven-grain cereal (she called it "peasant food"); three or four eggs scrambled with sausage, large chunks of German salami smeared with mustard, a wedge of dark bread, a slab of muenster cheese, and beer.

He was almost finished preparing the gargantuan feast when the doorbell rang. Probably one of Stephen's friends, he thought, as he walked down the half flight of stairs to the door.

Two men, conservatively but casually dressed, stood on the outside steps. One had reddish hair, the color of an Irish setter, and the other had slightly Semitic features and dark hair. Both were just over six feet tall, and looked to be in their mid- to late thirties. Walter wondered to himself if they were selling vacuum cleaners or religious articles.

"May I help you gentlemen?" he asked.

Jack spoke first. His voice was clear, confident, commanding; a voice trained to indicate that its owner was in charge.

"We think you can, Mr. Scholz. In fact, we are quite sure you can help us. May we come in and talk to you?"

Walter smiled, his usual charming smile. "May I ask who you represent, or who you are?" he asked.

"We represent the FBI," Jack said, "and there are some things we ought to talk about right now."

Walter kept a passable imitation of a smile on his face, but inwardly he struggled to keep his knees from buckling. How could they know? Did they know? Maybe they were just doing a routine check on a neighbor who had applied for sensitive government work. Maybe . . .

"Are you doing a background check on someone, perhaps?" Walter managed to ask. But even as he uttered the words, he knew they didn't sound convincing.

"It's much more serious than that, Mr. Scholz," Ed said, and then added "Or would you prefer to be called 'David.'"

The space in front of Walter's eyes turned a red-black color, and he thought for a moment that he might be having a stroke or a heart attack. But the color went away, and Walter found himself still standing in front of the two FBI agents, his mouth dry but still molded into the shape of a smile. All his training, all those years and plans and everything he had ever worked for would be gone; his entire life would be rendered worthless. What would happen to the family? His mind raced. Maybe they were just bluffing; they could have found just the name David somewhere and decided to try it on him, just in case. But they would have to do more than just say a name to break him. His legend would sustain him. He had the documents to prove it. There *was* a Walter Gottfried Scholz born in a village in the Sudetenland the same year Tomas Most was born. The boy had died of a childhood disease, but his family was killed during the war and the villagers were dead or scattered about. Everything would check out, Walter thought, as he remembered what they used to say about the young Lieutenant Most at KGB School 65 in Kiev twenty-four years ago: His legends were golden.

Walter tried to make his voice sound strong. "Certainly," he began, and then trailed off. "Certainly, there must be some sort of mistake. Who is David? Perhaps you have the wrong house."

But Walter could not control the perspiration that began to coat his face, even though the house was air-conditioned. He thrust his hands into the pockets of his Bermuda shorts so that the agents wouldn't see them trembling.

"Mr. Scholz, we're sure that there is no mistake, and perhaps after we talk awhile you'll be just as sure as we are," Ed said. "Or should we have you booked right away on espionage charges and you can call your family later from jail?"

Playing the good cop, Jack interjected, before Walter could speak: "I think Mr. Scholz would rather talk to us, Ed. Maybe we can come to some kind of an agreement."

· · · ● · · ·

Mark woke up late that morning, after eleven, and was surprised for a moment when he rolled over and found a warm body next to him. Maria had returned to Georgetown a week late after vacationing with her parents in Norway, visiting relatives and ancestral villages. He did not know exactly when she was scheduled to arrive in Washington, but was happy when she called near midnight the night before and said she missed him and would like to come over to his apartment.

She brought with her a bottle of good California champagne, and they drank it directly out of the bottle. Maria was drunk before the bottle was empty, and wanted to make love.

But Mark said he wouldn't until she proved she wasn't drunk by memorizing a claim on the champagne bottle's label that said, "It is a rarity that a select Champagne Cuvée is delicate enough to allow itself to be marketed in its driest natural form. It is a truly natural champagne."

Maria had laughed, wrapped her tanned, thin arms around his waist, and said, "Why don't you market yourself in your natural form?"

They kissed, and it was like it had been before, only better after the anticipation of a summer apart.

Remembering, through a slight hangover, the events of the night before, Mark suddenly felt a surge of affection for Maria. He was puzzled by it, because he had promised himself that he would not become emotionally involved with her. It just would not be convenient. But he heard a voice inside him that said, "Don't love" evaporate for the moment as he traced his forefinger down the narrow ridge of translucent hair running from the nape of Maria's delicate neck to the small of her back. He moved closer to her, and molded his body to fit her sleeping form.

"Mmmmm," she breathed. "I like when you do that."

She turned over to face Mark, naked except for a pair of pale yellow panties.

"I'd like to kiss you," she said. "But my mouth feels like the sewers of Paris."

"It's okay," Mark said.

But Maria suddenly sprang out of bed, a panicked look on her face. She had seen the clock.

"Oh, shit," she exclaimed. I didn't think it was so late. I have an interview for a job at this French place on M Street at noon. I have to run. Sorry."

She pulled on her clothes, and kissed Mark wetly on the mouth at the door. They made plans for the evening.

Ten minutes after she left the apartment, there was a heavy knock at the door. Mark opened it, and did not recognize the two serious looking men who stood there.

· · · ● · · ·

"Leave a note for your wife and son," Ed said, gripping Walter firmly above his left elbow as Jack patted him down for weapons. "Tell them that you had to go away suddenly on business, that everything is okay, and that you'll call later tonight. I'm sure it will be no great shock to them. You've disappeared suddenly before."

"I'm sure I can explain everything," Walter said.

"I sincerely doubt that, Mr. Scholz, but it will be interesting to hear you try," said Ed. "Now write that note so we can get out of here."

"How long will I be gone?" Walter asked, his voice straining.

"That depends on how cooperative you are," said Jack. "It depends on what kind of deal we can make."

"I don't make deals," Walter said. "You have the wrong fellow."

"We'll see," said Jack. "We'll just have to wait and see, won't we?"

A blue Chevrolet sedan was parked in the driveway, and Walter noticed as he was being led to it that there was another man in the driver's seat. He got into the back seat with Ed, and Jack took the front passenger seat.

They drove west on the Cross Westchester Expressway, over the Tappan Zee Bridge, and then south through north central New Jersey. The heat began to get uncomfortable, even with the breeze, so the driver pressed a button that rolled up the windows, and turned on the air conditioning.

After almost an hour of silence, Ed spoke first. "We already know who you are, Mr. Scholz. It's time you were introduced to us. I'm Ed, the fellow with the red hair is Jack, and the driver is Matt."

"My pleasure," Walter said. Since they left Woodvale his mind had been overwhelmed with thoughts so numerous and disturbing that he felt like he would explode any minute. But he could not escape the years of training that had drilled into him exactly how to behave in such a situation. Stick with the legend. If you stay with it, they'll never be able to break you. But there was something they had never discussed at the Center, a question that disturbed Walter immensely as he rode through New Jersey flanked by three FBI agents. How would they have found him in the first place without at least some good evidence? Did they pick his name out of a hat? Or had they turned a KGB agent who gave them his name. That was always a possibility, but one he preferred not to think about. He would stick to his legend.

"Tell me, Mr. Scholz," Ed began, as if in a casual conversation at the local watering hole. "Tell me about your vacation with your family this summer."

Walter breathed deeply, trying to keep down the bile that was rising in his throat. They had been following him. "Just an ordinary vacation," he said. "Like the ones we take every summer."

"Do you always fly first class, Walter? It's okay if I call you Walter, isn't it? Or David? Whatever you please is fine with me, but I do think we should be on a first name basis."

There was more than just a trace of sarcasm in Jack's voice, and it annoyed Walter. There was a certain superior attitude that the FBI man affected, he thought; an attitude that seemed to say: "Everything I stand for is good and right, and you are a scum Communist spy." But he kept telling himself to remain calm, not to react to anything that they said to him and possibly reveal anything. Just stick to the legend as long as possible.

"Doesn't first class stretch your budget a bit, Walter? Or are the boys at the Center paying a decent salary these days?"

"I have a good business, gentlemen," Walter said. "I can afford to fly my family first class if I want to."

"You left on July 16," Jack said.

"You and Mark left your wife in Munich on July 20," Ed quickly added. "Who did they stay with?"

"Cousins of Else," Walter snapped back. "Josef and Anna Behr."

"Um hum," Jack frowned. He looked at Ed, and the pair remained silent for the better part of a minute. Walter felt the panic coming on again, because he knew what questions would come next.

"Tell us how you managed to cross the Czech border without any notification on your passport, Walter? Can you do that?"

"What makes you think I ever crossed the Czech Border?" He would test them, and make them document every accusation. He would not give up until they could prove that they had enough to charge him with espionage.

"Okay," said Jack. "Suppose you didn't cross the Czech border. Then perhaps you can tell us what route you used to get to Moscow."

"Perhaps," said Walter, "we can put an end to this foolishness and you can find somebody else to play your games with."

Ed removed a folder from a briefcase on the floor of the car. He opened it, and handed a small stack of photographs to Walter.

"Take a look," said Ed. "Maybe then we won't have to waste our time with foolishness anymore."

With a feeling of dread, a feeling, he thought, like the one you have in your dreams when you're falling from a precipice and don't know when you'll stop, he looked down at the first picture: Walter and Mark in a Moscow store for visiting foreign dignitaries. Next picture: Walter and Mark sitting on a bench in a Moscow park.

"Is it a crime to visit Moscow?" Walter asked.

"Keep turning," Jack commanded. Next: Walter, Mark, and Filikov entering a safe house in Moscow.

"Mr. Filikov is getting on a bit in years, isn't he, Walter?"

The moment Ed mentioned Filikov's name, Walter realized there was no further use in denying his identity. But he would not be their patsy. He would not allow them to use him to the detriment of the Soviet Union or to the betterment of the United States.

"Cat got your tongue, Walter?"

"I have nothing to say," Walter said in a voice barely louder than a whisper.

"Suit yourself," said Ed. "There will be plenty of time for talking where we are going. Nice and quiet, no interruptions, and we'll even have a little surprise for you."

· · · ● · · ·

When they reached the Delaware Memorial Bridge, Ed placed blindfolds on Walter. After another forty minutes of driving, Walter could feel that they were going over another bridge. The car left the highway soon after it crossed the bridge, and headed into the rural countryside.

"It's really beautiful around here, Walter," Ed said earnestly. "We used to come fishing in this area when I was a kid."

The car stopped at the end of a half mile long gravel driveway, and the FBI agents led Walter into a small white farmhouse.

10

In the Safe House

When the two husky men knocked at his door, at first Mark thought it was some sort of a joke, though he couldn't readily figure out who would know enough to pull it. The FBI identification looked real, but he knew only too well that authentic looking documentation was easy to come by.

But when they didn't smile, and brusquely demanded that he pack an overnight bag, he began to panic. His face suddenly lost all color, and he bolted for the door, only to be stopped by the thick arm of one of the men, who choked him in the crook of his arm until Mark stopped resisting.

They had counted on Mark not reacting as calmly as his father, and welcomed the opportunity to use enough force to frighten him enough so that he might talk more than Walter when the time was right. They quickly hustled him down the freight elevator, and into the van waiting at the service entrance. Before one of them pushed him into the closed-off rear section of the vehicle, the other one warned him not "to cause any more trouble."

"We have your father, 'young Mister Hope,' he said, "and he's told us some very interesting things. We just want to make sure you say them, too."

The back of the van was completely dark, and before it had even pulled onto the highway next to the apartment building, Mark lost all orientation.

His heart was beating more rapidly than it ever had before,

and he suddenly felt like a trapped animal. A picture came to his mind of a small brown rabbit struggling to free its foot from a trap.

· · · ● · · ·

The van came to a rattling halt, and the bright mid-afternoon sun caused Mark to shut his eyes tightly before relaxing into a squint.

"Get out," said one of the men. "Billy is inside waiting for you. You'll like Billy. Everybody likes Billy."

They led him to a room in the back of the house, a small odd-shaped room with an old fashioned, wide-planked oak floor and plain white walls. A comfortable looking leather couch was against one wall, with a narrow metal folding chair facing it about a foot away. There was nothing between the sofa and the chair.

"Sit in the chair and wait," Mark was told.

Ten minutes later, the door opened, and a man with a neck the circumference of a medium sized tree walked in. His eyes were small and close-set, and his fleshy cheeks glowed pink like the center of a raw pork chop. His hair was cut to within a half inch of his blocky head, and the thick folds of his scalp merged a few inches above his collar with the reddened creases of his neck.

He was short, maybe five foot seven or eight, and probably close to 200 pounds.

"Mark," he said. His voice was coarse, and pitched slightly higher than Mark expected. "I'm Billy. You're in my chair. Get out of my chair."

Before Mark could move, Billy grabbed the top of the chair and pulled it out from under him, making him scramble for balance before losing his footing and falling on his back.

"Sit on the couch," Billy ordered. "You're wasting my time. I don't have time to waste with a little shit like you."

Mark decided to remain silent until he was sure that what they had on him was good enough. He would not, he vowed to himself, be intimidated by this Neanderthal with folds of flesh hanging from the back of his head. He had a theory that men with thick necks were idiots.

Billy pulled his wallet out from a rear pants pocket, and opened it to remove a small photograph.

"Take a look," he said, thrusting it in front of Mark. It was a photograph of Maria, lying naked on the bed with Mark in his apartment.

"You dirty son of a bitch," Mark shouted. "What right do you have to go taking pictures like that?"

Billy smirked, and flicked a pulpy tongue at the drop of saliva which had formed at the corner of his mouth.

"She happened to be there, that's all," Billy said. "It's not our fault you have naked broads in your apartment. And one thing more, Mark."

"Yes?"

Billy sat on the edge of the chair and leaned over until his face was close enough to Mark's so that they could have kissed. Mark almost gagged, and turned his face away so he wouldn't have to feel the ugly man's breath.

"We have the right to do any fucking thing we want to you. You have no rights, and don't go quoting the Constitution to me. It doesn't apply to people like you. We can put you in jail for the rest of your fucking life and the only people who would care are your Red friends."

Mark struggled to maintain his composure, and stared back at Billy. He did not speak.

"Do you want to spend the rest of your life in a stinking jail with scum?"

This ugly bulldog can go to hell, Mark thought, looking Billy directly in the eye. "Scum like Erlichman, Dean, Haldeman, Colson, Liddy?" Mark asked. "I'll be in the best of company."

"Don't get wise," Billy said, his voice threatening. "Now answer my questions before I decide not to be so nice. How long have you been doing the business with big Daddy? When did you first meet Filikov? Who is your control in Washington? What have they told you to do?

"I'm not answering any questions until you let me talk to my father," Mark said. "I must assume that you've taken him also."

"You're a smart kid. He'll be here in an hour or so, and just to show you that we're on the level, we'll let you see him for about a second when he arrives. But be smart like I know you can be. Would we let you talk to him alone and have a chance to come up with some bogus story that'll make our work more difficult? Why would we do that? See, you're not going to know what Daddy says and he's not going to know what you say, but we'll know what you're both saying so that when you bullshit us we'll know to tell the prosecutor so he can recommend to the judge that you get more time in jail for being uncooperative.

"But if you don't want to answer my questions right now," said Billy, "you can think about your answers for a while while I give you some more food for thought."

His tone seemed softer, less menacing, and he pulled the chair back a foot so that he didn't sit right on top of Mark.

"We have all your school records, and we're pretty damn impressed," he said. "I wish I had a brain like yours, what with knowing half a dozen languages and all. Now the only reason you got into this mess was because of your father, and you had no control over that. It wasn't your decision to be born into your family, so we can't blame your working for the Russians totally on you. You have a bright future in front of you, if you're smart about it. If you do the right thing."

"I've heard that before," said Mark.

"You've lived in our country for a long time, and you've adjusted very well—I don't think anybody could disagree with that. Except for one thing, which can easily be changed, you're not a bad fellow at all. It's just a matter of whose side you're on."

"I'm listening," Mark said.

"You're on the wrong side right now," Billy said.

"I'm on the winning side," Mark retorted. "America is falling apart at the seams. Vietnam, Watergate, and an army full of half-wits who can't even read their training manuals. America is the laughing stock of the world."

"We have our problems, as you point out," said Billy. "No system is perfect. But we don't solve our problems by repression and terror tactics. We don't have people who protest against the government declared insane and shipped off to a psychiatric prison. And it's obvious that our press isn't controlled by those in power, or you wouldn't have been able to reel off the Haldeman-Erlichman-Dean crap. But I don't have to sit here and give you a course in comparative government. I think you know enough to make the comparisons yourself."

Billy lit a large cigar, and began to puff on it. He blew the foul smoke into Mark's face, and began to speak slowly, as if discoursing to a group of trainees at the FBI academy.

"Let me put it to you this way," he said. "We don't give a damn whether you think Karl Marx is King Shit or what. We don't

care what you or your father think about anything. All we care
about is what you do. Who was it who said 'When you've got 'em
by the balls, their hearts and minds will follow'?"

"I don't know," said Mark. "Machiavelli? Westmoreland?
Nixon?"

"The point is that you've got two choices. Now, if I was
nineteen years old and had my whole life ahead of me, I wouldn't
want to spend it in jail. I would want to spend it doing exactly
what I wanted."

"How would that be possible?" Mark asked.

"With a few minor restrictions," said Billy, attempting a
smile. "Nothing would change. You would continue to do exactly
as before. Report to your Washington control, to Filikov, do
exactly what they tell you. The only difference would be that
you'd report everything back to us."

"What would happen when they want us all to return for
training?"

"We'll worry about that when the time comes," said Billy.
"We'll try to avoid that situation by making you seem so valuable
to them that they won't want you to appear suspicious by leaving
the country. You'll get just the kind of job they want you to have
when you graduate, courtesy of the Federal Bureau of Investigation. We'll work together to make sure that everything goes
smoothly."

"What if it doesn't?"

"Then we'll put the resources of the FBI into making sure
that your family is safe. We'll ensure that as long as you're in this
country, you won't be harmed . . ."

"Where's the bathroom?" Mark asked. "I have to go to the
bathroom." When Billy did not move Mark added, "I won't try
to climb out of the window."

"It doesn't have a window. You'd have no chance."

With three FBI men standing outside the bathroom door,
Marked leaned over the toilet bowl and vomited until he gasped
for breath.

"Are you all right in there?" Billy yelled.

"Leave me alone," Mark managed to gasp. "I'm fine. I'll be
out in a few minutes."

He sat on the toilet seat, holding his head in his hands and
trying to think. What was it they had told him over and over
again? He could practically hear Filikov's words: "If you have to,

if they have the goods on you, and you have absolutely no other choice, play along with them. If you end up in jail, all we can hope for is an exchange some day, depending on the political climate. If you're free, even if you're under heavy watch, eventually they'll loosen up and we can get you out. It could be a year, five years, ten, or twenty. As long as we get the signal, we will take care of you. As long as you don't betray the party . . ."

But later, home in Woodvale, he told Walter what Filikov had told him, and Walter threw back his head and laughed, and then told him not to be so naive, that once the FBI even knew to say hello to them, it was all over, and their careers were over. And maybe even worse.

"Once people in our position are discovered, my boy, we are in a very grim predicament, indeed," he said. "All the FBI need do is mention our names to our friends at the Center, or to any journalist, and we are done for. Our effectiveness instantly becomes zero, and we are suspect the rest of our lives, by both sides. You see, they have us all ways. We work for them, and eventually there is some conflict and we are discovered by the Center, and the rest of our lives is spent in terror. Or we refuse to talk, and we are returned to the KGB, and they think we have been turned and sent back to betray the Party. The last alternative is the honorable one, the one chosen by our comrade Colonel Abel. He stood trial, and he revealed very little, and he went to jail until a deal was made. Now he is living out his life as a hero in Moscow, one of the Center's finest trainers. He did the honorable thing. He did not betray."

Honor and betrayal. First they were words, just words, maybe on a spelling test in sixth grade, maybe on a test he took soon after moving to America. That was when the rabbit got caught in the trap, and the Russian man came and took Dad away.

· · · ● · · ·

"Okay, Mark, it's about time you come on out of there now. We have some work to do." Billy's voice reached Mark through a haze.

The image of the rabbit came back, and the rabbit was jumping and screeching, and doing everything it could to free itself from the trap. And then, out of nowhere, Walter appeared in the trap, struggling to get out. The rabbit was gone. Walter opened his mouth and tried to scream, but only rabbit noises came out. He was reaching out to something that was not in the picture, and then in the next frame, Else was in the trap with him.

And then, Mark saw himself in the trap between his mother and father, and he, too, was making strange animal noises and trying to get out.

11
Decisions

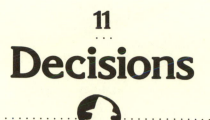

Ed sat on a rattan sofa in the living room of the safe house after lunch Monday afternoon, and addressed Walter and Mark matter-of-factly, the way he might lecture his children about caring for the family pet.

"There's no further point in staying cooped up here in the boondocks and talking, gentlemen," he began. "We're all satisfied that we understand each other, aren't we?

"We are," he answered himself. "Do either of you have anything to say?"

"There is nothing more to say for a while," said Walter.

"Meaning?" Ed asked.

"Meaning we must know our choices before we can tell you anything."

"Since we in the United States believe in free will," Ed said sarcastically, "we will give you some choices, and two days to decide on them."

"I don't know if we need two days," Mark said.

"Shut up," Walter snapped.

"Now, now," Ed began to chide. "This is no place for family disputes. You'll have plenty of time for that later. We're taking you back to suburban splendor this afternoon, back to your cozy American home in your nice, quiet, bourgeois American neighborhood. For the next two days, the two of you and the wife— I strongly advise against letting young Stephen in on the deliberations—will have the luxury, courtesy of the Federal Bureau of Investigation, of deciding what you want to do with the rest of your lives."

"Some choice," Mark mumbled.

"Shut up."

"Of course," said Ed, "we would be most delighted if you would join our ball club. Right, Jack?"

"Yes sir, we sure would love you people aboard," said Jack, as he stood by the kitchen door, sipping on a soft drink.

"What assurances would we have?" Walter asked.

"Everything would be kosher, Walter," said Ed. "We got you a bona fide lawyer, we draw up an agreement, you be nice to us, and we'll be nice to you."

"What if you're not?"

Ed smiled. "Trust me," he said. "We have nothing to gain by screwing you. Unless you don't cooperate, that is. We have to return you to Woodvale today so that your *spymeisters* don't start wondering. But if you wait too long to make the right decision it really won't matter, will it, Jack?"

The auburn-haired Bostonian seemed to take a sort of idiot's delight in playing the yes-man to his partner. In fact, it was a well-rehearsed role that both men could act out equally well. He ambled over to the sofa, sat down with his legs splayed, and took another sip of his Dr. Pepper.

"Nope," he said. "If you make the wrong choice, your Russian friends won't have to do any wondering at all. They can just pick up a newspaper and read all about it. They can even come to the trial if they want, and I'm sure they'll want to."

"Just think about it, Walter. You'd be a star. Reporters, flashbulbs popping, TV cameras. It wouldn't be a bad exposure for us, either, would it, Ed?"

"My mother in Philly would be so proud," Ed said. "We'd be big shots, Jack, imagine that. But we're not so hungry for glory that we wouldn't give the Scholz family the benefit of the doubt. We'd rather keep everything quiet and have you people on our side. So here's the deal. Wednesday, at eight in the evening, you two will leave your house and go down the hill to the restaurant for a fribble or whatever. Walter, you'll go outside to a phone booth, and call a number that we'll give you. You'll tell us what your decision is. If it's the wrong one, you'll be arrested immediately and with great fanfare. If you tell us what we want to hear, we'll make further arrangements. Either way, I'm sure you realize that from here on in you are being watched by the intelligence agencies of the world's two greatest superpowers. Don't try to contact them, Walter, because we'll know. We'll tell them before you will, if you try anything funny. Our eyes are ever vigilant."

· · · ● · · ·

Else sat at the kitchen table with her head in her hands, wiping tears from her eyes for almost a half hour after Walter returned home Monday evening, accompanied by Mark.

The first thing Walter said when they entered the house was, "There's been some trouble." He hugged Else tightly, urgently. He allowed her to hold him but as she began to comprehend the situation she pushed back and began to pound on him with her fists, lightly at first on his chest, and then, as he turned from her, violently on his back. Mark averted his eyes and stood silently in the entrance hall. He had witnessed similar scenes, when Walter returned from an unannounced mission, but Else had never before displayed such anger.

"I wasn't so worried when I saw your note," she began weakly. "But then I called Mark, and he wasn't in, and I kept calling until all hours of the night, and then I called Maria, and she was worried because they had a date and he disappeared all of a sudden, and nobody had any idea where he was, and I thought the two of you had gotten into some awful trouble."

"We have," Walter said. "Terrible."

"I stayed up all Saturday night, and I tried not to let Stephen know that I was worried, but he's not so dumb, you know. He knows when something's wrong, even if he doesn't know exactly what. And yesterday I just paced the house all day, and I'm afraid I sounded very bad when Bev Rosenfeld called and asked if we'd like to go with them to the theater in two weeks, and I said nothing, but she knew and asked if I'd like her to come over for some coffee, and I said no, I just don't feel like it right now but thank you anyway, and I wanted to talk to someone so badly but of course I couldn't. . . ."

"That's enough, Else. I've never known you to carry on so," Walter said sharply.

"I knew something was awful, something had happened. I just felt it in my bones. But you're all right. You're okay."

She looked at Mark, and then put her head down and cried some more. "Darling," she said, looking up at him, "come over here."

He walked stiffly to the side of the table, like a small child meeting a distant relative for the first time. Else reached out and pulled him to her, and continued to weep softly.

"Why aren't you in school?" she asked. "Where have you been? Why didn't you tell anyone where you were going?"

Walter opened the refrigerator to get a beer, offered one to Mark, and then sat across from his wife.

"I wish you would stop crying so we can discuss a very serious matter rationally," he said. "At least listen to me. We have been arrested, captured, discovered. The FBI has found us. They know who we are, what we do."

"They will kill us!" Else shrieked, burying her head in her hands again.

"They won't kill us," said Walter. "They will either put me and Mark in jail or we become double agents."

Her body wracked with sobs, not really listening to what Walter was saying, Else's eyes began to take on a wild look, like she had just received an electric shock.

"The Russians will kill us," she said softly, almost in a whisper. "You will be in jail or dead, and they will come for Stephen and me. It will happen as I always knew it would. The family will be destroyed, one way or another."

Mark left his mother's side, and paced back and forth across the kitchen floor.

"Where's Stephen?" Mark asked. "Is he in the house?"

"He's gone," said Else.

"What do you mean he's gone? Where did he go?"

"A class trip," she said. "They went to spend two days on an old ship in Mystic Seaport. I forgot to tell you."

"It's better he's gone," said Walter. "Because we have only two days until they start the proceedings against us. We must decide what to do by Wednesday evening. But I have already given it great thought."

"We should explain everything to Mom," Mark said. "We can't make the decision ourselves, either you or me."

"I make my own decisions," Walter said, glaring at Mark. "I know what the best thing is."

"Well then, what is the best thing, my darling espionage

agent? What shall *Herr Doktor* do now to get out of the mess he's in?" Else's face was red as she began to shout at Walter.

"What if we do what they want? Then what?" she asked, gesturing with her palms turned upward. "Do they protect us? Do they change our faces? Do they make us sign pledges of allegiance in blood?"

Walter rose from the table, spun around, and pounded the side of the refrigerator with his closed fists.

"Goddammit, I would rather rot in jail than help those lousy sons of bitches. How could I help them, after giving my whole life to the KGB, to the Communist cause? What kind of man would I be, succumbing so easily to their threats? I would be nothing. I would be shit. And then how could I ever trust them to protect us? They hate our guts. They wouldn't care what happens to us after they get what they want."

"Where are they?" Else asked.

"Around. Close by, in the street, tapping the phone, the radio equipment, I don't know. Maybe they can hear us now, for all I know."

"Walter? My love."

"Don't try to convince me otherwise."

"Walter, does it really mean that much to you? More than Mark, more than Stephen? More than me? Are you really so committed that you would give up everything for an idea, a way of life that you have never really experienced. What is so wonderful about what you do? I haven't seen any results. I haven't seen any more peace in the world, or less poverty and hunger. Do you think you make such a difference?"

"Every person who dedicates himself makes a difference," Walter said. "Someday, if this had not happened, I would have meant something. Mark would have meant more. We would have been national heroes."

Else turned from her husband, slapping his words away with a broad, sweeping gesture of her arm.

"What nation?" she asked with undisguised contempt. "Whose hero would you be? You are a German, remember? The Germans are more American than the Americans today. They don't love you for your deeds."

"Communism knows no national borders," Walter said. "And millions of Germans are committed Communists."

"Through no choice of their own," Else said.

"Look," said Walter, "all of this doesn't matter. What it comes to, no matter what a man does for a living, or why he does it, is that you can't just go and turn your back on your life's work. You make a decision to do something when you are a young man, and you do it for the next twenty-five years, and then all of a sudden you renounce it all? What kind of a man would do that?"

"A man who loved his family," Else said. "A man who cared more about those who love him than a philosophy or a political system. Or is that what you care about most, Walter? Are you really so dedicated to the Communist ideals, or are you just another man who blindly follows his career to wherever it leads him, even if it kills him? What happens inside a man's head that makes him risk the things dearest to him for something remote? I can't say that I really understand this husband of mine. Some of the things he's done in the name of this great mission he feels compelled to perform for a people who would just as soon kill him as make him some sort of perverse hero."

"Don't you talk about me like I'm not in the room, like a person who speaks another language," Walter shouted. "Don't you dare question my motives in such a high-handed manner."

"Then how may I question them?" Else snapped, standing and placing her hands on her hips in a defiant gesture. "No one in this family can ever question your final decisions, can they? Well, let me tell you something. I'm all finished with your decisions that seem to lead us to disaster. No more. You do what you want to, but leave the rest of us out of it. Enough."

"It's not that easy any more," Walter said, his voice almost cracking. "We are all in this together now, if we weren't before. The government won't have it any other way, I'm afraid."

"You mean Stephen and I would also have to go to jail?"

"No," Walter said. "Other arrangements would be made. They might deport you, I don't know. But certainly life would not be the same."

"I don't know what to do," Else said flatly. "Ever since I have understood that my life was not to be the same as the others, I haven't known what to do. It was always you who made all the decisions, and I just sat quiet in the house and pretended to be the happy wife. I went to the store, and took the children to their appointments, and arranged for us to have a happy social life with all the happy neighbors so we would look to be just like the rest.

Well, we're not, are we? We're not like the rest and now we can't pretend that we are any more. The game is over and now we must pay the price, and I'd like to pay it as painlessly as possible."

Mark slowly dropped to his knees, as if to pray. Tears welled in his eyes, and soon his body began to tremble ever so slightly. He was silent for a while; he merely kneeled and looked at his parents in a way they hadn't seen before. The expression was almost one of defeat, perhaps of supplication. The words between Walter and Else ceased as they gazed at Mark.

"Why don't," Mark began in a near-whisper, struggling to control his emotions. "Why don't you ask me what I think? Why hasn't anyone thought to ask me for my opinion?"

"But of course. . . ." Walter started to say.

"After all, am I not the kingpin, the hope, the second generation spy to end all second generation spies? Aren't I the *raison d'être* of the whole thing?"

"Don't make yourself larger than life, my boy," Walter warned. "Don't make yourself into the tragic figure."

"But he is, Walter," Else said, her voice trembling. "I've been telling you that for years. He is the tragic figure, and it is his future that is at stake. We've dragged him through enough already, haven't we? Isn't it time we let him make the decisions that are important? We'll be old before you realize, and then when you do, it will be too late. But there is no reason that Mark has to suffer under the same burden you did, he can get out of it now if he wants to."

"I told you it's too late for that," Walter said. "Mark's choices are very limited. He goes to jail, he turns against the Center and cooperates with the FBI, or maybe, at best, he is deported to East Germany."

"What makes you think I would want to go back to East Germany?"

"It's your homeland," Walter said.

"It's your *homeland,*" Mark shot back.

"Didn't you hear what I said?" Walter asked.

"What? I don't want to go back."

"Not that. I said your choices are limited. But they're your choices, do you understand? Your mother is right. They're your choices."

"Am I hearing right?" Mark asked.

"Do you agree, Else?" Walter asked his wife.

She began to laugh, tears again flowing from her red-rimmed eyes. "Do I agree?" she sputtered. "What have I been saying? What have I been begging you? You, me, we have no right to tell him what to do any more."

"It's up to you," Walter said to Mark, as the son stood up to embrace his father. "Whatever you decide, we will do."

· · · ● · · ·

They ate dinner in silence that night, speaking only to ask for a dish or salt shaker. It was like this when something was wrong or about to go wrong, and when they knew that talking about it would not solve the problem. Avoiding sensitive discussions was something that members of the Scholz family had become adept at. At times it was a matter of survival, mostly it was just a condition of life.

A warm, hazy dusk enveloped the early evening like a cocoon when Mark left the house after dinner. The muffled cries of playing children echoed through the full-branched oaks and maples, their noises blending in with the cyclical patter of automatic lawn sprinkling systems set out every night this time of year to guard against late summer parching. He walked to the dead-end part of the road, and then to the woods where he had spent hours playing as a child. Down the hill were the railroad tracks that whisked thousands of fathers from their sprinkler systems to their New York offices, to read reports and write memos and have important meetings over expense account lunches. They would return each night to homes at the end of a driveway, the reliable old "station car" clunking to a stop just before it knocked over a new ten-speed bike that was supposed to be in the garage.

The palm frond trees, which were really just overgrown weeds, arched over the railroad tracks to create a tropical atmosphere. They didn't look like they belonged in New York, but they grew almost uncontrollably fast by the railway bed, as far down as the Bronx or even Harlem, where the train burrowed underground for the final five-mile stretch before disgourging the Westchester warriors onto the battlefields of Manhattan.

A fence separated the track from the woods, but the neighborhood boys would often climb it to play close to the trains. The favorite game was to place pennies on the rails and remove them, hot and flattened, after the train passed over them. Mark remembered the time a slow train with a card marked "Brewster" came to almost a complete stop when the brakeman saw them putting pennies on the track, and then the man started shouting something at them, something about how the police were coming and they were in trouble. They ran back up the hill at breakneck speed, about six or seven of them, and made quick work of hopping the six-foot tall fence, until Timmy Moller got his pants caught on the top. He reached over with his right arm to unsnag the pants, and then the soft part of his arm, in the crook of the elbow, got caught in the fence and the rest of him fell, and his arm opened up all the purple and white where the bone was showing. Later, he remembered, Timmy bragged about the stitches in his arm: "Ten inside and fifteen outside."

The woods were dark, the neighborhood quiet, when Mark got back to this street. He walked back toward the house, looking at the ground as he used to do when he was a child. He would walk down a busy street in White Plains with his mother looking at the sidewalk, because once, when he was about eight or nine, he found a worn-out Mercury head dime with the date 1928 on it, and considered it an important token because 1928 was the year that Walter was born.

On his first trip abroad with his father, he was admonished for doing it. "You look like a drunk," Walter said. "The people at the Center will think you're a drug addict or something if they see you walking around like that."

"But here on the dark, quiet street, he could do what he wanted. Walter was not there to tell him not to look at the ground. His mind began to wander; scenes from past years, from years before he really knew the secret, flashed like the filmstrips they used to show in school, where a man with a deep and boring voice said something like "America, from her agrarian past to her increasingly technological future." Then there would be a beep, and the picture on the screen would change.

The sound of a car engine startled him, and he turned around to see a dark Chevrolet sedan moving very slowly toward him. Instinctively, he froze, much as he might have if a large, angry dog were sniffing around his feet. As the car drove by, a man whom he had not seen before looked out of a window at him solemnly.

"Isn't it past your bedtime, Mark?" he asked.

· · · ● · · ·

His sleep was surprisingly sound and dreamless, but he was troubled when he awoke because of the man in the car the previous night who must have been an FBI agent. He wanted to walk around town all day so he could think and he didn't want a blue sedan following him. When he told Walter of the problem, his father left the house, drove to a phone booth in a shopping center and called E.

"He just wants to walk around town by himself," Walter said. "He's not going anywhere. My wife and I will be in the house all day. He'll be home by six."

"Ed said," Walter later repeated to Mark, "that the agents would try to keep a low profile, and that you would probably not notice them, but they would have to maintain their watch."

"Maybe I shouldn't go out," said Mark.

"Fuck them," Walter said to Mark. "Go wherever you want. Just be home for dinner."

There were a few things that he had to see before making his decision, Mark had resolved the night before. First, the pet cemetery.Then, for balance, the high school. Then, the highway. He wouldn't actually go right to the highway, because the blue sedan, or whatever it was today, might think he was hitchhiking to Argentina. So he would just go to the cliffs over the highway, and imagine. But then maybe they would think he was going to avoid the whole messy future by flinging himself a hundred feet through the air into the traffic. But if they imagined that, he reasoned, they must not have done their homework on him. Suicide would not be a reasonable alternative; it would be admitting defeat, and Mark had long ago determined he would never be defeated.

The Woodvale Canine Cemetery, founded in 1881, was a fixture, if a somewhat humorous one, in the town. Within its five acres lie the remains of thousands of members of the animal kingdom, from dearly departed cockatoos to snakes to, it is said, a once-famous circus elephant.

The cemetery offered, under its century-old trees, refuge from the sun on hot days, and a resting place for kids cutting through it to get to the high school. But more than that, for Mark, it offered a chance to think about America. What better place, he thought, than in the middle of a prime real estate graveyard for expired pets of rich Americans, to consider the argument for not betraying the KGB. In fact, the cemetery was always the example Walter used when declaiming on the imminent collapse of capitalist society.

He chose a grassy spot under a large elm to sit and look around. It was on a high piece of ground, at the back of the graveyard near Washington Avenue. About five feet in front of him was a weathered pink granite headstone, about the size of a folded newspaper, with the name "Colonel" engraved across the top in block letters. "1916–1932," the line below read. Below that, "A brave companion. A trusted friend. Beloved member of the Alfred G. Osborne family, Scarsdale, New York. We will cherish your memory forever."

To the right of Colonel's headstone was a newer one, a polished gray marker distinguished by the engraved likeness of an exaggeratedly adorable cat, whose name was Sabatha. Sabatha had died only a few years before, in 1973, leaving behind a heartbroken family. "We miss you Sabby, love Mom, Dad, Jennifer, Amy, and Jason Grossman," the inscription read.

Down the hill about ten yards was a Lhasa Apso whose pedigree and record of dog show awards were listed on the tombstone. Just behind it was a horizontal marker, flush with the ground, which revealed that there was a family of tamed raccoons owned by a man from Greenwich, Connecticut. The masked animals, the stone said, had all perished together "in an unfortunate and tragic mishap."

Everything that Mark planned to do and see that day he thought would disclose, by their very nature, what his decision would be. It was a form of Marx's dialetical materialism, in a way. The opposing forces, even if only opposed in his own mind—the good and the bad—would be pitted against one another and somehow, reality would emerge. The true. There was no right and no wrong, really. Just a force and its opposite. And if properly chosen opposites were allowed to come up against each other that day, then there would somehow be truth at the end. It sounded good, he knew. It sounded good in the Marx-Engels readers, and it sounded good coming from the mouths of tweedy professors whose lives were as far from the ideal envisioned by the socialist thinkers as Mark knew life behind the Iron Curtain was from what the Communist world's leaders pretended it was to the rest of the world.

He looked again at the tombstone of the long-dead brave

companion from Scarsdale, "Colonel" Osborne. He wondered how Colonel had spent his declining years. Supping from a silver bowl, perhaps, a bowl with his name engraved on it, placed on the kitchen floor every morning, brimming with freshly ground meat, by a white-uniformed maid? Did Colonel eat better in Scarsdale during the Great Depression than did children in the slums twenty miles south? Did Alfred G. Osborne own factories in which children worked fourteen hours a day so that Colonel could eat steak from his silver bowl and be buried on a hillside in what was then the country?

But there were other questions that could not be answered by sitting under a tree in Woodvale Canine Cemetery. What privileges did the old men in the Politburo receive while the vast majority of Soviet citizens struggled through lives marked by scarcity?

Blat, as the Russians called influence, gave considerable advantage to the *nomenkatura,* the high government officials, scientists, members of the foreign service, editors of the *Pravda* and *Izvestia,* artists, and similar persons who were more equal than others in the "classless" Soviet society.

They were the ones who spent their summers in choice "dachas" in the rolling hills southwest of Moscow and drove un-Soviet cars made by Mercedes-Benz and Citroën.

There were things wrong with the capitalist world, he knew, but there were things very wrong in the Soviet Union, and East Germany and Czechoslovakia, or wherever Walter might have decided to settle when he retired a hero. That's what Walter often talked about: the dachas and fancy cars and special stores, and all the luxuries that would be waiting for him when he returned to the Communist world after his service was over. Somehow, when daydreaming about the life he would enjoy in his old age, Walter would never mention the fact that his present life was every bit as comfortable as the one he spoke of in the future tense. And he would never admit, or even discuss, when Mark asked him, the seeming contradiction between Communist ideals and the way it really was.

"You will understand when you are older, when you are forced to compromise," he once said when the subject was broached. "Ideals are not everything."

As he rose from the tall, dry grass and walked down the hill, weaving in and out of the miniature headstones and speeding up to a jog as he approached the street, a single piercing thought entered Mark's mind: "Maybe he's right."

. . . ● . . .

As he reached the edge of the woods, Mark saw the buildings of the Woodvale High School through the underbrush. In his mind the high school was more or less neutral. He had once believed it was the embodiment of a classless society. But no, he later decided, it really wasn't so much a classless society as one that was quite mixed. You couldn't say it was a rich school or a poor school, or even middle class; not black, white, Jewish, or Italian. It was all of these. Some of the community's more liberal members maintained that class and race did not count at the school, and that it was an experiment that worked. Others, in particular those who attended it, were likely to say that the students at Woodvale were as class conscious as any, even if it wasn't fashionable to talk about it.

At the high school, Mark stood at the edge of the woods by the soccer field and watched a gym class play touch football. The scene didn't mean much one way or another as far as making the decision went, but it was important for balance because, whatever it meant, it was a big part of his life. He was not just a tool of the KGB when he was at the school. He was just another kid, a bit smarter perhaps, and more worldly than the rest, but nothing more as far as they knew.

The cliffs over the highway were for college, for the two years he had spent at Georgetown before the secret was lost. It took him about twenty minutes to walk to the highway, cutting through Woodvale Country Club, and then through Midview, a predominantly black section halfway between Elmsford and White Plains, along Tarrytown Road.

The cliffs rise about 100 feet over the Cross Westchester Expressway, the traditional dividing line between southern and northern Westchester County. When Mark was a sixth grader at the J. W. Holcombe School after they moved to Woodvale, some of the boys in his class would sneak off from the schoolyard during recess, dash across the highway, and climb the cliffs. They called themselves the "Indian Club," and had an initiation rite that consisted of walking across a foot-wide ledge that hung precariously over the speeding traffic. From the top of the cliffs they could see the buildings in White Plains to the east, and the Tappan Zee Bridge to the west. The club was unceremoniously disbanded when the mother of one of the boys caught them in the act when she happened to drive by one morning.

But the cliffs were for college, for an emotion he felt during a five-day trip he took in his sophomore year with four of his freshman year dormitory hallmates. Brian Flanagan, his freshman roommate, called him late one night, obviously drunk, and invited him to join a bunch of the guys from the dorm who were going to New Orleans for Mardi Gras.

"But it starts tomorrow doesn't it?" Mark asked.

"Yeah. We'll be there," Brian said.

"You're driving straight through?"

"It's Brew-boy's car," Brian said, too loudly. "He's from down there. Says the car can get there on automatic pilot while the boys have some brews."

"Brew-boy?"

"Pelletier. Says he never missed a Mardi Gras and he's not going to start now. We're leaving in an hour. You gotta go, Mark. It'll be a great time. Brew-boy's got a plantation."

"With slaves?" Mark asked.

"I dunno," said Brian, giggling stupidly. "Hey, Brew," Mark heard him shout. "You still got slaves down there?"

"He says no, not since the liberals took over the country. Mark, we gotta go now. We'll be over to get you soon. Be there. Aloha."

Being on top of the cliffs by the Cross Westchester Expressway reminded him of what Brian later referred to as "The Road Trip" because at the top, looking down on the free-flowing highway, he could look at the cars disappearing into the distance, maybe over the Hudson and up into the mountains, or maybe up through New England, through the industrial towns on the way to Boston, and then on into Maine, north past Bangor, and into the wide-open land of Aroostock County where potatos bouncing from trucks roll across the New Brunswick Highway.

On the road trip last year, there had been five of them, Mark, Brian, Brew-boy, Wilson "Skip" Perkins, and Jackson Kirbo "Bo" Lanier. They weren't his type of guys, but they had gotten along well together in their freshman year, and in a pinch he could slug down "Greenies" (Heineken beer in green bottles, a perennial favorite) with the best of them.

What he liked most about the whole thing was the spontaneity of it: we got a car, we got some money and a full tank of gas, a few cases of beer—let's blow. The essence of a college road trip.

They left at midnight, and soon after 2 A.M. they were in the mountains, near Charlottesville. Bo, who had already consumed the greater portion of two six-packs, was howling about how he wanted to stop and see his best buddy from prep school (Virginia's Woodberry Forest School), Blake something or other, who, he proudly pronounced, "is screwing and drinking his way through UVA in the finest Woodberry tradition."

But they continued on, driving south on Interstate 81 toward the Cumberland Gap. The conversation centered on which girls liked it which ways, and how a guy from their hall had shown up at Clyde's with the ugliest warthog imaginable, and that the girl should be put out of her misery and the guy who asked her out should be committed.

Mark fell asleep in the back of the station wagon outside of Roanoke. When he woke up about nine that morning, they were coming out of the Smokies in northeast Tennessee, about an hour from Knoxville.

They were only a few hours from Fayetteville, in the south central part of the state, and they would be within eighty miles of it when they got to Chattanooga around noon. He didn't want to think about Fayetteville, because he and Walter had had a terrible argument before they went there to locate some dead-drop sites. It had only been a few weeks before the road trip, and he had had to break a long-planned date with Maria to fly off to Nashville in the middle of the night to meet Walter. There was no real reason that Mark had to go, except for one: "You must know everything that I know," Walter told him.

They got to New Orleans near midnight, and stayed at Brew-boy's "ancestral home," as he called it, a large, white, columned affair in the Garden District, complete with hanging moss and servants. Brew-boy's parents were not home, but in the city, tending to their duties with Comus, the most elite of the carnival crews.

For the next two days, they existed in a near-stupor, sometimes prone on Canal Street, at other times in oak-shaded hammocks in the side yard of Brew-boy's home. They left New Orleans two days earlier than they first expected to because Skip decided that they should all "take a little detour" and go to Daytona Beach to sit in the sun and let the alcohol coursing through their bodies get absorbed by the rays.

So they went, and although Mark had some work to catch up on back at school, he didn't protest because he wanted to be part of what seemed to him a wild, hedonistic, basically aimless adventure.

Brian suggested that they stop at Panama City, on the Gulf side, because it was so much closer and almost as warm as Daytona. But Brew-boy and Skip both wanted to drive on the resort's hard sand. So they went to Daytona, drove on the beach, slept in the station wagon because they didn't have enough money for a hotel room, and tried unsuccessfully to bed down a quintet of young lovelies from Michigan State University.

When he thought back on the trip, the memory was mostly of an open road: broad, uncluttered interstates which bisected mountains and forests and the vast low-lying tidal marshes of coastal Georgia and South Carolina. There was a certain easing of the soul that he had experienced in the back of a car filled with free-flowing beer and invigoratingly mindless conversation, moving at sixty-five or seventy miles an hour behind a convoy of interstate haulers equipped with CB radios, fuzzbusters, and other anti-police paraphenalia.

· · · ● · · ·

On top of the cliffs, a slight wind was blowing. It felt good on his heat-flushed face, and he stretched out on a wide ledge to rest. He knew the decision could not wait any longer, but he also knew that it was not really a decision. It was just, he realized, an admission of something he had known for a long time: which Mark he really was.

He would have to compromise, and he would have to reveal many things he had sworn with all his soul not to. But he would never, he promised aloud to himself, under pain of torture or threat of death, breathe a word about the file in Filikov's office. He wanted the "American Friends" all to himself, because some day he would find them. He would find SPRINTER, and they would have a few beers together, and it would be like finding his twin.

12

In the Middle

Walter and Else said nothing when Mark told them of his decision, but later, when Walter was downstairs playing with his cameras, Else hugged Mark tighter than ever before.

"It could all end here," she said, "or this could just be the beginning."

There were papers to sign, confessions of some sort, that they "were, in fact" agents of a foreign intelligence agency, namely, the Soviet Union's KGB.

A lawyer was assigned to them, but told them that if all went as planned, there would be no need of his services.

Then there were days of debriefings, at times with Walter, Else, and Mark all present, and at times seperately. Tape recorders ran throughout the sessions, and they were constantly reminded that there would be ways, if not now, then later, to verify the information.

It was tedious, and at times Mark felt as though he might get physically ill at any moment. They were questioned about everything, from Walter's childhood in the Sudetenland to his ideological adoption of communism, to his sparkling career as an intelligence officer after the war. The first day Walter did almost all of the talking, and Mark watched as his father was transformed into a person he hadn't known before as he spun the tale of his life. It seemed almost cathartic for him, a huge relief, to release the things that had been for so long kept carefully locked away.

After he got used to the routine of his interrogators, Walter relaxed, and appeared to relish in talking about himself; for once, perhaps for the first time since he had become a secret person, he was on stage, and no longer had to hide behind the mask of espionage. He did not gush, though; there was still a natural reserve that the FBI questioners could not penetrate with their queries. He was careful in his answers, and, as far as Mark could ascertain, he was telling the truth.

Names were named, with the assurance by the agents that Soviet illegals in the country under diplomatic cover whose identities he disclosed would not be immediately declared *persona non grata,* and that if and when action was taken against them, it would be done in a manner so as to make it appear that those expelled were at fault for their own discovery. Besides, explained Vincent, a middle-aged veteran of the bureau's Soviet desk, the FBI is not nearly as interested in KGB agents posing as diplomats, all of whom are suspect anyway, as it is in others whose professions and identities would not automatically lead to suspicion—people who appear to be just like the guy down the street.

"People like you, Walter," Vincent said. "That's who we're interested in. People like you, and your fine young son here, and your beautiful wife. You're the people who are most interesting, because you're the people who can do us the most harm, in the long run. Who do you know, Walter?" he implored. "Tell us who you know."

Mark sat silent and swallowed hard. He was not asked, so he did not speak.

"Who do you know, Walter? You must tell us."

"I don't know any of the others in our category," Walter said in a flat, unemotional voice. "You don't think they would be stupid enough to tell me anything like that, do you?"

"You never know when certain things don't seem so stupid to some people," Vincent said. "For instance, it wouldn't be so stupid for you to know some of these people if a war ever broke out, would it? If diplomatic relations were broken, and if suddenly you had to mobilize all the troops, so to speak? If there were young people like Mark, their educations complete and firmly in place where they could provide valuable information to your friends at the Center, and if you were the focal point of all this, then it wouldn't be so stupid, would it?"

"I would never know information like that, about other agents like us, until I absolutely had to. No one based in the

United States would know those things; it is quite unwise, as I am sure you realize, to have such operations too centralized, especially to have it rest in the hands of someone who possibly could be caught."

"Such as you have been," Vincent said with a smirk.

"Don't jerk me around," Walter said. "You want to know certain things, and I will tell you. But please try to be decent about it."

"Would you care to take a lie detector test?" Vincent asked.

"Whatever you please," Walter said. "I suppose I don't have much choice."

"We'll take care of it later," Vincent said. Then they moved Mark to a different room, by himself, to question him. He told all he knew, except for the secret he had promised himself never to reveal. And they believed him.

· · · ● · · ·

After the first few weeks, every effort was made to bring things back to normal. Contact with the FBI was kept at a discreet minimum, though three members of the Scholz family knew that they were always being watched. It was not a particularly comfortable feeling, but it was one they were fairly well used to. They had always been watched. The only one who didn't know to be uncomfortable was Stephen, who was unaware of the change.

When Mark returned to Washington after a week-long absence, he called Maria and told her that he had to rush home the previous Saturday because the doctors thought his father might have cancer, but that the tests turned out to be negative and everything was okay now, and he was sorry he hadn't called her earlier, and he would do anything to make it up to her.

"I've heard that line before, Mark," she said. "And it doesn't impress me. I'm sorry about your father, and I'm glad he's okay, but I can't take this disappearing act any more. I love you, but not in the way you think. I can't love you in a normal way, because you're too strange in ways like disappearing last Saturday. And believe me, I've known strange people, but not anyone quite like you. Maybe that's why I'm so attracted to you, Mark, but I can only take so much."

"Things will change, Maria," Mark pleaded. "My life is different now, things will be better."

"What are you talking about?" she asked.

"There have been problems with my family for a while that I didn't want to bother you with," he said. "But we've resolved them during the last week, and things will improve, I promise."

"I guess we'll just have to see," Maria said.

When Mark got off the phone, he sat on his bed and cried for a minute. He looked at his watch and made sure that it was no more than that, because it was bad enough he was crying, without doing it uncontrollably. As long as he could turn it off when he wanted to, he reasoned, he was still in control of himself. And that was the important thing.

It wasn't so much that he feared losing Maria; he had a good time with her, but there would be others. What terrified him was the possibility that ever since he made the decision, on top of the cliffs, he might have been deceiving himself. He had thought, perhaps for no good reason at all, that things would get better just because the family was willing to turn against the Center. But why would they? he asked himself as he lay on his back, staring at the ceiling. The only difference now was that there were two governments breathing down their necks instead of one. The Center would still demand the same of them, and the FBI supposedly would do its best to help them satisfy those demands. But then there would be pressure from the FBI to do more, to do so well in their work for the Russians that they would be trusted with even more sensitive information, more plans, more plots, more names. They would all be pushing, and they would all be pushing with Mark Scholz in the middle.

But at least it was a new start.

. . . ● . . .

For several months life was normal. Mark went to classes daily, joined the staff of the student newspaper, the *Voice,* as a photographer, and saw Maria fairly regularly. The family went on a skiing vacation at Sugarbush Mountain in Maine during Christmas, and tried very hard to pretend everything was normal. But then they had always been that way, and, Mark supposed, it was not much different now than it ever had been. Just a bit more complicated.

He had gotten to know Jack and Ed better over the months following the decision; they met occasionally at park benches and public monuments around the city, but only after Mark carefully did his dry cleaning to make sure that no one might discover them. He had dinner at Ed's house one night, steak and spaghetti, a combination he found rather unusual. Ed's wife, a plain looking though intelligent woman in her early thirties, tried her best to make Mark feel comfortable, and although she knew who he really was, she asked only about his courses at Georgetown, his favorite restaurants in Washington, and wasn't it beautiful this time of year when the blooms were just appearing on the cherry blossom trees? When two girls about eight and ten came downstairs after dinner and announced that their homework was finished, Jack introduced them to Mark as Linda and Julie, and told them that Mark was a college student who was interested in learning more about Daddy's work. They shook his hand ceremoniously, and then Linda, the younger one, asked him if he had any little girls of his own. When he said no, they seemed to lose interest in him, and returned upstairs to watch "Little House on the Prairie" on television.

In early April, the Monday of the second week in the month, Ed met with Mark and told him that an urgent message had come to Walter the day before from Moscow instructing him to show up at a pizza restaurant in Brooklyn the following Saturday with Mark, where they would be met by a man identified only as Helmut.

Ed relayed the instructions to Mark: "Arrange for Hoffnung to arrive independently of you, at or before 4:30 P.M., April 15, at Sal's Pizza Restaurant at the intersection of Eighty-sixth Street and Bay Parkway in Brooklyn, New York. You will arrive at the same time, same place by public transportation, best by subway. Relay same to Hoffnung. Be seated in the back and order. A gentleman will enter the establishment and join you, introducing himself as Helmut. You may speak to him in German, if you wish, so that your conversation is not understood by the other patrons, who are likely to be of Italian descent in that neighborhood. Helmut has no official connection to any Soviet agency or delegation in the United States. He is a businessman who is friendly to the Soviet Union. Helmut will have in his possession the text of a report that we believe to be true, and which must be made known to the appropriate persons. This will be Hoffnung's duty, and will be explained further by Helmut. Reports on the success of this assignment will be expected."

"What do you suppose it is?" Mark asked Ed.

"Have you ever been involved in disinformation before?" the FBI agent responded.

"Walter has," Mark said. "Wasn't he debriefed on it?"

Ed paused a moment, chewed on his upper lip, and said, distractedly, "Yes, that's right. That ridiculous letter to NASA in the late 1960s wasn't it. Well, this sounds like it could just be a bogus message they want you to sneak into the editorial pages of the *Washington Post* or the *Times*. I don't know. But I'd sure like to find out who Helmut is."

"A German," said Mark. "We seem to give you a lot of trouble."

"Yes," Ed said. "I would agree with you." He smiled, shaking his head from side to side. "First we beat you in a war, then twenty-five years later we beat you in another one, then we rebuild your economy for you, then what do we have to show for it?"

"We come and spy on you for the Russians," Mark said, adding, "Our personalities are quite suited to the profession, you know, like the British. Perhaps it's a genetic predisposition."

"Just remember which country your genes are now predisposed to," Ed warned, in a mock serious voice. "Helmut is probably just another one of hundreds, maybe thousands of East Germans posing as political refugee businessmen, based in the West. They have an international network of contacts that you wouldn't believe. They're very helpful to the Russians, and they're the hardest for us to catch."

"Besides us?"

"Yes, Mark," Ed said. "Besides you. You and yours were a prime catch. The fishing couldn't have been better. Now this is what is going to happen with Helmut. You'll get into New York about one, fool around for an hour or two, and take the subway to Brooklyn so you're within sniffing distance of Sal's by three-thirty."

"The subway is putrid," Mark said. "It's beneath human dignity to ride on that thing."

"So take a cab," Ed said. "I don't care, it's your money. When you get there, after you meet your father, order a large pizza with anchovies and garlic."

"Why anchovies and garlic?"

Ed leaned forward, cupped a hand around his mouth, and

whispered into Mark's ear: "It's an old Bond trick. You breathe on the guy, he passes out, we grab his wallet, his ID, his documents, make copies of everything, put everything back in place before he comes to. It's like slipping the guy a mickey. An Italian mickey."

"An Enzo," Mark said, laughing.

"This is what you do when he's revived. Don't worry about taking notes, or trying to remember what he says. We'll have ears all over the place. I'm sure Sal will accommodate us. Don't worry about talking to the guy in German, either; we have plenty of translators."

"The thought didn't cross my mind whether I shouldn't speak German with him," Mark said. "That's such an American thing, to think that if something isn't in English, there will be all sorts of problems."

"You get on my nerves with that Americans-do-this-and-that routine, Mark. Maybe you would be happier if you learned to appreciate this country for its good things rather that taking every opportunity to knock it." Ed sounded testy; Mark realized he had been obnoxious for no good reason, and decided to keep such feelings to himself in the presence of his new overseer.

"I'm sorry," Mark said, "What do I do with Helmut?"

"Your father has the same instructions, but you won't get to talk to him about this between now and Saturday, so listen carefully. This fellow may just be doing a small favor for some KGB guy who helped him out in the past. He'll have instructions for you, I'm sure, but probably won't know exactly what you know. So you play the call-my-bluff game. Pretend to know a lot more than you do. Flatter him. Ask him isn't he the fellow General So-and-so of the First Department spoke so highly of, and he'll probably want to brag like all you Germans."

"Watch that," Mark cut in with a smile playing on his lips.

"We're one for one on the day now," Ed said. "Let's quit while we're even. So he'll say 'You must mean General This-and-that, not General So-and-so.' If you get enough of that kind of stuff, we can build a trail of reports to whom and how the whole network is set up, that kind of thing."

"Are you going to arrest Helmut?" Mark asked.

"We couldn't do that without risking you." Ed replied. "Unless we follow him long enough to catch him doing something else, something far enough removed from his business with you and your father so that they don't make the connection. It's probably not worth it for this, but we'll wait and see what he gives you. Just play it cool."

"Cool is my middle name," Mark said.

· · · ● · · ·

He was short of money when he got to New York; the train cost more than he thought it would, and he had blown some with Maria at an Afghan place on M Street the night before, so Mark was forced to do the unthinkable: he took the subway from Penn Station to Brooklyn. He encountered none of the horrors that he had been half expecting. The cut-in-half man on the skateboard must have had the day off, and maybe the roving youth gangs were out setting the Bronx on fire. There were just a few middle-aged women on his car, an old wino, and a group of teenage girls with wing-tip hairdos and disco clothes. There was even, Mark noticed with incredulity, a young woman wearing shoes with four-inch lucite deck heels, which were filled with water and had what appeared to be goldfish swimming around in them.

Walter was already sipping on a coke at a small, brown for-mica-topped table in the back of of narrow pizza place, which was filled with noisy teenagers. They greeted each other, and then Mark went to the service counter to order a garlic and anchovy pizza, large, heavy on the garlic. Walter roared with laughter when Mark told him the reason for that particular type of pizza.

They were halfway though the pizza when a thin blond man in his late twenties, obviously a European by the way he dressed and walked, entered Sal's. He immediately walked to the back, sat down at their table, and introduced himself. "I am Helmut, and it is a fine day out there, so I won't waste your time," he began in German. "This is for you," he said taking a white envelope out of his jacket pocket and handing it to Mark. "There is a young man who attends college with you, though I am told he is a year more advanced, in his last year, I believe. His name is Farouk Mustafah, an Egyptian, and from a very influential family. His father is ambassador to Italy."

"I know Farouk," Mark said. "We're in a Mideastern politics class together."

"I know," Helmut said. "That is why this will be so easy."

"I don't know how wise it is to get Mark involved with his classmates," Walter interrupted, displaying what was for him an abnormal degree of belligerence. "These Arabs are not like his American friends, you understand. They're not as likely to take things at face value, they will be suspicious of any obvious gestures Mark makes."

"Precisely," snapped the German. "Precisely because of this trait will the mission be successful. Mark will make no personal contact with the young man. Are you listening, Mark?"

"Go ahead."

"The professor, a Doctor Harrison Finch, I believe, is a part-time instructor at the University. Most of his time is spent as a top-level consultant to the State Department on Middle Eastern affairs."

"He's a brilliant man," Mark said.

"Regardless," said Helmut. "You will engineer a way to give the young Egyptian the impression that he has discovered the document in the professor's possession, and it is for that reason authentic."

"How would he do that?" Walter asked.

"I don't know exactly how. I'm not responsible for details," Helmut said. "Details are your concern. Be creative. Pretend you are writing a spy novel. They come up with the wildest things in those books, and a lot of them probably work."

"Why an Egyptian?" Mark asked.

"Look," replied Helmut, glancing nervously around the pizza parlor, "everything will be clear to you when you examine the document. Don't ask me any questions. I can't linger in this ridiculous place any longer. The information in that document is necessary so the Arabs know exactly who they're dealing with. We are sure that this fellow, Mustafah, will get it to the right people." Helmut rose from his seat, and smiled slightly. A thin, cold smile, the smile of a man who might have tortured small animals when he was a child.

"Wait," Mark said, "one last thing."

"Sorry, gentlemen, but I must leave. You will, of course report back to your superiors on the outcome of this little task."

"Hey," Walter shouted to the German as he strode briskly down the narrow aisle toward the door. "Don't be rude to your countrymen. Stay and have some pizza with us. We ordered the anchovy with extra garlic just for you."

Helmut paused for a moment in the open door, while a group of six or seven youths, chewing on a few pizzas at a corner table next to a pinball machine, looked up at the commotion.

"Yids," one of them said under his breath. "Why can't they learn to talk American like everyone else?"

"Auf wiedersehen," Helmut called out, and then he disappeared onto the bustling sidewalk.

"Shithead," Mark said. "Son-of-a-bitch bastard."

They finished the pizza, and walked two blocks to a corner where they caught an express bus for Manhattan. Between Brooklyn and the FBI safe house in Greenwich Village, they switched buses twice, and took a cab eleven blocks, checking all this time for a trail. Satisfied, they climbed four flights of stairs to the FBI apartment, and showed the document to Jack, who had preceded Mark to New York.

There were several typewritten pages of notes, it appeared, taken by an aid to Secretary of State Cyrus Vance on the secretary's recent trip to several Mideast nations. Across the top was scrawled the words "For the President."

The trio sat at a table and read the document. It read:

. . . .

FRIENDS:

Secretary of State Cyrus Vance sent two reports on his Mideast tour to President Carter. I have not read the report written by Vance's aides who accompanied him on his trip; the report was signed only by the Secretary of State. However, I had an opportunity to read the report written by Vance himself. It contains his impressions and views, as well as the hints about future U.S. policy and tactics in the Arab part of the world. As I consider it a plot, I have summarized the principal thoughts of the report and arranged for their large-scale dissemination.

It is impossible for me to publish them in the papers. My identity would be revealed and my life endangered. *Therefore, I appeal to all honest journalists to inform the world about this plot.*

Excerpts from Vance's Report

Israel

1. The talks confirmed and elaborated Israel's *standpoint,* which is well known.

2. The present internal problems limit Israel's foreign policy moves.
3. Rabin is optimistic and confident. He has good reason for his optimism and confidence.
4. We shall respect Begin's outright refusal of the Palestinian participation in the talks. This attitude will serve as proof that we have freed ourselves from the actions affecting our relations with our closest and most reliable allies in the past.
5. It turned out that our past approach has undermined Israel's confidence as far as sincerity of our actions is concerned. Our future steps have to be influenced by this fact so that Israeli leaders are able to see the difference between our strategy and tactics.

Egypt
1. The talk with Sadat proceeded as expected.
2. Sadat was eager to persuade us that we should consider him the key personality among the Arabs.
3. Egypt, yes, Egypt is of the first importance. This does not apply to Sadat, however.
4. Sadat may even think that Egypt could take over Israel's role.
5. His concepts of what the United States should do in relation to Egypt are unrealistic, even absurd.
6. It is hardly possible for our Mideast policy to be too closely linked with Sadat.
7. I was under the impression that he paid more respect to Rabin than to Assad and Arafat.
8. As far as the Palestine problem is concerned, Sadat will go still further. In fact, he will not oppose our plans.

"What a blatant, unconscionable forgery," Jack said between clenched teeth when he finished reading. "What lousy bastards, and they can't even do a good job of it."

"I take it the document is intended to throw a few kinks into Mr. Carter's efforts to strengthen the U.S. relationship with the Arab world," Walter said. "It is not the first time, you know. These things have been done before, though I have not done them personally."

Ed paced the small apartment, both hands in his front pants pockets, his head bowed. After two or three minutes—a period of strained silence—he walked to an open window and slammed it shut.

"You become paranoid after awhile," he said, in an effort to explain his impulsive action. "I suppose you have no choice but to do it," he said, sounding agitated. He began to pace again, like a caged animal, finally pounding his closed fist on the windowsill. "But I really don't think you can," he said, talking to Mark but staring out of the window. "In fact, the more I think about it, the more dangerous it sounds. What if you were successful, if you somehow got this Egyptian to believe the forgery is authentic, then the State Department—not to mention the Scholz family—is put in a very uncomfortable position. How would they explain it without exposing you?"

Walter suddenly sprang from his chair, as if propelled by an electric shock, his face flushed and lips tight. "What an absolute idiot I was to think for a second this deal would work out," he shouted. "Look what a bind we're in now, we're in trouble either way we turn."

"What did you expect, Dad?" Mark asked Walter quietly.

"Shut up, you little prick," Walter retorted

"Shut up, both of you," said Ed. "We'll work something out. That was the promise, and we'll do our best. Just take it easy and trust us."

"Trust," Walter said. "Hah!"

13
A Message from Moscow

"You have failed?"

Mark nodded his head slowly in the affirmative. "I guess you would call it that," he said. "But I tried."

Romankin walked along the river shore, looking at his feet. After a minute, maybe two, he kneeled to inspect the rocky ground more closely, and began to pick up flat, round rocks, about as big around as an egg. Squinting his narrow, close-set eyes, he crouched into the stance of a discus thrower, spun once, and skimmed one of the stones across the gray surface of the Potomac. It rebounded eight or nine times, the most impressive exhibition of stone skipping Mark had ever seen.

"I was always best at this when I was a boy in the Komsomol summer camps. Maybe it would have made you a bit more energetic in your work."

"You get on my nerves, comrade," Mark said. "Did I ever tell you that?"

The Russian sat on a large, smooth rock and looked at Mark. "I must file a report," he said. "You must tell me exactly what happened, in detail how you fouled up, and I must believe every word of it."

"What do you mean? I wouldn't lie to you."

"I will be brutally honest with you, Mark. We have not been pleased by your performance for a while. It is as if you are not giving all your efforts. I don't know how to say it any more delicately."

Mark swallowed hard, as his throat turned dry. He hoped Romankin hadn't noticed. The feelings of panic were coming more frequently since the FBI ordered him not to carry out the KGB disinformation mission, though Walter had ranted and pleaded. They assured him that nothing would come of it, that a valid explanation could be found to satisfy the Russians. But Mark was not so sure. He knew exactly how they thought of him: American enough to be valuable in later years, and possibly American enough to forget who his father was someday. They had never said it quite so plainly, but he knew the suspicion was there.

"You don't believe me?" Mark asked, his voice rising.

"I didn't say I didn't believe you. I said I was not pleased with your performance. There is a difference. When I don't believe you, then you are in trouble."

No kidding, Mark thought.

Romankin took a small notebook from the inside breast pocket of his poplin suit jacket. "Well," he said, "Let's get this over with. Tell me what happened, and make it good. Kanayev may be reading this."

He knew the story by rote, after practicing it dozens of times with Ed and Jack. It was believable, he knew, and there was probably no way they could check it without arousing suspicion.

"Well?" Romankin asked impatiently.

"The opportunity was there. I don't deny that," Mark began. "In our Middle Eastern politics seminar, we have individual question-and-answer sessions with Dr. Finch to help prepare for our final papers. Two weeks ago, on a Tuesday, Finch passed a sign-up sheet around the class for appointments to meet him in his office. I made sure to sign up after Farouk. I let him sign up first, and then I found a time just before his. It worked fine; he signed up for the eleven o'clock slot. I noticed later that nobody had signed up for the ten-thirty, so I came at ten-thirty on Thursday morning and told Dr. Finch I had a conflict at eleven, and asked if I could see him a half hour early since he had nobody else on the list."

"Get to the point," Romankin said.

"So we talked about my paper, and finished at eleven, and then I walked him to the coffee shop. He said he was only going to be a minute, so he left his office door open a crack. He really doesn't keep much in there anyway. My plan was to sneak in his office when he was in the coffee shop and arrange the document so that Farouk couldn't help but read it when he came in before Dr. Finch. And Dr. Finch was going to be late because I was going to run to the coffee shop and tell him my other appointment fell through, that I had a few more questions about the paper, and could I talk to him for just a little longer. He's very accommodating, and besides, I'm one of his favorite students. I always ask the right questions. But it didn't work out that way, because when I went to his office to sneak the document onto his desk, one of the department secretaries was buzzing around in the office next door. She knows me because I have been by the office before to drop off and pick up papers. So I was in Finch's office, ready to arrange the document, and this lady pops in and say's 'Hi, Mark, do you have an appointment with Dr. Finch?' I almost dropped dead. She stays there talking my ear off, and Finch comes back in and I told him I had a few more questions, and then Farouk comes in early, and the whole thing was blown. I'm sorry."

"Couldn't you have tried again?" Romankin demanded. "Couldn't you have thought of something else?"

"I'm sorry," Mark said. "I was so prepared to do it this way, and I guess I got a little flustered. Maybe this isn't the best line of work for me."

"It's too late for career choices, I'm afraid," Romankin said. "You disappoint me. There's nothing that can be done about it now, except to do a sloppy job. Anyway, it's too late. They wanted it done by now. I'll have to report back that the assignment was a failure, and that they will have to do it some other way if they still want it done. Are you satisfied?"

"I did my best," said Mark.

· · · ● · · ·

There were no more assignments from the Center that summer, and Mark spent most of his time with Walter making a film for a large oil company about life on off-shore drilling rigs in the Gulf of Mexico. They spent three weeks on a rig, getting to know the roustabouts, mostly native Louisiana Cajuns and roughhewn imports from Texas and Oklahoma. They followed one of the rig workers, a young Cajun named Aldes Voisin, to his hometown of Houma, and filmed him dancing with his girlfriend at the "fais-do-do," a southern Louisiana version of a country dance.

In September, Mark returned to a sticky, uncomfortably hot Washington to begin his final year at Georgetown. It was a difficult time for him, time to start thinking about the future. And whenever Mark was forced to think about the future, it meant thinking about things like the Center, the FBI, the family, and Maria, and most of all, how uncertain everything was. He sometimes felt himself inevitably hurtling through his surroundings toward a frightening uncertainty; maybe not a final, terrible end, which would be more dramatic, but rather some state of being that he could not now envision. It might be better, he thought, than the way it was now, but he had thought after the arrest that the way it was now would be better than the way it was before. He felt confused, though not so confused that he was rendered useless to his family. For the forseeable future, usefulness meant obeying the FBI first, and the KGB second. There was inevitable conflict between his roles with the two organizations, he knew, but it was something he understood from the beginning, even before he made the decision high on the windy cliffs almost a year ago. Only recently, however, had he clearly understood through the aborted disinformation assignment, that regardless of where his sentimentalities lay, his actions would be directed first for the benefit of his captors, and then, only if it could be done with no harmful effect on the United States, a token gesture for Mother Russia. It was likely, he suspected, to lead to problems in the future that he didn't really want to think about just then.

Maria was another problem. The more Mark thought about her, the more he realized that he had treated her for the last three years, and perhaps she him, as incidental parts of each other's lives. And now he understood the reason, at least for him. It was easier not to get involved to a degree where solid commitments were necessary, because although he never consciously admitted it to himself, he knew that he could not get involved in anything even remotely permanent until certain things were resolved. But he didn't know if they ever would be, and even then, they might very well turn out in such a way that it would be better never to make any promises.

They saw each other frequently, but there was an unspoken understanding between them that it didn't have to last, that it didn't have to be anything special, that it was tentative by mutual consent.

Students at a university such as Georgetown are by nature planners and achievers. Mark was no different. Many entered the university knowing exactly what they wanted to do with their lives, often down to a medical specialty or a desk in the State Department. At the beginning of their senior year, these young paragons of ambition apply to law schools, medical schools, business schools; the best graduate programs in history and languages; the advanced foreign service schools; jobs with Morgan Guaranty Trust; or that special desk at the State Department, or perhaps with the Foreign Service. Several students openly talked about applying to the CIA, and about visits to the headquarters building in Langley, Virginia.

In October, the first Sunday, Walter received a message for Mark from the Center.

"URGENT," it said on the top.

"Inform as to your progress with employment following graduation. Refrain from contact with Romankin, send all messages radio through David. Do not apply for employment with top-security agencies. Establish good record first with a subsidiary agency or group, and gain trust of someone who can find you later employment in CIA, NSA, Senate Intelligence Committee. Center must approve any employment offers. Also, send list of classmates applying for employment at CIA or NSA. Immediately send list of employment possibilities for Hoffnung."

"They've been telling me the same thing since I was in tenth grade," Mark told Ed later. "You'd think they wouldn't be so hyper about it by now, that they'd assume I could repeat their instructions backwards in Bulgarian."

"They're nervous," Ed replied. "Intelligence agencies are always nervous. You should know that by now. They want reassurances, so give it to them. Tell them what you're doing, who you're talking to, what your best prospects are."

"What are they?"

"I told you, we have something lined up for you."

"Will it make them happy?" There was anxiety in Mark's voice.

"As happy as they can be, under the circumstances," Ed said.

"What are the circumstances? Please be direct with me, you have no idea what pressure I'm under."

"I have a very good idea," said Ed. "And I'm sorry, I really am, that your life is in such a mess right now. But given the alternatives at this stage of the game, Mark, you should count your blessings."

"Communists," said Mark with a grin, "Don't have any blessings to count. We're not allowed."

"By the power invested in me by Billy Graham," Ed bellowed, imitating a southern preacher, "I declare thee an honorary theist."

"Thank you," said Mark. "But let's get serious. What am I going to next year? What should I tell them?"

"If I knew exactly, I still couldn't tell you just yet. We're working on it, but nothing's definite yet. Just stall them, that's all I can tell you."

"What if they start getting suspicious?"

"What if, what if, what if," Ed shouted. "How the hell do I know what if? What if the sky falls tomorrow? We're not your babysitter, and I think you're losing sight of what our main concern is. It's not the safety of Mark Scholz. It's the security of the United States. We come first, get it?"

Mark didn't reply; there was no use. He would just roll with the tide, just like always.

· · · ● · · ·

During the winter of 1978, Ivan Filikov was not a happy man. It seemed the things that had been going wrong for him over the last several years were getting worse by leaps and bounds, and now there was "the matter"

Maybe it was just old age, he had thought at first. But he was only sixty-two, a mere youth compared to many of the most powerful Soviet leaders. His age would not wash as an excuse with his superiors. Maybe, he reluctantly admitted to himself, he was just a washout, a used up remnant of the brilliant espionage agent he had been. In his youth, he was known as a master recruiter and trainer; the best, perhaps, in the Illegals Directorate. Some said the best in the entire KGB. Now he was little more than a tolerated functionary, with few real responsibilities and little power. Since "the matter," they had even taken away his one window office with it's view of the courtyard, and replaced it with a windowless cubbyhole between two corridors, next to the men's bathroom. No, things were not good for Ivan Filikov.

Sometimes men would even walk into his office and start to unzip before they realized they were in the wrong room.

His decline had been a long time in coming. It started well before attention was called to "the matter." He wasn't good at office politics. That was part of the beginning of the problem, but it was more than that. When he was fifty, after being passed up three times for promotions he thought he solidly deserved, Filikov began to lose interest in his work. Eventually the slow and gradual malaise showed up in the form of absent details on reports, and laxity on security matters. He began to think that his work was in a sense ridiculous, just a way for grown men to pretend they were playing a game that was important to the whole world.

The other thing bothering him was his ulcer. Until he was in his early fifties, Filikov had been a healthy man. Not robust, to be sure, but never ill enough to miss even a day of work during the most miserable stretch of weather, when half of Moscow was home with colds and flu. The doctor told him that the ulcer was because of stress on the job, and that he should take it easy for a while and not be so tense about his work.

But the ulcer, Filikov suspected, was his punishment for just that. For taking it easy, and for not being nearly as careful as he should have been. For letting "the matter" happen.

During the summer of 1973, five years before, the Illegals Directorate had begun computerizing some of its most sensitive files, including ones Filikov maintained in his office. Filikov was asked to go through his files carefully, and to remove and shred useless and outdated ones. It was a long and arduous task, for Filikov had never been one for neatness and order in his office. At home he demanded that his long suffering wife, Mascha, keep everything immaculate and in its proper place, but those strictures just didn't apply when it came to keeping his workplace in order. It was a common source of joking around the illegals wing: "We should keep all our secrets in your office, Filikov," a colleague joked, "because if the enemy ever invades the Center, even if they get into your office, they'll never be able to find anything."

Filikov's responsibility, for the most part, was the illegals in the United States alone. At one time he had coveted the job of assistant director for North America, but now was resigned to finishing his career as subdeputy for the United States. To many of the younger men in the directorate, it was an enviable job; certainly one of the most important. But that didn't console Filikov, who had always wanted more. Now, he just wanted out.

During the months in 1973 when Filikov was actively purging his files, things were in more disarray than usual. One of those things was Filikov. It was then, in July and August, that Mark Scholz had reported for extensive training, and Filikov had had to supervise his stay. That was a part of his job that had bothered him. He was supposed to be an executive, a higher-up, but he was still stuck with such tasks as looking after kids during the summer, when he would rather be relaxing at the Black Sea. It was not only Mark. A number of young Americans were placed under Filikov's care when they were shipped into the Soviet Union for training.

The most secret of his files was the "American Friends" drawer in an old cabinet. Sometime during that summer, Filikov had left the file unlocked while he sorted through his papers, trying to get everything in a semblance of order so that he could take his vacation as soon as the Scholz kid was gone. Once, when the office was in a particular shambles, the director of the Illegals Directorate, Kanayev, had walked in and chided him for the mess. "Sloppy surroundings, sloppy mind, sloppy deeds," Kanayev said.

Later, when the matter became known, Kanayev told his top aides that he could have predicted as much.

Before Mark visited Filikov's office that August, Filikov had inventoried the "American Friends" file, recording the five-digit number stamped on each page into a small black notebook. He was exceedingly careful double-checking every entry, re-counting the number of pages. But though he was obsessive in some details, he was inexplicably careless in others, as a dieter counts calories maniacally, then eats a quart of butterscotch ice cream at one sitting.

He left the file unlocked before Mark's visit, and then trusted the young spy to stay alone in the room while he left the office "for a few minutes."

A year later, September 4, 1974, Filikov had to make a final check of all the files before programmers started to feed the information into the computer system. He checked the file, page by page, against the numbers in the notebook he recorded the previous summer. Almost immediately, he noticed something was wrong. The numbers were out of order. Upon further examination, he realized that the succession was faulty in the SPRINTER folder, that something had been changed since the last time he had added anything to the file.

When was the last time? The question perturbed him, because for all his appearance of disorganization, he had a remarkable memory. He could recall under which pile of papers and trash he placed an important memorandum months ago, and he could even remember the last time Kanayev smiled at him and bade him good evening at the end of a day. He sat in his stiff wooden chair, a relic, he imagined, from Czarist days, and leaned back against the wall in the way that used to earn a swift smack with the teacher's stick when he was a boy in the Caucasus.

Then he remembered the directive from Kanayev that came toward the end of last summer, and retrieved it from under a stack of old training manuals that he had authored in his more productive days. He read it:

. . . .

TO: All Sub-department Heads
FROM: Y. I. Kanayev
SUBJECT: Phase-in to Computer Storage for All Materials Classified Top Secret
As of September 1, 1973, all additions to top secret files will be stored on computer tapes for eventual insertion into the new system. Existing files will be processed when the system is nearer completion.

. . . .

Nothing in the file cabinet, the "American Friends" file, since September 1, Filikov mumbled aloud as he searched his mind for the source of the confusion. Around September 1, where was I? With the Scholz boy? No, he left before that. Then where? He rummaged through several desk drawers and pulled out a dog-eared calendar. It showed that Mark left Moscow with his father on August 18, 1973. The scrawled notation for August 19, read: "Leave for Sochi," the Black Sea resort town. Yes, now he remembered; the two weeks at the sea were later than usual because of the Scholz visit, and then he stayed at the resort into the first week of September. So Mark Scholz would have been the last person in the office before the Kanayev directive went into effect.

Could the boy have gotten into the files? Filikov wondered. Was he ever left alone? Filikov searched his memory, trying desperately to remember details of Mark's visit, to reconstruct the few hours they spent together in the room.

They had talked for a while; he had baited Mark about his training at the deft hands of Natanya. Then the telephone had rung, and he was called out of the office. By whom? He couldn't remember, but it must have been important. But would he have let the boy stay alone in the office with the files in such disarray? It was against regulations to leave him there in any circumstances; in fact, it was probably against the regulations to have him in the Center at all, because his identity could be known only by a few top officials. But that was part of Filikov's problems for a while; failing to comply strictly with regulations, and that was why he was a very lucky man indeed to end up with a windowless office instead of a windowless prison cell. He had done the unforgivable, and worse yet, he had waited years before reporting it to a superior. But Kanayev felt sorry for him, and decided that it would be easier to remedy the situation abroad, if necessary, than it would be to have poor old Filikov suddenly disappear one day and have people whispering about him forever. Better to hide him next to the lavatory.

It was not long after starting to review what had happened the day Mark was in his office that Filikov realized with certainty that it couldn't have been anyone else but the boy. But what could he say? Who could he tell? It would be easier, he reckoned, just to let sleeping dogs lie and hope that Mark could be trusted with the names. He would talk to him, confront him with it, and frighten the life out of him. But how would he talk to him? When would they meet again? Certainly he could not send a radio message to the house in Woodvale without risking others finding out about it. But the longer he waited, until Mark was scheduled to return to Moscow, perhaps, the greater the risk was that something catastrophic would occur.

Years of planning would go down the tubes, and the loss of the valued agents would be devastating, fatal, even in the event of war. It was too horrible to think about, so Filikov didn't think about it much after a nip or two of his favorite vodka. For a year, two years, almost three years, Filikov said a word to nobody about his fears. He kept close watch on Mark, and was distressed to hear in the spring of 1977 that he was performing poorly and creating problems for the people in Washington. That summer, the drinking became worse than ever and he missed several days of work because of it. They knew, Kanayev and the rest of them, that he had been drinking too much, but they wouldn't say anything about it. It was so common, such a fact of life, like sex and waiting in line, that it was not worth mentioning. If he couldn't do his job, then they would find something else for him to do. If he was doing it, then he could drink all the vodka in Moscow and they wouldn't care.

On his way to work one day, he collapsed in the street, and was taken by police to hospital. They diagnosed his malady as a bleeding ulcer compounded by a generally debilitated state of being. "Lay off the vodka," the doctor, a matronly woman, told him. "And start taking it easier on yourself or you'll soon be a memory."

During his week-long hospital stay, Filikov determined that he must reveal his grave error before the tormenter inside him got any worse. They could do with him as they wished, and he would probably deserve whatever befell him. He was not scared of the possible punishment so much as he was tired of the whole thing. He just wanted to live out his years peacefully, enjoy a good meal and a hearty drink, when the occasion permitted (the doctor made him promise to cut down, and he agreed), and two weeks by the sea every year. Maybe he could have it if he confessed right away, he hoped. Maybe it wasn't too late.

· · · ● · · ·

"You are sure?" Kanayev asked, his heavy eyebrows moving closer together as he frowned. "There is no doubt in your mind that the boy has had access to these files."

"It pains me to say so, sir," Filikov glumly replied, staring at his feet as he sat on a small, uncomfortable chair next to the director's large oak desk, "but for almost three years I have pondered the question, and the more I study my records, the more I am convinced that this conclusion is accurate."

"You have put me in an awkward position, Comrade Filikov."

"I am prepared to submit my resignation immediately, sir," Filikov said.

"Something like this could cost you a lot more than your job, I must tell you," Kanayev said, grimly.

"I'm aware of that, sir," said Filikov, unable to plead with his superior. "But I am willing to offer whatever assistance I can to resolve this problem."

Kanayev lit a cigar, and his fleshy jowls quivered ever so slightly as he inhaled deeply on it. He glowered at Filikov, and after several minutes of silence, flicked some ashes from the end of the stogie toward him.

"The best thing you can do for me right now," Kanayev growled, his voice threatening, "is to discuss this matter with no one, just as you have done for the last three years. You will still no longer oversee the progress of young Hoffnung. The seriousness of this matter cannot be overstated, but there is no use in making it known to others around here. Why destroy more reputations than necessary? One is quite enough, at this point, don't you think so?"

"What will you do?" Filikov asked.

"Shut up and get out of here," the director barked. "Just go back to your office and write some useless reports and don't get in my way."

"Yes, sir," the chastened Filikov answered.

"Out, get out of here."

Yuri Iosifovich Kanayev was a meticulous planner and plotter, and years before it was necessary, he arranged to handle situations such as the one Filikov just related to him. When he took over the stewardship of the Illegals Directorate in 1964, it was poorly organized and understaffed. But what it lacked most of all, he believed, was a special operations officer, just one man, who would be responsible for enforcement. One man whose job it would be to make sure that any KGB agents who were becoming threats to the organization, for whatever reason, be eliminated. His salary would be paid out of a contingency fund which Kanayev did not have to account for, and the only people who would know of his existence would be Kanayev and the KGB director, Yuri Andropov. In 1968, Kanayev had dispatched such a man from Moscow. He was called "S." Yes, thought Kanayev, this is just the sort of situation which calls for his special skills.

On any given case, S knew only as much as Kanayev told him. He was excellent at surveillance, but his primary duty was far more specific than that. S was so good at what he did, such a master of his craft, that he could walk past you on a city street, stumble, and touch you lightly with the end of his stylish umbrella so that you would probably not even notice it. Five minutes later, your leg, or perhaps your rump, would begin to itch, like an insect had bitten. An hour later, you would lie down with a mild headache. The next morning you would be dead.

Kanayev wielded his power so effectively because he had taught those working under him not to question him. He would ask a question, and he would get an answer. He gave an order, and it was carried out.

During the fall of 1977, and into the winter of 1978, Kanayev gave the following orders: He told Romankin to watch Mark very carefully, and to report back to him every week. He sent a message to S, telling him what the problem was, and that his services might become necessary. "We hope it won't come to that, because Hoffnung is a very nice boy," the message said. "Consider this a preliminary alert."

14
...
The Working World

Two weeks after graduating from Georgetown, Mark was back at his apartment in Rosslyn to begin his new job at the Computer Information Council, a computer industry lobby group with offices in a box-like, black glass building only a few blocks from Mark's apartment.

For months before graduation, Romankin had been hounding Mark about stepping up his job search, saying that the people back at the Center were beginning to get worried because "such tardiness of action is very uncharacteristic of you."

Mark told him not to worry so much, that he was waiting for just the right job offer, and that it would be unwise to rush things. Two weeks before graduation, after his final exams were over, and just before he was ready to leave for a five-day camping trip to Assateague Island on Maryland's eastern shore with some friends from the *Voice,* he got a message from Ed to call him as soon as possible.

"We have a job for you," he said. "The one we've been trying to line up since January. Our man agreed to do it."

"What is it?" Mark asked.

"I don't know the specifics of the job, but basically, it's an entry-level thing at a computer lobby in Rosslyn. You'll be working on a newsletter, doing administrative things, nothing too heady. The good part is that you can sleep until eight-thirty and still be at work on time."

"How was it arranged?" Mark asked. "What are my obligations to this place?"

"You're just an employee, a kid out of college trying to make it in the big, bad world of Washington lobbying. The only person who knows about you is the president of the group, a guy named Vernon Chase. He's a very reliable fellow."

"Any connection with you guys or the Company?" Mark asked.

"Like I said," Ed replied, "He's a very reliable fellow."

"What will I say to Romankin?"

"Tell him exactly what you are doing, who you're working for, you can even mention that Chase seems well connected in the intelligence community, and if they're smart, they'll be able to confirm that. Believe me, Mark, this is the perfect job. It's not too spooky so that they'll be suspicious, and it's not too far removed from what they're looking for so that they'll be pissed off. They know that the computer industry is vital to U.S. intelligence and military operations, and that connections in the industry can get you pretty far. It's no secret that the people who know what's going on in computers have access to all kinds of information. Don't worry, they'll be happy. They were pressing you for the big stuff, but they really didn't expect it. It's better this way, anyway; your security clearances will come slower if your second job is with a defense or intelligence consulting firm, but you'll have built up a track record with CIC, which will help a lot. If you have a guy like Vern Chase vouching for you, it's bound to help in the future. Romankin will be pleased as shit."

· · · • · · ·

He walked up the hill from his apartment down near the river, up Wilson Boulevard past the glass boxes that house lobby groups and consulting firms, conservative newsletters, and liberal think tanks; the very things that gave Rosslyn and other recently developed locales in the Washington area their identities. Halfway up the hill, he passed the entrance to the new Metro station, where hundreds of suited men and women whose jobs are to occupy the glass monoliths stream out of a hole in the ground marked by a pillar with the letter "M" on it.

Looking at the young men striding purposefully to their skyward cubicles, Mark realized that he was dressed the same as at least half of them, in a light poplin suit, crisp blue Oxford shirt, and red and blue rep tie. He even wore loafers with little tassels on them. He hoped that he didn't look too much like John Dean.

The new clothes weren't his idea, but Romankin's, who himself favored the crisp American classical look, and told Mark that he couldn't expect to be successful in an American organization if he dressed like a Parisian student. The KGB agent even gave Mark a gift-wrapped copy of a book called *Dressing for Success,* by a dapper and intimidating looking man named John Molloy.

He took the elevator to the nineteenth floor, then walked down a corridor to a door marked "Computer Information Council, Inc." Inside, the receptionist smiled at him and said that Mr. Chase would see him in a few minutes.

Vernon Chase was short, broad-faced, and had the look of someone who would be more comfortable at the wheel of a tractor than behind a desk. His ruddy cheeks seemed out of place in the airless environment of a computer lobby; in fact, he enjoyed the company of his prize Brahma bulls at his small farm near Chantilly far more than he did the computer company executives whose gripes he had to listen to daily.

When he was hired to head the group several years before, Chase knew little about computers or the computer industry. But he was valued for his years of experience in areas of government that could serve the industry well, and most of all, for his extensive contacts at the highest levels of several key agencies crucial to the well-being of computer and computer-related concerns.

He was a graduate of Oregon's Reed College, and did extensive graduate work in Asian affairs at Stanford in the early 1950s. After that, according to his resumé, he spent nearly twenty years with the State Department at a half dozen posts in the Far East. It was rumored that he had strong ties with the CIA, but such was the rumor about so many people who worked in Washington that nobody got too excited about them.

Mark entered the spacious, sunny office, and was greeted warmly by Chase.

"Glad to have you on board," the man said.

Mark laughed to himself, wondering why the nautical reference was so often used when welcoming new employees. But his face remained straight as he mustered up his heartiest voice and said "Glad to be on board, sir."

"Did you have a hard time finding the office?" Chase asked.

"No," Mark said, "I'm familiar with the area. I live just a few blocks away, down at Potomac Towers."

"Well," Chase said, his smile dissolving into a more serious expression. "I guess we can be frank with each other."

"Of course," said Mark. "I understand the situation."

"As well you should," said Chase. "And rest assured that I understand it also, probably better than you do. I've been involved in this kind of thing before, but luckily for both of us, you're very well qualified to do the job. Just another smart kid out of Georgetown."

"What exactly is the job?" Mark asked.

"For the most part, you'll be my right hand. We put out a newsletter every two weeks, the *Computer Fortnightly*, which is a lot of press releases, industry trends, and some classed-up gossip. You'll be our contact point with some industry types, mostly p.r. guys, and you'll help prepare my speeches and testimony for committee hearings and the like. It's a very good introduction to the business, frankly, and you should learn a lot."

"It sounds interesting," Mark said.

"I'm sure you'll be very valuable to us. By the way, what exposure do you have to computers? Are you familiar at all?"

"A bit," Mark said. "I took two courses, and I know COBOL and FORTRAN pretty well. And I learn pretty quickly." He paused a moment, then said: "I hope you don't think this is rude, asking you this now, but I don't even know what my salary is. I didn't think to ask when they told me I had a job."

"It's one thousand a month, to start, with raises coming every six months if you're good."

"I'll be good."

"You'd better be," Chase said with a smile. " "Come on, I'd better introduce you around."

Only twenty people worked in the office, mostly secretaries and subprofessionals who were referred to as "support staff." Two people were assigned to producing the newsletter, and four "client liaison representatives" spent most of their time traveling around the country, meeting with member companies of the CIC.

He settled into the office routine quickly and easily, polite to his co-workers, and eager to establish himself as a reliable and efficient employee. The work was not difficult, though it took a while to become familiar with computer industry jargon. It was not too exciting, either, not nearly as much as traveling the world with Walter making films and learning how to be a spy. But maybe, Mark thought, he had had his share of excitement for a while; maybe working nine to five like the rest of the world wasn't so bad.

Romankin was pleased when Mark delivered to him a copy of the transcript of the testimony he wrote that was given by Vernon Chase at an International Trade Commission hearing in September. It wasn't anything earthshaking, just a summary of the problems the U.S. computer industry was facing because of Japanese "dumping" of microchips and other products. Romankin agreed, as Ed had predicted he would, that at least Mark was getting to know influential people.

"But perhaps," the KGB agent urged him, on more than one occasion, "soon you can try to get another job with a related firm where security clearance of some sort will be necessary. The Center loves security clearances. It would make them very happy."

"I'll do the best I can," Mark told him.

Toward the end of September, Mark began having lunch regularly with one of the full-time newsletter writers, a twenty-four-year-old Chicagoan named Darrell Ventura. Darrell was quiet, but friendly, not at all shy about inviting people he wanted to know better to have lunch or dinner with him. The first few times they went out together, they spoke of nothing more exotic than what was going on in the office, who was getting separated or divorced, who had just bought a condo on Connecticut Avenue for a ridiculously high price, and who was incompetent.

After a while, when they were more comfortable with each other, Darrell began to express his unhappiness with the job, his desire to do something closer to a career in journalism. He was disappointed that he hadn't been able to get a better job after earning his journalism degree from Marquette, but thought that coming to Washington for any job that had anything to do with writing would be better than staying in the Midwest. Lately, he had begun to think that perhaps he was deluding himself: "I can see myself forty years old and still writing about fluctuations in the software market for our little newsletter," he told Mark.

"What do you want to end up doing?" Mark asked.

"Covering the White House for the *New York Times.*"

"Can you see yourself doing everything it takes to get there?"

"No," Darrell said dejectedly. "That's the problem. I think big, I'm ambitious deep in my heart, but somehow I just don't think I have the push, the something special it takes to make it big."

"Some people just don't," Mark said. "It's nothing to be ashamed of."

"You can see it right away," said Darrell. "I don't want to sound like Norman Vincent Peale, but you can just look at somebody and tell if they're going to make it. The way they talk to you, how they carry themselves; some people just have the words 'I'm going to be a success' written all over their faces. Like you. You're a winner."

"You think so?" Mark wanted to sound him out, not beg for a compliment; he wanted to hear his impressions.

"A lot of people think you have to wear your ambition on your sleeve, that you have to be like a pushy, glad-handing insurance salesman, but it's not true. Successful people come in all packages. You, for instance. You're quiet, you don't try to grab attention, but you're obviously determined and you know how to make a good impression on people. I've heard it around the office."

"What?"

"You're an up-and-comer, according to the word."

"Who's the word?" Mark asked.

"Just general talk. Chase likes you, and some other people have seen your memos and speeches, and they're pretty impressed. It's obvious you've got what it takes."

Mark laughed, "Takes for what?"

"For whatever," Darrell said. "You're a 'can-do' person."

"That's football coach talk," Mark said. "A boy scout leader would say that. It's nonsense. You can do as well as I can. We're both can-do people. You just have to have more confidence in yourself."

· · · ● · · ·

They grew to be close friends, Darrell and Mark, at least as far as Darrell was concerned. Mark enjoyed talking to Darrell most of the time, found him thoughtful and interesting, but sometimes a bit too melancholy and introspective. When they went out, often to after work places like the Pawn Shop on North

Fort Myers Drive in Rosslyn, Darrell liked to talk about himself, and Mark was happy to listen. But one evening, just before Thanksgiving, Darrell drank more than usual and began to talk louder and more aggressively than he ever had before, and at one point said the simple words: "Tell more."

"Tell more what?" Mark asked.

"About yourself. I'll tell you what I know and you tell the rest. This is what I know: You think you are a renaissance man. You speak every language in Europe, and then some. Maybe even Esperanto. You're close to your family, and all you remember of your youth is making corporate movies with dear old Walter. You sort of love Maria, but you don't see her that much any more because it's time to start breaking things off because she's probably going to take off for Paris and be artistic and dilletantish the rest of her life. And you guard some things very carefully, but I don't know exactly what they are."

Mark was annoyed, even angry. He had allowed himself to become more than just an acquaintance of Darrell because he perceived him as someone who wouldn't pry too much, who would just leave things alone. Maybe, Mark had thought, that's why he couldn't make it as a journalist. But now, his line of questioning was making Mark uncomfortable, and he didn't know quite how to respond to it.

"Well," Darrell said, challenging him with the tone of his voice, "are you going to sit there in a Central European funk, or are you going to talk to me?"

"You're upsetting me," Mark said quietly. "You have to understand that I'm just not like you, that I'm not as open about myself. There's nothing very interesting about me other than what you already know, I can assure you of that."

"I'm not so sure," Darrell said.

"Such as?"

"Now don't go and get mad at me for repeating gossip, you promise?"

"I promise," Mark said.

"I heard it from Kathy, who said she heard it from Anne the bookkeeper."

"What is it?" Mark demanded. "And which Kathy are you talking about?"

"Kathy Atkins, Kathy Lee Atkins," he said, mimicking a Scarlett O'Hara accent and emphasizing the middle name. "The one who's always coming over to your desk and making goo-goo eyes."

"What'd she say?"

"She didn't tell me exactly, but sort of hinted that Anne said that something funny started happening with the books after you were hired. She was wondering if you had anything to do with it."

"What are you talking about?" Mark hoped that he didn't sound desperate, begging. It was probably something stupid, innocent, just a little thing that some stupid gossipy women decided to make a big deal out of. But he could never be too sure.

Suddenly a change came over Darrell. His face and gestures became less animated, and his voice dropped several decibels. "I'm sorry." he said contritely. "I was just an ass even to mention it. Kathy's a dope, anyway. Just forget I said anything, will you?"

Mark rose from the table, and politely excused himself. He did not feel well.

· · · ● · · ·

Because Romankin was good at what he did for a living, the FBI agents assigned to keeping him on his toes took advantage of his considerable skill at determining exactly when he was being trailed. For a while he never seriously suspected that they were watching him for any specific reason. The on-again, off-again Russian watch seemed just part of their routine. The only times problems arose because of this was when Romankin wanted to do a little surveillance of his own, perhaps don some casual clothes and sneakers, take a leisurely stroll through Rosslyn, and get a glimpse of Mark walking out of his office building and down Wilson Boulevard to a restaurant a few blocks away.

He just wanted to make sure that Mark wasn't with any people he wasn't supposed to be with; the people from his office, all of whom he had taken photographs of were okay. But stiff looking men he hadn't seen before; men with short hair and dark, conservatively cut suits were not. He would usually just sit around near where Mark was likely to pass by, his face hidden behind a copy of the *Washington Post.* On more than one occasion, the Russian became so engrossed in the newspaper's gossipy features section that he forgot to look around when Mark was scheduled to walk by. He especially enjoyed reading the rare snippets about his boss, Dobrynin.

But Romankin never did have a chance to see Mark in the company of anybody other than his co-workers, and eventually he began to have strong suspicions about some of them. But he checked them out: their names were on CIC's employee roster, and they walked in and out of the building everyday, so there was nothing, really, that he could do about it.

On days when the FBI was following him, he knew it would be very foolish to appear anywhere near where Mark might be, even if his premise was that the Bureau had no interest whatsoever in the young man. One could just not take those chances.

So on the increasingly frequent occasions when Mark was called to meet with Ed or Jack, a team of FBI agents would be dispatched to tail the Russian in a manner so obvious that he had no reasonable option but to retreat to the embassy and sit at his desk the rest of the day. For a while, he paid no attention to it, but after several months Romankin began to see a pattern emerging; not a distinct one, where he could predict which day they would follow him so closely that he could, and did, flip them his middle finger, but nevertheless there was some reason beyond routine duty, he sensed, for their behavior.

In early December, 1978, Romankin transmitted the following message to the Center:

It is with apologies I report that contact with Hoffnung has been sporadic of late. I am unable to determine whether this is through fault of mine, Hoffnung's, or whether other forces are intervening in some manner. I believe there is some sort of an effort to prevent me from observing Hoffnung at certain times. I have no proof of this, but my trained instincts alert me that something is wrong. Please advise. V. A. Romankin.

The next day, through an illegal agent outside of Washington, Romankin received this message sent from the Center:

Continue your efforts, but also be aware that others are watching him also. Alert Center to days on which you believe efforts by the FBI to observe and intimidate you are greater than usual. There may be some significance in these days. Important to maintain as much normal contact with Hoffnung as possible. Observe, if any, outward changes in his manner. Awaiting reports. Yours, Y. I. Kanayev.

Mark and Romankin met in McDonald's in Alexandria on December 10, and immediately the Russian noticed that Mark was tense and distracted.

"What's wrong?" Romankin asked.

"This is stupid," Mark said. "Half the FBI lives in Alexandria. Someone's bound to recognize you. They know who you are."

"Don't worry," said Romankin. "My collar's turned up and I'll keep my ski hat on. Since when are you worried about the FBI, anyway? Is this something new with you?"

Mark chewed on his Big Mac. The special sauce dripped down his chin. He didn't have much to say to Romankin.

· · · ● · · ·

On a Friday in the middle of December, Mark woke up with more enthusiasm than usual, looking forward to his participation that day in what he considered a strangely American ritual: the office Christmas party. He had never been to one before, but Walter told him stories about the ones he used to drop in on when he was making films for the large corporations.

Nobody did too much work that morning, and after lunch the secretaries started to set out the food and drink. Mark immediately noticed how much liquor had been purchased, as well as gallons of heavily spiked eggnog.

Vernon Chase, dressed in a Santa Claus suit, popped out of his office singing "Chestnuts roasting on an open fire, Jack Frost nipping at your nose" to start the festivities.

Mark nearly laughed aloud at his boss' choice of song, thinking that there wasn't even an open window in the building, much less an open fire. But the members of CIC's Christmas party committee had done their best, festooning a real Christmas tree with lights and ornaments, as well as with yards of narrow yellow computer tape.

After a few glasses of eggnog, Mark ambled over to a corner of the reception area where "Santa" Chase was holding court and drunkenly singing Christmas carols. He was sitting on an easy chair, a bit woozy and enjoying the performance, when he noticed Kathy Atkins giving him the eye from across the room. Normally, he probably would have been too shy or embarrassed to stare back, but the Christmas spirits had taken their toll, and he flashed her a smile and a wink.

Kathy Lee Atkins was thrilled by Mark's response. She had been trying to get his attention for months; she would even walk over to his desk on the pretext of borrowing a pen or eraser, staying to make small talk until he indicated that he had to return to his work.

"Enjoyin' yourself?" she asked, sashaying into a position that she imagined was casually sexy, one hand on her hip and the other playing with the layers of her shag haircut.

"Are you?" Mark responded. He decided to play with her.

Kathy Atkins, Kathy *Lee* Atkins, giggled. She giggled a lot, thought it was charming.

"Markie, with all this booze, honey, no way I'm not gonna be havin' a good time."

Nobody had ever called him Markie before. The fake endearment made his stomach turn, but he just smiled at the girl and let her talk.

"How come you're so quiet and shy, Markie?" she asked, trying her hardest to look directly into his eyes. "A good looking guy like you shouldn't be like that. Loosen up!"

"It's an experiment," Mark said.

"What?"

"An experiment, not talking more than I have to. It's for a research paper I'm doing."

"Oh," said Kathy, her mouth hanging open for a second more than politeness dictates. "For what?"

"Secret," Mark said.

"Oh. Are you putting me on?"

"Hey," Mark said, holding his palms up in front of him. "Would I put you on? I happen to think you're a very nice and charming person."

"You do?" Her voice was a bit slurred. "I was wondering if you were a snob. I couldn't figure out if you were just shy, or if you were a snob."

Mark didn't answer her; he preferred to wait for her to continue, to say something stupid because she was afraid to let the attempt at conversation lull.

"Where did you go to college?" she asked.

"Georgetown."

A smile lit up her pale face. "So did I!" she exclaimed. "I went there too."

Mark smiled at Kathy, waiting for her to explain.

"You don't believe me," she said.

"Of course I do," said Mark in a patronizing voice. "Which division were you in? Arts and Sciences? Foreign Service? Languages?"

"I went to the Georgetown College of Secretarial Science," she said, smirking. "See, I told you. Well, it's Georgetown, isn't it?" She began to giggle.

"Yeah," said Mark, beginning to weary of the conversation. "I guess it is."

"Well don't get so huffy about it," said Kathy. "It's only a joke. It's only what I say. When people say where did you go to school, I say Georgetown. Just for fun. Let 'em think what they want."

Mark leaned back against a wall and looked at Kathy, checking her over like a horseplayer might examine a filly before a race. She was twenty, maybe twenty-one, still schoolgirl thin. Her full breasts were incongruous with the rest of her, and when she wore a push-up bra on occasion, it made her look ridiculously out of proportion; like one of those "life size—feels like real skin" inflatable dolls advertized in the sleazier skin magazines, Mark thought. Her face was the face of an ingenue, but whether by nature or design, he couldn't tell. She had wide-set, saucer-round sea green eyes, a tiny, unformed nose, like a child's, and a swath of freckles dancing across her cheeks. Her thin lips were glossed, even buffed, he thought, and extended beyond their natural boundaries for what was supposed to be a voluptuous effect. She tried hard to look the way she thought men would like her to look, though the look was not one that Mark was usually attracted to. But tonight she would do.

"What are you looking at?" she drawled.

"It's just that I'm not busy now," Mark said. "When you come over to my desk, I'd like to talk to you, but I'm always busy. They work me like a dog around here. But now I'm not busy. I have plenty of time to get to know you."

"It's sure a shame, isn't it, Markie?" she asked. Her voice was full of the honey tones of her native Lynchburg, which she left after high school with two of her best friends. "People could work together for all this time, they spend *one-third* of their whole lives at a place, and never get to know the folks they work with."

"It's never too late to start," Mark said.

Kathy batted her eyelashes from behind the wine-filled paper cup she was holding. "I'm a Lee of Virginia," she said. "I'll bet that you didn't know that was what the Lee in Kathy Lee is for. We're descended through my daddy's momma.

"I'm very impressed," Mark said, trying to sound sincere. "You must be one of those FFVs."

"That's right," she said. "The First Families of Virginia. That's pretty good for a Northerner."

"I know all that stuff," Mark said. "Why, I'm from an FFB."

"What's that?"

"First Families of Brno."

"Come again?" she asked.

"Brno," Mark said. "Don't tell me you've never heard of Brno. It's the swingingest place in all of Moravia, maybe in all of Czechoslovakia. We're descended through my father's mother, also. She was a Hruka. Very prominent people in Brno. Don't tell me you haven't heard of the Hrukas of Brno?"

"I'm sorry," Kathy cooed. "They don't have a branch of the family in Lynchburg, I guess." She laughed at her own joke.

"Not last time I checked," Mark said. "Look," he added. "There are some people I sort of have to mingle with, like Santa Claus and some other honchos. But I agree with you, we should get to know each other better. How about dinner tonight?"

Kathy raised her eyebrows, trying to look skeptical of Mark's invitation. "A gentleman will usually ask a girl out more than a few hours in advance."

"It's no big deal," said Mark. "I just thought we could get together after work. Not like a big production or anything, just a little dinner for two." He smiled, a smile that some might have considered lascivious, but that Kathy thought charming. "Just me and you," he said.

"OK," she said. "But I need time to get ready after work. I look like an aich-oh-gee hog." She scribbled her Alexandria apartment complex address on a piece of memo paper, and tucked it into Mark's hip pocket, letting her hand linger just a second too long.

"Later," she said.

He would woo her, charm her, make her think that she absolutely enchanted him. That was the key, he believed, to gaining the affections of a woman. Make her think that she is beautiful, or brilliant, or whatever she likes to think of herself as. Make her feel good about herself, and she will follow you anywhere, including straight into bed. You gotta be like a salesman, Mark used to say. Get them into the habit of saying yes: Do you want to have dinner with me? Yes. Do you want to come up and see my record collection? (C'mon, that's the oldest one in the book, but okay, yes.)

Dinner was at a place Mark detested, but knew Kathy would enjoy and brag to her friends about. It was called Victoria Station, one of the small chain of restaurants built around the remains of boxcars and cabooses, with the predictable stained glass and train memorabilia. There was a salad bar, and the menu featured slabs of beef and ribs. The night they went was all-you-care-to-eat ribs night.

While they were waiting for a table, sitting in the caboose lounge with a wicker basket full of little goldfish crackers between them, Kathy consumed two strawberry daiquiris. She had another one with her meal. Later that evening, at a Georgetown bar called Mr. Smith's, she had a few more.

"They're my favorite." She breathed into Mark's ear after she asked him to order another one.

Her eyes were half glazed when Mark started to play the game with her, a game whose bait he knew she would rise to.

"So," he said, "I hear you know all the secrets of the office. Care to spread them around? Just a little?"

"What's it to you?" she asked.

"A kiss." He kissed her lightly on the lips. "And more to come."

"All I know," she said, "is that somebody is very mysterious."

"Anybody in particular?"

"I'm talking to him," she said. "But that's okay. I don't mind a mystery man."

"I wish I knew what it was that was so mysterious about me," Mark said. "Maybe you could tell me what you think it is."

She winked at him. "Later," she said, standing, grabbing his hand, and leading him out into the cold night air.

· · · ● · · ·

After it was over, and Kathy lay covered by a sheet in Mark's bed, smoking one of his Player's cigarettes, she turned to him and said, "You know, I like you. You're real nice. But . . ." Her voice trailed off.

"But what?"

"But I wish I knew more about you."

This was it. He had her.

"Shoot away," he said. "Ask me anything you want."

"How did you get your job?"

"I applied for it," Mark said. "A professor from Georgetown told me there was an opening at CIC, so I applied."

"How much do they pay you?" she asked.

"Isn't that a little personal?"

"It's not like you're president of the damn company," Kathy said. "If you tell me, then I'll know if what I know means anything."

He didn't know what she was leading to, but he had to find out. What difference could her knowing his salary make anyway? "Twelve thousand a year," Mark said. "Big deal, right?"

"A thousand a month," said Kathy. "That's what Anne said."

"What did Anne say?"

"Right after you started working at CIC," she said, then began to hesitate. "I'd better not. I promised Anne I wouldn't tell anybody."

"You already have," Mark said. "I'm not the first one."

Her eyes looked frightened, and she stammered a bit when she spoke. "I'm sorry," she said. "It's probably no big deal. . . ."

This time Mark resolved not to let up, not to let the subject die. "What is it?" he asked coldly. "Tell me."

"Promise not to tell anyone I told you," she said. "Promise."

"I promise."

"Anne said that right after you started working, a thousand dollars appeared on the books. Mr. Chase entered it. It's been coming every month."

"So what?" Mark said.

"She didn't know where it came from. There wasn't enough in the payroll account to cover your salary when you were hired, and then this money started coming in."

"So?" Mark asked.

"So she asked him where the thousand was coming from, and you know what he said?"

"What?"

"He looked at her real funny, and he said, 'Don't ask!' That's all he said, 'Don't ask.' He told her not to bring up the subject again."

"So what do you think?" Mark asked Kathy.

"Promise you won't take it personal?"

"I promise."

"I think your daddy got you the job," she said. "I think you must have pretty good connections, and that's how you got the job."

She couldn't know, Mark decided. There was no possible way she could know the truth. But she was suspicious of something; she wanted to believe something about him so he would let her. "Connections help," Mark said. "I have to admit it."

"Is your daddy rich?" she asked. "Like all the Georgetown snobs? Because this is my theory. Promise you won't get mad, and I still like you."

"I promise," Mark said. He was beginning to get bored.

"My theory is that your daddy is friends with Mr. Chase, and you had a hard time getting a job after you graduated, and your daddy asked Mr. Chase if he could give you a job. But CIC's been having some money problems for a while, it's lost some clients and all, so Mr. Chase told your daddy he'd like to help out, but they just didn't have money in the budget for it. So your daddy said he would pay your salary until CIC was doing better, and told Mr. Chase not to let anybody know about it. He'll probably be real mad if he knows you know, so please don't say anything about it. Please."

"Okay," said Mark. "Don't worry about it. I'm glad you told me. You know, I've been wondering about the same thing myself, wondering if my crafty old man would go to that length to get me a job. But you never know with people. Sometimes they'll do the strangest things."

"You're not mad?" Kathy asked.

"No," Mark said. "How could I be mad at someone like you?" He felt like laughing, like telling her what a silly fool she was, but instead he kissed her.

15

S

.... ∩ ....

The killing wasn't the part that S minded; it was the waiting. He was an impatient man, bored easily, and always ready for a new challenge. That's why he enjoyed his job so much. The killing part, he reasoned, was just an incidental tacked onto the end of the whole thing, but an unavoidable incidental. It came with the territory. The fun part for S was the planning, the anticipation. He became irritable between assignments.

He smiled at his good fortune whenever he recalled the day in the summer of 1968 when he had been summoned into Kanayev's office after the argument with a co-worker over a paperweight. He was amused by the absurdity of dying over a paperweight. Just the way for a bureaucrat to go, he thought. A bureaucrat's death had given him new life, a most comfortable life.

He hadn't intended to kill the man, but when his face was slapped he responded reflexively with a series of offensive moves learned while studying the martial arts during his father's Education Ministry assignment in Japan.

As a specialist in the elimination of undesirables for the Illegals Department, he could follow the free-roaming life he enjoyed. Especially in the United States, where he found the lifestyle most agreeable. He was a natural for the territory, having mastered four different American regional accents. S favored the broad-voweled speech of New England.

He was nearing forty, but a perfect physical specimen. He

had never been married, and never really been in love. There once was a girl, a beautiful Brahmin from Bombay, who interested him for a while, but he had to move on and leave her behind. His job was too much fun to give up for a woman. And it was not the kind of job one could just up and quit.

He checked into the hotel under the name "W. M. A. Saltonstall" two days before Christmas, on Saturday, December 23. His room, as he had requested, had an excellent view of the river. He could even see the buildings across the river in Rosslyn, the buildings he would get to know more intimately in the days to follow.

The next day he rented a car, drove up Wisconsin Avenue to Hudson Bay Outfitters, and bought a kayak and a wet suit. He drove, with the craft on the top of his car, to a spot near Cabin John, about ten miles west of the White House, and launched the craft in the icy water. The currents were swift for several miles, but not treacherous. He would have preferred to test himself on the headwaters of the Rappahannock in the Virginia mountains, but there wasn't enough time. Maybe after the job was done. In the early afternoon, he brought the kayak to shore in southeast Washington, after paddling a short distance upstream on the Anacostia River. Two black teenagers were standing on the litter strewn river bank when he brought the kayak out of the water, and they looked at him as though he had just landed from a distant galaxy.

"You want a kayak?" he asked them.

"You crazy, man?" one of the youths declared.

"You want a kayak?" S repeated. "It's a lot of fun. Or you can sell it."

"Got no money," the other youth said.

"Take it," said S. "I don't need it anymore. It's yours." He reached through the rubber spray skirt of the kayak, and removed his clothes. Stripping off the wet suit down to his long underwear, he put on his sneakers, jeans and a heavy gray wool sweater. He left the wet suit on the frozen ground, and walked several blocks to South Capitol Street, where he hailed a cab to take him back to Cabin John for his car.

That night, Christmas Eve, S was bored. He wanted a woman. He wanted something to occupy his fancies for a while. He had the names of a few of the fancier call girls around, but didn't want to bother with them. He preferred something raunchier. In the Yellow pages, he turned to the section where massage parlors advertised their "outcall services." There were lots of them: "Candy Johnson Unlimited. Quality Service. Credit Cards Welcome" and "Apex Outcall Massage. Anywhere in Washington, Maryland, Va." and "Debonair Outcall. Service After Six." He chose "The Circle of One Hundred Club," which claimed to be "one of the finest massage services in the area." They accepted, S noted, Diners Club and Carte Blanche cards. From S, they would have to accept cash.

· · · ● · · ·

According to the reports S had been furnished by Kanayev, CIC would be closed all of Christmas week and New Year's Day. It would re-open Tuesday, January 2, 1979. But many of the other offices in the building would be open every day except Christmas and New Year's Day, the report noted, so S would have ample opportunity to take care of his business.

He had a blueprint of the nineteenth floor of the building, and a schedule of the security guards' nightly rounds. Sewn into the lining of his long wool outercoat was a locksmith's kit which, combined with his skillful fingers, had never failed him. A small but powerful flashlight, a miniature Minox camera, a few chocolate bars, some light reading. That was all he would need—that and some patience—and the job would go without a hitch.

Tuesday afternoon, at three-thirty, S walked past the security guard in the lobby, flashing a forged identification badge. On the nineteenth floor, he took a quick look down the hall at the door that said CIC Incorporated, and then opened the door of the men's room with a key made a few days earlier, after his first visit to the building. In less than a minute, he pushed in one of the fiberboard squares in the dropped ceiling, crawled through the opening, and replaced the square. He then strung a mesh hammock from the same steel supports from which the ceiling hung. It was time for a nap.

The alarm in his wristwatch buzzed at midnight, awakening him. He would have to wait eight minutes, according to the report, until the guard left the floor. After that, there would be plenty of time to do the job.

He unlocked the main door to CIC in three minutes, a bit longer than planned, but within acceptable limits. It took a while longer to determine which file cabinets held the personnel and payroll records, because the office had to remain dark, except for the narrow beam from his flashlight. He was not nervous. The word never really applied to S. But the erratic hummings and thumpings of the building's internal mechanisms distracted him to the point of annoyance. It was difficult to tell if the noises were the building's normal noises, or whether a guard had heard something unusual, a KGB agent perhaps, and had decided to investigate.

The files were locked, but the locks were cheap things which came with the cabinets. There had been nothing of secrecy or value in the CIC files until recently, and Vern Chase decided that changing the locks would draw more attention than necessary. Either way, S would have had minimal difficulty breaking in. The inexpensive locks just made the job that much easier.

There were only nineteen folders in the personnel files. S checked and double-checked them as rapidly as he could. There were only two names under the S's, and Mark Scholz's name was not one of them. Strike one.

The payroll records were dated, week by week, from 1976 to December 30, 1978. The employees had already been paid for their 1978 vacations. S turned to the last week of May for 1978, just in case they entered Mark before he started working in June. They hadn't.

Then S heard footsteps. Two sets were approaching the door of the office. He checked his watch. Only seven minutes had elapsed since he left his perch above the bathroom ceiling. Quickly, silently, he crouched under a desk. There was an unmistakable sound at the door to the reception area, the door from the outside corridor. The door opened, squeaking a bit, and he heard two voices, the voices of black men, he thought, speaking in normal tones.

"You think Theisman's got what it takes?" one man asked the other.

The beam from a flashlight flickered about the room haphazardly. The voices remained at the door. "I hear his restaurant's better than his arm is," the other man said. "Last time I got to the stadium for a 'Skins game, it was so cold I'd like to freeze my butt off. And then they went and lost."

S felt his pulse quickening, but made sure to keep his breathing under control. He sensed no real danger; the guards had merely deviated from their routine, or were bored and decided to make their rounds together to talk about Washington Redskins football. Still, S was slightly uncomfortable.

The door closed, and the guards continued down the hall. When he could no longer hear their footsteps, S returned to the payroll sheets. Next to Mark's name was a notation that his base pay was $230.37 per week, but that the amount was not to be deducted from payroll funds until further notice. "Pay from discretionary fund, $1000 monthly. Authorization V. Chase," read a woman's rounded handwriting in the margin. S could not be certain that the handwritten notation corresponded to the entry next to Mark's name, but he had no time to find out. He suspected, however, that after the sheets were analyzed, they would be sufficient to declare the second strike against Hoffnung. That would put him right at the edge, thought S, because in America you play the American way: three strikes and you're out.

He removed the palm size Minox camera from his pocket, and snapped pictures of the payroll records. The personnel files contained no mention of the recently hired writer, but he took photographs of them anyway.

The next morning at a few minutes before eleven, after reading most of Harold Robbins' *The Betsy* by the light of his flashlight, he extricated himself from the hammock, smoothed his somewhat rumpled clothes as best he could, and strolled past the guard in the lobby.

"Have a Merry Christmas," he told the man.

"Can't complain," the guard replied.

· · · ● · · ·

Within hours after S transmitted his findings to the Center, he received a message in response. "Watch Hoffnung constantly, but without risk," it said. "We are in a precarious situation now, and must be neither too aggressive nor too neglectful of our duties. Report frequently, and maintain preparedness for a final signal."

· · · ● · · ·

Mark stayed in Washington Christmas week because he had promised Vern Chase to complete some research he had fallen behind on after a series of short trips out of town with Walter.

They had agreed, when he took the job, that he would be allowed to take days off when duty demanded, but also that he would not neglect his job with the CIC.

Thursday afternoon, Mark went to the Library of Congress to find some government documents about the history of trade agreements between the United States and Japan. The work was tedious, and after he handed a clerk at the huge round desk in the middle of the main reading room a long list of documents he needed, he was told the wait would be an hour, and probably more.

Now, he began thinking, would be the perfect time to do a little personal research, work that he had been putting off for years. Ed and Jack weren't around, and the stuff would not be too difficult to find. The problem was what to do with the information once he had it. Was the time really right? he wondered, considering the notion more carefully. Or was it, at this point, just an indulgence that was more likely to do him more harm than good?

It had been more than five years since he had seen the name in Filikov's secret file, five years during which he could have tried to find out more, to get closer to uncovering the secrets that would lead him to the boy. No, he wouldn't be a boy anymore. He would be about the same age as Mark, twenty-one, and he might not even be in Tucson anymore.

He sat down at one of the desks ringing the cavernous room, next to a bearded young man wearing a turban reading from what looked to be an Indian medical journal written in English. Only ten yards away was a room filled with telephone books, every telephone book printed in the United States. Every little county and town, every shoe repair store, everything. The KGB, he suspected had probably managed to collect as many phone books as the Library of Congress; it was a fetish with them, he thought. They loved lists of names, thought there was something vaguely secret about them. They didn't even publish a phone book in Moscow, for fear the enemy might use it to his advantage.

But he would need more than a phone book, more than the city directories and newspapers; he would need to actually go to Tucson, to spend some time there, hang around the high schools and find out who was a very popular member of the class of 1974. "I don't remember the guy's name," Mark would say, "but he was a real good athlete, and his father was in the silver import business. Maybe you know him."

It could be done, he knew, but could it be done without serious and irreversible consequences? What if the FBI found out, and suddenly swooped down and arrested a few dozen Soviet agents in placid, unsuspecting neighborhoods throughout the country? The thought was too disturbing to dwell on. But there really couldn't be too much harm in just casually walking over to the phone books, and taking a quick look at the Tucson yellow pages. Or in calling up a few microfilm reels of the Arizona *Daily Star,* and looking in the high school sports pages in 1973 and 1974. It would just be an academic exercise, a test to see if his sleuthing abilities were up to acceptable standards.

Soon he had forgotten the Japanese trade documents and was in the phone book room looking for the Tucson directory. What he didn't notice was that an elegantly slim blond man had moved to a desk in plain view of the phone directory area, and was watching him from behind a copy of *Le Monde,* the Paris daily newspaper.

He took the Tucson directory, which included a section of yellow pages, to the desk where he had been sitting, next to the turban wearer. Then he found where business and street directories from almost every city in the country were kept, and removed the two Tucson directories—the *Polk Directory* and the *Cole Directory.* He didn't notice that the man who was behind the French newspaper had moved closer to his desk when he returned to it with the two heavy books.

In the next several hours, he managed to excavate from the bowels of the great library not only the commercial directories he originally set out to find, but also U.S. Geological Survey topographical maps of the city and surrounding areas, and a book about the founding families of Arizona (it described a particularly interesting man, Sidney P. Osborne, governor of the state during the 1940s. The idiosyncratic Osborn never attended a governors' conference because he believed the people of Arizona elected him to attend to affairs of that state, not to socialize with the nation's other governors at resort spots; the door to his office was always open, and he would meet with anyone who happened to walk through it; he usually answered his telephone himself, and would fire any secretary who asked, "Who's calling?"). Such obscure details fascinated Mark, but he was more interested in finding out about the Tucson of the 1970s, the place where a person who had occupied his thoughts for five years lived a special existence.

He found a guidebook of Tucson, and a brochure published by the city's Board of Realtors extolling the virtues of exclusive neighborhoods like El Encanto and The Foothills, located north of the Rillito River. He even managed to find a copy of Catalina High School's 1968 yearbook, and stories about Catalina "Trojans" football exploits in back copies of the *Daily Star.*

With the books and guides, newspapers and maps stacked around him, Mark began to search through them with an intensity he rarely exhibited. First, he turned through the yellow pages, looking under jewelers, silver dealers, and importers. He copied down the names of the businesses' owners, after cross-checking them in the two commercial directories. Many of the silver businesses, he noticed, were near the intersection of Broadway and Stone Avenue, and on the fringes of El Encanto, around Country Club Road. Many of the larger dealers, he found, by looking in a street by street directory, lived in El Encanto, which, according to the real estate brochure, was an old neighborhood of typically southwestern houses in the $150,000 to $200,000 range.

He found by cross-referencing the names of students in the Catalina High School yearbook with those in the nearby neighborhoods that a number of the students were the sons and daughters of silver importers. One of the directories listed occupations next to the names and addresses.

He recorded the information in his notebook, copying such details as the names of Tucson high school athletes mentioned in the sports pages of the *Daily Star* from 1972 to 1974, and whose last names matched those listed as being involved in jewelry or silver in the Polk and Cole directories. It was just a confusing jumble now, he knew, but after he sorted through it, maybe even devised a computer program to make more sense of it, it would lead him to SPRINTER. Not now, maybe not for years, but someday when things were better, he would take a trip to Tucson and put the information to good use. Someday.

The library closed before Mark finished his research, but he promised himself he would come back later in the week to complete it, and to start on the Japanese trade documents.

He was forced to leave all the Tucson material on the desk, which made him uncomfortable. He knew it was a groundless feeling, that the person who re-stacked it had surely seen things far stranger than research material on the Arizona city. Still, he had a thing about not leaving traces of himself behind.

And for a good reason, on that occasion. S managed to linger in the library a minute longer than Mark, just long enough to walk past the desk stacked with everything you ever wanted to know about Tucson. He even noticed that the yellow pages were open to "Importers—Silver," and that there was a high school yearbook among the material. He had no idea of its significance, and doubted that it meant anything except perhaps research for something Mark was doing at work. But S was trained never to discount anything, so he made a few notes about Mark's activities of that afternoon, and returned to his hotel.

That night, he sent the following message to Kanayev:

Hoffnung spent several hours from his vacation performing what appeared to be research tasks in the Library of Congress today. He first requested extensive material concerning U.S.-Japan trade agreements and such, and then proceeded to ignore the material. Instead, he went through the library and collected information of all sorts concerning the city of Tucson, Arizona. The books and other material included: Tucson "yellow pages," an alphabetical listing of businesses open to section marked "Importers–Silver." A *Cole Directory,* listing persons by their address and occupation. A *Polk Directory,* more of the same thing. A topographical map of Tucson. A yearbook published by Catalina High School, with pictures of the students. The Arizona *Daily Star,* issues from 1972 to 1974. Particular attention was paid to high school sports pages. Hoffnung appeared a touch on edge.

Please advise. S.

Kanayev wasn't terribly surprised when he received the message from S, but it disturbed him a bit nevertheless. He liked to consider himself a fair man, a man of conscience. He lapsed from his ideals sometimes, when circumstances demanded, but mostly he tried to behave in such a way that a judicious and rational person looking back would declare: "Yuri Iosifovich Kanayev did the right thing."

And now, he knew, there was laid before him a decision that called for weighing the consequences with a view toward the judgment of that nameless man. He had read once, a long time ago, some selections of the writings of British philosophers of the eighteenth and nineteenth centuries who embraced a school of thought called utilitarianism. As best as he could understand it, the rightness of an action was based on what would bring about the greatest good for the most people. It was, he thought, somewhat similar in that regard to Marxist-Leninist teachings. But when Kanayev had to make important decisions, he preferred to think of his own reasons for them, rather than relying on rigid dogma.

The Hoffnung problem was difficult only in that Kanayev did not relish the thought of ordering the death of a pleasant enough young man who had held such promise. But when he considered SPRINTER, and HOMER, PARABUS, and ELITE, and the others who represented years of delicate planning and crucial steps on the road to the downfall of the capitalist nations, the decision was really not that difficult.

He would call them all "victory units," except for young Hoffnung. The boy and his family had apparently been compromised, had fallen deathly ill, and could no longer be counted among those units. So there was one former victory unit, and possibly more. When more intelligence was gathered on the rest of the family, they could learn just how far and deep the cancer had spread. So, of course it would be morally reprehensible to allow one fallen unit to destroy many healthy and valuable ones, if he had not already. But what if he already had? Kanayev wondered. The damage would be irreparable, but the boy would still have to be dealt with severely; he would have to be held up as an example to others. Kanayev wanted to discuss the problem with somebody, but he could not just call any one of his underlings into his office and say, "Look, I've got this problem with one of our agents in America, and we'll have to get rid of him. What do you think about it?" He wanted to maintain silence about the Hoffnung matter as long as possible, until there was a good time and acceptable way to explain the unusual disappearance of the young man and possibly his kin to the only higher-up who would have to know about it—the director of the KGB, Yuri Andropov.

The only person he could discuss the matter with was the bumbling fool who caused the mess in the first place, Kanayev decided. He liked Filikov personally, but tried not to let that interfere with his taking certain measures to neutralize the deterioration of the man's work and his probably fatal security lapse. Personal feelings really had no place in handling a matter such as this. Still, he felt it was bad enough punishment for Filikov to

live the rest of his life knowing he was responsible for the events
to follow. The man was loyal, and after all, just incompetent. And
Kanayev wanted to remind him of where the blame lay every day
he continued to occupy his cramped office next to the lavatory.

He dialed two numbers on the interoffice phone.

"Filikov," he barked into the receiver. "Get your ass in here
immediately."

A minute later, Filikov was sitting next to Kanayev's desk,
awaiting the next blow.

"Well what do you suppose is the occasion?" Kanayev asked
Filikov.

"I suppose," said Filikov, with a sad, resigned tinge to his
voice, "that you have received some bad news about our young
friend."

Kanayev smiled, a dour smile, not really a smile at all. "Not
only do I have bad news for you, but I have its natural successor:
worse news," he said. "The bad news is that an examination of
Hoffnung's personnel and payroll records at his place of employment indicates that he has been compromised by American authorities for quite some time."

The words left Filikov momentarily numb, and he could not
think of anything to say in reply.

"Of course, if Hoffnung has been compromised, then it is
safe to assume that the whole family, our dear David and his
lovely wife and younger son, are all working against us as we
speak. Isn't that safe to assume, Mr. Filikov? I want to hear your
expert opinion."

"I would think," began Filikov in a near-whisper, "that the
American authorities would treat a family such as the Scholzes as
one unit."

"Precisely," said Kanayev. "I was just about to bring up that
topic. Units."

"Pardon?"

"Let us imagine that our 'American Friends,' as they are
called in our ill-fated files, are victory units. They are the tools,
the items, by which we will achieve victory over the capitalist
powers in years to come."

"If it isn't already too late," Filikov glumly said.

"Don't interrupt me," Kanayev commanded. "So we'll call
them victory units. And what, my dear bumbling Filikov, would
a rational person do when afflicted by a cancer?"

"He would cut out the diseased part," Filikov replied.

"Precisely," said Kanayev. "It warms my heart to see that we are sharing these thoughts. Because you have only heard the bad news. Now comes the worse news."

"I shudder to think," Filikov said.

"It seems that you were correct in your suspicions, comrade. For how else could one explain our young friend spending hours in the finest library in the United States pouring over information about the city of Tucson, Arizona?"

Filikov swallowed hard, "It could just be a coincidence," he offered.

The directory of illegals smiled his wan smile, and then slowly wagged his head from side to side. "Would you also call it coincidence," he began to ask, "if the fellow exhibited, in his research, a particular interest in silver dealers in the city of Tucson, Arizona? And in athletic contests in that city's secondary schools during the same years our boy SPRINTER attended secondary school? Would you call that coincidence, Mr. Filikov?"

"I would think not," Filikov said, "if your intelligence is as good as I'm sure it is."

Kanayev leaned back in his chair, and swung his feet up onto his desk. He was both furious at and amused by Filikov, a man whom he should have, by all rights, had thrown into prison on grounds of treason by negligence.

"That's an interesting turn of the phrase to polish the apple with, comrade," Kanayev said, "and we won't pursue it further. My intelligence is impeccable. The question now is how and when to proceed with what we must do."

"Remove the cancer?" asked Filikov.

"You like that phrase, eh?" Kanayev sneered. "Well, maybe you're a part of the cancer, did you ever think of that?"

Filikov began to sputter, but his superior cut him off before he could manage anything intelligible.

"Oh, don't fret so, Filikov, you're too old and useless to bother with. As far as I'm concerned, you can spend the rest of your life soaking your toes in the sea and dreaming of your girls. Don't you know when I'm joking with you? Look here, the reason I summoned you was because you know the boy and his family, and I wanted to ask you a few things about how they might react to some aggressive action on our part."

"Beg pardon," Filikov offered, "but what if the 'American Friends' information has already been revealed by Hoffnung?"

"I doubt he would have been doing that work in the library if he told them," said Kanayev. "And I also think that if he's as smart as he seems to be, he would hold back on such vital information in case he ever needed certain favors from the Americans. He may have teased them with some useless tidbits, but I don't think it's too late for us to intervene. This is what I wanted to ask you: What do you think would happen if we asked Hoffnung to return to the Center for some additional, extensive training?"

"It depends how the message was phrased," Filikov replied.

"You don't think they would be suspicious of our motives?" Kanayev asked.

"Maybe," said Filikov, "but they would have to decide whether it's a risk they should take. Think of it as they would: if they cooperate with our request, then in due time Mark will return to the United States, and all will be well. If they don't, then of course we would have no choice but to assume that they have turned against us, and would have to take necessary measures. They are aware of what those measures are."

"So what is the true test?" Kanayev asked.

"The true test," said Filikov, relishing the opportunity to salvage the last bit of his reputation, "would be to tell them that Hoffnung is being recalled for an indefinite period. At the first sign of hesitation, we would then move in."

"Very good, comrade," Kanayev said. "But I must tell you this: they may have been alerted by the authorities that information concerning Mark's employment was stolen. This would make them very uneasy. It might push them to the brink."

"But you have your own way of taking care of things, sir," Filikov said. "We must give them one last chance, or we'll never be as sure as we can that we're doing the right thing."

"We must do the right thing," said Kanayev. "Thank you, comrade. Dismissed."

· · · ● · · ·

"Job well done," the message to S began. "Remain in the area of Washington, and await further instructions. Pending communication with David, you will be given the final message. Center."

16
Final Warning

When Anne McMullen walked into her tiny bookkeeper's office at CIC on Tuesday, January 2, she immediately sensed that something was wrong.

She was an orderly woman, orderly sometimes to the point of neurosis. If everything wasn't where it was supposed to be, it made her uneasy to the extent that she couldn't do her work until everything was set right again.

That was one reason that the plumpish, gossipy thirty-year-old woman liked her job so much. She controlled the order of the little figures in the books that she kept so meticulously. The numbers were well behaved; they wouldn't go and do things that would make Anne McMullen unhappy and nervous.

The first thing she saw was that someone had taken a tissue from the Scott's tissue dispensary on the upper left corner of her desk. She knew this because she always made sure, before leaving the office for the day, that the tissue was tucked into the box, and not flapping outside the oval opening as it would naturally after one of the squares is pulled out. That would be too disorderly.

Then she saw that the payroll drawer of one of the file cabinets was not pushed all the way in. There were two positions in which the drawers could look, to anyone but Anne McMullen, like they were pushed in, but Anne could tell if they were merely in place or if they were clicked into place with the little slipguard button on each drawer.

Anne McMullen knew something was wrong.

She opened the payroll file drawer, and saw immediately that the files had been tampered with.

It was only seven forty-five, and no one else was in the office yet. Anne always liked to be the first one in; it made her feel virtuous, but now she was feeling angry. She would tell Mr. Chase as soon as he walked through the door in an hour or so, but before he arrived, she called the Arlington Police Department and reported a break-in.

"That was a stupid thing to do," a livid Vernon Chase informed the woman when she told him, as soon as he walked into his office that morning, that two detectives would be coming soon to investigate.

"But there was a break-in," the woman whined. "Someone broke into the office during vacation and got into my files. I'm sure of it."

"I'm sure you're right, Mrs. McMullen," Chase said, doing his best to control the words, "but you should have waited for me. You don't really know anything. It would have been . . ."

He stopped himself, realizing that he was about to say something he didn't want to.

"What's done is done, Mrs. McMullen," he said. "I'm sure that you called the police out of honest concern for CIC, but next time something like this happens, please tell me before you do anything else."

"I'm sorry, Mr. Chase," the woman said. "I didn't mean to cause any trouble."

Chase got rid of the police as soon as he could, but only after they had looked the entire office over and discovered other evidence of a break-in: tape over a latch in one of the doors, and a thin calfskin glove in the space between two file cabinets in Anne McMullen's office. The glove, Mrs. McMullen assured the police officers, was not hers and she had never seen it before. It was most unusual, she assured them, for a glove to be in such an awkward position in her very orderly workplace.

Vernon Chase closed his office door after the police left, and thought hard about what steps to take next. Before he made a decision, he jumped from his chair and went to his locked personnel file to see if the intruders had paid a visit to it. They had. The cheap lock had been sprung, and the brown manila folders had been separated, by a hand other than his own, at the space where Mark Scholz's file should have been. But there hadn't been a

Mark Scholz file; the FBI told him several times that they were working on one that would be safe, but they hadn't delivered it to him yet, and so there was nothing in the file where there should have been. Except for a space, a most conspicuous space, left by a person who apparently knew that the space should not have been there. It was as if the intruder was telling Vernon Chase something.

Feeling weak, he returned to his desk and loosened his tie, before dialing the number of his friend at the Bureau who had convinced him to hire Mark.

"What now?" he asked the man, whom he had known since both were in the same fraternity at Reed.

"Try to keep the local cops out of it as much as possible," the man said. "They'll just screw things up. I'll send over the two guys assigned to Scholz. Just take it easy, Vern. And I want to reassure you that your favor will be returned some day. We won't forget you, Vern."

"Thanks," Chase glumly replied. "You've made my day."

When Ed and Jack arrived, they made a brief inspection of the files that had been broken into, and then went with Chase into his office. Mark, who had heard brief snatches of conversation among some of his co-workers about some kind of a break-in over the holiday, was then called into the office with the three men. As soon as he saw Ed and Jack, he knew something was wrong, and he had a gut feeling that it had to do with the break-in. And before they said anything, he had an even stronger suspicion that the break-in had something to do with him.

Uncharacteristically, Mark spoke first.

"The break-in," he said.

"Yes," said Chase.

"We can't be sure it's them, Mark," said Ed, "but we can't figure out why anyone else would be interested in that kind of information. It's almost as if they wanted us to know they did it; it wasn't a very smooth job, from the looks of things."

"So what do we do?" Mark asked.

"We play it very, very cool for a while," Jack replied. "They're not going to do anything rash until they've exhausted every possibility. They'll contact you again, once, twice, maybe more. Don't worry. It's very dangerous for them to start playing any war games on our territory. They'll keep you talking to them as long as they can. And that's what we want them to do."

"You mean," Mark said, skepticism registering in his voice, "that's what you hope they'll do."

"Look," said Ed. "I'm sorry. What can I tell you except we'll do our best."

Inside, Mark felt cold, hard, like everything beneath his skin had turned to stone. It was not the first time he felt that way. The sensation now was almost like an old friend, a trusted companion who would come and visit whenever things were looking bad. Whenever he felt like the world was a horrible place, like there was no escape from the tangled web he seemed to have been born into, there was always that impenetrable hardness beneath the surface that allowed him to behave rationally, to carry on, to do what must be done.

"They want to kill me," Mark said. It was a plain, simple statement of the facts as he saw them, and nothing else. He was not looking for agreement, or sympathy. It was a thing he had thought before, it had always been in the back of his mind. They might want to kill him one day. He knew they weren't crazy people, the men from the Center in Moscow, but they were people who wanted very badly to do a certain job, and they wanted him to help them. And if he got in their way, well, they would just have to kill him, plain and simple.

"They might," said Jack. That's a possibility we can't discount. "But besides the strong possibility that they know you've turned, in which case it wouldn't necessarily be worth it for them to want you and your family dead, is there any other reason? Is there any way in which you could hurt them more than you have already by remaining alive? If you don't tell me, Mark, our job is going to be tougher than it already is."

"Nothing," said Mark. "There's nothing more. But you don't know how they think as well as I do. It's a matter of principle with them more than anything else. They want to keep their people terrified."

"You don't know any other reason?" Ed asked.

He wondered if they could tell he was lying. But he was such a good liar in tight spots like this, it was almost second nature.

"Remember," Jack cautioned, "what you're telling us now, and what you've told us in the past, every briefing session we've had, anything even remotely connected to this, that you've done or heard or said. I'm warning you, Mark, this is no joke. This is very serious business."

"Look," Mark seethed, his jaw muscles knotting as he clenched his teeth to contain his rising anger, "I don't know what you're accusing me of. All I know is these goons know that I'm working for you, and if I know them, I'm a dead man. And all you're telling me is that I haven't been leveling with you. Well, fuck off. You know all you're going to know."

"Mark!" Ed admonished.

"Do you believe they want you dead?" Jack asked.

"I don't know," said Mark. "They always warn you, sort of let you know very subtly when you're over there that certain defectors who have been caught later haven't fared so well. They let you know that they don't let double-crossers relax. It doesn't have to be because you know any secrets that will make the whole KGB come crashing down to its foundations. They don't care if you don't know anything. They're just worried about their image, it looks very bad when all their agents end up working for you guys. I mean, how many CIA agents defect to the Soviet Union?"

"What do you want to do?" Ed asked.

"I don't know," said Mark. "Why don't you ask my father, my mother, my little brother, for all I care. Ask him. Ask Stephen. They never let the poor kid make any decisions in his life, that's why he's so confused. He doesn't even know what this whole thing is about, he probably thinks Dad makes porno films and got into a bad deal with the mob or something."

"Answer the question, Mark."

"I don't want to die," Mark said. "That's what I want to do."

· · · ● · · ·

An agent in New York contacted Walter at home that day, and told him about the break-in.

"I guess it's about time they found out," Walter said. "I was just waiting for it. We really couldn't go on like this forever, you know."

"We're not 100 percent positive that the break-in was ordered by the KGB," the agent said.

"It was them," Walter said. "I know it was them."

A twenty-four hour watch was set up in and around the house in Woodvale. Neighbors who asked were told that the men were plainclothes police officers on a "burglary prevention" patrol. An agent slept in Mark's old room over the garage, the room next to Stephen's.

The plan for the days after the break-in, until more was known and a final course of action decided, was to stall and to protect the family. The night of the break-in two agents moved into a vacant apartment at the end of the floor Mark lived on in Potomac Towers. And, with the cooperation of the building manager, they installed tiny closed-circuit television cameras at every entrance of the building.

· · · ● · · ·

Kanayev had decided to keep everything as normal as possible. Certainly they would be confused by such an obvious break-in, but then the message would arrive on Sunday, the normal day for messages to arrive. The message, however, was considerably different in content and tone than the hundreds of others Walter had received in the basement of the house on Sycamore Road.

"Greetings, David," it began,

It has been several years since a representative of your fine family has visited us in the Soviet Union. It is our opinion that Hoffnung should be the one to do so. He has performed quite well to date, but we believe that if he is to serve in the many years to follow at his maximum capacity, then he should return to the Center for further training. We realize this creates several problems. First, Hoffnung is becoming established in his job, and it would be difficult later on to explain his extended absence. However, we will eliminate this problem by producing evidence that Hoffnung was taking graduate studies at a university in West Germany. Hoffnung is in need of advanced training in several areas which cannot be mentioned here for reason of their complexity. Therefore, you will deliver him to Hotel Holzkirchen, Munich, on February 2 at 3 P.M. This will allow him ample time to put his affairs in order before departing. There can be no assurance of when he will return to the United States, as the type of training he will undergo is experimental. During his stay in the Soviet Union, you will be kept informed at regular intervals of his progress. However, it will be impossible for you to communicate directly with him during this period. Between the time you receive this message and the time Hoffnung is met in Munich, the Center will maintain contact with you, and with Hoffnung through an agent in Washington. Respond immediately to this message. Center.

An FBI agent watched over Walter's shoulder as he deciphered and translated the message. As its meaning and peculiar phraseology became increasingly apparent, Walter's expression became anxious, and his hands began to sweat. He knew it was coming, but still, he wasn't prepared to accept the finality of it.

The agent snatched the completed document from Walter's hands after he wrote it down on a pad of legal size paper.

Angered, Walter yelled, "Give that back. What are you doing with it?"

"It goes to the Soviet desk at headquarters," the agent said. "We'll have to give it to one of our experts to see exactly what it means."

"What do you think, I'm a moron?" Walter shouted. "I've been reading these damn messages for twenty-five years. I know exactly what they mean. You don't have to give it to some jerk in Washington who wouldn't know a KGB agent if he were kicked in the balls by one. Which is exactly what they're doing to me now, the bastards. They're kicking me right in the balls while I'm sitting here like a bird on a fence, just waiting for their hunters to open season."

"Calm down, Walter," the agent said in an unassuring monotone. "We're here to protect you."

"The bastards know," Walter said. "They're just playing with me, teasing me, until they strike."

"Calm down, Walt."

· · · ● · · ·

The Soviet desk people in Washington said the same thing that Walter knew from the moment he began reading the message, except they wrote a ten-page report about it and used important sounding words.

Their findings, essentially, were that the message was merely a device to force the family into a situation where there could be no doubt about their allegiances. And as soon as it was obvious that they had no intention of, or were wavering about complying with the demand, they would move in and take "whatever they deem to be appropriate action, which in our opinion would be one or more assassination attempts," according to the FBI report.

Walter and Mark were amused, as amused as they could be under the circumstances, by the FBI report.

"Of course," Mark told Ed over the telephone after he was told of the Bureau's interpretation of the message. "You think I couldn't have told you the same thing? There's no way they would call me over there for an indefinite period if everything was going as they wanted it to. They would never call me away from a job that has the potential of leading to just what they want. It's much too risky; I can't just slip away like I did in high school and college anymore, and they know it. And the stuff about not being able to communicate directly with my family. They always arranged for us to communicate, in one way or another. They did their best to treat us well, to make us feel vital, wanted. But now there's only one way they want us, I'm afraid."

· · · ● · · ·

They wanted to have a family conference, but the FBI said that Mark couldn't leave Washington under any circumstances, that it would be much too dangerous to take off from work in the middle of the work week and arouse the suspicions of the Soviets, who surely must be keeping track of his movements.

Ed and Jack, after meeting for several hours with their superiors, and after discussing it themselves until the early morning hours at Ed's home, decided to advise the family, in the strongest terms possible, that they should take advantage of the Bureau's offer to obliterate the Scholz family and create another one, hopefully one that assassins dispatched from the Center would never be able to find.

A conference call was arranged after checking, as they had been for the past week, to make sure that the phone lines were free of bugs. The whole family was on the phone; Mark speaking from his apartment in Rosslyn, and the three others from the three phones in the house. In addition, Ed was on the line from the FBI field office, insisting that he serve as moderator lest emotions get in the way of what he called "a cool, eminently rational decision, one you'll have to live with a long time, or maybe not too long at all, if it's the wrong one." He couldn't force them, but he could scare them, Ed reasoned. It was just for their own good.

Stephen's voice was shaking, frightened; Mark wanted desperately to reach out and hug him, something he had never wanted to do before, and tell him that everything was going to be okay.

"Why didn't anybody ever tell me the truth?" the boy sobbed into the receiver. "How could you not tell me about this for so many years? Mark, how could you do that?"

"I'm sorry," Mark offered weakly.

"It was for your own good," Walter said sharply. "Now stop crying."

"It was bad enough," said Else, in a tremulous voice over the phone to the son in the same house as she, "that Mark had to become so involved. There was no reason for you to be involved too. It was because we love you."

"Please," Ed interrupted. "I don't mean to be insensitive, I know you have a lot to say to each other, and hopefully you'll all be together soon to talk for as long as you want to—I hope. But we can't do that now. We have to make decisions."

"This sucks," Stephen blurted, in a voice made coarse by screaming and crying. "This really sucks. This whole thing, my whole life, you all suck."

"Stephen, goddammit, just shut your mouth for once," Mark tersely commanded.

"Everybody, please, we can't talk if we're all screaming." Ed's voice showed a tinge of weariness, or frustration, like an inner city social worker who had labored too long without seeing any change. He knew that if he allowed the conversation to degenerate into what should be a private, intensely emotional family scene, no decisions would ever be made.

"Look," he said. "Everybody be quiet for a minute and listen to me. Stephen."

"What?" the boy answered.

"You know the Mafia movies, "The Godfather," "Valachi Papers," that kind of thing?"

"What about it?"

"You know what happens to the guys who squeal, who testify against the big daddy Mafiosi?"

"Yeah," said Stephen. "They cut out their tongues, and then they cut off their balls and stuff them in their mouths. Or they strangle 'em with piano wire and dump 'em in the bay near Kennedy Airport, or they put a bomb in their car that blows up when you turn the ignition."

"Yeah, that's what they want to do, Stephen. But what do you think they do when they have to testify against these thugs to save their own asses? You think the government just lets them back out on the street to get wiped out? If we did that, those guys would rather spend the rest of their lives in jail. What we do to protect them is we make them into new people."

"I heard about that," Stephen said. "You change their identities. You slip them away for a while, and then they surface somewhere else later on, and nobody knows who they are."

"That's right," said Ed. "You understand. Now let me ask you something, not just you Stephen, but all of you. Haven't you ever wanted, when things are going bad, just to forget about who you are now, just to drop yourself off somewhere and start all over? Haven't you ever said to yourself, 'Boy, if I could just start all over in life, I'd do things differently, I'd be a better person?'"

There was silence on all ends of the conversation for a moment, for several moments.

"I suppose we all feel that way sometimes," said Walter. "Sometimes we all feel it would be wonderful to have that *tabula rasa,* that blank slate on which to start building another life. I have often thought it must be an exciting proposition."

"It's odd you should say that, Walter," Else said. "Because you have already started over once, and now you want to do it again?"

"I could never see my friends again," Stephen said. "What would I do if I saw them on the street in ten years or something?"

"You have to understand, Stephen," Ed soothingly told the boy, "this is forever, it's like being born all over again. Inside, you're the same person. But outside, where people can see, there's no more Stephen Scholz. You can keep him to yourself, but to everyone else, he's gone."

"Dead," said Stephen.

"Just gone."

"It's the only thing to do," Mark said. "I've thought about it, and I've decided I'd rather live as someone else than the way I'm living now. It would be a challenge."

"We'll think about it on this end," said Walter. "It is an interesting proposition."

"Think quickly," said Ed, "because there really isn't very much time."

· · · ● · · ·

They advised Walter to send the KGB a stalling message, to buy as much time as possible while they got things in order.

> We have discussed your request for Hoffnung to return to the Center for intensive training, and agree that it is a wise proposition. He will be at the named location on the named date, as you requested. He asks advice, however, about how to gracefully explain his departure with such short notice. He believes the university excuse will not suffice, as he has never mentioned such plans to anyone before. Mary is upset, but that is to be expected. Could not some arrangements be made for more direct communication than you have proposed. David.

The FBI analysts were pleased by the message; they thought it was both agreeable enough to please them but also raised enough natural parental doubts to be believable to the Soviets.

· · · ● · · ·

In Moscow, they were not quite so convinced as the FBI would have liked them to have been. Kanayev decided to push to see just how far he could take them.

He returned a message the following day: "David, plans have been changed," it began,

> Hoffnung's training must begin immediately, therefore he shall report to same location 15 January at 3 P.M. We are sorry to inconvenience him, but this revised plan must be adhered to. Reply immediately. Center.

Walter was told not to reply. Whatever he responded with, they told him, would be subject to misinterpretation by the Center. The Soviets would not do anything until they had time to determine why Walter hadn't responded.

· · · ● · · ·

By Wednesday evening, when Kanayev had still received no reply from his last message to Walter, he knew that he could delay the inevitable no longer. He had taken the test to its limits, and he knew all he cared to until the mission was completed. That same night, in a plush hotel room, 4876 miles away, a small but terrifically powerful receiver alerted a sleeping assassin that there was some news for him. He woke up and received the message, and when his head again touched the soft pillow, he was ready to kill.

· · · ● · · ·

A mood settled over Mark that week, as he was preparing to leave himself behind and start over again. It was a feeling he remembered having as a child, especially the few weeks before they were to move from Toronto to the United States. There was a boy in his class at school; he seemed to remember the name George, but he couldn't be quite sure. The boy had taken to tormenting him for no particular reason the spring before they moved, and it continued in the neighborhood during the summer, until one day Mark challenged him to a fight. They fought, and there was no discernable winner, but the whole affair left him with a sad feeling; the neighborhood children crowding around and chanting, teasing. He wanted to get away, to go somewhere else, a place where they hadn't seen him standing ragged and panting, his dignity stripped away like an overcoat in winter, leaving him exposed to the raw cruelty that young children are so good at displaying.

He was both anxious and serene, walking through the last few days like he was watching everything from a far-off place, like he was no longer part of it.

· · · ● · · ·

"I guess you knew all along, that's why you've been acting so strange all week," Darrell said as they had lunch together Thursday, at a small restaurant. "How did he break it to you?"

Word had gotten around the office that morning that Mark had been the first among what was expected to be a number of termination notices by Vernon Chase. The industry was having temporary hard times, he had been saying for a while, mentioning almost as an afterthought that if things didn't get better soon, CIC would lose clients and be forced to lay off employees according to the last hired, first fired rule.

"He was very nice about it," Mark said. "You seem more upset than I am. Don't worry about me, I'll be fine."

"What are you going to do?"

If only he knew, thought Mark. If only he knew the truth.

"I'll go back home to New York for a while," he said. Maybe help out my father with some films for a while. I don't know, I'll find something."

"When are you leaving?" Darrell asked.

"Saturday," said Mark. "But I'm not coming to work tomorrow, even though I'm not officially through until the end of the day. Chase said it's okay. I just don't want to hang around all day, people feeling sorry for me and wanting to take me to lunch and everything. It just makes me uncomfortable."

"I hope we'll get to see each other soon," said Darrell. "I don't mean to be sappy or anything, but you've been a real friend. I can't explain it. There's something different about you. You listen to me without having to always get your two cents in like most people do, myself included. You're a good listener, that's very important."

Mark began to blush. "Don't make such a big deal . . ." he began.

"No, I mean it. I'll be sad to see you leave. I'd really like to keep in touch, but I know we won't."

"I'll write," Mark said.

"No you won't," replied Darrell. "You're just not the type. I'll write you, and you won't write back, but that's okay. That's just how things are, I guess."

Mark looked at his friend and smiled, an easy, relaxed smile. "One way or another," he said, "you'll be hearing from me. I guarantee it."

17
Fatal Switch

Mark's phone rang at eight Friday morning. Sleepily, he turned over and reached for the receiver on the night table by his bed.

"Hello, Mark?"

"Darrell!" Mark's voice was more surprised than pleased. He liked to tie things off neatly, and thought he had when he told Darrell goodbye the day before.

"Mark, I have a favor to ask." Darrell's voice was tremulous, and a bad telephone connection made it sound even shakier.

"Sure, Darrell. What is it?"

"I know that you're busy getting ready to move and everything, but something just came up. You know how I am about asking favors, Mark. It makes me nervous."

"Anything I can do to help you, Darrell," Mark said.

"My mother just called and said my grandmother had a heart attack and that she's probably not going to make it through the weekend. They want me to come home tonight, and the only flight I could get was out of the Baltimore airport. If it were National, I'd just take the Metro, but it's hard to get all the way out to . . ."

"I'd be happy to take you, Darrell," Mark interjected. "Please stop apologizing. I'm your friend, and we won't be seeing each other for a long time. It's the least I can do."

"You're sure it's no problem?" Darrell asked.

"What time?"

"About six-thirty, that's when we should leave," Darrell said.

Mark knew he would be busy all day, and shouldn't leave the apartment, but felt an obligation.

"I said I would," Mark snapped. "Can't you take yes for an answer? Just come to my apartment after work, and if I can't take you, Maria will. She's free today, and would be glad to help out. No more whining."

"Thanks Mark. You don't know how much I appreciate this," Darrell said. "I'll see you later."

· · · ● · · ·

Maria had no classes Friday, so she took the Metro to the Rosslyn stop and went to Mark's apartment soon after she woke up around 10 A.M. Mark had already called her and told her he had lost his job and was moving to New York, but he insisted he would visit as often as possible.

Ed and Jack were not happy about Maria coming to the apartment, but agreed to stay out of sight while she was there.

Mark had planned "an elegant dinner" at the apartment for their last night, and though Maria wanted to go out she finally relented, after telling Mark, "You're so stubborn."

When she arrived at the apartment, Mark took her in his arms amid the half packed boxes and suitcases and began to kiss her.

At first she didn't refuse his advances, but after he kissed her the second time, she said quietly, "We agreed not to. We can't. Don't get me any more upset than I am, with your leaving all of a sudden like this. I don't want to get involved again, especially not now."

"Okay," Mark said. He tried to smile, but couldn't. "I'm just trying to curry your favor because I want you to do something for me later."

"Anything but marry you."

"Anything?"

"Almost anything," she said. "What is it?"

"Darrell's grandmother is croaking, and . . . ."

"Don't be so insensitive," Maria commanded.

"Sorry. Anyway, the old bag is dying, and . . . ."

"Okay," Maria said, laughing. "You've made your point. I award you the golden medal of crudeness."

"He has to get to Baltimore-Washington Airport tonight to catch a flight, and I'm feeling a little overwhelmed with all I still have to do. Could you drive him in my car when he comes over after work?" Mark started filling a cardboard box with books as he asked the question.

"Sure," she said. "I assume you'll be packing and sautéing those medallions of veal at the same time, so that when I come back we can stuff our faces."

"Our last supper," said Mark. His voice was strange, distant, as if there were some greater meaning in the words.

"Invite me to the crucifixion," quipped Maria. "I wouldn't miss it for anything."

"Can you stay over tonight?" Mark asked urgently. "There are some things we should talk about before I leave. Important things."

"I don't know," said Maria. "I don't think so. Why can't we just leave them for some other time."

"There might not be another time," Mark said. "I have some important things to explain to you. Maybe when I do, you'll understand why we didn't work out the way we could have."

"You're getting weird," Maria said. "I hate it when you start getting weird. I don't want to start up with you again, Mark. We have an agreement."

Their relationship had evolved, during the last year, into one marked more by friendly affection than by love. They saw each other a few times a month, but rarely on weekends.

"I'd really like you to stay over tonight, Maria." Mark said, almost pleading. "I have to tell you these things about me, because I trust you. You can keep a secret for a while, can't you?"

"As well as you can. But I don't know if I want to go into a head trip with you just before you leave. I don't know if it would be the best thing."

Mark laughed, but without joy. It was an inside joke, and he was the only insider.

"As usual, I don't know what you're laughing at," Maria said. "But if you really want to talk about anything important, we can talk today. We've got all day while you're packing. Anyway, it's too late for the important things. Obviously, I'm not important enough, or you wouldn't be frothing at the mouth to get back to New York the minute you don't have a job. There are billions of jobs for someone like you in Washington. I don't understand why you're doing this."

"There are a lot of things you don't understand about me," Mark said.

"No kidding," Maria said caustically. "Why do you think our relationship has just about gone down the tubes in the last couple of years?"

"We're still good friends," said Mark.

"I'm good friends with the stuffed animals I got when I was a kid," said Maria. "I wanted more than good friends, but your schedule just wouldn't permit it. It wasn't just the schedule, either. It was the way these unexplained emergencies would spirit you away. Poof, you were gone, poof, you were back, and it never seemed to faze you a bit. Are you in the Mafia?"

"You should know better than that," said Mark, "considering your background."

"What do you mean?"

"I just can't tell you now. Maybe tonight was a bad idea too. Maybe I'll just wait until everything is resolved."

"Forget it," said Maria. She picked up a book and put it in the box by Mark. "I'll just take you as you are for the short time we have together. Maybe I liked you in the first place because you were a little odd, so I shouldn't complain too much. But just tell me one thing. Why do you have to get to New York in such a rush?"

Mark considered the question for a moment, and realized that his answer would reveal more than any complicated explanation.

"I have to work on a film," he said. "My father needs me."

· · · ● · · ·

At six that evening, Darrell knocked at the door of Mark's apartment. He went undisturbed by the FBI since Mark had earlier informed Ed that he would come to the apartment and that Maria would drive him to the airport while Mark remained inside.

"I hate to be a bother," said Darrell, once he stepped into the living room.

"No problem," said Maria. "I hope your grandmother is doing better."

They had been sitting and talking at the kitchen counter for about ten minutes when Darrell frowned and said, "Oh, no."

"What is it?" asked Mark.

"I'm only wearing this," said Darrell, pulling at the lapel of the heavy tweed sportcoat he was wearing over a bulky sweater. "I forgot my winter coat at the office—my Chicago winter coat. My mother will be furious. All I need when I step off the plane is to have my mother screaming at me about being irresponsible for not bringing a coat."

"I'll lend you one," Mark said. "I have two ski parkas. Take one and send it to my New York address when you get back."

"Are you sure it's okay?"

"Darrell, please. I said I have two." Mark stood up from his stool, and pulled Darrell up by his shoulders.

"We are the same height, same weight, same build," Mark said. He went to his closet, and removed a down-filled ski parka with a V-shaped red and white pattern that he had been wearing frequently for the last few weeks.

"Here," he said, and threw the coat over Darrell's head. Darrell grabbed the cuffs of his sportscoat with his hands and put them into the sleeves of the parka.

"Same size," said Mark, placing his hands on Darrell's arms. "Prost," he added. "To your health. This is a one of a kind authentic Austrian *schnee-jacke,* endorsed by ski champions from throughout the Tyrol."

Darrell pulled the collar away from his blushing face. "I'm touched," he said. "You don't know how much I appreciate . . ."

"I know," said Mark. "Believe me, I know. Now why don't you and Maria just take off before you miss your plane." He picked up a red stocking cap from the kitchen counter, and tossed it to Darrell. "Put this over your ears and leave," he said. Darrell put on the cap.

"Let's go," Maria urged. "Don't get the ogre angry."

"Just remember what I said yesterday about you being my friend," said Darrell, as the trio walked to the front door.

Mark extended his hand to Darrell, and felt a sudden twinge. Sadness? Regret? Relief? He wasn't sure what he felt. But it made him shudder. "Goodbye," he said. "I hope your grandmother gets better."

· · · ● · · ·

After he had awakened in his hotel suite perched above the Potomac Friday morning, S had checked the sunrise-moonrise calendar he kept folded inside his wallet. For January 12, 1979, under the column for forty degrees north latitude, moonrise was at 4:35 P.M. and sunset was at 4:55 P.M. Washington was just south of the thirty-ninth parallel, so he interpolated for one degree and determined that moonrise and sunrise would both be two minutes later than in the chart. He could have checked the morning newspaper, but it was more interesting this way. Something to do while biding his time.

At one minute after sunset, when the sky over the river was still a purplish hue, S drove his rented red Camaro to the most remote section of the parking lot next to Mark's building. On the seat next to him were a dozen photos of Mark, taken over the course of the past several weeks. In seven, Mark was wearing the red and white ski parka.

It was his first day on the final patrol for this assignment, but S was confident it would also be his last. Mark's pattern of activity had been quite regular for the past several weeks. He went out each Friday and Saturday night, usually after 8 P.M., but S liked the idea of arriving just after sunset. It was a nice image, he thought—the hunter closing in on his prey just as the sun sinks into the horizon. Sometimes he was so pleased by the images he created that he toyed with writing a novel about his adventures. But that would have to come later.

There were two entrances to the apartment building, one on the side, which led to the parking lot, and one in the front, which people used when they were on foot. During the week S had observed, Mark used the front entrance. On weekends, when he often took his car across the river into Washington, he used the parking lot entrance.

As the darkness settled in on the cloudy night, S leaned back in his seat to wait. After an hour and twenty minutes, he saw a familiar sight. He checked once, then again, to see if the pattern on the red and white jacket was the same as in the photographs. It was. He smiled, and momentarily felt light-headed, as his unfortunate victim, carrying a suitcase, began to walk with the familiar blond-haired girl toward Mark Scholz's old Peugeot.

S stroked the pearl handle of the umbrella which lay across the seat next to him, and smiled again, ever so slightly, as the images played across his mind.

· · · ● · · ·

The traffic on New York Avenue heading out of Washington was still heavy when Maria turned the Peugeot onto the thoroughfare from Sixth Street. The traffic thinned out when they turned off onto the Baltimore-Washington Parkway, and by the time they passed the Bowie exit a few miles outside of the beltway, there was an open road ahead of them, and only one car in the rear view mirror.

It was seven-fifteen when Maria parked the car in the short-term parking lot, in a spot about fifty yards from a walkway which led to the passenger terminal.

"You could have just dropped me off in front of the United gate," said Darrell as Maria switched off the engine and they got out of the car. "You don't have to go into the airport with me and spend money on parking."

"Too late," said Maria. "We're parked already, and anyway, I have instructions to treat you with kid gloves. The boss wants his *schnee-jacke* back in one piece."

"Do you think you'll be seeing him much after he goes to New York?" Darrell asked as Maria opened the trunk and he took out his suitcase.

"Who knows?" Maria said. "We have a rather odd relationship, I suppose. We're parting as friends, and as to what will happen in the future, I have no idea. Maybe he just needs to get away for awhile."

"You can't tell with Mark," Darrell said, and they began walking toward the terminal.

· · · ● · · ·

When S stopped at the mechanical gate of the short-term parking lot, he took the ticket from the machine, tore it up and stuffed the pieces in his pocket. It would be wiser, he thought, to pay the full amount when he left and leave no record of when he entered.

He pulled into the first space he found, and walked quickly to avoid losing sight of the young man in the red and white parka, the young man, he reassured himself, who would soon be just another tally on his scorecard.

As he walked through the cold night air, he took stock of the situation, and realized that it had markedly worsened in the last forty-five minutes. There would probably be no second chance, since Hoffnung was flying off somewhere. There might be FBI agents in the airport and on the plane to protect him. It was not a pleasant situation, but S took it in stride. It merely heightened the pleasure of the accomplishment.

S held the umbrella parallel to the ground as he walked, and checked with his free left hand to make sure that its cap still covered the tip. Maintaining his distance at fifty yards behind the couple, he followed them through the lower concourse, and up the elevator to the ticketing area. S was glad that the areas around the ticket counters were crowded. Sometimes he preferred isolation, but for this task a crowd was better—a milling, confusing, disorienting crowd.

In a casual, fluid motion, S removed the cap from the umbrella tip, and glanced at the gleaming quarter inch-long needle protruding from it. He pulled up slightly on the umbrella handle and the needle disappeared into the metal tip. He pushed down and it reappeared.

Retracting the needle again, he held the umbrella close to his body as he entered the crowd around the United Airline ticket counter where his prey had joined a line.

S kept his stride even as he approached, and tightened the grip of his right hand on the umbrella. He looked at his ring, his golden tiger, and its piercing emerald eyes, and then he allowed himself to stumble.

It was a perfectly executed misstep, which seemed to have been caused by stumbling over the man's suitcase, and the umbrella darted out to touch his pants leg with seeming innocence as S faltered.

The jab was squarely in the center at the back of the right calf, and S said "Excuse me" to the young woman beside him as he recovered his balance. Seconds later, walking away from the ticket counter, S turned, unable to resist a final glance at his victim.

He saw the young woman first, and then a young man in a red and white parka, but the ski cap was off now, and something looked strange. The man's hair seemed darker, his features coarser. It was the first time S had actually seen his face that day. It was the wrong face.

S walked quickly to his car. His mouth was dry.

$\cdots \bullet \cdots$

As Maria leaned forward to give Darrell a goodbye kiss at the security gate on the way to the plane, he bent down to scratch his right leg.

"Scared of a little kiss?" Maria asked.

"No," he replied, embarrassed. "That's not it. I must have gotten bit by a mosquito." He hiked up his right pants leg to reveal a raised red welt the size of an aspirin on his right calf.

"There aren't any bugs around this time of the year," said Maria. "Maybe it's an allergy."

"Could be," he said. "I was a very allergic child." He bent and scratched again.

"Leave it alone," Maria warned. "It'll go away." She kissed him on the cheek and left.

$\cdots \bullet \cdots$

Airplane travel made Darrell nervous. He knew the statistics, that it was safer than driving in a car, but when the engines started up and the plane rumbled down the runway, the numbers didn't help his anxiety.

Whenever he had to take a plane, he tried to fall asleep as quickly as possible. He would have a drink or two and recline the seat as far back as it would go.

This time, as he drifted off to sleep when the aircraft had only just begun to pass over the mountains of western Maryland, he was surprised at how quickly the alcohol seemed to have taken effect.

Fifteen minutes after the airplane landed at O'Hare Airport in Chicago, a stewardess was even more surprised when she couldn't awaken the young man, and when she felt for his pulse she couldn't find it.

18

The Red Dot

He had failed the Center, but worse than that, he had failed himself. S could never remember being so miserable as he drove back to Washington from the airport. He had violated the most important rule of assassination: Be sure that you kill your intended victim only.

He felt no remorse for having killed the other one, only for not having killed the defector Hoffnung. Of course, it made things more complicated, but there would be no way the authorities could determine how the young man died. The poison would disappear from the bloodstream within a few hours, and it would appear to be a normal cardiac arrest, except for the fact of the victim's tender age. But that was not S's concern.

The Center was expecting a message that night, so he would send them one. He could fail once, but not twice, and to ensure that, he would tell the Center what they wanted to hear.

"Mission completed," the message read. "Hoffnung has been eliminated. 12 January 1979. 2030 hours. EST."

There was no reason the Center should know of his miscalculation at the airport, because the real victim would be dead soon enough. He would just have to get more aggressive, perhaps take a greater risk than usual. But the job would get done. Fool me once, thought S, the image of a disembodied red and white ski jacket in his mind, shame on you. Fool me twice, shame on me.

S stared at the emerald eyes of the golden tiger on his finger. *They* gave him strength. There would be no twice.

· · · ● · · ·

It was a crisp evening for that time of year; not bitter cold as the last several days had been, but comfortably cold, bracing, just the way S liked it. He took his position in the winter-bare overgrowth next to the George Washington Parkway just after sunset, setting into a ready crouch that he would be able to maintain until the sun rose over the frozen Potomac the next morning.

This part of the waiting wasn't as bad as the others, because now at least he knew there were no more changes. Before it was just wait and follow, report back and wait some more, be very careful, and wait some more. Take a kayak trip if you want, have some fun with the ladies, but wait. Be very cautious.

Of course, he still had to be cautious, and he had taken measures to ensure that they wouldn't catch him. That is, if they even tried to. They might have a few crack men from the Bureau get into it, but he was sure that they were loathe to involve the local cops in such a thing. Regardless of who was out looking, they would never find him, if only for the reasons that he could wait in any number of thickets for as long as he had to, and that, when the victim was fired on, the only clue they would have to go on was a tiny red dot playing across his heart, or maybe across his forehead. That would be more interesting, he thought; the little red beam, cutting through the blackness from 150 yards away, doing a brief dance just above the boy's eyes. Maybe he would know what was about to befall him, but probably not. Nobody ever expects such a thing.

He fondled the weapon, stroking its smooth stock like he might a woman's thigh after an especially pleasant union. He had considered, briefly, using it without the stock attachment, but he rather liked the feel of it against his shoulder as he aimed the Austrian-made AM-180 in the direction of two doors on the ground floor of the apartment building. He didn't know which one Hoffnung would come out of, but eventually he would walk through one of them.

He was eager to try the laser-aimed weapon on a person; to train the deadly accurate red beam on a real piece of flesh and watch the rounds stream out at a dizzying rate.

He had spent hours filling each of the hollow point bullets with the deadly poison curare, and then sealing each projectile with wax. The curare was just a precaution, but S believed it necessary to take all precautions.

The bullets would follow the red light to their destination, tearing into a small section of heart, brain, or gut.

The assassin S cradled his weapon, and smiled down on it as if it were a sleeping infant. And then he waited some more.

· · · ● · · ·

The veal was superb, the wine, a Pinot Chardonnay, was just right. But the evening was not going well, Mark realized, almost as soon as Maria returned from the airport.

"Did he get off okay?" Mark asked.

"Yes. As far as I know. But there was something strange."

"What was it?"

Maria seemed distracted as she sat down to the dinner table. "I don't know, really. I thought I was having flashbacks to my childhood. I don't really know what it was, it was just weird. Forget it, I just get like that sometimes. Maybe it's from hanging around you for the last three years."

They talked after dinner, mostly about Maria and her hazy plans for the future. After a while Maria turned the conversation around, and started asking Mark about himself. When he began to drop the same lines about helping his father with his documentary business, and about not being too upset about losing his job with CIC Maria lashed out with uncharacteristic venom.

"You're such a bullshit artist, I can't believe it," she shouted. "What was all this great secret stuff you were going to tell me?"

"Don't be so hostile," Mark said. "Not on our last night together."

"Screw yourself," spat Maria. "I don't even know why I agreed to come over tonight. The only thing that happens when we've been together the last few times is that I get upset."

It degenerated from there. Mark suggested that Maria stay overnight so that they could "iron things out," and that only enraged her more.

"You just want to get laid," she said, tears springing to her eyes. "One last fuck for the road, that's all you're interested in."

"That's not true," Mark said. He wanted to cry, but couldn't. "There are other things I want, more important things."

"Forget it," said Maria, rising from the sofa. "Maybe sometime later. Maybe a lightning bolt will strike you, and you'll come back and we can start acting like normal people together. Maybe then."

She left, and for the first time he could remember since he was a small child, he cried until it hurt.

· · · ● · · ·

"No," Mark said, his hand almost losing its grip on the telephone receiver.

"Yes, I'm afraid so," replied the woman's voice. "The Good Lord works in very mysterious ways sometimes, but I suppose He had a reason to take Darrell away from us."

The woman's voice was calm and matter-of-fact when she called Saturday night a few minutes after nine.

"Are you the young man who worked with my nephew Darrell Ventura?" she asked him. "His mother told me he had spoken very highly of you. Well, I have some very bad news. When Darrell's plane landed last night, he was dead. They say it must have been a heart attack, that he just stopped breathing and his heart stopped pumping while he was sleeping on the airplane. They say he must have had a heart condition all these years and we didn't know about it. Darrell never was a very robust boy, but you never expect something like this to happen to such a young man. It came as quite a shock to everybody."

"I'm sorry," Mark said. "I had no idea anything was wrong." But now he did have an idea that something was wrong. First there was Maria returning from the airport talking vaguely about something strange, and now this. He tried to remember what she had said.

"We called Darrell's office and they said they thought you had driven him to the airport after work yesterday," the woman said." We were wondering if you noticed anything unusual."

"No," Mark said. "Nothing." They should know the truth, whatever it is, Mark thought. They should know why he died. Maybe later.

"You loaned him your jacket," said Darrell's aunt. "There was a name tag inside. Did he complain of being cold? Did he look pale? Why did he borrow the jacket? Didn't he have one of his own?"

"I think he just forgot to bring it with him when he showed up at my house," Mark said. He hoped his voice wasn't betraying his emotions.

"I'm very sorry, ma'am. I feel like . . . I feel so terrible, I don't know what I can say. Tell his mother I'm very sorry. When is the funeral?"

"Monday morning at eleven at Saint Francis of Assisi Church here in Des Plaines. We hope you can be here. Darrell's mother said he spoke very highly of you."

"Yes. I'll try," Mark said. "Thank you for calling. You must be a very strong woman, the way you're taking all this. Thank you."

"I always handle family emergencies," the woman said. "They always call on me."

"Goodbye," said Mark, "I'm very sorry. Goodbye."

· · · ● · · ·

He hung up the phone and stood motionless while a thousand thoughts raced through his head. Darrell was dead, Maria was gone in a final burst of anger and frustration. And there was one reason for it all, he knew, one terrible reason. He, Mark Scholz, was the reason.

He knew what the FBI had told him, time after time during the last several days. Stay inside. You'll be okay if you stay inside. We'll protect you, and after Saturday night, you'll be gone and safe.

But he had to know, he had to know more about what strange thing Maria had experienced at the airport. He picked up the telephone again and dialed 411 for information.

"Le Petite Canard bistro on Wisconsin Avenue in Georgetown," he said breathlessly to the operator. Maria would be working there until at least midnight, he remembered her saying yesterday.

The line was busy. Two minutes later, it was still busy. There was no choice. He would have to go there.

The problem was, he realized after hanging up the phone, one of the FBI agents might catch him going out the door, and give him a hard time. At least it was worth a try. They would probably be too busy watching other things to notice, he hoped.

Just in case they discovered his absence, he left a note saying that he was visiting a special friend and would be back in time to leave as scheduled. Everything was already packed, the note said. "I hope you'll understand, I had to do this," the note ended.

· · · ● · · ·

The story was unusual by the standards of Woodvale, New York, but not really that unusual coming from the Scholz family. They had lived all over the world already, and that guy Walter was always traveling around the globe on business, so it made some kind of sense.

Stephen's last day of school was Friday, and it was only then that he was permitted to tell his friends and teachers he was leaving. Walter had notified the principal earlier in the week, but asked her to keep quiet about it until they left. "It's kind of a shock for Stephen," he said.

Stephen's friends were puzzled by the news.

"How come you're moving to Guatemala?" they asked him. "Where the hell is Guatemala, anyway? Why would your father want to go there?"

Stephen's explanations were weak, something about how he had to do a long-term film project among the Indians there, and he didn't want to leave the family alone for such a long time.

"Well, now you have to start learning Spanish for real," his Spanish teacher, Mrs. Lefcourt, told him. "I'll bet you wish you had paid more attention in class for the last two years. Good luck."

Walter explained it with his usual heartiness and enthusiasm, but somehow the pose did not come off as well as it always had in the past.

Else had become depressed, not enough to be incapacitated, but she didn't smile or laugh once during the last week.

"I'm going to miss my friends," she said. "The people here have been so nice to us, for all we are and could have done, for all the years we were doing this thing right under their noses, and they took us in like one of their own."

"Don't get melodramatic, Else," Walter said.

Else insisted on having the Rosenfelds over for dinner the last night, Friday night, over the objections of the FBI agents who were watching the house.

She was teary during the whole affair, and Sheldon Rosenfeld tried to cheer her up with mildly dirty jokes. After dinner, when the two men were downstairs looking at some of Walter's new photographic equipment, Rosenfeld asked Walter, with true bewilderment in his voice, "Why would someone want to leave a nice place like this to go to some godforsaken place you've never even seen before?"

"Maybe someday I can explain it to you," Walter said.

· · · ● · · ·

It was all to be done in a matter of minutes. Ed and Jack would show up at the appointed time, check the building's entrances, and make a quick visual sweep of the surrounding area, which would not do much good anyway, because of the darkness. They didn't want to use a power beam for fear of attracting attention.

By nightfall, though, Jack was getting nervous and wanted to get out of the house. He drove to Ed's house and found that his partner was feeling the same way. They decided to start early. It couldn't do any harm, they reasoned.

The traffic was light, and it took them only twelve minutes to drive the eight miles from Ed's house near Fall s Church to Mark's apartment.

Both had worn several layers of warm clothing, because they were reluctant to keep the motor in the car running for so long, since it might attract attention. They parked on the end of the parking lot closest to the building, but still about thirty yards away from the nearest of the two entrances. There would be nothing to do, nothing to watch for, they were sure, but they wanted to be nearby. Just in case.

They began to talk, about Mark, the family, their own families, what a terrible strain it must be on them. "They were the enemy, I suppose," said Jack, "but they're still a family. They're no different than yours or mine."

They talked, and drank coffee from a thermos Ed brought along, but it wasn't long until a peculiar sight caught their attention.

· · · ● · · ·

He had never killed this way before, from such long range, but he had always been an excellent marksman, so the necessity of dispatching Hoffnung by this method didn't bother him much. Of course, there were much more clever ways of doing the job, but he strongly suspected the boy was under heavy guard. He could not risk getting too close.

He wanted so badly to complete the mission on this clear winter night. Not only had he committed himself with the message, but he was anxious to use the weapon. He enjoyed weapons, and this one more than others. It seemed so wonderful to him that out of such a simple looking object could rain a hail of death so quickly and so easily. There were bigger weapons, and ones that shot decidedly more powerful ammunition, but this one was as awesome in its effect as any he had seen.

The AM-180 had been around only a few years, and was advertised as being for sale only to military organizations and police departments. But gun dealers had gotten hold of it. The price ran more than $3000 when fully equipped with the laser-sighting attachment, rifle stock, and silencer. S needed all the extras.

It was called the "laser-sighted super gun," and that description was accurate. The Thompson submachine gun favored by Prohibition era gangsters fired at a rate of 700 rounds per minute. But his AM-180 fired at a rate of 1800 rounds per minute. Its .22 caliber bullets were small, but when propelled from the barrel of the AM-180, which could empty its 177-round magazine in about six seconds, the bullets could do unspeakable damage.

The reason was that the weapon had virtually no recoil, and that the slugs would unerringly strike within an inch or two of whatever spot the red laser beam is trained on. The beam, which emanated from an attachment underneath the barrel, was visible for a mile on a black night.

· · · ● · · ·

Mark left his apartment at nine-thirty, estimating that it would take ten minutes to drive to the Georgetown restaurant. He left the note on the kitchen counter, and then pulled on his hiking boots. He put on his ski parka and a pair of buckskin gloves Maria had given him for his birthday.

He stepped quickly out of the apartment door, darting across the hall to the stairwell, instead of walking all the way down the hall to the elevator, which was closer to the apartment the FBI had recently occupied. He walked the twelve flights of stairs down to the basement, and toward the exit that led to the south parking lot where his car was. It was the parking lot from which, on a clear night like this one, you could look out across the river and see the Watergate and the Kennedy Center.

He stepped out into the night, under the spotlights that were mounted over the door, and he hesitated a moment while he tried to remember where he had parked his car.

He couldn't have been plainer in the view of his assassin's binoculars.

S felt the adrenalin surging, his body began to move almost instinctively, like a jungle cat about to pounce on its supper. He was sure this time. There was no mistaking his victim, and he was ready to complete the mission.

He raised the weapon, and activated the laser beam. He aimed it first at a point halfway up the side of the building, just to check it, at the same time keeping an eye on his still immobile target, then brought the beam down on Hoffnung, stopping at the upper part of his chest.

At the same time Jack noticed a heavily clad figure standing in the doorway, he saw a strange beam of red light cut through the sky from the direction of the river. He saw the red dot on the wall of the apartment building, and didn't know what it was. A second later, when he saw the dot land on the chest of the figure in the door, he grabbed Ed by the arm, pointed across the parking lot, and said, urgently, "Look."

Terror gripped Ed. He knew exactly what the red beam was.

· · · ● · · ·

Mark saw the red spot on his parka, and wondered first if it were a stain he hadn't noticed. Then he realized it was a beam of light, and followed its straight path to the blackness down by the highway, next to the river.

The assassin S was enjoying himself. The poor boy didn't seem to know what the little red dot was. Well, thought S, maybe he would have a better idea if the deadly beam was more direct about its intentions. Mark began to walk, and S quickly raised the barrel of the weapon just a hair, so that the light was trained on the space between his eyes. His finger was on the trigger, and it was just a matter of. . . .

. . . ● . . .

It was more of a shriek than a shout, a strange sound that Ed had never heard before and it came out of his own mouth.

"Mark, drop," he screamed. "For your life, Mark, drop."

The assassin heard the shouting, but could not make out the words.

Mark turned and saw Ed, standing by a car, frantically gesturing to him, with a look of horror frozen on his swarthy features.

He dropped, and one hundred seventy-seven .22 caliber bullets went flying five feet over him, thump-thump-thumping into an earth embankment twenty yards beyond. There was no report from the weapon, just the thumping of the errant bullets, so concentrated that not one strayed from a path the diameter of a silver dollar.

Mark lay panting on the cold macadam. He knew that something terrible had happened, but not how it happened. His palms were scraped raw, and small stones were embedded in them.

The next thing he knew, Ed's strong hands were dragging him into the front seat of a car, and they were careening madly down the narrow roads of the apartment complex. Jack drove as fast as he could without losing control of the car, through the residential streets between Wilson Boulevard and Arlington National Cemetery, until he was sure that they were not being followed.

Soon Mark realized what had happened, and reacted in a way that he never would have imagined. He felt a joyous relief, a surge of exuberance, the magnitude of which he had never felt before. He was free, and it was over. They had tried, and failed, and now he didn't have to be Mark Scholz anymore.

They were on the parkway heading northeast away from Washington before Ed spoke.

"By all rights," he said, "your body should be splattered all over the goddamn parking lot."

"I'm alive," Mark squealed, unable to control the emotional surge, "I'm alive, I'm alive. They couldn't kill me.

"It's not over yet, Mark," Jack said, "but you're on your way."

"I'm alive," Mark screamed. But then, an image crept into his mind and quelled his manic exuberance. It was the image of a weeping mother, and a dead young man. The mother would probably never know what killed her son, and the son would have apologized, if he had known, for getting in the way. Mark wasn't sure what killed his friend, or who, but as he considered the possibilities, being alive wasn't as great as it had been the moment before.

19
...
Discovery

"I have to see Maria," Mark told them when they reached the house. "My friend Darrell is dead. Maybe Maria is next. I have to see her. I have to know she's safe."

Ed grabbed Mark by the arm and shook him. "Look," he said. "Don't be a horse's ass. Maria's safe, we've taken care of that. We don't know about your friend. We'll have to look into it. But you can't see her. No way. You're not going to see anyone from your other life for a long time, just get that straight in your head. Just forget about it."

"I can find out a lot of information you'll want," Mark pleaded. "There's a lot she knows about Darrell. She was there. She knows. I have to see her."

"Forget it," Ed said with finality.

"I have to," Mark insisted, his voice starting to crack. "You can't stop me, I've kept my part of the bargain, and I don't care if they kill me. I have to see her."

"You can't see her," Ed repeated, this time in a more conciliatory tone. "But maybe we can arrange a phone call. But we'll have to listen in on it."

"No," Mark said. "You have to trust me. You can't listen in on my whole life. You have to leave me alone with things like this."

· · · ● · · ·

His first words to Maria were, "I love you."

"They had to tell me, Mark," she replied. "The FBI. When I noticed they were watching me, they told me about you. They were scared I'd start asking what happened to you. My reaction was unusual. I didn't get upset, or angry. I didn't cry or go crazy. You know what I did? I laughed. I wasn't surprised. Everything makes sense now, after they told me what happened. I think of everything that's happened between us, and I can't believe that I didn't figure it out for myself. I guess we just don't think of things like that."

"They shot at me, Maria," he said. "They tried to kill me. I'm alive."

Maria's voice became softer. "They didn't tell me that," she said. "They just said that you might be in danger. Thank God you're alive. I'm sorry for everything I said. I just had no idea. I want to see you."

"I wanted to," Mark said. "They won't let me, at least not for a while. I have to ask you some things. I have to tell you something terrible. Darrell is dead."

"Oh, no," she cried. "What happened?"

"I don't know," said Mark. "But I think it might have been meant for me. He was wearing my jacket. He was with you, in my car. You said something strange happened to you at the airport. What was it? Try to remember."

"He kept scratching his leg," Maria said.

"What about the flashback? You said something about your childhood. What was it?"

"It was a scene in Oslo," she said, hesitating. "And it happened when Darrell and I were waiting in the line at the ticket counter. The same thing."

"What?"

"Remember my Norwegian cousin, the girl I met in the village with my Grandfather when I was eight or nine? I *told* you about her—Astrid?"

· · · ● · · ·

The twin! Astrid was the girl Maria told me was like her twin. She told me about Astrid when we met, and it made me feel closer to her. She told me how wonderful it had been to meet someone with whom she had a special bond, and I knew just how she must have felt. I had the same feeling when I found out about SPRINTER; that there was someone out there who could share my secrets. I could never really feel that way with Maria or Darrell, but at least they were there. They meant something to me. Now, they're gone, and it's not a game any more. It's not a game, like it used to be.

· · · ● · · ·

"What happened?" Mark asked.

"Astrid came to visit from Möslund. It was the last time we would see each other before we moved to Copenhagen. I met her at the pier, I think, and then we took the train to the Try-vanns Tower. It's a spectacular view over the fjord and the coun-tryside, and we always liked to go there. It was a special place for us."

"What happened?" Mark asked again.

"When we got to the top, everybody was gathered around the railing. A man had fallen off, but I didn't see it happen. I remember it because of my tiger. My stuffed tiger, Lief. Grand-mother had just sent it for my birthday present. There was a man leaving the observation deck when we got up there, and he was wearing a ring, a gold ring in the shape of a tiger head, with little green stones for eyes. It was frightening, but Lief is so cute. The contrast made an impression on me.

"I had the strangest feeling that I saw the same image, or maybe the same exact ring, at the airport, when we were waiting on line. I had the strangest feeling, like déjà vu. And both times I saw the ring, something terrible happened."

· · · ● · · ·

It was so much fun in the beginning, such a game, and so abstract. I would come home from school, and Dad would be sitting in the living room, sipping a beer, and he'd get one out of the refrigerator for me and put his arm around my shoulder and make me feel like I was important. We'd go down to his workroom, and he'd show me how to develop the microfilm, and how to use the transmitter and receiver. We'd go into the woods, and leave something in a hidden place, and he'd tell me I was really learning, I was really doing well. It was so much fun.

· · · ● · · ·

"What happened in Oslo?" Mark asked.

"The next day in the newspapers, it didn't say very much; I remember I looked, I was so upset about it. It ruined a beautiful day that Astrid and I had planned. The newspapers didn't say much, but I heard my parents talking. My father said he heard the man was a KGB defector and they thought he might have been murdered, maybe pushed off. All I could keep thinking of was my stuffed tiger, and the horrible ring.

"I swear, I got the same creepy feeling at the airport when I was standing next to Darrell, and I saw a man walk by, and he was wearing the ring with those little green eyes. It was the same feeling I had ten years ago in Oslo."

"It was the jacket," Mark said, his voice starting to break with emotion. "The assassin thought Darrell was me. I was a fool to lend him my jacket. We look the same from behind. What a fool I was. I can't think of anyone but myself sometimes. They made me like that."

"You had no idea," Maria said. "How could you have known?"

"I knew," Mark said.

· · · ● · · ·

I knew sooner than I'd like to admit. I knew when I went with Dad to California to find the defector. I saw him, I saw his eyes. But it was just a game then, and I didn't want to think about what would happen to the blue-eyed man. Deev, I think his name was. It was an adventure, and if I thought too hard about what we were really doing, it wouldn't have been fun anymore.

They kept it interesting, so that I would forget about the terror I saw in my father's eyes when the Russian came to that house the day of the rabbit. It's funny how I think of those two things together; my father's fearful eyes and the poor, trapped rabbit who had to chew his leg off.

· · · ● · · ·

"I love you, Maria," he said. "I wish you could have understood everything before. I wish Darrell could have."

"It's too late for that," Maria said. "We're both gone from your life. You've lost us. I guess we're all just victims of circumstance, aren't we? None of us had any idea of what we were getting into." She bagan to sob softly into the telephone.

· · · ● · · ·

They kept it interesting, providing me with my very own older woman-sex goddess when I went over there the summer after tenth grade. But then they told me what I would be doing every minute of the rest of my life, and it wasn't so much fun anymore. But I really felt it the worst when I began to love Maria, and I wanted her to know everything about me. I wanted her to love me the way I was, but I couldn't let her know who I was. So I don't think she ever really loved me.

I caused the death of my friend, that poor insecure bastard. He thought I was the greatest, and I can't understand why. He trusted me, and I killed him. But they killed me, a long time ago.

· · · ● · · ·

"Yes," Mark said. "It's too late."
"Goodbye, Mark."

20

Tabula Rasa

Baltimore is only thirty-five miles away from Washington, but in image and temperament the two cities are worlds apart.

Where Washington is a city of transients, Baltimore is a city of family roots and revered traditions such as the Flower Mart and the Preakness.

Although it has recently started to cultivate the image of a modern American big city, with fancy new buildings in the downtown and harbor areas, most Baltimoreans like their city the way it still is beneath the patina added in the last fifteen years by civic boosters. It is a city of ethnic neighborhoods, each a small town unto itself.

Baltimore is better known by sailors than by diplomats, more for the Lacrosse Hall of Fame and Johns Hopkins University than for being a hotbed of espionage activity, which it never was. In fact, the last reputed spies to have any association with the city were Whittaker Chambers, who lived in several different neighborhoods, and under varying degrees of secrecy during the 1930s, and Alger Hiss, who grew up in H. L. Mencken's Union Square neighborhood.

In such an unassuming, workaday town, the FBI believed the family would be safe from inquisitive or murderous KGB agents, who were more likely to look in several western and southwestern cities that were known as refuges for people enrolled in the Justice Department's witness protection program, or in the Bureau's program to hide defectors.

It made the family nervous to be so close to both New York and Washington, where dozens of Soviet agents, they imagined, were kneading their hands and preparing to flex their muscles over the family's disappearance.

But it would only be for a short time, they were assured, just long enough to get their papers in order, to create substantial and credible backgrounds for each member of the family.

The FBI, they learned, maintained safe houses throughout the United States, places whose identities were carefully guarded, but which are often in the middle of bustling cities. In Baltimore, the family was taken to a turn of the century townhouse in a neighborhood near Johns Hopkins University's Homewood Campus. The neighborhood, Charles Village, is an interesting mix of students, aging hippies, young couples who spend their free time scraping wall paper and plastering ceilings in houses that always seem to be under renovation, and a great many pairs of spinster sisters who have lived together in their six bedroom, dumbwaiter-equipped house since mother and father passed away twenty years ago.

The family occupied the top two floors of the three-story house. The ground floor was taken up by an attractive young couple, both of whom were FBI agents. When the elderly woman who lived two doors away inquired, she seemed quite satisfied when the woman agent told her that she heard the new family, who seemed to stay to themselves, were connected to the university.

Mark, who had always been stick thin, was told to gain twenty pounds while working out with weights, to start growing a beard, and to switch from glasses to contact lenses. He spent most of his time in the house eating Else's heavy German cooking, and trying to cheer up both her and Walter. They both seemed so depressed, which surprised him since he had been feeling so good since the assassination attempt. He was eager to get on with his new life.

Walter complained that the FBI wasn't moving fast enough, that he wanted to get out of the East as soon as possible, far away from his "predators," as he had begun to call them. Walter was informed of the assassination attempt, but Stephen and Else were not. For the first time, he began to talk about the United States in kind terms. "They would never do this for Americans in the Soviet Union, but I just wish they would do it faster," he said.

The family grew closer during those weeks, and Stephen seemed to change almost overnight from a whining, troublesome boy to a thoughtful young man. One night, after Walter and Else had gone to sleep, Mark and Stephen sat up late talking in the kitchen. Mark said that he was very proud of Stephen, that he seemed to have been matured by the recent events.

"That's not really it," said Stephen. "It wasn't the fright and the danger that made me change. It was just that I suddenly understood everything, all the late night arguments between Mom and Dad, the strange callers, the unplanned trips that stretched into weeks and months; I was always angry and jealous —I knew something was going on, and I didn't know what it was, and nobody would tell me. The only thing I knew was that whatever it was I couldn't play. You know how when you're a kid and you go outside and the other kids think something's wrong with you and they don't let you play with them? Well, I always felt like that. That whatever our family was doing, it was something important, and I couldn't be a part of it. I thought it was because you were so smart and I was so dumb."

"You're not dumb," Mark said. "But maybe you just started thinking you were dumb and it became a self-fulfilling prophecy."

"But I understand everything now," Stephen continued, engrossed in his own flow of thought. "It's not that they hated me."

"Nobody ever hated you. We loved you. We still do."

"I believe what Mom told me. That you were Dad's son, and I was hers, and she wasn't going to let me go through the same thing that you did. I don't know how you did it. I would have cracked up years ago. I guess I'm glad they did it the way they did."

"People are made differently, Stephen," Mark said. "It will take you a long time to really understand everything. Maybe even your whole life. But you can make what you want of it now, remember that."

· · · ● · · ·

In the middle of February, the whole family began to make trips that Mark and Stephen jokingly called "the midnight express." A car would come and pick them up soon after midnight, and whisk them down the Baltimore-Washington Parkway, through Washington on New York Avenue, and into a special entrance of the new FBI building. In a conference room there they met a Mr. Porter, who said he would be helping them out in the months, maybe the years, to come.

He looked to be in his late forties and had a pixieish face; a mouth that always seemed to be smiling, and sparkling blue eyes set off by shiny, smooth pink skin. He looked as though he never had to shave.

"I take great pride in my job, and my job is to help you make new lives for yourselves," he said. "I will be honest with you from the beginning. These programs don't always work as well as they should. I'm sure you've heard about problems with the Justice Department's witness protection program."

"I have," said Walter, "and I'm concerned about them."

He had heard, among other horror stories, of shoddily forged documents, of court records accidentally opened to the public, of resumés prepared by program officials that contained gross inaccuracies, such as spelling the name of a college incorrectly, or listing a former address that would be in the middle of a swamp.

"I've taken great care to make sure that we make your transition as smooth as possible," Porter said. "After all, you're not just another bunch of Mafiosi who squealed on your own kind."

"We squealed," said Walter.

"Yes," replied Porter, an odd smile lighting up his face, "but your case is different. This is national defense. This is so the Russians don't overrun this magnificent land of ours. It's not just a bunch of Italian thugs from New York we're dealing with." His voice was rising, almost pleading with them to agree. "You understand, don't you, why this is so important?"

Please, Mark thought to himself, don't let this guy be an American version of Filikov.

"How much say do we have in this thing?" Walter asked. "I would like to go to Arizona or southern California. I like the climate."

"Sorry," said Porter, still smiling. "No can do. Arizona's all filled up. Unless you want to live on the Hualapai Indian Reservation. Ha ha ha." The laugh was brittle.

"No thank you," Else sternly said. "We will not live with the Indians."

"I was only kidding," said Porter. "Now listen, I've been working on a plan. I think it would be nice to have you somewhere in the middle of the country. That's where I'm from, the American heartland. Fine people, fine places to raise a family. I'm from Cornland, Illinois, myself, little town just outside of Springfield. Some name eh? Cornland."

"I would like to be near a city," Else said.

Porter furrowed his brow, and chewed on his lower lip. "I suppose we can arrange for that," he said. "But one thing, I think Mark should live away from the three of you. It would be best if Stephen was separated also, but that's up to you."

"I didn't expect to live with them," Mark said. "That's fine."

. . . ● . . .

On the second and third visits, they learned more about their new lives, and their fabricated pasts. Walter spent his whole career with the Army Intelligence Agency, and just retired after twenty-five years' service. He spent his childhood in Germany, but left before the war, and could never shake his accent, "just like Henry Kissinger," Porter suggested he say. Else would simply be the dedicated wife, following her husband around the world as his career progressed. Mark and Stephen had both attended a number of different American schools overseas, and had records to prove it.

Mark had transcripts and a diploma saying he graduated with a bachelor's degree in history in 1977 from the University of Maryland, a school so large that his "classmates" would not think it unusual that they didn't recognize his name, since no student knew more than a very small percentage of his graduating class.

Their most recent address was listed as that of a house in the planned town of Columbia, Maryland, midway between Baltimore and Washington. It belonged to an FBI agent who worked under Porter, and who would say, in the unlikely event he was asked, that yes, the gentleman, an Army type, lived here before he did.

Walter's legends had always been golden, and he was expected to have no more trouble maintaining this one than he had his other one for the last twenty-seven years. Except this time, he promised himself, there would be no dire necessity to use it.

At the end of March, 1979, Porter summoned them for the last time to his office at the end of the dark corridor in the massive FBI building on Constitution Avenue.

He gave them each a handshake and a telephone number to call if there were any problems.

"Good luck," he said. "God be with you and keep the Red devils far away from you."

21
Epilogue

By late fall of 1979, a store called the Jolly Lensman was doing a brisk business in a shopping mall twenty miles west of a large midwestern city. It had been opened that August by a middle-aged couple who told their customers, in accents that many of the area's German Americans remembered hearing at grandfather's knee, to call them Karl and Eva.

Eva was quiet, but attentive to the people who wandered into the combination camera shop and photographic studio. Karl was more outgoing, and would pull a customer aside to tell him a joke or ask about the crop forecasts.

They had moved into the comfortable town, which linked the suburbs to the expansive farmlands, at the beginning of spring, and spent several months looking for the right location for their store. A substantial loan from the Small Business Administration, which came in sooner than expected, made them sure they had made the right decision.

The house they bought was a red brick colonial, three bedrooms, with a family room and a sun porch, on a half acre plot in an older neighborhood where people liked to know the folks next door. The day after they moved in, a grandmotherly woman named Margaret Ruppert knocked at the kitchen door and deposited an apple pie in Karl's hands.

"Welcome neighbor," she said, explaining she lived across the street, and spent the better part of an hour recommending stores, service stations, doctors, and anything else she could think of.

"You wouldn't happen to need a podiatrist, would you?" she asked.

"Thank you," said Karl, "but our feet are still in good repair."

A few days later, Margaret and her husband Warren, a retired electrical contractor, had the new couple and their teenage son across the street to the Ruppert's house for dinner: leg of lamb, creamed corn, okra, stewed tomatoes, and freshly baked dinner rolls.

The Rupperts pried in a friendly way, asking no questions that they wouldn't have answered about themselves: What brings you to our town? Where are you from? What do you do?

The conversation flowed smoothly, and no one noticed when Karl smiled across the table at his son, nodding his head barely perceptibly as if to indicate, "You're doing fine, keep it up."

"It's good finally to settle in a place and not have to move around all the time and see your friends come and go," the boy told his new neighbors between mouthfuls of lamb.

"Yes," said Warren Ruppert, a tall, bald man in his early seventies whose handshake and voice were still firm. "It's nice to set down roots somewhere, to walk down the street and have folks say hello. Other military people have settled here before. Some just happened to be driving through and noticed how pretty and peaceful it is. That's as good a reason as any, I suppose.

"It is," said Eva. "It's the best reason there is."

They went to a Lutheran church that Sunday with the Hupperts, and eventually joined the congregation, "just to play the game," Karl insisted to his wife. "It will be good for business."

With Eva working in the store the same long hours as her husband, there was little time for the clubs and associations she was invited to join. But she was an industrious woman, so she used her time at night and on Sunday afternoons to write out invitations and help arrange bake sales, or whatever she was able to do.

At the local Rotary Club meetings, Karl became known for his quick and sometimes scatological humor, and soon was elected to a minor office. "A fine fellow," one Rotarian said of the new member. "And he seemed to fit in so quickly."

Epilogue

· · · ● · · ·

The boy made a list of resolutions before he moved with his parents to the new town, and was surprised by his ability to stick to them.

There were ten:

1. Lose twenty pounds by the time school starts.
2. Run two miles each day and work out and get in shape.
3. Join the football team and stick with it, and always try my hardest, even if I ride the bench all season.
4. Don't be loud and disruptive in school.
5. Take pride in my appearance, and try not to make Mom angry by being a slob.
6. Don't be jealous of my brother, because I know people are different.
7. Don't be selfish.
8. Don't try so hard to make people like me, because it never works.
9. Find a girl friend.
10. Try to understand my father, as hard as it is to do that.

By mid-October, after the team played a few games, the boy, Scott, had so impressed the coach with his determination, if not by his ability, that he began seeing a few minutes of playing time at the end of the fourth quarter if the game was not too close.

"By the time you're a senior," the coach told the tenth grader, "you could be our starting center. Just stick with it."

When the season ended, he continued his running program and increased the distance he ran each day. He would rise in the December pre-dawn darkness, run past the neat and substantial neighborhood homes, past the school, and down a straight county road that cut through a cornfield. Sometimes he would imagine that there was someone waiting for him behind the next stand of trees, someone who might want to hurt him, but he would always push the thoughts away and keep on running.

As the winter drew to an end and he learned that his father would travel to Washington for a few days to take care of business, an old anxiety returned. He felt like they were leaving him out again, hiding important things from him.

"Tell me what it is," he demanded of his father at breakfast one morning in February. "You have to tell me."

The father reached across the table, over the platter of scrambled eggs and bacon, and held his son's hand in his own, and as he did, he realized that the boy's hand was larger. Maybe, he thought, it was time for the son to know everything that the father knew.

He looked at the son's face, at his soft features and fine hair, at his eager and innocent eyes.

"I'm going to put this whole thing behind us for good," he said to the boy. "I have no choice in the matter, so I just have to go and make the best of it. You'll read the newspaper stories. They'll make a big deal out of it for a day or two, and then I'll be back here in our cozy town selling cameras again. It will make you feel funny, probably, seeing everything like that in the newspapers and on television."

"It kind of makes it official," said the boy. "It makes it final."

The mother sat down at the table and, as she often did in such moments, said nothing. Her son saw the long worry lines in her brow, and the way she twisted the skin of her right forefinger with her left hand.

"It'll be all right, Mom," he told her. "Everything is working out. It's better than it's ever been."

The woman touched her hand to the boy's pale temple, and stroked her fingers between the strands of his golden hair. "We're a family," she said. "We'll do our best."

· · · ● · · ·

There had been many days that marked passages in Walter Gottfried Scholz's life, but this one was different because everyone would know about it. Until the past several years, Walter had prevented, with the greatest of ease, others from knowing what he did not wish them to know. This day would be worse than the others.

· · · ● · · ·

For several days before the March 3rd press conference in the auditorium of the FBI building at Tenth and Pennsylvania Avenue, a highly placed member of the Bureau spent much time on the phone with a dozen of the nation's most influential journalists, casually mentioning halfway through each conversation that a press briefing of major importance would be coming up soon.

"Just thought you'd want to know," the FBI member would say.

The game would begin, of course, as it always does when a journalist is baited by a good source. Little by little, so as to make it seem more important, giving the impression that whomever he was talking to had the inside track on the story, the FBI man would release the details.

"He's the biggest one we've caught since Rudolf Abel."

"He'll talk, but you won't be able to see him."

"I can't tell you much more now, but believe me, you'll want to leave a big news hole for the story."

And so it happened, in the carefully controlled manner of news leaks, that by the time the media event was ready to begin, the news, to those in the inner circles, was already yesterday's, but the rest of the world had yet to hear the story about a short, gregarious man, his family, and a mission.

· · · ● · · ·

He was introduced to the media representatives as "Colonel Walter Gottfried Scholz, a Soviet KGB illegal resident who was 'doubled' by Bureau agents."

Seated behind an opaque screen that blurred his already tampered-with features, Walter spoke into a microphone that served the same purpose for his voice as the screen did for his appearance. The elaborate precautions were taken not only to frustrate the three reporters and photographers from the Soviet News agency, Tass, but also to add to the mystique which should rightfully surround a spy billed as "a big fish."

The Soviet journalists, who were, to nobody's surprise, KGB agents, had known for several days that the agent to be publicly exposed was undoubtedly Scholz. There was little they could do during the event, except to watch and listen carefully for indications of the seriousness of Scholz's situation.

· · · ● · · ·

Walter Scholz knew, as he sat behind the screen, that he was carefully being watched by the KGB, the FBI, and any number of journalists familiar with the intricacies of international espionage. He was also on display for all the world to see, dangled before an America that was eager to retaliate in whatever cold-warish manner possible against a Soviet Union that was being increasingly perceived of as a very real threat.

But Walter Scholz was not in a position to explain what the real reasons for anything were. He was only in a position, as he had been nearly all his life, to do and say exactly what he was supposed to, and nothing more. With that firmly in mind, he leaned back, as well as he could, in the metal government-issue folding chair, and filled his pipe with a sweet cherry tobacco. And he wondered what Kanayev was saying right now to Filikov, and how the nameless assassin would be dealt with for failing his mission.

· · · ● · · ·

After a brief introduction, during which a Bureau public information officer said Walter Gottfried Scholz was the highest ranking illegal Soviet agent apprehended in the United States since 1957, the questions began:

"Why did you agree to this press conference, Colonel Scholz?"

"Either I would cooperate with the FBI or I would be given to prosecutors . . . it was part of my deal with the FBI."

"Your son, Colonel Scholz," asked a young wire service reporter. "What role did your son play in this mission? What were the plans for him? What is his name?"

Walter Scholz kneaded his hands. He did not like to answer questions about himself, or about his family. But Colonel Scholz was a rational man, and he knew that the most rational thing to do was to cooperate, to do as he had been told. Colonel Scholz always did as he was told, if the authority was imposing enough.

That he spoke through a microphone which altered his voice rather pleased him. For most of his life, he had lived in altered circumstances. Why, he asked himself, should it be any different now?

"My son," he said, "accompanied me on many trips. Some were abroad, and some were within the United States or Canada. He attended a university, studying political science and history. He was preparing to attain a high, hopefully sensitive position in the U.S. government someday, and would have supplied information to the Soviet Union."

"His code name was Hoffnung," Walter continued.

"The hope."

· · · ● · · ·

"Okay," the young graduate student said to the fifteen freshmen in the Introduction to Western Civilization section he taught once a week, Thursday afternoons at two. "Bad government is better than no government at all. Who believed this, and why?"

"Mr. Cairnes," the young teacher said, nodding at a student who was usually well prepared for the class. "Give it a try." He knew it was an academic affectation, calling a seventeen-year-old freshman "Mr. Cairnes." It probably made the kid a bit uncomfortable, but the graduate student's faculty advisor liked the touch of formality, so he played along.

"It was Thomas Hobbes, I believe," the freshman said. "Hobbes shaped much of eighteenth century political thought. He said that the people, the natural subjects, will submit themselves to the sovereign, or even create one, for their own protection. He talked about a covenant, a binding agreement to create political order."

"Thank you, Mr. Cairnes," said the graduate student. "Very well said."

When the hour was over, a sensitive looking girl who liked to wear long skirts and shawls stayed in the classroom to talk to the graduate student. It was the third consecutive week she had done this, and the graduate student was both annoyed and flattered.

She started to address him as "Mister" but he cut her off quickly: "The third time someone stays after to talk," he said, "they can call me Matthew."

"Matthew," she said, somewhat apprehensively, "would you care to join me for coffee? I'd like to toss Rousseau around, if you don't mind."

The graduate student smiled at the freshman and replied with only a touch of condescension, "I don't mind, if Mr. Rousseau doesn't."

The university was one of the largest, and also one of the most respected in the nation. It had an excellent reputation for graduate studies in history, and if he performed well during the four or five years it would take to earn his doctorate, they assured him, he would have no trouble finding a teaching position with a top-notch institution.

He was beginning to form a good relationship with his faculty advisor, a wild-haired old man whose preeminence in his field of colonial American history had him dubbed "The Wisest" by the department's two dozen graduate students.

Life was not quite as exciting as it had once been, but he was content for the present. Sometimes, though, sitting alone in his off-campus apartment, he would be stricken by a feeling that everything might suddenly come crashing down around him; that all was not as well as it seemed to be.

He had always thought of himself as strong, as able to handle anything that life might throw at him. But in recent months, since the previous winter, he found that he was more fragile than he used to be.

It was more important, he knew, to concentrate on what lay ahead of him than to think about the past. But little snippets of horrible scenes sometimes kept him awake at night; they would march across his mind, leering and laughing maniacally: the man with the Oriental face and the blue eyes from the cabin in California; the bumbling but vengeful Filikov; the screaming rabbit from the woods near the house; the faceless assassin from the blackness by the river. They were all there, and he had to struggle to convince himself that they did not belong to him anymore.

In the middle of the night, when he couldn't exorcise the tormentors, he would dial a long distance number and wait until a voice with a familiar accent sleepily answered "Hello?"

"It's me," the graduate student would say. "I'm sorry to awaken you."

"That's okay," the voice would answer. It was soothing.

"I can't get them out of my mind."

"They'll leave," the voice would respond, "someday they'll leave, because it's all over now, and they have no business overstaying their welcome."

The student would take a deep breath, maybe another one. "You're right," he would say. "I'm sorry; it's all over. Good night."